CONFIDENTIAL

ALSO BY ELLIE MONAGO

NEIGHBORLY

CONFIDENTIAL

ELLIE MONAGO

LAKE UNION
PUBLISHING

Text copyright © 2019 by Holly Brown
All rights reserved.

Published by Lake Union Publishing, Seattle

www.apub.com

Amazon, the Amazon logo, and Lake Union Publishing are trademarks of Amazon.com, Inc., or its affiliates.

ISBN-13: 9781503904224 (paperback)
ISBN-10: 1503904229 (paperback)
ISBN-13: 9781542040082 (hardcover)
ISBN-10: 1542040086 (hardcover)

Cover design by Rex Bonomelli

Printed in the United States of America

First edition

CONFIDENTIAL

CONSENT TO TREATMENT

I'm Michael Baylor, licensed clinical psychologist. Welcome to my practice.

The therapist/client relationship is a unique one. My approach is unique, too. You won't find any cookie-cutter techniques here, and there are no easy answers. This is a revelatory process, and you may be surprised by what you learn. Please remember that it's not like a medical procedure where your main job is to show up and the doctor does the rest. This is a collaboration, and in our sessions, you gain only by participating fully.

Therapy can be of enormous benefit, but it's not without discomfort. Excavating old wounds often hurts; changing long-held beliefs and long-standing habits can hurt, too. But I will never abandon you. All I ask is for the chance to earn your trust.

CONFIDENTIALITY

In general, the privacy of all communications between a patient and a psychologist is protected by law, and I can release information about our work to others only with your written permission. But there are a few exceptions.

If I believe that you may do harm to yourself or to others, I am required to take protective actions . . .

PRESENT DAY

PSYCHOTHERAPIST FOUND DEAD IN HIS OFFICE

The body of Michael Baylor, a licensed clinical psychotherapist practicing in the affluent Rockridge section
of Oakland, has been discovered. The police are not yet
releasing any details . . .

BEFORE

ONE YEAR AGO

CHAPTER 1

FLORA

"Happy anniversary, baby!" I said it breathily, like Marilyn Monroe to JFK, and I was wearing a negligee and holding a cheesecake. That's Michael and me: the perfect intersection between sexy and ironic, between sleaze and cheese.

No, there's nothing sleazy about us, despite what anyone might think if they knew how we met, all the jokes they could make about therapist-client privilege. My love for Michael was boundless; I had opened up to him in ways that I never thought possible before. I hadn't even known to want them.

And now he was all mine. That's what we were celebrating.

Hard to imagine that when I first met him, more than two and a half years ago, I hadn't even been attracted to him. Now I was borderline obsessed.

But in a healthy way.

He would know, right?

"I love you, Dr. Michael," I whispered, lowering myself so that he could take in my cleavage, pillowed in red silk, as I placed the cheese-cake with its two burning candles on the table in front of him.

He rewarded me with a grin. I called him Dr. Michael only on special occasions, and it always turned him on.

"Blow them out," I urged, and he complied. Then I dredged my fingers through the cheesecake and put them in his mouth.

He licked them clean, slowly. "You think of everything." He was looking at me in the way only he could, so full of love, lust, and admiration, like I was a marvel. *A force of nature,* he liked to say.

Then he pulled me down to the floor, and the cake after us, which made me giggle. We smeared it on each other's bodies, like finger paint-ing all grown up. No, it was like our wedding, but without any observ-ers; there was no need for smashing confections into faces. Where did that tradition come from anyway? So much passive aggression. How could that bode well for any union?

But when Michael and I came together on my dining room floor, it was certainly portentous. After, we curled around each other, serpentine and spent. I put my head on his chest and listened to his heartbeat. It was even faster than my own. Good. A pulse can't lie.

Not that I thought Michael lied to me, but we had been a secret for two years. Sometimes I just needed some sensory confirmation of his feelings. After what happened with Young, that was to be expected. Michael would say that himself.

He kissed the top of my head, and my stomach lurched just a little. I knew what that meant.

He gently extricated himself to pad across the floor, naked. He'd gotten in better shape these past two years, doing Pilates. I hadn't known men did that, but it'd almost entirely eradicated the belly he had when we first met. He'd told me that he needed to get fit to keep up with me. I used to only like blonds, but Michael broke me of that. Now I was all about his thick brown-black hair and the tight whorls on his chest.

Darkness seemed manly. And Young just seemed, well, young. He was part of my misspent youth.

If it hadn't been for Michael, I might have just kept banging my head against that wall, thinking that because Young and I were married, we had to grow old together like my parents had. We'd met when we were twenty and said our vows a few years later in a Miami ballroom. How could anyone be held to decisions they made at that age? I was now ten years wiser, and Michael had ten years on top of that, so I knew I was doing the right thing.

But he was walking away from me, and I suddenly felt cold on the hardwood floor. I heard him start the shower, and I pulled the negligee back over my head. Time to scrape up the cheesecake. In the throes of passion, I didn't mind a mess, but the rest of the time, I kept a spotless house. Well, apartment. A lovely apartment, from the early 1920s, with light oak floors, lots of sunlight, and built-in bookshelves, though it initially chafed that we had to sell the house in the divorce. My monthly rent for this one-bedroom in Rockridge was nothing short of ridiculous, but it was walking distance to scores of restaurants and boutiques, plus the BART station where I took the train to San Francisco for work. It was also fairly close to Michael's office, not that I'd been there for the past two years. I'd been tempted, but I always managed to stop myself. That would have been too risky, and he would have been so angry. I hated seeing Michael angry.

Once my apartment was scrubbed, I yanked the negligee off and dropped it on the floor of the bathroom, parted the curtain, and stepped inside the claw-foot tub. I noted with disappointment that Michael was standing in the spray, already done with the soaping. I positioned myself near him, hoping he'd take the bait and lather me, but even though he was right there, he felt remote.

I'd never liked that he always showered right after, like he was getting rid of all evidence as quickly as possible.

He pecked me on the cheek. "I'll give you some privacy," he said, beginning his exit.

For someone who reads people for a living, he could sometimes be a little dense. If I wanted privacy, wouldn't I just have waited until he was done?

I put a hand on his arm, the lightest restraint. More beseeching, really, which wasn't the most comfortable position for me. "Stay." I smiled. "We need to make plans."

"Oh?"

"For the big reveal." His face was disconcertingly blank. "What's the best way to go public?"

The American Psychological Association says that former clients and their therapists must wait two years after the termination of therapy before they can become romantically involved. Today marked two years from when Young and I had our last session with Dr. Baylor, when we "processed" my decision to end the marriage.

In my mind, Michael and I had taken the moral path. Our first sexual contact had taken place after Young and I split up. I hadn't cheated. It was a shame that the APA was so rigid, that it failed to recognize different circumstances. Sure, the rule existed to protect vulnerable clients, and I understood that. But I hadn't been vulnerable; I'd been fully capable of making a clearheaded decision and protecting myself. Ironically, the APA and its well-meaning bureaucrats had been the only real threat to my mental health. It was rough, keeping a love this big underground.

"We can't go public the second the time elapses," he said. "It would look suspicious."

"To whom? Who's looking?"

"Young, maybe. He could report me."

I scoffed. "Young lives in Pacific Heights. We haven't spoken since we finalized the divorce. You know that."

"Don't underestimate a man scorned. It's hard to lose a woman like you."

I felt a flush of pleasure that Michael thought so, though I highly doubted Young would agree. He was likely relieved when I ended it. He could tell his parents that we'd done counseling and, more important, that he'd done all he could but that I wasn't willing to continue. I was sure he had told them that. Then he began to date immediately, according to the one friend we still had in common. I'd bet he never had any problems getting it up for all those girls from Tinder.

The flush of pleasure vacated my body instantly, and I felt a wave of self-consciousness. I shouldn't have started this conversation with Michael in the shower. Far better would have been with full makeup on, with my lips accentuated and my nose deemphasized.

It wasn't like I'd ever had trouble being noticed by men or being regarded as fuckable. Not until late-period Young. And Michael had just fucked me, vigorously.

But he didn't want to be seen in public with me. That's what he was saying. He wanted to keep me his dirty secret.

I'd waited two years! Two years!

Michael could see that I was getting worked up, so he started soaping me. At his caresses, the adrenaline started to abate. I felt soothed, like a cat being pet in a sunlit corner.

"I've risked everything for you," he said. "That's why I just need for us to take it slowly. You know how I feel about my career."

His hand moved between my legs, and my head lolled back almost involuntarily. What that man could do to me.

CHAPTER 2

LUCINDA

I was hurrying down College Avenue, my fluffy dishwater-blonde hair flying behind me, dodging the myriad pedestrians who were darting into their chosen eateries, from the lowbrow crepe place to the small-plate French bistro with sixteen-dollar cocktails. Every third storefront was a restaurant; therapists populated every fifth building. Discreetly, a bit set back from the main street, sometimes around a courtyard, with bronze plaques full of names followed by initials: MSW, MFT, PhD, PsyD.

Michael Baylor was a PsyD, meaning he had his doctorate in clinical psychology. And he was mine. Only until 6:50, though, and it was already 6:04.

Stupid, stupid. Every missed minute cost money I barely had, money that could never be replaced because the San Francisco Bay Area was a leaky sieve and I worked as a proofreader for a small press in Berkeley. I was twenty-six, an introvert with four roommates. You could say things were not going particularly well.

Truthfully, though, it wasn't really the money I was upset about. It was that I didn't want to miss a minute with Dr. Baylor.

Christine had caught me on my way out the door, and I'd always been the worst at telling people *no, I really have to go*. I hated interrupting. I just stood there, trapped in the conversation like a fly in amber, waiting and listening for a substantial-enough pause. The right-size opening never seemed to come. I never wanted to hurt anyone by giving the impression that what he or she was saying wasn't crucial or fascinating.

Dr. Baylor had pointed out that this was a toxic pattern for me: I was always aggrandizing others, thinking their time was more valuable, their desires and preferences worthier of satisfaction and their feelings more important. I knew he was right, and I didn't want to admit that my lateness was because I'd done it again with Christine, who was a terrible boss and an even worse person.

I punched in the code that opened the outer door to his building and raced up to the second floor. Bursting into the small waiting room with no receptionist, two chairs, and a side table with a fan of *Psychology Today* magazines, I felt ungainly. I had that feeling a lot, since I'm more than six feet tall, which makes it hard to be as inconspicuous as I'd like to be. Dr. Baylor says I should embrace my height, that when you also factored in my "almost incidental beauty" (another way of saying I should brush my hair more?), I could own any room I went in. It was hard to believe that, though he looked so sincere, but it's even harder to believe he'd lie.

There he was, in the doorway to his inner sanctum. "Lucy!" he said, his face creased with pleasure at my arrival. "Come on in."

"I'm so sorry," I said. "You know I totally value your time—"

"I do know that." His smile was sympathetic, and beautiful, really. I imagined he owned any room he was in. He was like the therapist version of George Clooney. He's so much better looking than the head shot on his website that if the photo had been more accurate, I never would have called him. I thought that what I wanted was someone smart and compassionate, with an average and nondistracting appearance. How wrong I'd been.

Distraction wasn't as much of a problem as I would have expected, though. Dr. Baylor had a knack for keeping me focused. He was such a good therapist that I was grateful for the lousy photography that brought us together.

His office was all blond wood and white furniture, with a brightly colored braided rug and some tapestries on the wall from his travels to I wasn't sure where (I wasn't well traveled myself). The bookshelves weren't full of only clinical tomes but also novels and nonfiction on a host of different subjects, as well as stacks of the *Economist* and the *New Yorker*. It made it seem like I was seeing him in his natural habitat, where he felt at home. I couldn't help noticing that when it came to reading, his tastes mirrored my own. That helped me feel at home, like for once I could relax.

Since I'd started seeing him, I had made lots of progress on my critical self-talk. When I heard the negative voice in my head, I could just turn down the volume. He'd taught me that I didn't have to buy every thought I had, that some were just conditioning from a less-than-optimal childhood.

I settled on the white couch, trying to slow my breathing.

"Put your feet on the floor and get centered," he said serenely. "You're here now."

I did as I was told.

"Are you feeling centered?" he asked. I nodded. "Good. There's something I want to talk to you about."

Oh shit. He was firing me. It was only the third time I'd been late, but he'd had enough. He had a busy practice, with a wait list. There were plenty of other clients who'd covet my evening slot.

Or he was leaving his practice, retiring early. He was moving to Bora Bora. He had a brain tumor.

"Are you okay?" He must have seen my panic, that I couldn't handle losing him.

"I'll be fine. What did you want to talk about?"

He studied me an extra second, then said, "Starting today, there'll be no charge for our sessions."

I stared at him. "You mean, we'd keep meeting every week, and I wouldn't pay you?"

"Yes. I do a certain amount of pro bono work—"

"You mean like charity?" He pitied me. I knew it.

"I'm aware of how stressful it is for you to pay for the sessions, and I'd like to remove that stress."

"But I'm in a six p.m. slot. That's prime time."

"I can afford it." He smiled. "Let me do this for you. Please."

I stared down at my jean-encased legs, struggling to compute what he was saying. My old friend shame rose like bile. "There are people out there who have it way worse than me. You really should give them the pro bono slot."

"No one deserves it more." His tone was so kind that the shame got even stronger. I'd never been able to take a compliment, and I certainly couldn't take this. "You'd be doing me a favor. You're one of my favorite clients, and at some point, you might have to make a choice between therapy and other essentials, and then you'd need to stop. You have so much potential that I don't want that to happen. Really, it's selfishness on my part."

He was saying I was special. One of his favorites. I'd be doing him a favor to rob him of $150 an hour, four times a month—$600 of missed income?

Special. My cheeks were in flames.

"I love our conversations. I love our work. It feels almost"—he looked like he was feeling around for the word—"wrong to take money for them."

11

I felt something happening in my body that definitely wasn't shame, but when I registered what it was, I managed to be even more embarrassed. I told Dr. Baylor everything (well, within reason), but I wouldn't tell him this. It was just too clichéd, a girl in love with her therapist.

No, I wasn't in love. They were just feelings, that's all, and not even precisely romantic. I'd been in love with only one man, and that was a disaster of, like, illegal proportions.

Dr. Baylor was watching me, waiting.

"Everything else will stay the same?" I said. "Everything else from the Consent to Treatment still applies?" As in, we would still be purely professional. The only difference was, I'd get to keep my $600 a month. It was almost too good to be true. If I hadn't known Dr. Baylor's reputation, if I hadn't been well aware of his good heart and his commitment to his work, I might have had some reservations.

But I did know those things. What I hadn't known before was that I was special to him. Precious.

"Everything will stay the same," he said.

Even though I'd been the one asking the question, I was disappointed by the answer. Because normally I could tamp down the thoughts; I could tell myself how ridiculous they were because obviously someone like Dr. Baylor had a significant other, someone beautiful and poised and established, his equal, but just then, I had to face the fact. I wanted so much more.

CHAPTER 3

GREER

"I picked you because I really liked what you said on your website, about how adaptable you are, that you're not the same therapist with every client," I said. "It's not easy for me to ask for help, but I've come to the conclusion that I need to adapt."

"Adapt to . . . ?" Michael prompted.

"Some people might say I'm a control freak, and that's been okay, for the most part. It's made me successful." I stared right at him, refusing to soften the remark or to make any apologies for my ambition. "Lately, I've been thinking that I want a baby, which is highly inconvenient." I was thirty-nine years old, but I didn't have to tell him that; he should have read my age on the intake. "Babies make your life unpredictable, and I've certainly never wanted that, but I . . ." To my mortification, I felt myself on the verge of tears.

He nodded with a simple, "Go on."

At work, I didn't waste a word. But in this office with its IKEA aesthetic overlaid with nomad chic, I found myself rambling. It was as if I'd been in captivity and had finally been released. "I'd be doing it alone. I don't have a partner, but I wouldn't especially want one, either. I can't imagine all the compromises and accommodations with a child involved. Then I think maybe I could hire someone, but I'm not having a baby so someone else would raise him or her. If I do it myself, though, it'll be chaos, and that terrifies me. But it terrifies me more to never do this thing that I suddenly want so desperately, yet it may obliterate me. I'd have to become someone else entirely."

He nodded again encouragingly. He was better looking in his photo. Maybe it was an old picture, as he had more gray now and a few more laugh lines. He looked kinder, though. Less professorial.

"This isn't how I normally sound," I said. "If you met me in another situation, you wouldn't even recognize me."

He gave a slight smile. "If you met me in another situation, you might not recognize me, either."

"I need help. I'm not used to that. I really hate it."

"You hate being here?"

I looked at him with surprise as I realized, "No, I don't."

"It's okay to have some ambivalence about this process."

"I'm not an ambivalent person. I'm used to deciding on a goal and pursuing it wholeheartedly. But the things I want are in direct opposition to each other."

"Career and family are in opposition?"

"For me, yes. I'm single. I'm in charge of my company, and I work a lot of hours. But it's more than that. I have to be a certain kind of person to run my business, and that is not the maternal type. I feel like motherhood might make me a schizophrenic."

"That's a common worry."

"Really? Schizophrenia is a common worry?"

He laughed. "The fear of losing yourself to motherhood is common. If you joined a moms group, you'd hear that a lot." He must have seen the horror on my face. "Support is critical with such a big life change."

"Sitting around with a bunch of women leaking milk? It just doesn't sound like me."

"You'll have to expand your concept of who you are and what you're capable of. You're right, it'll be scary, but it's likely to be worthwhile."

"Only likely?"

"There are no guarantees."

I had foolishly hoped he'd reassure me, that he'd tell me having a baby doesn't necessitate a radical lifestyle change, just a few tweaks.

He wrote in his Consent to Treatment that there are no easy answers. Yet I'd managed to hope that in this case, there would be, like what I really wanted was a charlatan psychic and not a mental health professional.

"You seem disappointed," he said. He didn't wait for my response; he was that sure he had me pegged. "I know it's your first time in therapy. Did you have an idea of what our conversation would be, and this is somehow falling short? It's good to talk about expectations."

"I'm not used to sharing my feelings, especially not with men."

"What are your relationships with men usually like?"

"They're brief. I want a successful man, but successful men don't seem to want their equals. They find me 'intimidating,' apparently. I'm not bitter about that. I haven't put much energy into the search, and I've never tried to be a truly good partner to anyone. We have a few dates, and then a part of me is relieved when I don't hear from them. Or if I do hear, I find fault with them. Maybe I'm looking for someone who'll work harder at the relationship than I will, which isn't fair. I want a beta to my alpha, yet I wouldn't be attracted to anyone but the top dog. It's a catch-22."

Had Dr. Baylor put some truth serum in the water he gave me? I shifted uncomfortably on the couch, wishing I could stop, knowing I probably needed to go on. That's what Dr. Baylor was saying with his nods.

Here came another one. Maybe they weren't even intended as communication; it could have been the therapist version of hiccups or gas, a bodily function gone awry.

But I wasn't paying him for a staring contest. "I haven't had a real relationship in years," I said. "I'm almost forty, and there's no time to find one. If I want a baby, I need to start the process soon, on my own, and I need you to help me figure out what that'll mean for me, since so much of how I see myself is work. I go and go and go, and I'm afraid of what I'll find when I slow down. And I know motherhood will slow me down. So why do I want it?"

"That is the million-dollar question."

"I'll write you a check, you tell me the answer, and we'll be done with it, then."

He met my eyes. "Now where's the fun in that?"

PRESENT DAY

CHAPTER 4

DETECTIVE GREGORY PLATH

I've been at this a long time, but I've never seen a case quite like this one.

The victim's a doctor but not the real kind of doctor. He's a head shrinker. I'm not supposed to think that, here in Progressive Land, but after that accidental shooting fifteen—no, more like twenty—years ago, I had to "see someone," and it pretty much confirmed what a bunch of bullshit all that is. Not just bullshit but self-indulgence. We are what we do. You want to have higher self-esteem? Go do something to be proud of. You had a rough life? Go make something of yourself. I did it. You can, too.

I guess you could say I'm biased. But I'm fifty-seven years old. If you're not biased by then, if you haven't developed some opinions, there's your problem.

I don't prejudge, though. Like these three women. I'm not going to assume I know who they are until I bring them in. Then I'll sit across from them and I'll see what they're made of.

Now, if I could get my hands on Dr. Baylor's records, it would be a hell of a lot easier, but lucky for them: my request had to go before the judge, and he's taking his sweet time in making a ruling. There's no love lost between us from the Nicholson case. That guy holds a grudge.

Now those guys—they ought to be called "prejudges." It used to make me crazy but not anymore. What would a head shrinker say? I've learned coping skills.

Based on his reputation in the therapy community, Dr. Baylor was a stand-up guy. Lots of people said they'd recommend him "without reservation." Well, they used to. I doubt he's getting any referrals wherever he's found himself.

I asked about the couple of complaints against him to the professional board, the ones that never went anywhere, and I was told that's par for the course. "It's an occupational risk," one female therapist told me. "We work with emotionally unstable people, Dr. Baylor most of all. He never shied away from a challenge. I sent him some of the hardest clients—people with histrionic personality disorder, borderline personality disorder, complex trauma—and he didn't hesitate. He changed their lives."

You could say that they had a reason to want to rose-color this guy. For one, he was dead, and it's true, people generally don't like to speak ill of the dead. But for another, this wasn't exactly good PR for the profession. The first news reports didn't say the cause of death, but now the word is out: we're looking for a murderer.

What I've got so far are three people of interest. I can't say they're suspects yet, because it's all circumstantial. But it's a hell of a circumstance: three of Dr. Baylor's clients and former clients meet up at a dim sum restaurant, and hours later, someone beans him in the head with the alabaster bust of some classical composer or philosopher or who-the-hell-ever from his bookshelf without leaving a trace of evidence, almost like they had their own forensic cleaning service on speed dial.

Not that the office was spotless, though. Far from it. There were plenty of hairs and fibers everywhere else—a whole lot of clients passed through that office in a week, and people shed their personal detritus at an alarming rate—but none on or immediately around the body. Nothing I can use.

Three very different women with only Dr. Michael Baylor in common meet in a dim sum restaurant. Sounds like one of those old jokes: a priest, a rabbi, and a Buddhist monk walk into a bar . . .

I wish I had those records—that would make this whole thing a lot easier—but I've gotta sit tight. That's in the works. Until then, I just need one of these women to talk. Get one of them to crack. Apply enough pressure and most people do. It's like they can't help themselves. A little bit of genuine curiosity and people are dying to spill their secrets. That's something Michael Baylor probably figured out, too. He and I, we've got something in common.

Unless they're professional liars or professional killers, everyone cracks.

BEFORE

CHAPTER 5

FLORA

"He whipped it out under the table, right there in the restaurant?" Nat's mouth was hanging open. Jeanie was in hysterics, so much so that she nearly slid off the U-shaped couch in the darkened lounge area of our favorite after-work bar.

"Yep, right there!" I said. It didn't even feel like a lie. It was just a performance, and an entertaining one at that.

My divorce had been finalized for nearly a year. I couldn't expect my friends to believe that I'd stayed entirely single and celibate all that time. After I'd feigned grieving, they were after me to get back on the horse, and I couldn't tell them that I already had, and my stallion's name was Dr. Michael Baylor, not without risking his career. I had no choice but to invent this life where I was freewheeling around Tinder. And the storytelling could be fun, like I was the one living vicariously through my own made-up adventures, in an alternate universe where I'd never met Michael. We all need to be the person others expect us to sometimes. Most of the time.

It was easier to fool Jeanie, in that she was gullible in the kindest sense. She wanted to believe me. But it was harder in that I felt much guiltier misleading her. Nat and I were more after-work cocktail pals, while Jeanie had cried on my shoulder many times during the IVF process that ultimately culminated in her having twins, now almost three years old. If she found it suspicious how little I'd cried over Young, she never said it to me. She'd also never protested about the downgrade in our intimacy, that we had lunch these days rather than dinner, that it was more laughs than heart-to-hearts, but she must have felt it. Michael was so consuming that I didn't have the bandwidth to miss her like I should have.

"You make my dates look good," Nat said. She was around my age, early thirties; never married; and had a profile on four different dating apps. Attractive as she was with her long blonde hair and mint-green eyes, it had been hard for her to find men who wanted to get serious. She'd sworn off casual sex. They had to buy the cow. She seemed envious that I didn't seem to mind giving the milk away for free. If she only knew.

Jeanie was older, in her early forties. She always laughed the hardest at my tales, and while there was nothing condescending in it, I had the impression that it validated the benign and mundane domesticity of her marriage. She was attractive, too. It was a job requirement, as we were all pharmaceutical reps.

"Which restaurant?" Jeanie asked.

She wasn't trying to catch me in a lie; there was no suspicion in her tone. But it occurred to me that I should have worked out all the details. Before I could even think, it was out: "Zuni Café."

"Zuni Café?" Jeanie and Nat responded in unison.

"He's spending two hundred dollars on dinner and then yanking his wank at the table?" Nat said with a touch of incredulity.

"That just made it even weirder," I answered, though I'd averted my eyes, presumably to sip my champagne. "He ordered the sixty-minute chicken for two . . . Wait, that must have been why he ordered it! I couldn't walk out when the world's best roasted chicken was still to come."

"Speaking of coming," Jeanie said, and then they were both laughing again, and I thought, *Whew, I got away with it.*

But I felt this twinge of sadness at the reminder of how distant I'd become from my own friends. I'd been trying to enjoy my double life, I really had, and sometimes I succeeded. Clandestine sex can be hot. Yet at some point, it stopped feeling like our secret and instead, I just became his. Two years was a long time, and lately I'd just been running out the clock.

Only the buzzer had gone off, and he was still stalling. I could share my frustration only with Kate, because she was family, and because she'd never judge. She heard the story of Michael and me the way I wanted her to: like it was a great romance. Nat wouldn't, and I couldn't be sure about Jeanie. So Kate it was.

"I can't believe that in all this time, you haven't found anyone who deserves a second date," Jeanie said. "You must have terrible radar. Show me your phone. I need to do your swiping for you."

"I'm not trying to get serious," I said. When I finally introduced them to Michael, I'd have to pretend that we just met at a grocery store or somewhere serendipitous, and it was love at first sight. He'd made me change my whole way of thinking. It was true; only the timeline was a fabrication.

"Maybe you're more hurt about Young than you've admitted to yourself," Jeanie said. "Maybe you could use therapy. You thought your couples therapist was awesome. You could go back to him."

"I should get his name," Nat said. "Maybe if I got rid of my baggage, I could finally find someone decent."

The last thing I wanted was Nat seeing Michael. It would practically be incest. "You don't want to go all the way to the East Bay for therapy. There are a million good therapists in San Francisco."

"A million therapists," Nat corrected. "Not a million good ones. You've vetted him for me."

That was one way to put it. "I'll reach out and see if he's taking new clients," I said. "He's very in demand." I swigged the rest of my champagne, but out of the corner of my eye, I saw that Nat was giving me a strange look.

"Let me see your phone," she said, and was I imagining it or was her tone ominous?

"Why?" I tried to keep mine light by comparison, helium to her lead.

"Isn't he in your contacts? I can just call him myself."

The moment was fraught. We'd entered a standoff. Jeanie must have felt it, because she interceded, her maternal instincts kicking in. "If you go to him," she told Nat, "then Flora might feel less comfortable going back. And she had him first, right?"

How I loved Jeanie. She could finesse any situation. It's why she was the best sales rep on the team, even though she was the oldest.

Nat saw Jeanie's wisdom and nodded slowly. Then she brightened. "I have a great idea! We should both pull up our apps and then Jeanie can do the swiping for both of us. She can show us the error of our ways."

Jeanie clapped her hands, no longer the truce-brokering mom but instead, a giggly twelve-year-old. "Tin-der! Tin-der! Tin-*der*!" she chanted. Her impeccable auburn bob was percussive, swaying to and fro.

The twentysomethings on the next couch glanced over at us; they were holding their eye rolls until we looked away. So I kept staring at them challengingly, and they had to yield, dropping back into their own conversation.

But they weren't really my problem; they were a delaying tactic. My problem was, I had no Tinder account.

"After Chicken Guy, I'm taking a break," I said.

"Don't let him scare you off," Nat said. "There are lots of great men out there. I mean, there have to be, right?" She looked to Jeanie for confirmation.

"Of course! Just put yourselves in my capable hands. I know how to spot a douche a mile away. It was a lot of trial and error before I got to my husband." Jeanie turned to me. "Come on, it'll be fun. Let me swipe for you."

"That sounds really racy!" I joked.

"Come on!" she said again. She was tenacious, another reason she was the number one salesperson.

Nat was watching me, too. I had a feeling I totally hated: that I was being a buzzkill. But I couldn't help it. There was no way I was going to come clean now, not when I was so close to being able to introduce them to Michael.

I had an inspiration: "After Chicken Guy, I temporarily deleted my account."

They went back to their drinks, and my mind went to Michael. Since he was taking so long, I could probably start laying the ground-work. *Funny thing*, I'd tell Jeanie and Nat at our next happy hour, *I met someone, and he's actually a psychologist in Rockridge; he probably even knows my old couples therapist, wouldn't that be crazy?*

Or, *I ran into my old couples therapist right in the neighborhood, and we just hit it off . . .*

Or, *I called him to go back into therapy and we acknowledged that there'd always been a hint of mutual attraction, so . . .*

I had to think this through more and talk to Michael. Get our stories straight. It might be harder than it seemed, given how borderline suspicious Nat was acting. One thing I knew was that Tales from Tinder was ending tonight. Like I told them, I needed a break.

Michael's ears must have been burning because a text came in. It wasn't his name, of course, just his initials: M.B.

What are you wearing?

I turned the phone over.

"Is that him, Chicken Guy?" Nat said.

"Rookie mistake," I said. "I shouldn't have given him my number. He should have to message me through the app."

"Well, you were hopeful," Jeanie said. "That makes sense. He took you to Zuni."

Nat agreed. "How could you have known?"

"Sometimes," I said, "they blindside you."

CHAPTER 6

LUCINDA

"Are you sitting down?" Mom asked.

I was in publishing, which meant I was always sitting down.

I was also in a cubicle, in a largely silent room. Usually I could hear other people on the phone or talking to one another, or a stream from Pandora, some ambient noise, yet right then, it was only keystrokes. It was a converted warehouse, the drafty kind with walls that looked like aluminum rather than one with hip architectural details. Sound carried.

"Could I call you when I get home?" I said in a low voice.

"This can't wait."

"I'll call you back in a minute."

I grabbed my purse and walked outside. Verdant Publishing was housed in an industrial part of Berkeley that was rapidly developing. When I'd started a few years ago, we were the only inhabitants of the block and I had to bring my own lunch. Now we were being overrun by live-work lofts, and there were four restaurants within a couple of blocks (though they all closed by three p.m. The neighborhood was gentrifying, but nightlife still fell outside its parameters.). So at four thirty, with everyone inside living and working, the block had gone still.

Again, I would have preferred some ambient noise, but there were no benches or trees. No camouflage.

Fortunately, there were also no windows in the aluminum-sided warehouse, so none of my colleagues could see me, not unless they took a smoke break, and since it's a boutique publisher in health-conscious, eco-conscious, formerly-hippie-and-now-mostly-just-hip Berkeley, no one smoked—or at least, no one wanted to be seen smoking. When the college kids in town vaped, it was organic and vegan.

It wasn't that long ago that I was one of them. Never as carefree as some, but it had been a liberation of sorts. Though it was only a few hours from where I grew up along the river in Guerneville, I treated it like a trek through the Himalayas. Mom missed me, but she'd stopped pressing. She must have known, on some level, that I needed space and time. Light and air. She just didn't know why.

She never called me at work. Full of dread, I rang her back, and she said, again, "Are you sitting down?"

"Yes," I lied. I leaned against the building, since it was the closest approximation.

"I didn't want to worry you before there was anything to worry about, but it's Adam. It's cancer."

I should say something. What kind of cancer? I'm sorry? But before I could come up with it, she added quietly, "Pancreatic. Stage four."

Stage four meant dying. I mean, we're all dying, but stage four meant soon. My stepfather wasn't even fifty years old yet, and he probably never would be.

What should I be feeling? What was I feeling?

"How are you?" That was a better question. Safer.

"I'm scared." Then she was crying, hard, and I'd never heard that before. She loved him so much. I'd always known that. I used to wonder if she loved him more than me.

But this wasn't about that. It was about how I could help her right then. My mother's a good person; the strain in our relationship wasn't her fault. "You're going to get through this," I told her.

"It's advanced, so there aren't many options. They can try chemo, but he doesn't want to do it. His mother did chemo, and he said that it took everything out of her and she died anyway." More sobs. "He's just going to let himself die."

"Oh, Mom. Mommy." I was crying, too, not because of him—at least, I was pretty sure it wasn't—but because she was in so much pain.

"Come home and talk to him," she said. "You know how he feels about you."

I wanted to help her, but I never wanted to go back. "If he's not listening to you, he's not going to listen to me."

"He thinks you're smarter than me. You're the one who went to Berkeley."

"I'll call him."

"Something like this, it has to be in person."

My first visit in . . . how long had it been? A year, or more like two? "Does he look sick?"

"No. He just looks like Adam." I heard her stifling her tears, and the effort at containment was just as heart-wrenching as the weeping. "Please, Lucy. Come home. I need you. Not just to talk to him."

She needed me to be there for her. She was falling apart. The man she loved was dying.

It sounded like he was ready to die. Maybe our job was just to let him go.

Was it evil to feel the teeniest bit of anticipatory relief, to think that my secret would die with him?

I was torn. I didn't like to say no to anyone, especially not to Mom, and especially not right then, because that would be monstrous, but I didn't see how I could handle this. How I could be her confidante. Or his. The image made me shudder.

It was like I was shrinking, losing a year a second, and I was a kid again. I wanted my mommy.

But my mommy was asking me to be a grown-up. I couldn't let her down, yet I couldn't come through, either.

"I've never known anyone who's died," I said. All four of my grandparents were still alive; my father was, too, as I knew from Christmas cards and nothing else. He'd been on the East Coast and entirely uninvolved, not even aware of what was happening during Mom's drug years. Aunts, uncles, cousins—everyone was okay. Except Adam.

"Adam is not going to die!" she said fiercely. "He needs treatment, that's all. If he fights, he wins. We have to make sure he fights."

We. I was in this with her, whether I wanted to be or not. I couldn't tell her why I was hesitating. She'd never even asked why I didn't come home all through college. Like she hadn't wanted to know. Like she hadn't cared.

Suddenly, I was feeling the most unfamiliar emotion: anger.

Dr. Baylor would be pleased. He said I needed to get mad more often, that it was the building block of assertiveness, and that I should be standing up for myself.

It was a blessing and a curse that I was seeing Dr. Baylor that night. A blessing because I was in a horrible tumult, and because he's Dr. Baylor and I always wanted to see him, every day, and I thought of him more often than was comfortable in one sense, but in another, he was the ultimate solace. I liked knowing that he was out there, looking forward to our time together, maybe not the same as I did, but he must have had some anticipation. Otherwise, why would he do it for free?

But it was a curse because I was going to walk in there a total mess, and I hadn't told him much about Adam, or even about my mother. For a therapist, he asked remarkably few questions about childhood. I thought all therapists would insist we go there, but not Dr. Baylor.

Maybe there were things he didn't want to know, either.

"I'll come home this weekend," I said. It was the only way out of this call.

"Thank you, Lucy."

She sounded relieved; I was feeling the opposite. I was having trouble breathing, wondering if it was cardiac arrest or a panic attack. Best to assume it's a panic attack and to focus on my breathing. I told myself to think calming thoughts and visualize a serene place. Picture Dr. Baylor's face.

I didn't go back inside. I texted Christine and told her that I had to leave just a little bit early, I must have eaten bad shrimp. No one wanted to make further inquiries into other people's GI tracts.

Then I spent five minutes beating myself up: Bad *shrimp*? Who says that?

But those were five minutes not spent beating myself up for the far greater offense that lingered in the back of my subconscious, just waiting for an opportune moment to rise to prominence. Sometimes it was like I really did have a parasite living inside me, only it wasn't in my GI tract at all.

I tried to kill time in a café, but I was so antsy, so full of awful swirling thoughts, that I decided to go straight to Dr. Baylor's. Just being near him, even in the waiting room, could have a positive effect. I had to hope.

The intimacy of knowing the code to his building settled me a little. Seeing his name on the subscription label for all those issues of *Psychology Today* settled me more. I wasn't alone. He'd get me through this.

I knew it wasn't the same as having an actual partner. I did want a boyfriend to make me tea after a hard day. But all the rest of it—the expectations, the demands, the emotional sharing, the sex—was daunting. A lot of the time, I just wanted to curl up with a book. I flipped back and forth between the dreamy pleasure of my own company and self-flagellation. What guy was going to want that?

But for fifty minutes a week, with Dr. Baylor, I was at my best. If only I could stretch it out. After our sessions, I'd step outside his building feeling like some kind of superhero. A few blocks later, I was me again.

I started paging through the magazines. Narcissistic personality disorder seemed to be all the rage. How to know if you have it. How to deal with a loved one who has it. When to leave. Why you're not leaving. It sounded like narcissists often managed to find people with pathologies that clicked together with theirs, like a jigsaw puzzle. Dependent personalities.

His door opened, and a woman emerged. She was somewhere in her thirties, more put together than I'd ever been, with blow-dried hair and glossy lips. Her clothes had a sophisticated drape, and while they didn't reveal her shape exactly, you just knew she was skinny under there. She radiated confidence. She was pretty enough and, I'd guess, successful. I wanted to know her diagnosis.

She was laughing and saying, "See you next week!" Her voice was gay. It was like she was exiting a very good party.

I was envious of the way she carried herself and that airy tone. Envious that she'd just spent an hour with Dr. Baylor.

And he'd just spent an hour with her. She was the tough act I had to follow every week. Usually, I raced in at the last minute and she was already gone. I'd never before seen my competition.

I reminded myself she was paying for her sessions and I wasn't.

Of course, she could afford to pay for her sessions. She was probably about to meet her rich boyfriend for cocktails and small plates at À Côté. I was sure she would never think of me as competition.

All this flashed through my mind in the seconds before Dr. Baylor said, "Lucy! I'll be right with you."

He shut his door, and I was left with just one thought: I was utterly pathetic. Totally second-rate. That was without his even knowing the terrible things I'd done.

By the time he invited me in, I was in tears. I couldn't even look at him. He sank down on his knees in front of me, and I took the tissue he offered. He didn't say anything, just let his beatific energy wash over me. When I was ready, I stood up and followed him inside.

"Start wherever you'd like," he said. "Or we can sit in silence for a while."

I grabbed for the whole box of tissues from the end table beside the couch. I had absolutely no idea where to start, how far back to go, or should I be in the present? Should I just tell him that I might be in love with him, and I knew how stupid that was, and that nothing could ever happen between us, and that he would never feel that way about me, even if he'd met me under different circumstances?

He might say that we couldn't work together anymore. I could lose what we did have. All I had.

Besides, I was being a narcissist, focusing on myself at a time like this. I needed to think of Adam. No, I should think about my mother.

"My stepfather has cancer," I said.

Dr. Baylor didn't respond in the way I would have expected. He didn't say he was sorry. Instead, he nodded and waited.

"It's stage four, and he doesn't want to have chemo. My mother thinks I can convince him."

"That's a big responsibility. Why do you think she would put you in that position?" He was watching me compassionately but carefully. Again, not where I thought he'd go, but I trusted him. He knew better than I did.

"Adam listens to me. Or at least, she thinks he would."

"He doesn't listen to her?" When I was silent, Dr. Baylor did another nod, like something was coming into focus for him.

I was gripped with fear. He already knew. It was therapist telepathy, or maybe the precise ways I was fucked up matched the contours of what I'd done. I fit the profile.

"I guess he's not listening to her about this," I said.

"You've stopped crying," he observed.

I hadn't noticed.

"How do you feel about the prospect of Adam dying?"

"I believe in the right to die."

"That's a belief. It's not a feeling."

"I'm sad about it."

But I couldn't seem to conjure any tears. What I felt was afraid. Because Dr. Baylor was close to the third rail.

I explained that I hadn't seen my mother in a long time and that this task was probably beyond me and I really didn't want to let her down. It wasn't untrue. But I knew that my affect didn't match, that I was revealing myself in the discrepancy.

I hated keeping things from Dr. Baylor, but I couldn't tell him. I couldn't lose his good opinion of me.

He knew there was more, but he left it at that. He was letting me keep my secret. He told me in our first session that I was in charge of what got shared and when. "This is your time," he said, and I'd felt myself blushing.

"Adam hasn't been in my life that long," I said. "They got married when I was fifteen."

"Complicated age."

He had no idea.

Unless he did.

CHAPTER 7

GREER

Donor Profile #1017

Interview Notes

Donor 1017 was tall and handsome, with an infectious smile. His blond hair was short and neat, and his green eyes matched his polo shirt, which was tucked into jeans. He wore a matching brown belt and brown sandals. He laughed easily and was quick to joke, but he didn't shy away from uncomfortable topics, either.

Donor 1017 grew up in the Midwest, and he's proof that what they say about Midwesterners is true: he's just so nice! His parents have been married thirty-four years, and he grew up in a stable, loving home. He climbed more trees than he could count!

Donor 1017 was a high school soccer star. He was also on the debate team. It was important in his family to be well rounded . . .

Q & A

Describe your personality.

Fun-loving. Achievement-oriented. Hyphen-prone. :)

What are your interests and goals?

I love being outdoors. I hike a lot. I'm learning to sail. I'm interested in becoming an architect. I just started the coursework and so far, I love it. I want to have a family of my own someday, and I'll coach soccer for my kids. My dad was an amazing role model. But until then, I'd like to help other people have the families they're dreaming of.

Was this kid for real? A sweet, handsome Midwestern future architect with an incredible genetic profile and sperm that he just wanted to give to a good home. The interviewer was clearly smitten. All those exclamation points! I'd always disliked pairing "infectious" with anything except "disease." Made me think his smile could give me bubonic plague.

Donor 1017 had to be a plant. He was a test to see if you'd become too jaded and therefore were willing to turn down the perfect human.

If so, I'd failed.

I couldn't help but think there had to be a catch. No one could be that wholesome, or if he really was, I wouldn't want to hang out with him. Maybe his smile wouldn't give me the plague, but it would give me cavities. If I chose Donor 1017 and was successfully inseminated (ugh, what a word), then I would wind up hanging out with him, in a way. I'd be raising a child that was half Donor 1017, and someday that (boring?) child could go looking for him. Would that child be disappointed in Donor 1017 and, by extension, in me for making a substandard choice? Or would the child be infatuated with Donor 1017 and come to hate me?

I'd never been a neurotic before, and I would have thought that it was too late to start, but apparently, you were never too old to learn new tricks.

Part of my problem was that the majority of donors were quite young. No wonder they sounded so facile, so callow. Donor 1017 was a junior in college. He hadn't been seasoned by life yet, peppered by mistakes, failures, and letdowns. Reading the profile couldn't show me his true measure, who he would become. If I ever got a dog, I wouldn't pick a puppy; I'd pick one that was fully grown so I'd know what I was really getting. This decision was far more monumental, and what I had on my hands were puppies.

Not to mention that even though there would be no sex involved, it felt wrong to spawn with someone who was barely legal. I was no cougar.

If I were to use the sperm of men my own age, it seemed like it should come through normal channels. When I saw a profile of a donor in his thirties, the inevitable question was, "What's gone awry in your life that you're selling off your DNA?" Sperm donation was a young man's game. It was beer money.

Reading those profiles, I felt my eggs wrinkling, imagined them inside my ovaries like tiny shar-peis.

Enough about the dogs.

There was a knock on my office door, and I minimized the window where I'd been cyberstalking the future father of my child.

This wasn't me. When I was at work, I worked. From seven in the morning until at least seven at night. No breaks. Salads or sandwiches at my desk, unless it was a business lunch. That was how you got to helm your own headhunting firm in a market as competitive as San Francisco.

If a baby was this distracting now, when it was just an idea, what was going to happen when (if) it was a reality?

"Come in," I said.

My assistant, Chenille, pushed open the door. Chenille was an absolutely gorgeous woman, with ebony skin, long dark hair, and an hourglass figure that engendered rubbernecking. I once witnessed bike-versus-car when neither could keep their eyes off her. I knew nothing of her life outside work and vice versa. Boundaries were paramount, and Chenille got that, which was one of the reasons she was the best employee I'd ever had.

"I have some documents for you to sign," Chenille said, placing a folder on my desk and then stepping back gracefully, the admin version of ATM distance.

"Amazing that we still need to use actual ink."

For me, this qualified as chatty, and Chenille looked ever so slightly surprised. As always, she recovered well. It was another reason I valued her so highly. We were in a never-let-'em-see-you-sweat business. "I have to make myself useful somehow."

I gave her a quick smile as I bent to my task, grateful not to make eye contact. Even though I knew Chenille couldn't tell what I'd been doing just prior, the embarrassment persisted. It was like being caught seconds after masturbating.

Chenille departed, and I realized it wasn't long before I'd need to head across the Bay Bridge. I lived in the city, so getting to Oakland to see Dr. Baylor—Michael, he'd told me to call him Michael—was a definite irritant. But privacy was an overriding factor, and I'd wanted to make sure I wouldn't be running into my therapist out and about.

My therapist. Jesus.

No one knew I was seeing him, and I would never become one of those people who made casual references in conversation. I didn't really like calling him Michael; I'd prefer Doctor. He didn't call me a patient; he called me a client. Again, I preferred the formality of patient, with the sense that I was submitting to a necessary medical procedure, like getting a bunion removed. Six weeks of bed rest and good as new. I was hoping therapy could be that efficient. With forty looming, six weeks was about as much time as I wanted to devote to the decision-making process.

At the end of our last (and first) session, he asked me about my treatment goals. "What do you most want to accomplish here?"

I stared at him blankly.

"How will you feel; how will the world look? How will you know our work is done?"

More staring.

Those questions had haunted me all week. I wasn't sure whether to tell him what I came up with: Our work would be done when he had cured my baby fever. When he'd made me stop wanting to hold my very own bundle of joy. When he'd gotten me to see that parental love wasn't all it's cracked up to be. No, not just see it. Feel it, deep down.

I wanted him to convince me that it was better not to grow in uncomfortable ways. That I didn't have to spend my time reading the personal statements of prospective donors or use words like *insemination*. That I didn't have to walk this path in order to become a mother because my life was great just as it was. I was fine already. More than fine. I was precisely who I should be.

CHAPTER 8

FLORA

This was how I remembered the first session:

Young had found Dr. Baylor. It was important to Young that we meet with a man. My theory was that a man was supposed to understand how a husband loses that loving feeling toward the woman he's been with since college. Young was probably hoping that a man would set me straight, and I'd adapt to certain inevitable realities. Then we could live like roommates with a quickie a couple of times a month.

At first, I thought Young might get his wish. Dr. Baylor just seemed like such a nebbish, as my father would say in Yiddish. Unassuming, even a little hapless, Dr. Baylor let Young tell his side ad nauseam (literally, I was nauseated) and didn't say anything about Young's frequent interruptions when it was my chance to speak. For the first thirty minutes, it was The Young Show. I was seeing the two of us through Dr. Baylor's eyes, and I didn't like it. I was sure that couples therapists had an intuition about which ones were going to make it and which weren't, and Young and I were going to fall on the wrong side of that ledger, and Dr. Baylor wasn't man enough to do a thing about it.

Young was all I'd ever known. He was my first sex and my first love. I'd fought hard for those to be the same person, despite many temptations along the way and a whole lot of false rumors and innuendos. Our relationship wasn't perfect, but I was proud of the rings on my finger and the man on my arm. As I saw it, divorce was not an option.

Then I sat in that session, and I listened. I really heard, perhaps for the first time, all Young's excuses, rationalizations, and judgments (of me, not of himself). "I bring in two-thirds of the money, and I work seventy, eighty hours a week," he said, "and still, she wants more—"

"I want closeness," I interjected. Dr. Baylor didn't even look up from the yellow legal pad where he was taking notes that I couldn't read upside down.

"I want dinner." Young turned to Dr. Baylor. "You know how women are always saying they'd want sex if their husbands would ever do housework? Well, I might want sex if Flora would ever cook dinner. It's takeout every night."

"That's suffering? Oakland has incredible restaurants," I said, also to Dr. Baylor, a referee who wouldn't blow the whistle. "We can go a month without eating the same thing twice."

"*Expensive* restaurants," Young countered. "No wonder I have to work so much. But that's not the point. The point is feeling taken care of by your spouse. Home cooking is about a home."

Dr. Baylor's gaze was suddenly leveled at Young with an intensity that I hadn't seen coming. "Your wife wants to feel taken care of, too. She wants to feel full. She wants to feel sexy and desired and *sated*."

Perhaps it was the element of surprise or the absolute authority in Dr. Baylor's voice, but Young shut up.

"Flora, turn to him," Dr. Baylor commanded. "Tell him what you want. No, what you need."

Young was staring down at the floor sullenly.

"I can't," I said.

"Try."

"It's too embarrassing."

"You're a human being. Human beings have needs, and sex is among them. Love is among them. Do you feel loved?"

Out of nowhere, I was sobbing. I hadn't known I ached like this, that I felt so bereft.

Young's arms were around me, and he was telling me how much he loved me, how much he needed me, but when I looked up, Dr. Baylor—Michael—met my eyes, and the shake of his head was nearly imperceptible, subconscious maybe, but I caught it.

Young and I were a memory, an open grave. It was just a matter of time before the dirt fell over us.

CHAPTER 9

LUCINDA

Mom said Adam hadn't changed, but could love really be that blind?

He looked ravaged. He'd always been thin and rangy, but now he was skeletal. He must not have been eating for months before his cancer was discovered. I couldn't believe he just saw a doctor in the past few weeks. This had clearly been going on much longer. And the house was a wreck, too, like they'd become hoarders.

All the rooms were tiny, but after Mom got clean, they'd been well kept. Cozy. I used to love that house, sitting outside on the deck, journaling, the Russian River below. Now there were dusty piles on every surface, and it managed to smell actively rotting and musty at once. Again, this had all been going on much longer than a few weeks.

It already smelled like death, was the thing. Food left to decay and spoil, the scent of apathy and neglect.

It didn't seem like Adam was the only one who'd given up, no matter what Mom had told me on the phone. I wondered what had been happening between them over the past years, in my absence.

Adam was lying on the plaid sofa in the living room, under an afghan. Mom was slamming pots and pans in the kitchen. She'd looked pissed ever since I arrived, which was disorienting, as I'd expected to find her weepy and grateful. Adam appeared to be dozing, but he had to be pretending; I couldn't imagine who could sleep in all that racket, or maybe he was just that close to dead.

Finally, Mom walked into the living room with a tray holding some canned soup she'd heated up. My eyes hadn't yet adjusted to seeing her with gray hair and no makeup and sweats; it was as if someone were impersonating her. As if I'd wandered onto the wrong soundstage, and none of this was real.

She shoved a bunch of papers, magazines, and who knows what from the coffee table onto the floor and put the tray down with a clatter. The soup spilled. Adam's eyes flew open.

"Your daughter's here," my mother sneered. He'd come into my life as a teenager; she'd never left out the *step* before *daughter* before.

I'd also never seen her behave like this. But then, I didn't know what it was like to have your husband choose dying over living with you. Now that I'd seen the condition of their lives, though, it seemed like a far more rational decision.

"Hi, Lucinda," Adam said with a weak smile.

"I'm going out," Mom announced. "I'll leave you two to talk."

After the slam of the front door, Adam and I looked at each other.

"She knows," he said.

"Knows what?"

"The past." He glanced down at the soup as if he didn't know how it got there, and I realized my mother hadn't told me where the cancer had spread, but his brain seemed like a definite possibility.

"Whose past?"

"Ours." He gestured between us. "I told her. Deathbed confession." He tried to smile again.

I stared at him for one long, shocked moment.

Then I had the uncharacteristic desire to smash him in the face. The gall. The selfishness. He was on his way out, but I had to go on living, and she had to live knowing . . .

I stood up and started striding around the room, not sure what I could possibly say. He couldn't undo this. Neither of us could. He'd blown it all up. His life. His relationship with my mother. My relationship with her.

The anger was like a fire through my limbs. An unfamiliar fire. I didn't get mad; I got self-abusing. But that was under normal circumstances, and this was so far from normal.

"You're going to die," I said. "You're going to hell. But did you need to take us with you?"

"You're always so melodramatic."

Maybe cancer really was rotting his brain. Good. "I've never been melodramatic. I've always held in way too much." Then it dawned on me. "You did this so she'd let you go, didn't you?"

"She hasn't tried to convince me to do chemo since. And once I'm gone, she won't waste a lot of time grieving. She can go find someone who deserves her."

"That's not how it works. You don't love the people who deserve you. You love who you love."

"But you don't have to act on it," he said. "That was my mistake."

Crazy as it sounded, all I'd wanted was to protect my mother from the pain. The pain of knowing who I really was. Now I couldn't spare her.

I couldn't believe he'd chosen this as his final act. The man who both my mother and I fell in love with was riddled with cancer and, supposedly, conscience. He thought this was about mercy. I could see it in his face.

He was getting ready to leave, and Mom and I had to dwell in the wreckage. Well, I already had been for years. But she didn't have to. He and I had agreed to that years ago. He broke the pact, without giving me so much as a warning while I drove here, ostensibly to convince him of how much he had to live for.

"I'm sorry," he said. "Maybe I wasn't thinking clearly."

"Maybe?"

"Now you can go ahead and hate me, too."

He'd done this so I'd let him go, too. Then Mom and I could both hate him. "I'm going home."

"What do I tell your mother when she gets back?"

That I love her. That I'm sorry. That I should have told her sooner. That he never should have told her at all. That I shouldn't have done what I did. That I thought I couldn't help myself, but I know now you can always help yourself. That I'm an awful person.

That I deserved Adam, but she never did.

"That I love her," I said.

"I know you do."

"Do you think she knows it anymore?"

He looked down, color rushing to his face, as if he'd just then grasped what he'd done. "Maybe not right now, but she will again. Someday."

He couldn't know that. I certainly didn't.

"Goodbye," I said. I slammed the front door behind me, the identical sound to the one my mother had made just a few minutes before.

She had to come back, but I didn't.

Because there was nothing left. He'd seen to that.

CHAPTER 10

GREER

"Do we really have to go there?" It was too cliché, too paint by numbers. Go to therapy and exhume your childhood. My childhood was fine.

"We're going there," Dr. Michael said. I had noticed that from each session to the next, he was firmer. More alpha, really. It was only our fourth meeting. If we continued this way, he might be the Terminator by the six-month mark.

I actually preferred this Dr. Michael. Economy of speech and emotion was my bailiwick. But talking about my childhood? That was hardly in my wheelhouse.

"I wasn't a kid even when I was a kid," I said. "My earliest memory is age eight."

"What is it?"

"I'm just saying, my childhood memories are sparse, and they're not very relevant."

"Sometimes what we don't remember is the most relevant."

I rolled my eyes. "Okay, Obi-Wan."

He grinned. "You've got to trust me here."

"Is that how trust works? You just tell people they have to?"

"You're avoiding."

Actually, I was having fun. I was more myself than I had been the first few sessions. My diarrhea of the mouth had resolved. "My parents were lovely people."

"Were?"

"My mother died seven years ago."

"That must have been rough."

"I was an adult." If he wanted tears, he was going to be disappointed. "They had a good marriage. A model marriage. They were both ambitious and successful. They were true equals."

"It's interesting that you called it 'model.'"

"Why's that?"

"Because you haven't used it as a model. You don't want to be married."

"I never said that."

"I wrote it down in our last session. I underlined it."

"Something I don't even recall saying doesn't merit underlining."

"You're terrified of intimacy."

I shook my head. "You've just met me. You can't know that."

"You're right, I can't know for sure, not this early. But all the signs are there. I have to wonder: Do you have few childhood memories because you spent much of it alone?"

It felt like he'd just punched me, though I couldn't say why.

Gently, he asked, "Were you nurtured, Greer?"

"I was raised! By two lovely people!"

"You used that word before: lovely. Lovely or loving?"

I got frustrated sometimes at work. But this—it wasn't mere frustration; it was laced with something.

He saw me struggling and prompted, "Could you tell me what you're feeling?" No, I couldn't. "Do you know what you're feeling?"

After a long moment, I admitted, "No."

"We learn to define our emotions from our parents. You cry, and they help you understand whether it's sadness or disappointment or hurt. The differentiation is important. Knowing what you feel guides you. Emotions are information."

That wasn't how I operated. Was it how anyone operated?

"I feel like you're blaming my parents," I said. "You're blaming them for screwing me up, and I'm not a screwup."

"No, you're not. But we're all screwed up."

"Oh really? How are you screwed up?"

His smile—it's laced with something, too. "Conversation for another time. But you should know, I think you're fascinating."

I laughed. "I bet you say that to all the girls."

"Only when it's true." He squinted at me, appraising. "You know what? You're good."

"I'd say thank you, but I'm not sure you're giving me a compliment."

"You know how to create the illusion of intimacy. We're smiling, we're laughing, we're bantering. But the truth is, as you've gotten more comfortable with me week by week, you've managed to give less and less. You were vulnerable that first session, and you didn't like that. You've pulled back."

"I get it. You took this job because you like damsels in distress. You like to dispense your nuggets of wisdom and save people. Well, I don't need saving."

"What do you need?"

I did something uncharacteristic: I squirmed under his gaze. I made my living staring down men, proving that I could hold my own, that I could find them the right person for their executive position; no man could do anything better, or be any tougher, than me.

"What do you need?" he said again.

The answer came disturbingly quickly: "Love."

"Now we're getting somewhere."

He might have thought so, and I might have feared so, but the clock said otherwise. It was time to wrap things up in a neat bow and send me out into the world.

"Next week," he told me, "we'll look more at the messages you received in your childhood about love, marriage, and parenting, and what you might have internalized that's holding you back now."

"Goody."

"Next week, same time, same place?"

I assented with a marked lack of enthusiasm, and then I flew out of his office and through the waiting room. On my way down the flight of stairs, I stumbled. My ankle twisted, my purse went AWOL, and I glanced back up, relieved to find that he'd shut the door. He'd missed this little display, which meant he couldn't psychoanalyze it.

I got to my feet gingerly, putting the slightest exploratory weight on my ankle. It wasn't broken.

I felt a twinge of pain as I pushed the outer door open. It was lifted out of my hand. I recognized the woman from Dr. Michael's waiting room last week. She was tall and blonde, an Uma Thurman type who clearly didn't know how striking she was.

She recognized me, too, and said, "Are you okay?"

"Fine," I said through gritted teeth. Maybe she could see how I was favoring my leg, or maybe she could see what Michael had done to me in there, how discombobulated I'd become in only a month of sessions. Was this really how therapy was supposed to work? "Thanks for asking."

I pushed past her, my ankle throbbing as it hit the pavement of College Avenue.

My plan had been to go to a café and work for an hour or so until the traffic subsided. Now all I wanted was to get home to my condo along the Embarcadero, sit outside on my balcony with a glass of Chardonnay, and watch the light fade over the bay. That was my happy place.

At least, I'd always told myself it was. What was this bullshit about needing love? It was a radical revision of my whole life story.

It couldn't be true. I must have been under some kind of spell in there. Dr. Michael was doing a Jedi mind trick. Why else would I have made that weird Obi-Wan reference?

That wasn't me. I didn't talk Star Wars.

Was it possible that I didn't need a baby, I needed a man?

No, it was not possible. Besides, I wasn't into Dr. Michael. I couldn't be.

We're going there. You've got to trust me. You never want to get married. I wrote it down.

I hadn't seen it in my first session or even my second, but he was absurdly cocky. Worse than any Silicon Valley exec, as he trotted out all his Zen koans and his bullshit about feelings being information and his presumption that I hadn't been nurtured.

Nurtured, for fuck's sake.

Terrified of intimacy, underlined.

That prick.

I wasn't going back. Then he'd see how good of a therapist he really was. He couldn't even keep a client past the fourth session. That would show him.

Besides, I didn't need therapy. I'd find my answers somewhere else.

PRESENT DAY

CHAPTER 11

DETECTIVE GREGORY PLATH

This Flora—she's a piece of work. You know those teenagers who were told that being sassy and sexy will take you everywhere?

She still believes it.

I tell her what I know, which is basically the names of all Dr. Baylor's patients (current and former, he had them in different drawers of his file cabinet), though I haven't been able to open the files themselves. I know Flora is a former, and that she met with another former by the name of Greer and a current by the name of Lucinda at a dim sum restaurant, and that the timing was curious, to say the least: the day of the murder. Greer left first, and Lucinda and Flora stayed for another hour, maybe.

"Who told you that?" she asks, all pissed off. "Greer?"

The way she says it, I know there's no love lost between the two of them. I shake my head, but I don't give up any details. It wasn't Greer or Lucinda. It was Maureen Hillard, one of the women who filed a complaint and then withdrew it. She was the first former client I interviewed, the most obvious suspect, since the other complainant now lives across the country. Maureen had an airtight alibi, as did her husband, Cyrus, but she was quick to act as an informant.

According to Maureen, Flora had lain in wait by her car to invite her to the dim sum brunch. Maureen had asked who else was going, just out of curiosity, and Flora told her, and then Maureen said, "Sorry, I'm busy." It was sort of a bitch move, from where I was sitting, a way to try to get Flora's goat. So there was no love lost there, either, but after that, Maureen clammed up. She said that she assumed Flora wanted to talk about Michael, but it hadn't been said directly, which stunk up my office, it was so much bullshit. After she fed me my three prime suspects, she got cold feet. She didn't want to get involved. I see that all the time. People want to point fingers, but they don't want them getting broken off. Who wants to be in the crosshairs of someone who's murdered once? What they fail to realize is that homicide has the lowest recidivism rate of any crime.

But I digress.

Maureen hadn't wanted to talk about her complaint, either, whether it was true or false and why she rescinded. I couldn't make her spill, given that alibi of hers. I just had to be grateful that she'd told me as much as she had, that she'd led me to three people of interest, the first one of whom has no alibi to speak of. Flora says she was home in her apartment, alone.

If that trio had been cooking up something, the dim sum restaurant was an inspired location. The staff didn't speak much English, and the joint had apparently been jumping. No one working that day could describe the dynamics among the three women, whether they'd seemed friendly or not, whether they'd been upset or laughing or conspiratorial. They did know that the short, skinny one left before the tall, skinny one and the darker-skinned woman with the big nose (the latter presumably Flora, given her visage). I'm sure she'd love that description.

"Tell me how you knew these women," I say.

"Why do you want to know? Because you're *curious*?" She's using my word against me, raising an eyebrow like she's fucking adorable.

She's annoying, but that doesn't make her a murderer. Right now, all I've got them on is timing. Way too coincidental but also circumstantial. I need someone to give herself up or give someone else up. Either works for me.

"I'm trying to piece things together and find out who did this. I don't have a lot to go on right now. I'm following down all the leads."

"So I'm a lead?" That same eyebrow. "Or am I a suspect?"

"I'm hoping you're someone who's going to help me in this investigation. Am I right on that? This guy was your therapist." Or more, based on her demeanor. This woman could sexualize panhandling. "Don't you want to get the person who did this to him?"

"My therapy is my business."

"We'll see if the court agrees with you on that. The judge probably won't uphold doctor-patient privilege."

"But they might. I'll take my chances." She sits back in her seat, looking mildly self-satisfied.

She's so confident. Is that because she knows there's nothing to find? Because she knows she's innocent?

Or she's guilty and she's a fucking psychopath. She enjoys the cat and mouse with me, maybe the same as she enjoyed it with her shrink, until she killed him.

She's a former patient, so I don't know how long ago her professional association with the doc ended and if/when a personal one began. How long she was batting him around.

"There were two other women at that restaurant," I say. "Whoever talks first might be the winner."

She looks at me with frank astonishment. "What are you saying? You think I conspired with Lucy and Greer to kill Michael?"

She called him "Michael." Not "Dr. Baylor." And she called Lucinda "Lucy."

But I have to admit, her shock is convincing. "I'm not saying anything about conspiracies," I say. "I'm just saying that if whatever you talked about that day is relevant to my investigation, you want to be the first to tell me."

"Just because someone tells you what you want to hear doesn't make it true. And just because someone doesn't talk—that doesn't mean they're hiding something."

What kind of a riddle is that? "Talk straight, please."

"I could say the same to you."

Okay, so this spitfire thing does have a certain charm. "Let's get off the whole dim sum topic. Let's talk about you and Michael."

"He was my therapist. You know that. I saw him for couples therapy with my husband."

"How'd that turn out?"

"We're divorced."

"Sorry."

"Don't be. Sometimes things need to end."

I smile. "Is that really what you want to say to a homicide detective?" Wait, did she just get me to flirt with her?

"What I want to say is, I had nothing to do with Michael Baylor's death. Dim sum had nothing to do with it."

"So you weren't talking about the one thing you had in common?"

"How do you know he's the only thing we had in common?"

She is. She's enjoying this. That doesn't necessarily make her guilty. But I've got a strong feeling that she's not sorry he's dead.

What did this guy do to her?

BEFORE

CHAPTER 12

FLORA

"You're where?" I said, hoping I'd heard wrong.

"The ER," he said again. "But don't worry, I'm fine. Everything's under control."

"What's going on?"

"I can't say much. I need to get back. It's a client."

"You're having her committed to a mental hospital?"

I heard his impatience in the silence. His disapproval. He didn't like when I asked too many questions about his other clients, though he sometimes volunteered their predicaments. No identifying information, just the general outlines. It felt unfair that he was allowed to bring them up, but if I asked further, I was prying. Sometimes it was like he made all the rules.

"Doesn't she have a husband or family?" I couldn't help it; I was impatient, too. This didn't seem like a normal thing for a therapist to do, sitting with his client in the ER for what could be hours. And it was a her, wasn't it? He hadn't said that, hadn't used a pronoun, but other than in couples therapy, he didn't seem to have male clients. Or if he did, he didn't find them worth discussing, which was telling.

"I need to go." Then in a whispered hiss, "She's *suicidal*. Have some compassion." *Click.* He was gone. Back to her.

I hated how I felt right then. Petty and small. Abandoned. He was right; I should have had compassion for this nameless, faceless woman who wanted to die.

Or she was just pretending so she could get a few hours with Michael in the ER. He had that effect on women.

He'd told me his dating history had been full of women who'd misconstrued kindness, who'd held on too long with grasping fingers, and that he'd learned over the years that it was better to amputate. Don't give false hope. Be direct.

Was I the one with the grasping fingers now?

No, if he didn't want to be with me, he'd tell me directly.

There was no need for insecurity because I knew how Michael felt about me. But it had been creeping up lately. I wanted to meet his parents and his friends. I wanted legitimacy. Then I'd feel permanent. At that moment, I felt so insubstantial. Replaceable.

He said I was the only client he'd ever had true romantic feelings for. "But you must have been attracted to other clients," I said. "You're a guy. You must have wanted to have sex with some of them."

"That's normal. It's called countertransference."

It was getting increasingly difficult to take his reassurances at face value. I wanted them to be backed up with actions, and though it had been more than a month since our "anniversary," I was still in the shadows. We'd gone nowhere. Trips to his house remained infrequent, because he still didn't want the neighbors to catch sight of me. The vast majority of the time, it was still takeout dinners and sex in my apartment. Tonight, it wouldn't even be that, because he was with some other woman.

A client, I reminded myself. Suicidal threats were not foreplay. This was work. He was a responsible therapist and a caring human. I wouldn't want him to be less, would I?

Needing to get out of my head, I picked up my phone.

"Cousin!" Kate—Katerina—exclaimed. No mixed messages there; she was always glad to hear from me.

We grew up together in Miami, her trailing at my heels along the beach. A three-year age difference felt significant in childhood, and my head start in life meant that she was perpetually looking up to me. But I became a self-involved teenager, and she spiraled downward. All the drugs and all the men, some of them twice her age, because they were the ones providing the drugs. It was a dark time in our family, and I wanted to be the one to pull her out, back into the light, but I couldn't. She had to do that herself, and she did, finally, after her fourth stint in rehab. She'd been clean for several years now, and while the family was still wary of her, keeping her in black-sheep status, she and I had a loyalty, a bond, that was unbreakable. I trusted her completely, which was why she was the only one who'd known about Michael since the beginning.

"How's everyone?" I asked. Mostly, I meant my parents. Kate kept an eye on them for me, since I was across the country. They didn't have any particular health problems, but they were in their seventies, and I was their only child. The distance was hard on them. We spoke weekly, staccato exchanges of information, my fielding their yes-or-no questions. They would make terrible therapists.

"We all miss you, of course." Kate had never lived in Russia, but she had a faint accent. That's because her parents were the family members who had assimilated least. In her house, it was always Moscow: Russian food, tapestries, language. "Your parents are after me to visit you. Then I can give them the skinny."

I laughed. "Tell them there's no skinny. I'm fine. I'm great."

"You know they don't believe that."

They'd remained in a chronic state of worry ever since Young and I separated. Initially, they tried to convince me to patch things up, whatever it took. I told them I could survive on my own; I make decent money, and the divorce settlement was fair. Still, they'd gone into deeper mourning for my marriage than I had. For a time, Kate said it had been like they were sitting Shiva, always in black. They hadn't even liked Young that much; they just really liked marriage. They thought it was the only true safety net, and now, in their minds, I was adrift.

"What do I need to do?" I asked. "Show them my bank account records? A smiley Instagram account?"

"You know the only thing that'll satisfy them is if you move back to Miami, find a nice man, marry him, and have babies."

"They think nothing's keeping me here."

"Tell them otherwise. Tell them about Michael. Say he's a rich, successful therapist. A *Jewish* therapist."

We both laughed. "You think I can get him to convert before he meets them?"

"At the pace he's going, yeah, I think you have the time."

I didn't laugh.

"How is Michael?" she said.

"He's at the ER. With a client."

"Oh." She got it immediately. We'd known each other our whole lives. She knew what I'd feel before I felt it. "You have to remember, that's work. You're love."

"I used to be work."

"You know what this is? It's the Other Woman Syndrome. Even after men leave their wives for the other woman, she always wonders. She thinks, *If he did it once, he can do it again.*"

"And don't they? Do it again?"

"Not always."

"But sometimes."

"But not always," she said firmly.

I nodded, trying to take it in. I would be the exception. Besides, I wasn't the other woman. He hadn't been with anyone when we got together for real; I hadn't, either. Young and I had already split up before Michael and I even shared our first kiss. Sure, we had already admitted that we had feelings for each other before that, but feelings were not actions. Actions were what counted.

That was my problem. I was waiting for him to act, and I'd never been good at waiting.

Kate got it again. "Patience," she counseled. "That's your only move at this point."

"It's not the only move."

"What are you going to do, push him until he pushes back or runs away?"

"Tell him how I feel. Tell him how much this hurts me."

"Haven't you done that already?"

Sadly, I had. He'd empathized and commiserated; we were still on his timetable.

But he was the one with everything to lose: his professional reputation, even his license if someone found out what'd been going on these past two years. He was incredibly dedicated to his work, which was why he was being so cautious. He wished we could be a regular couple, too. This was hard on him, too.

No one knew, and no one would find out until the time was right. It was between him, Kate, and me. Not that I'd mentioned Kate. Well, he was aware she was my cousin and we were close, but that was it. What he didn't know wouldn't hurt him.

To get through this, I'd needed a confidante, and she was all the way across the country. If he'd told someone about me, I wouldn't have any problem with it. Actually, I'd be flattered. Validated.

"Come visit," I said. "Then you can report back to my parents, and you can be the first to meet Michael. Two birds, one stone."

See? There was another move.

CHAPTER 13

LUCINDA

All week, I'd been throwing myself into work. Amazing how something so tedious could be so absorbing. Normally, I bemoaned the fact that proofreading and fact-checking used so little creative brainpower—so little brainpower, period. I mostly did the job on autopilot. But this week, I was giving it all I had. It was a real exercise in mindfulness: do only what you're doing, completely. Dr. Baylor would be proud. I'd tell him in tonight's session.

What I'd learned was that I really did, unequivocally, hate my job. I'd always assumed my dislike was related to my lack of commitment and my half presence, along with some nascent resentment, since I wished I could be doing my own writing or even true editing where I'd get to critique plot and character like I had in my undergraduate fiction workshops. I'd thought it was professional jealousy, because no one was getting paid to improve my writing (not that I was actually doing any, but jealousy was an irrational emotion) and because I would never have chosen to acquire these books, yet there I was, tasked with making their sentences smoother and their points clearer, with making them honest. But no, that wasn't it. It was also the work itself. That was a depressing realization. Autopilot or not, though, I was still Verdant's best proofreader.

For a small boutique publisher, the breadth of books was startling, while the quality was fairly uniform: Last week, it was a truly cringeworthy coffee table book on refugees (what kind of person would want to advertise their social conscience that way? No one with an actual social conscience); this week, it was a self-help book called *The Art of Eating Disorders*. I begged Christine to rename that one because it didn't sound like it was about how art aids recovery from anorexia and bulimia but rather that you, too, could elevate your starving, bingeing, and purging to an art form.

Christine, predictably, maintained that no one would think that. I rarely voiced any strenuous objections, reserving it for the most egregious errors and miscalculations, ones where it would have felt sadistic toward the author not to speak up, and you might have thought that would give Christine pause. But no, she dug her heels in and defended, with a passion she'd never previously expressed toward the project.

What it meant was that I didn't merely spend my days suggesting that authors move commas on their execrable manuscripts but that Christine decided nine out of ten times that the comma would stay where it was. I felt like Sisyphus but with a whole lot less dignity. At least Sisyphus was rolling a boulder; I was rolling thousands of pebbles, and most of them were raining back down on me.

But minutiae can be consuming, and this week, I was grateful for that.

Mom hadn't called again. I hadn't called her. Every time I pictured her slamming those pots and pans, so unlike herself, my stomach hurt. I'd done that to her.

Then I thought of how long it must have taken for her house to devolve to that state, and again, how unlike her that was. She used to take pride in her home, and in her marriage, and in herself. Her hair was gray, and that couldn't have happened overnight, with Adam's diagnosis. She'd gotten old, which was uncontrollable, but she didn't care enough to hide it. That wasn't her, either. Adam's disclosure was devastating, but that house and that hair . . . they were preexisting conditions.

It underscored that I didn't really know her anymore. It had been six years since I lived in the river house. I'd hightailed it out for college at eighteen with a broken heart, and she'd called every week, and I hadn't wanted to talk to her. I didn't want to hear news about Adam. She'd won, which wasn't her fault; she hadn't even known we were competing. I was unfairly angry with her, and guilty over that, and mourning Adam's loss, though I'd never had him to begin with. In short, I was an utter mess. My classmates gave me a wide berth.

But she kept calling, never pushing, expressing concern tactfully, lovingly, letting me know that I could tell her anything and she'd always be there for me. It was unbearable. I answered every third call or returned them when I knew she couldn't pick up, like during her Monday night Narcotics Anonymous meeting, or I rang her while I was on my way to class and then told her, "Gotta go!" after five minutes. They were all tricks to keep my distance, and she was a bright woman. She must have known that. She just couldn't have known the reason. Now, though, she did.

Did she feel any relief at that, since we were all detectives at heart, wanting to solve the mysteries of our lives? Or was she now tortured by the knowledge of exactly what kind of child she had raised and what kind of man she'd married?

My heartbreak had worn off slowly; I can't say it healed, exactly. The guilt and shame rushed into the void, no longer background but foreground. I was aware of what an awful person I was and that I deserved to be alone. That made me want to keep hiding from her, keep avoiding her. I hid from everyone, really, in that all the friendships I started to make were superficial. By my senior year, she'd stopped calling every week or even every other, she no longer asked me to come home for breaks from school, and after I graduated, we could go a few months without speaking. Our calls were an exchange of facts, proof of life.

For a while, since therapy with Dr. Baylor, I'd been feeling a little better about myself, like I did have redeeming qualities and that if anyone could redeem me, it would be him. But now it had once again become stark, what kind of person I really was. I was going to see him tonight, and no matter what I said, he'd see through me.

I'd thought a hundred times about canceling. The policy was that if I canceled with less than forty-eight hours' notice, I was supposed to pay the full fee for the missed session. I wasn't sure how that worked now that I'd gone pro bono.

Canceling at the last minute after he'd entrusted me with a prime-time slot for free . . . I couldn't do it. It would be a slap in the face of the person to whom I felt closest. On shaking legs, I made it to his office.

Yet I couldn't even look at him, though his concern was palpable in the room. I was tucked into one corner of his couch, my knees drawn up to my chest, trying to disappear. My face was bright red. Almost ten excruciating minutes had ticked by, and I still hadn't formed words. I'd bumped into the client he had before me, the one who'd looked so put together last week, and her outfit was on point, but from her face, it was clear she was unraveling, too. Maybe it was contagious. Poor Dr. Michael, surrounded by disastrous women.

He told me to take my time—after all, he'd always stressed this was my time and I was in charge of it—but he probably hadn't anticipated that we could sit here for the entire fifty minutes in silence. Agonizing as that would be, though, speech would be worse. Once I started talking, there would be nowhere to hide.

"Did you go to see your mother and Adam like we discussed in the last session?" he finally asked at the twenty-five-minute mark. I managed a nod. "You thought it might be painful, seeing Adam like that and seeing how it was impacting your mother. From how you look today, I'm guessing you were right."

Another nod.

"Have you ever grieved before?"

I didn't even know what that meant. I shook my head.

"It hits everyone differently. It's not that unusual to become mute in the face of mortality, actually."

So he couldn't see through me. I was almost disappointed. I'd ascribed such inhuman powers of perception and insight to him that it was no wonder he couldn't match it.

"But I don't think that's what's going on here," he said. "Did your mother abuse you, Lucinda? Is that why you went away to college and never came home?"

This time, I shook my head with a force that was nearly spasmodic. He couldn't think something like that about Mom. I was the rotten one. She was innocent.

"Did Adam abuse you?"

"No." People might say that I'd been too young to consent and that Adam had been like a father, but it had never been like that.

"Do you know what complicated grief is?" Dr. Baylor asked.

No, I didn't.

"Simple grief is when we have simple feelings for the person we've lost or will lose soon. For example, a husband and wife are married fifty years. It's a loving marriage. When he dies, you'd think she'd have the hardest time coping, but no. The wife who has it worst is the one who secretly hated her husband, who had wished for her freedom. Then once it happens, she's full of guilt. She doesn't recover for many years, if ever."

"What if the guilt isn't because of the person who died?" I said. "What if it's about someone else who's been left behind?"

Dr. Baylor studied me. "Did Adam abuse your mother?"

"Not in the way you mean."

74

"Did he abuse you?" he asked again, softer this time.

"No."

"Let me ask another way. Did you and Adam ever have sexual contact while you were a child living in his house?"

"Define child."

"Under the age of eighteen."

I averted my eyes. "Yes."

"Oh, Lucy." He sounded so sad. "I'm really sorry."

I felt the tears, but they had no business in this conversation. I'd done a terrible thing. I'd hidden that terrible thing. But now she knew, and she was surely destroyed, and I hadn't even called her. She hadn't even gotten an apology from me, because the words were so disproportionate to the crime. I couldn't imagine how I'd begin to do penance. Yet here I was, accepting condolences from Dr. Baylor.

"I feel the weight of your guilt all the time," he said. "You slouch, did you know that? That's how heavy it is."

"I don't like being tall."

"It's a physical manifestation of the burden he caused you to bear. You were a child. He was in a position of authority. You couldn't consent."

"I said yes. Worse, I said please, come with me. When I'm eighteen, I said, leave my mother and we'll be together."

It was the most shameful declaration I'd ever made to anyone. It was unforgivable. Dr. Baylor was going to kick me out of his office. He was going to say, *No more free sessions for you. No, you'll pay double.*

"Tell me why you said that."

I was startled. He wanted to hear the whole sordid story? How Adam came into my life when I was a teenager, and I'd looked at him like a rock star, not a father, never a father? That I acted as adult as I could around him, because I didn't want him to ever see me as a child? That we talked like friends, right from the start? That I wanted to be more, right from the start, and I never thought it would happen, that he could actually develop feelings for me, and that he tried to resist, and I didn't want him to, I wouldn't leave him alone? That I was the one who should have had the greatest loyalty and devotion to my mother?

Yes, he wanted to hear all that, and I needed to lay my burden down.

I did what Dr. Baylor had always urged: somehow, I found my voice.

CHAPTER 14

GREER

"Come in, come in!" Alexis's enthusiasm seemed a bit strong for our employer/employee relationship, though she was out on maternity leave so maybe we'd entered a new phase. Maybe we were just a couple of gals hanging out.

Jesus.

I'd never been that kind of boss. In fact, I'd deliberately been the precise opposite of that. I was no ice queen—it was civility above all—but boundaries, people. That was my motto. When I didn't have to spend my time asking about everyone's weekend, I got a lot more done.

Now here I was in Alexis's house, using her for in vivo research. It went against everything I stood for.

But after my therapy session five days ago, after spraining my ankle trying to get out of there, I decided I was quitting. I did it by voice mail last night, making a pact with myself to gather the information I needed somehow. This was the how that came to me.

Alexis's baby boy was named Byron, and he was two months old. He had a strangely mottled complexion and a downy sort of fauxhawk. He was looking at me curiously from over Alexis's shoulder, and I was pleased to find that while there was nothing objectionable about him, I was in no way moved to touch him, not even that angel hair of his.

Alexis was a little manic, offering me this or that, tidying with her free hand. "I meant to do this before you got here," she said apologetically. "It's just, I don't know where the time goes, you know?" She let out an embarrassed laugh.

I really didn't know and perhaps would never have to. There was a normal amount of furniture, but the living room felt cramped, with baby-related linens draped across every surface, plus a staggering variety of chairs for the baby, one of which played music and vibrated, sending Byron into a torpor that's closest approximation might be an opium den. But he was out of the way, and now we could talk, and I had no earthly idea what to say.

I had time to figure it out, though, since Alexis was babbling nervously and sucking up all the oxygen. I was used to the highly competent, impeccably turned out Alexis from the office. Alexis's doppelgänger was wearing a T-shirt with a rainbow of stains that I couldn't definitively identify, her hair up in a precarious bun. I'd never realized that she drew on her eyebrows every day until now. Their absence gave her a startled appearance, or maybe that was just my effect.

I probably should have given her more warning instead of just calling and saying I was in the neighborhood. I had assumed that she wouldn't be as immaculate as if she were going to work, but I hadn't expected this extent of degradation, either.

Somewhere in her soliloquy, as she went on about all the expenses and stresses of motherhood, I got it: she was afraid I'd come to fire her.

It saddened me that she could think I was the kind of person who'd do that to a new parent. That may have been the flaw in my management style. While I was always on guard against people knowing me too much, they wound up knowing me too little.

I started to counter-steer, offering extravagant praise about what an amazing worker she'd always been, and how much we all missed her, and how we can't wait until she's back, at which point she began to look worried again, and I had to reassure her that of course we were going to wait until she was back. She finally relaxed. Then Byron let out the fart of a truck driver, and we all laughed, including him. The kid had timing.

"What's it like, really?" I asked her, since it felt like closeness was baked in after smelling the offspring's byproducts.

Alexis, who had just taken a seat across from me on the couch, froze. Then she burst into tears.

Emotions were information, all right. She'd just told me all I needed to know. *Let go of this ridiculous fantasy, Greer. Look around you. Look at the state of this house and of this woman in front of you, and look at the tiny being who created it.* The power imbalance relative to stature was absurd and terrifying. He was cute, but he wasn't all that. *Let it go.*

I thought I'd be able to, as Alexis talked about how sometimes it was boring and sometimes it was overwhelming, like when he cried and cried and she couldn't figure out what was wrong. "Loving him so much makes me feel a little bit out of control all the time," she said.

I nodded, thinking I didn't ever want to know. I was dodging this bullet, no question. Therapy schmerapy.

"But you hold him and you can't imagine anything better. Like here"—and before I could protest, she was across the room and scooping her son out of his opium chair—"try it."

There was no graceful way to refuse an actual person. There could be no bigger rejection than saying, "No, I'd prefer not to touch the fruit of your loins." That was why I found myself with Byron on my lap, more than a bit awkwardly, and as Alexis laughed through her fast-drying tears, she advised me to lift him to my shoulder. When I did, I just hated what happened.

Which was that I loved it. I loved his smell—which was not farty at all but sweet, and not just like baby powder but like Byron—and I loved his heft. He was the perfect size. Really, he fit me like a glove. I was flooded with something that felt chemical. Oxytocin, wasn't that what made nursing mothers' breasts leak when they heard their babies cry?

I didn't think I could be having oxytocin for another woman's baby, but I swear, it was like something was overtaking my body. It was a calm—all ocean breezes and waves and piña coladas—only natural, created from within rather than without. After all, there was nothing more natural than the drive to be a mother. So soporific, like I could have fallen asleep right there and slept for a hundred years and it would have been the best hundred years of my whole life.

Oh God. Oh shit. I wanted this feeling, but then I thought of Alexis's tears. I certainly didn't want *that* feeling. It was unlikely that you could have one without the other. If you loved a helpless creature so much, you inevitably had . . . not the opposite, not hate, but out of control, which was a form of pain that I had never tolerated well. It was what I'd always feared, on some level: that love made you painfully beholden.

Fear of intimacy, just like Dr. Michael said.

But did I need love, like I'd blurted out, badly enough to risk the pain?

I gently returned Byron to his mother, feeling equal parts relief and regret, and told her how happy I was that I got to see her in her element (she clearly liked that). Then I beat it the hell out of there.

On the street, I was shaking. I still felt it, the weight of him. That little baby who wasn't mine but could be. Well, not him, but something similar. Maybe even one a little cuter, if I got lucky. If I picked the right sperm donor.

Jesus.

I was walking down the street, faster and faster, like I could just leave it all behind, like I could pretend that the experiment hadn't led me to an inevitable, terrible conclusion. I wanted more love in my life, possibly in the form of a ten-pound soul-sucking monster. I turned my phone back on, hoping for some work-related emergency that would require my full attention, but instead, the only message I had was from Dr. Michael. An eye for an eye. A voice mail for a voice mail.

"Hi, it's Michael," he said. Not Dr. Michael, just Michael. "I got your message, and I owe you an apology. When I meet with someone as compelling as you, sometimes I get overexcited. I get ahead of myself, and I make presumptions. Sometimes I push too hard. I think that happened in this case, and I appreciate your feedback." Feedback. That's a creative euphemism for quitting. "I'd like to ask you to give me another chance. I do think you need to be pushed, at least a little. Don't go finding yourself one of those 'How does that make you feel? Umm-hmm' therapists. You're too good for that. And even if I'm not right for you, let's talk about that in person, okay? Because if you leave like this, it could just be another sign of—don't shoot me—that fear of intimacy we talked about. That you're afraid to let someone care about you, which I do. Let's meet on our usual day and time, okay, Greer? I promise you I can do better."

He was practically begging for a second chance.

I couldn't say why, but I was smiling.

CHAPTER 15

FLORA

"I'm really glad to have her here," I tell Michael. We're in the kitchen, and Kate is sitting at the dining room table. I dump another container of Burmese takeout onto a serving platter while Michael smiles at me affectionately.

"No one does takeout like you," he says. I smile back. I especially appreciate his appreciation, since that proclivity of mine had been such a bone of contention in my marriage.

I can't help wishing, though, that we weren't in my apartment yet again. I'd offered to make a reservation at any restaurant he wanted, requesting a back booth, and we could even arrive in separate cars, and besides, even if someone recognized us, he could just introduce me as Flora. He didn't even have to say "my girlfriend, Flora." Not yet. All those concessions, but he said he wasn't comfortable with it yet. Soon, he promised.

"Is anything wrong?" he asked.

"No." I smiled wider. I didn't want Kate to feel any tension. She was my guest. Moreover, she was the first one seeing Michael and me together, and I wanted her to approve. Funny, she'd always been the one seeking my approval, and now the tides had turned. I put out my hand, and he took it. Then he pulled me into his arms.

"Mmm," he said. "New perfume?"

He was the best noticer I'd ever been with. Always the first to compliment me on a new dress or a new scent. To compliment me on takeout, for fuck's sake. Where did I get off complaining just because he needed more time to get comfortable? I wanted him comfortable.

"We have forever, right?" I asked him.

He drew back his head so he could look into my eyes. "That," he said, "is the plan."

We kissed, and then Kate yelled, "Get a room, you two!" and we laughed as we started carrying the serving dishes and platters out to the dining room.

Kate looked beautiful by candlelight. Since I last saw her, she'd started dyeing her hair dark red and was wearing matching lipstick. With her creamy pale skin, she looked like the mysterious woman in an espionage novel, the one disappearing into the night in a well-fitted trench coat.

We started eating the tea-leaf salad. Michael made an appreciative noise, as if to play along with the ruse that I'd done more than procure, and Kate chimed in. "This is really delicious! I've never had this kind of salad before, with all these nuts and seeds and spices," she said. "I don't even know exactly where Burma is."

"It's really Myanmar," Michael said. "Bordered by India, Bangladesh, Thailand, and China."

"Michael's one of those people who just knows everything," I said. "I love that about him."

"You love everything about him!" Kate said.

Michael did a double take. This visit was supposed to be when she first learned about him, but that remark made it sound like she'd been hearing about him for months.

"Since I landed," she clarified, "it's been Michael, Michael, Michael."

Fortunately, he seemed mollified. "In my head," he said, "it's always Flora, Flora, Flora."

I smiled at him and touched the back of his hand. "It's amazing that we can feel so strongly in such a short time. I've never been caught up like this before, with anyone."

"I know! When you got together with Young, it was just such a checklist, you know?" Kate took an enthusiastic sip of her wine. I knew that her addiction wasn't to alcohol; it was to everything else, but still. I wished she'd given up drinking along with the rest of it. "Young was handsome, and she knew he would make lots of money, and sure, he treated her like a princess most of the time, and yes, they got along really well and they were in love, but—" She stopped talking and shook her head with a rueful laugh. "Sorry, I don't know where I was going with that."

"The checklist," I said, my smile tight. "How I loved Young because I thought I was supposed to." Whereas Michael was the opposite. I loved him despite every impediment.

"Right," Kate said, but she didn't elaborate.

Michael finished his glass of wine. "Young was a starter marriage. Flora and I are completely different."

I stiffened slightly. I had the strangest desire to defend my marriage to Young, even though what I wanted most was for Kate to see how superior Michael was. How much more evolved my new love was than my old. I chose Young when I didn't even know myself. What I had with Michael was exponentially more profound.

Kate had this look on her face that I'd never seen before as she watched Michael. I wanted Kate here because she never judged, but now

I realized that what she was doing, right then, was actively withholding judgment. I'd been hoping for a judgment in my—in Michael's—favor. I wanted her to be taken with him, to be taken in by him, to see what I saw and what we had.

But it was like the jury was out.

For me, it wasn't. This was my man. He was meant to be my man. That's why he came into my life when he did, in the way he did. Yes, it was taking a while to work out the kinks, but wasn't Kate the one who'd urged me to be patient?

"What was Flora like when she was younger?" Michael asked Kate.

She started to tell anecdotes, and he was laughing, and I joined in, though I'd heard these stories too many times to be truly amused by them anymore. I'd even told one to Michael before. Watching him, you wouldn't have been able to tell that. He was giving Kate his full attention. It was his gift.

The atmosphere had noticeably shifted, and by the time I was clearing the table of the various curries and noodle dishes, I felt like he'd done it. He'd won her over. She saw his charms, and more than that, she saw that he didn't merely love me; he was fascinated by me. He endeavored to know me inside and out, much more so than Young or anyone else I'd ever met, except for Kate herself.

When I came back after doing just a little cleanup, Kate was leaning into Michael and they were speaking in low tones. I sat down, and I would have felt like I was interrupting something personal except that they didn't let me interrupt; they just kept talking like I wasn't even there.

It was about Kate's past drug abuse. There was no way she'd brought that up herself, not in the five minutes I was gone. That meant it had to have been Michael.

When I told Michael her past, I never specifically told him he couldn't mention it to her. I just assumed he'd know better than to do that with a virtual stranger. This wasn't a therapy session. This was my family.

She didn't seem to mind, though. He was telling her, "I get it. That pull. That sense that nothing else could ever be as potent. That everything else is secondary."

Was he talking about his feelings for me? Or was he speaking from the perspective of addicts he'd worked with in the past? He'd never told me that he had any of his own problems with substance abuse.

"The future is what I care about now," she said. "I'm not looking to get pulled back into anything."

"It's so hard to content yourself with that, though, isn't it?" I didn't know what to make of his smile. "That gauzy dream—that's powerful stuff."

"No. Prison is powerful stuff."

"I've never been. How long were you in?"

"Three months. It was before my last time in rehab, before I got clean for good."

"Glad to hear it," he said, "that kind of confidence you have that it was the last time."

"She takes her recovery seriously," I said. That was if you didn't count the alcohol, and it wasn't like I'd seen her really drunk since she came out of rehab. "We're all really proud of her. The whole family."

Kate gave me a smile that was just a little bit sad. I was lying. I was the one who was proud of her; everyone else in the family was just waiting for the relapse. I'd told her before not to take it personally, that they were all fatalists. That was how they maintained control, so that when anything bad happened, they could say they knew it was coming. Nothing awful is surprising, that was the family motto.

"Are you an addict?" Kate asked Michael.

"Not exactly. A hedonist, maybe, which is a related vulnerability."

"What does that mean?"

"Pleasure is incredibly important to me." He shot me a meaningful sideways glance. It kind of turned me on, and it kind of pissed me off. I didn't want him referencing me like a concubine in front of Kate. Yes, we had incredible sex, but we were a whole lot more than that.

"What about love?" I said.

"You love what brings you the most pleasure. That's just human nature."

Love had to be more than that. Otherwise, how did you survive hard times?

Young might have asked me that same thing. Or maybe I gave him the answer: You don't. I hadn't.

"There are a lot of ways to get a rush, though," Michael said. "I'm lucky that way. Like my work, getting to connect with people in really deep ways."

I could feel Michael's hand on my knee under the table, reassuring me, but I stood up. "I'll be right back," I said. "I left the dishes soaking."

He must have detected something, because a few minutes later, he was pushing up against me from behind, my pelvis slamming into the cabinets below the kitchen sink. He sucked on my neck in the way that he knew I liked, and without volition, my head toppled backward. I felt fucking helpless. And I never thought I would, but I liked it.

I was no hedonist, but sometimes I thought I might be a masochist.

CHAPTER 16

LUCINDA

I'd seen Dr. Baylor three times this week, all free of charge. He said this was the moment, the open window when we could do the intense work. "You're ready," he said. "*You're* open."

He was right. For so long, I'd avoided talking about what happened with Adam, but this really was healing me. It was like having leeches all over my body, sucking out the poison.

It was probably because I was finally calling things by their right names. All this time, I'd been thinking that I was the guilty one, the one doing the seduction, but Dr. Baylor pointed out how well it served Adam to let me believe that. "It didn't matter if you were the instigator or not. A grown man saying that a fifteen-year-old girl is irresistible?" Dr. Baylor said. "We all have dark impulses. Adults are responsible for resisting them."

Adam wanted me to think I was the villain when he was an abuser. A predator.

Adam and I had our everything-but-sex affair for three years under my mother's nose. We stole moments when we could, and because it wasn't every day, the anticipation was torturously sweet. Adam was practically all I thought about: what it was like to lie in his arms, to whisper in his ear, to roam over his body. Then there was all the strategizing and the choreography to get my mother out of the way and have him all to myself. It eclipsed everything else.

Sometimes I felt like I hated my mother because she'd become this impediment to what I wanted most. The jealousy was so intense, and then afterward, I'd be flooded with shame. She was trying to connect with me, but I couldn't even look her in the eyes anymore. She asked me what she had done and how we could repair things, but I went monosyllabic. I told her that I just needed my space, and, finally, she had no choice but to give it to me.

Adam never used the word *love*, but it was implied. I felt it coming from him, reverberating through my body, syncopating with my own. Love, love, love, love. How it pumped. How it drove me. Contorted me from a girl who'd always done the right thing to one full of dreams and machinations, who would scheme against her own mother.

I'd put all that distance between Mom and me because I couldn't live with myself otherwise. I reminded myself of how she'd basically abandoned me years ago when she was on drugs, and even though she'd become an exemplary mother since then, it was too late. She'd made her bed, and I was going to lie in it.

When I first told Dr. Baylor, it was excruciating; now our talks were a kind of freedom. All these years, I'd been feeling like an evil person when really, I had been under the spell of an evil person.

I couldn't wait for Adam to die.

Dr. Baylor said that my self-absorption and tendency toward rationalization while in the throes of first love and hormones were completely understandable, given the developmental stage I'd been in. "Adolescents can seem immoral, but really, they're amoral. It's like morality is on pause because there's so much else happening in your body. In your life. That's all it was. You were a teenager who was led astray."

The day I turned eighteen, Adam and I were finally ready to consummate our relationship. I recalled the day so vividly: the new bra and panties I'd bought, the perfume I'd worn, the anticipation, the release. It hadn't even hurt; I was so primed to be with the man I loved.

Adam had insisted we wait until I was of age. He said that I needed to be legally able to consent, which entailed a level of premeditation that Dr. Baylor was quick to point out. "That's not about conscience," he said, "that's about calculation."

I was such a fool. We had sex the one time, and I thought it was magical, though of course I had no frame of reference. Adam must have felt otherwise, because he told me that we—he—couldn't do it anymore. I was leaving for Berkeley in the fall (it was a feat that I'd managed to get in, given how much space Adam occupied in my brain), and he told me, "I'm an old man. What will your new friends say?"

"I don't care about friends. I care about you!"

"Shh," he said. "Your mother's sleeping."

"I don't care! Let her hear. Let this be out in the open. We have nothing to be ashamed of."

It was a ridiculous contention. We had everything to be ashamed of. But in that second, it seemed true. How could love ever be wrong, regardless of the circumstances in which it had been born? We belonged together.

He shook his head like he couldn't believe how impossibly naive I was, all that I had to learn. But he wasn't planning to teach me, was he? He'd put in all that time, three years of foreplay, and I'd turned out to be a lousy fuck, so he was done with me.

I slapped him across the face, shocking us both. I'd never once been violent toward another human being. The rejection was so acute, like a blade through my stomach. He'd had me once, and now he didn't want me anymore.

"I'm going to tell her," I said.

"Then I'll be gone for good, and your relationship with her will be shit forever. Is that what you want?"

He was what I wanted, and now I couldn't have him. We would occupy the same house for another four months until I left for Berkeley. He'd be tantalizingly across the hall but completely out of reach. He'd made sure of that. For the remainder of our time under the same roof, when I tricked my mother into leaving the house, he went with her. He wouldn't allow us to be alone.

But then one day he was home sick. Mom went to work. I went to school just for a couple of periods, and then I headed back to the house, snuck in the bed beside him, and kissed his feverish head. I stuck my hand in his pajama bottoms, and he shook his head no, but his body responded. "Yes," I told him, climbing on top of him like I'd seen women do in the movies. It was only my second time; what did I know? But he began to move with me, almost against his will, and I pushed my face against his neck, letting his sweat wash me clean.

Then he mustered his strength and threw me across the bed. He was shaking with anger, and it would have been funny, the sight of it: his red face, his still-erect cock. Only he was glaring at me with what felt like true hatred. "You are one fucked-up girl," he said. "Stay away from me."

"I love you. I just want to be with you."

"You know what they'd say if you were the guy? They'd say you raped me."

"No, I just—"

He closed his eyes. "Get out of here."

"Please, Adam. You can't do this to me. I've never loved anyone; I'll never love anyone else. I need you."

"Get out. Stay out."

Afterward, we could barely look at each other. He was right: I'd basically raped him. He'd shaken his head no, but I was too intent on what I felt I needed—no, what I deserved. They say rape is about aggression, not sex, and truthfully, I'd been furious with him. I felt like he'd thrown me away, and I wasn't going to let him get away with it. The fact that I also loved him, that I also wanted our relationship back, had been secondary. That had been revenge sex.

I'd never been comfortable with anger, but I knew that I was capable of rage. That I was capable of violence. That continued to scare the hell out of me.

Dr. Baylor had already absolved me of so much, but what I did that day—that he could never know.

CHAPTER 17

GREER

Donor Profile #2206

Interview Notes

Donor 2206 recently graduated with his master's degree in anthropology. He said that part of his desire to engage in this process is anthropological, as he has an insatiable curiosity and craves new experiences. "I don't like life to get too ordinary," he says.

He is short and stocky, with brown hair and brown eyes. He is fairly intense and serious, though he is not devoid of humor. He got married three months ago, and his wife is supportive of his being a donor, since they don't intend to have children of their own.

He grew up in Southern California to what he calls "free-spirited parents." He has one brother with whom he is close . . .

Q & A

Describe your personality.

Introspective. Adventurous. Devoted.

What are your interests and goals?

I'm planning to spend the next few years traveling in an Airstream with my wife, figuring out whether I want to pursue my PhD in anthropology. Academia seems so confining, but since I'm not independently wealthy, I know I need to find a career that's personally meaningful and full of variety.

"An Airstream," I told Dr. Michael. "A friggin' Airstream. What am I doing?"

"You're weighing your options."

"I'm reading about business majors, mathematicians, budding documentary filmmakers, tree huggers, future cancer researchers. I can get any combination of hair color, eye color, and height I want. And it's a waste of time. No one's right. Maybe that's because this isn't right. You shouldn't have the baby of someone you've never even met."

"Are you rethinking motherhood?"

"No, I'm pretty sure I want it. Ever since I held Byron, I can't stop thinking about that feeling. It was the strongest feeling I've ever had, and it was maternal. But when I think of my options for how to get from here to there, I come up empty."

"This is the challenge we talked about right from the beginning. Your adaptability. Finding a way to want what you can have."

The truth was, I hadn't wanted things very deeply in my life. Even in my career, I made a decision and I pursued it ferociously, doggedly, because that was how my parents had trained me.

There it was again: that dog reference. My whole life, I'd been a dog with a bone, but I was starting to think it was the wrong one.

"I comb through these profiles obsessively," I said, a lump in my throat, "and I have someone else's thoughts. For example, you can't see the donors' current pictures, but you can see their baby pictures. I started thinking that I could take the baby picture and pay someone to photo age it, like they do with missing children, and then I can evaluate whether that's a person I'd want to sleep with. I'm trying to create some connection, any connection, so I'm not just turkey basting with some stranger. Is that normal?"

"It's normal to wonder if you're normal, I can tell you that much." He stroked his chin reflectively. "I've got this instinct, and I want to follow it. I want to steer us away from Byron and back to your childhood."

I exhaled loudly. "Wrong tree, Doc."

"It's never the wrong tree. It's the template for everything that follows."

"I just got back here. Do you want me to bolt again?" Actually, it had been three weeks, and we both knew I wasn't going anywhere.

"No, I very much don't want that."

Did that qualify as flirting? It went straight to my head. "This doesn't feel like the right time to talk about my parents."

"What would you prefer to talk about?"

Again, was that flirting? He hadn't changed his tone in any measurable way. There was nothing strange about a therapist asking a client what she wanted to talk about. But the effects were undeniable, like I'd been drinking champagne.

"I want to talk about how to get from here to there," I said. "I want to be a mother. I know it in my heart and in my gut, and I don't believe I've ever heard from those parts of my body before, not truly."

"I can't think of any better definition of progress." He smiled. "Let's get you there."

PRESENT DAY

PRESENT DAY

CHAPTER 18

Detective Gregory Plath

"I'm prepared to cooperate fully," Greer says. "I want to make sure you find the person who did this. Not only that, but I want to see a conviction. No one should get away with murder, no matter how good they think their reason is."

"I appreciate that," I say. "Cooperation would be great. It saves me some time."

"Oh?"

"You can just give me access to your therapy records. That way, I'm not wasting valuable time getting a subpoena for them like we're having to do with some of his other clients and former clients. We can devote all our resources to catching the killer."

She blanches, just a little.

Everyone wants to cooperate when it's to tell you about someone else. Of course, I wouldn't mind knowing more about Flora and Lucinda. They're not officially suspects, but they're the closest thing I've got, especially since Greer is yet another woman who was home alone on the night in question.

What people don't realize is that when they're eager to dish on others, they're really telling me just as much about themselves. Though this Greer—she's a cool character. I'm not getting much of a read on her so far. She's just sitting there in her oversize top and skinny leggings, with her no-makeup makeup, perfectly composed. Yet there's something else going on. Something's seething. I can't put my finger on it, but it's in the room.

"I don't think my records are relevant," she says.

"Have you read them?"

"No."

"You worried at all about what's in there?"

"No, because I trusted Dr. Michael."

I can't resist a smile. "That's what you called him?"

She clearly doesn't appreciate my tone. "A man's dead. He doesn't need your mockery, and neither do I."

This woman grew up with money, you can just tell, and I know she lives well now. She thinks she's untouchable.

But I'm not about bringing her down, unless she's guilty. And I've got this feeling . . .

"You say you want to help, but you didn't show up here on your own," I tell her. "I had to bring you in. And now you're telling me what's relevant and what isn't. Doesn't seem like cooperation to me."

"You're taking an adversarial tone with me, and I don't really understand that. Would you want someone in law enforcement to read through your mental health records? Those are my private thoughts, as transcribed and analyzed by someone else. Dr. Michael was an excellent therapist, but people get things wrong. They misremember. They misinterpret."

She's not wrong. I wouldn't want anyone combing through the records of my talk with the department-mandated therapist I saw years ago. And yeah, I do feel kind of adversarial toward her. There's just something about her manner, like she thinks she's better than me.

I need to check myself. This isn't about me.

It's about Dr. Michael Baylor, who seems to have led a low-key, under-the-radar life: never married, engaged once more than ten years ago and it ended amicably, in private practice for more than twenty years with a sterling reputation. If the math stopped there, it wouldn't have added up to murder. But I'm counting the last five years, in which two women filed and withdrew complaints alleging sexual misconduct, one who's on the other side of the country and won't return my calls and the other who's aimed me like a drone strike toward three other women who were unprofessionally involved with him. What happened over the last five years? Did he just fall off a cliff, ethically speaking, or was it more of a slippery slope? Or did his MO let him down and his misdeeds caught up with him and he ultimately got what he deserved?

I'm a homicide detective. On the record, nobody deserves to get murdered. Off the record . . . like I said, I have opinions, just like everybody else.

"I want to see the killer brought to justice," Greer says, "and I'll tell you all I know that can make that happen. But that doesn't mean I lay myself bare. I had no personal involvement with Michael, and I'm not going to answer any invasive questions without a lawyer present, but I am going to tell you what's relevant. Like what was said at dim sum."

I could almost believe her, except for that slip of the tongue, when she dropped the "Dr." and called him Michael.

BEFORE

CHAPTER 19

FLORA

It was only Kate's second visit since I'd moved to California, but she'd already developed this annoying habit: She'd insist we go out for Cuban food, and then she'd make subtle digs the whole time. Sometimes it wasn't even verbal; it was just her expression after she'd sampled the *ropa vieja* or the arroz con pollo. Tonight she looked dubious from the second we walked in and she saw the exposed brick, like, *That's not how they do it in Miami.*

But that wasn't what was bothering me most. It was that the second we'd ordered our mojitos, she asked, "So where's Michael tonight?"

"Working," I said. "That's the problem with being a therapist. He keeps some evening hours."

She nodded, but that look . . . it was pretty similar to the one she'd wear later after we tried the empanadas and paella. Sour.

She wasn't reserving judgment anymore.

But she wasn't coming out and saying anything, either, which was what put me over the top. "What?" I demanded.

"I was just thinking that's not the only problem with his being a therapist, that's all."

"What's your problem with it?"

"I don't have one. But if he were my man, I'd hate sharing him."

"I don't share him."

The mojitos arrived, and we both started sipping away. Neither of us liked the tension, but sometimes it was unavoidable. We were family, and we told each other everything. That had its pitfalls.

"What?" I said again.

"He basically told you he gets off on being close to other women. All the stuff about his hedonism and getting pleasure from his work."

"He never said 'women.'" She raised an eyebrow just slightly, but I caught it. "It feels like you're digging, looking for reasons not to like him."

"I thought he was charming." It was becoming obvious that she didn't trust charming. "I just don't want you to have blinders on, you know? I'm here to protect you."

"That's not why I asked you to come."

"No, you asked me to come so you could push Michael into going public. And guess what? It didn't work. We're here, and he's not."

"Because he's working."

"But he could join us later, right? He doesn't see patients until ten o'clock, does he?"

"He calls them clients," I practically mumbled. She had me on my heels, which was not at all where I expected to be when it came to Kate. She had always been the one nipping at my heels. I'd wanted her to come out here and put her seal of approval on my relationship. Instead, I was more insecure than before she arrived.

I shouldn't blame Kate; I knew that. But I resented that she was putting me on the defense.

I preferred offense. "What was that stuff at dinner about how great Young and I were together?"

"I never said great."

"You really think I would have been happier staying with Young?"

"I said it was a checklist marriage. But if we're being honest, you've put up with more shit from Michael than you ever put up with from Young."

My eyes widened. She had to be kidding.

"Sure, you were unhappy with Young, but he knew it. You stifle yourself with Michael. You let him call the shots."

"Only about going public."

She shook her head. "It's more than that. You defer to him. I've never seen you behave like that with anyone. It's like you think he's above you, and maybe he thinks so, too."

"That's not true! We're equals. He just has a career to protect."

"Did he give you a date or a plan?"

"No."

"He just tells you he's sorry and he understands. He does all the therapist shit. Lots of empathy, no action. Since when do you put up with that from a man?"

The server approached our table, smiling, and I told Kate just to get whatever she wanted, get everything, we'd split the whole menu, but I'd lost my appetite. When I had been Michael's client, he did have more patience and empathy for me. He did seem to care more. It's like I'd been demoted.

I hadn't allowed myself to fully admit it before, but I *was* jealous of those other women, the nameless, faceless clients who sucked all his energy and gave him so much pleasure. And maybe I was putting up with too much shit. Sure, he used to say I was a force of nature, but I hadn't heard that in a long while. If I used to be a cyclone, now I was just some wind whistling through the trees.

"I need to get out of here," I said.

"We just ordered a shitload of food."

"Do you want to stay and eat it? You can take an Uber back to my place later, or we can have them wrap it up. Whatever you want."

"What I want is a night out with you."

"I'm sorry, okay? I wish I could stay. But I'm going to confront Michael."

Her eyes lit up. "Finally! That's my girl!" She smiled at me. "I'll see you at your apartment later with doggie bags."

I guzzled the rest of my mojito and kissed her cheek, then hurried out.

As I drove toward his office, I ignored the voice that told me to turn back. Kate was right; I'd been doing everything on his terms, and what did I have to show for it? I didn't have a date or a plan for us going public. I was letting him be the boss when I was a boss bitch, and he needed to see that.

It was one of the reasons he fell in love with me, right?

CHAPTER 20

LUCINDA

"We've established that Adam was a bad guy," I said, "but what about Mom?"

Dr. Baylor finished making a note on his pad and looked up. "You tell me. What about her?"

"Is a parent guilty for what she doesn't see, even when it's right in front of her face?"

"You said that you and Adam took great pains to keep her far away."

"But isn't that, in itself, suspicious?"

"Denial is a protective mechanism. It keeps us from knowing what we can't psychologically handle, from what would destroy us."

My stomach dropped. It wasn't what I'd hoped to hear.

All week, I'd wanted Mom to be guilty, because after I'd reached out to tell her how sorry I was, I'd gotten nothing back.

I didn't only say I was sorry, though. I said that I'd come to realize that while what I did was wrong, I had been a child and a victim of sexual abuse. I could have had Adam arrested, and I probably still could. But I wouldn't do that. I'd let him live out the rest of his life in peace. Judging by his appearance the last time I saw him, there wasn't much left.

I meant it as something of a peace offering. If she wanted to stay with Adam until he died, she was welcome to do it; I wouldn't interfere.

If Mom was in the wrong, too, then I didn't have to worry so much about her lack of response. I wouldn't have to think about the condition of that house. Like derelicts were living there. Like drug addicts.

Mom had been clean for so many years that I never thought of her that way anymore. Since I was six, she'd been more than clean; she'd been an example. She went back to school, got her life on track, made her amends, and sponsored other addicts who looked up to her. She became a loving and attentive mother. To my knowledge, she hadn't had a relapse in almost twenty years.

But the love of her life was dying—and she just found out that love was a pedophile who'd betrayed her with her own child.

There was a clatter in the waiting room, like someone was knocking things over. Not throwing them, exactly, but a racket that loud didn't seem entirely accidental, either.

Dr. Baylor got this unsettled look I'd never seen before, no matter what I told him, and he said, "I'm so sorry, I just need to make sure everything's okay out there." He opened the door, stepped out, and closed it behind him.

There were two sound machines—one inside and one outside—and they were emitting soothing, masking white noise, so at first, I could only hear only snippets from where I was sitting on the couch. Still, it was enough for me to gather that whoever was out there was no client. It was a lover, and it wasn't going terribly well.

I knew I should stay where I was, that I should respect Dr. Baylor's privacy, but this was my chance, my glimpse. I moved over to the door, putting my head flat against it.

The woman was telling him that he couldn't keep letting her down. "I deserve better than this, don't you get that? It's not fair." His response was a low, comforting murmur, but she wasn't having it. "Do you have any compassion left for me, or is it all reserved for them?" She sounded aggrieved, near tears, and I could make out that he was telling her that of course he had compassion for her, but he was at work, he was in with a client, they'd talk later. She burst out, "Fuck your clients, just like you've fucked me!"

I took a chance, and I turned off the sound machine on my side of the door. Then I could hear him say, "Don't run away like this." He told her that he had just one more client and then they could talk all night. "I love you. I'll meet you at your place as soon as I can."

"Unless I'm meeting you at yours, don't bother," she said.

It sounded like they were close to a resolution, as both their voices had dropped. I turned the sound machine back on and scooted away from the door, back to the couch. Several minutes passed. I didn't hear how it ended.

I was dying to crack the door and catch sight of the hysterical woman Dr. Baylor loved. I wished there was some subtle way to get to the window and see her walking away from the building. But he was coming back in.

I had no idea how to play this, whether I could pretend I didn't hear any of their confrontation. I couldn't even remember what I had been talking about before the interruption. I was too shocked by what I'd just learned: Dr. Baylor was in love with someone, and she was crazy.

I should have figured he had someone in his personal life. Plenty of women would want him, and he had needs, just like any other man. I'd just opted not to think about it. My fantasy was that he existed only for me, that he lived for our fifty minutes together.

"I apologize," he said, taking his seat. He was visibly disheveled by the encounter, as if he'd been repeatedly running his hands through his hair. I'd never seen him embarrassed before.

"It's okay," I said, pleased to absolve him for once.

"Let's just be straight with each other." He leaned forward, his gaze direct. "What do you think you heard?"

Such strange phrasing. It wasn't what I thought I heard; it was what I did hear. Why was he acting like I was the crazy one, when his girlfriend was?

He was just embarrassed. I could understand that. He probably wanted me to think that his life outside this room was pristine, that he had everything in hand, and honestly, before my eavesdropping, I would have assumed that.

If he chose one crazy woman, he could choose another. I might really have a chance.

He was waiting for me to tell him what I thought I'd heard. "Your girlfriend was obviously very upset," I said.

"I'm not going to confirm or deny that." Was he making a joke? He didn't smile. "I don't really like my personal life to be on display."

"The good news is, now we're even." I smiled so he'd know for sure I was joking, but he remained grim. Purposeful, rather.

"You can't repeat what you heard."

"I wouldn't."

"You, of all people, know that love is complicated."

It felt like a dig or even a threat. Like he was using my past against me. But he wouldn't do that. I must have misunderstood.

Maybe I was pondering the wrong question. The right one being: What did he *think* I'd overheard?

He didn't know that I'd stopped listening. In those last few minutes, I couldn't know what was said; I might not even want to know.

"Are you in love with her?" I asked, because it was probably the only chance I'd ever have. He was the one who'd talked about windows of opportunity. This was a door, and right then, it was cracked.

He sighed, and he seemed genuinely tormented. About his love for her? About what I may have heard?

Finally, he said, "I don't know what I feel."

"She's clearly in love with you."

"Yes." He didn't sound happy about it.

"Do you want to break up with her, but you're afraid of what she'll do to you?" I ventured. "She sounded really angry."

"I'm afraid of what she'll do to me and of what she'll do to herself. I'm afraid of all of it. But I'm not sure I want to lose her, either."

"Because she's exciting." It was like I could see into him the way he'd been seeing into me.

"Excitement can get exhausting. Constant reassurance can get boring." He slumped a little in his chair, and we were both quiet for a long minute. Then he reanimated. "I can't ask you to forget this ever happened. That never works. I tell you not to think of pink elephants and that's all you'll think about."

"What do you think happened? That I learned you have a private life? Shocker!" I smiled at him, and he finally smiled back. "You couldn't be as good a therapist as you are unless you'd lived a little, right?"

He laughed. I was warming to this role reversal.

I wasn't sure what I'd learned tonight, but I knew I didn't want to forget it.

CHAPTER 21

GREER

He meant it to be romantic, sitting on a bench by the water, gazing out at the lights installation along the Bay Bridge, which looked like a giant harp made of incandescent strings. But the thermos full of hot chocolate laced with Baileys just felt sad, as if we were playing at being twentysomething bon vivants instead of a couple of established professionals set up by eHarmony.

Yes, eHarmony. What the hell was I expecting? To find my soul mate? I neither wanted nor believed in those. Even if I did, I certainly wouldn't need one in order to have a baby. But somehow, I got sucked into a free communication weekend, where I messaged all my matches in one late-night wine-fueled binge. I hadn't been able to resist the efficiency.

I didn't want to admit to anyone I'd done this, not even to Dr. Michael. Least of all to Dr. Michael. What would he say—worse, what would he ask—if he knew that I'd messaged only men who already had children (young children, I hoped)? That I'd stopped replying when I learned said children were more than five years old? That I'd been hedging my bets, wishing I could fall in love with someone who conveniently had a baby or a toddler who could feel like my own for only half the week? Then I could indulge my loving maternal feelings with impunity and minimal disruption. Maybe there could be some other way to scratch this terrible itch.

Ron was not going to scratch shit.

He wasn't bad-looking, and he was nice enough, and he was an orthopedic surgeon. But there was the thermos and his use of the word *irregardless*. Most of all, though, there was the subterfuge. In one of the pictures on Ron's profile, he had a gorgeous towheaded kid on his shoulders who couldn't have been more than three, and it never even occurred to me that it had been taken nearly a decade ago.

". . . she's a soccer star," he was saying. "And I love watching her play, I really do, but sometimes it's with visions of torn ACLs dancing in my head—"

"You really shouldn't do that," I said sharply.

"You think she can tell?"

"No, I mean you really shouldn't use such an old picture in your profile. It's false advertising."

"Oh." He averted his eyes, turning toward the Christmas tree bridge. "I'm sorry. I just don't take a lot of pictures of myself."

He probably hadn't intentionally hoodwinked me; he might have thought a twelve-year-old was as good as a three-year-old. But that level of denseness irritated me. There was a world of difference between three and twelve. The way they smell, for example. The way they cuddle. Their ability to bond with a new person and love that person as if she'd been around since they were born, as if she were practically a real mom.

I was using words like *bond*. That might have been as bad as *irregardless*.

"What about you?" he said. "How old are your kids?"

"I don't have any." I glared at him. "Did you even read my profile?"

"Of course." He looked flustered as he downed the rest of his hot chocolate, his Adam's apple bobbing in a ferociously unappealing way.

I stood up. "I've got to go."

He followed suit. "Are you sure? I've really enjoyed talking to you. And I find you really attractive. I was hoping we could—"

"No, we can't. You're not what I'm looking for." *You don't have what I'm looking for.*

Irregardless of his thermos and his daughter, this was a bad idea. There was no substituting another man's family for the baby I wanted.

Ron looked miserable. He probably didn't normally get rejected that flatly.

I couldn't believe what came out of my mouth next. "It's not you, it's me." Not only was it a cliché, but it was never true. It was always at least a tiny bit you, too.

How much was me? For so long, I'd substituted workaholism for passion, but it was all a diversion from whatever was wrong, whatever was missing. Like a bloodhound, Dr. Michael could smell it, and he was following that scent all the way back to my parents. I didn't know if he could fix it or if a baby would, but I had to find out.

CHAPTER 22

FLORA

I let myself into Michael's house, using the key under the flowerpot. It was a rare pleasure, making myself at home while I waited for him. It had always felt like foreshadowing, that this was what it would be like when we were married.

I'd loved Michael's house from the first visit. It was a Craftsman, and in the living room, shining oak built-ins surrounded a fireplace while the couch and settee were layered with afghans from all around the world. It was the kind of house where you wanted to curl up on a cold night and never leave. You wanted to curl around the man who lived in such a house and never leave. And tonight, we'd taken a huge step forward. I hadn't expected that barging into his office could end so well, but in addition to his usual professions of love, he'd added a promise: after Kate left, we were going public. Being a boss bitch had its perks.

I poured myself a whiskey neat and lay down on the couch, scrolling through Instagram. I saw pictures of Nat draped all over her new man. He wasn't nearly as handsome as Michael. I couldn't wait to show him off to the world.

I was daydreaming about what my first Instagram post would say, and then I started to actually dream. I hadn't been sleeping that well since Kate had arrived.

I woke to the sound of the front door opening and to Michael's grim face. Sitting up, I beckoned to him.

He shook his head, his face angry.

How long had I been sleeping? What could have happened between our interlude in his waiting room and now to make him look that way?

"What is it?" I asked, my heart pounding.

"You lied to me," he said.

"About what?"

"About Kate. She's known about me for months." I froze. "Don't bother denying it. She already told me."

I glanced down at my phone, seeing her text. *He knows.* I'd slept through her warning.

"I went to your apartment before I came here," he said. "I had this feeling, and I confronted Kate, and she admitted it. Happily, it seemed like."

My head was spinning. Finally, I got the words out: "I'm sorry."

He glared at me. "Is that all you have to say?"

"It's what I feel. I'm really sorry."

I stood up and went to traverse the continent between us, but he stepped back. "You betrayed me."

"It wasn't like that. She's family. She lives on the other side of the country."

"Oh? Was there an exception clause that I'm forgetting? When we said we'd tell no one, I assumed that meant no one. Not a single living being, here or abroad."

I hated when he got mad and talked down to me. Even though he was right, I wasn't a wayward child. I was his girlfriend, and I planned to stay that way. We were about to go public! He told me so!

"I didn't think . . . ," I started, and then under his withering stare, I couldn't continue.

"You didn't think I'd find out," he finished. "You thought it's better to seek forgiveness than permission."

Yes and yes. But I couldn't say that. He didn't care about my remorse, so what was left?

"And now she clams up!"

I hated when he narrated for an imaginary audience. "Can we just have a drink and sit down and talk this out, like normal people?"

"Like 'normal people'?" he parroted, his eyes narrowing cruelly. "What are those?"

"Civil people, I should say. People who love each other and want to make things work. People make mistakes, but it doesn't have to be irreparable."

"I risked everything for you." His tone was glazed with wonder. "I believed in us."

"You should."

"You told her." The wonder had turned to acidic incredulity. "She's known this whole time, hasn't she? She could have blown the whistle whenever she wanted these past two years. You were willing to jeopardize my career and lie right to my face."

"She would never—"

"You couldn't know that for sure!"

"She's my cousin. I've known her since birth."

I betrayed Michael by telling Kate, but I never would have guessed that Kate would betray me like this. When he asked her, why didn't she just deny it? Why didn't she protect me?

Because she was sabotaging my relationship. She basically goaded me into leaving the Cuban restaurant and confronting him at his office. And then when that hadn't worked, she got lucky. He showed up at the apartment, and she ratted me out. Sure, he asked, but she could have lied. She was a recovering drug addict. She'd lied convincingly to our family for years.

I didn't think someone could get a bout of jealousy as suddenly as food poisoning, but maybe that was how it worked sometimes.

I'd wanted Kate to be taken with Michael, and maybe that's what had happened. He really had charmed her at dinner, and she'd always wanted to be like me, so maybe she wanted what I had. But could she be so crazy as to think that breaking us up could benefit her?

Maybe. People could be plenty crazy. I'd learned enough about Michael's clients—minus the identifying information—to know that.

But why had he gone to my apartment to talk to Kate? After all the affirmations in his waiting room, he said he'd come straight back here so we could do what people in love do. He'd seemed eager to see me later. Instead . . .

He'd been looking for a loophole. He didn't want to fulfill his promise. He didn't want to go public with me.

No, it couldn't be that. He'd learned his lesson; he was direct with women. What he said was what he meant—in his office when he was telling me how much he loved me and now, when he was telling me how angry he was. Understandably angry.

"You realize," he said, "she still could blow the whistle."

"No, she can't. We waited two years. We're in the clear."

He shook his head, infuriated. "No, we've been together secretly for two years. And I'm sure she can prove it. I'm sure you must have texted about me."

"She would never—"

"You don't know what she would do!" he shouted. "You didn't see her face when she told me, like the cat that ate the canary. Are you the canary or am I? That's the question you need to ask yourself."

"You don't know her like I do."

He turned away, and I watched him, stunned. How did we get here?

Kate, that's how.

Earlier tonight, in the waiting room, he couldn't bear the idea of losing me. And now?

His back was to me, and his face was in his hands, and I realized: he was crying. I'd never seen that from him before.

Tentatively, I approached him and placed my hand on his convulsing back. When he didn't resist, I put my arms around him, and he practically collapsed against me, sobbing.

"I can't trust anyone," he said. "No one at all."

"You can trust me." His body was pressed to mine, and I could feel him trembling. I didn't like that he was crying that way, but I was glad that it was over me. "I'm sorry that I put us in this position, but I'll make it right."

"How?"

"I won't let her do anything to hurt you. Because hurting you kills me. I love you so much, Michael. It's been so hard not to have you all to myself these past two years, and I leaned on her when I shouldn't have. It was a terrible mistake. But I'll make it right."

I felt his sobs quieting, his body growing still.

"Forgive me," I whispered. "Please. I'll do anything."

"No one," he whispered back, "does anything."

CHAPTER 23

LUCINDA

I'd continued to leave messages on Mom's cell and her work voice mail. I did my best to let her know that I was genuinely sorry and increasingly scared. Even if she chose not to ever speak to me again, could she please just let me know she was alive? She could have relapsed. She could be in some strange man's house with a needle sticking out of her arm, like the bad old days. "You don't have to call," I said, "just text."

So far, nothing.

I'd gotten in my car several times, intending to drive to her house, but I couldn't turn the key. I was afraid of the most likely scenario: My own mother was ignoring me. She liked that I was worried about her; she wanted me to suffer. She hated me for what I'd done. And I understood that, I really did.

I'd been losing weight steadily since I first heard from her, and in the last session, Dr. Baylor told me that I needed to focus on my self-care. So tonight, I was making a tofu stir-fry with lots of vegetables. The smell of the sesame oil was nauseating, even as my stomach rumbled with hunger. My cell phone was on the battered counter next to me in the aged kitchen with avocado-colored appliances. The wooden cabinets were in a state of disintegration, half of them falling off their hinges. The oven barely worked, topping out at four hundred degrees. Our landlord was disinclined to do any repairs or upgrades when he could already command outrageous rents for each of the three apartments in this decrepit Victorian in Berkeley, and given that there was rent control, he was probably eager for us to depart so that he could raise it even more on the next tenants.

I was hoping that all my roommates would stay gone for the next half hour. If they came home while I was cooking, I clearly had more than enough, and it would be rude not to offer them a plate. Then I'd be stuck with a dinner companion I didn't want, with my head full of thoughts I'd never share. There was nothing objectionable about my roommates, but I hadn't moved in to make friends; I just couldn't afford even a studio apartment on my salary.

A few more minutes and the stir-fry would be cooked through. Then I could take it up to my room and gobble it down, undisturbed. Though who was I kidding, I felt nothing but disturbed these days. My only respite was when I thought of Dr. Baylor and imagined him thinking of me. I replayed that conversation I overheard between him and his girlfriend, and I wondered. And fantasized. And escaped, albeit briefly.

My phone rang. I saw the name and lunged for it, spatula clattering to the floor. "Hi, Blythe!" I said. "Thanks so much for returning my call!"

"Hey, stranger!"

Blythe was in her forties, one of the women Mom used to sponsor. They became good friends, and she'd been like a second mother to me. While I was relieved to hear the warmth in her voice, it was an indication that she wasn't in the loop. She didn't know what I'd done.

"How are you?" she inquired.

"Oh, you know . . . ," I said vaguely. "Same old, same old. Still in Berkeley."

"I love Berkeley."

She told me that every time. I knew I should ask how she was, but she was capable of great and useless detail, and I just didn't have the stomach for it. "Have you heard from my mom?"

Long pause. "No one has."

"No one?"

"None of our shared friends, I should say. I think her energy must be going to Adam, which we all completely understand. Since she took a leave of absence—"

"Wait, what?"

"She's off from work. I assume it was so she could devote herself full-time to caring for Adam."

I smelled burning and hurried to turn off the flame. "When did she do that?"

"A couple of weeks ago."

So after she learned about Adam and me, she decided to freeze me out and leave her job to take care of him? I was her daughter. He was the guy who'd taken advantage of her daughter. Her child.

"Are you there?" Blythe said.

"I'm here."

"Did something happen between you and your mom?"

"You could say that."

"Do you want to talk about it? We're only as sick as our secrets."

It was a platitude I'd heard many times, Twelve Step speak. Mostly, I thought it was true. But I was already sharing my secrets (most of them, anyway) with a licensed professional. Blythe was well meaning, but she had no training, just a million meetings under her belt. Besides, she was Mom's friend. Or at least, she used to be.

"Did something happen between you and my mom?" I said.

"Not that I know of. She just hasn't been returning anyone's calls or texts. It must be overwhelming, taking care of someone with cancer. Luckily, I've never had to experience it myself."

"Yes," I finally said, "it must be consuming." Then I thanked her and told her my food was burning, that we'd talk soon.

I couldn't take the smell, so I wrote a jolly "Help yourself!" note and affixed it to the counter. Then I ran upstairs to my room, hurling myself on the bed and crying into my pillow like a teenager.

Mom was standing by her man, even when that man had abused me, and she wouldn't even give me so much as a text to ease my mind.

That meant that she was a truly terrible person, or I was.

PRESENT DAY

CHAPTER 24

DETECTIVE GREGORY PLATH

"Here," I say, "have another Kleenex." I slide the box closer to her across the table. Lucinda's already gone through a dozen tissues, at least.

I started out sympathetic, but she's trying my patience. I've got a job to do, and histrionics just slow me down. Besides, I'm not sure if the tears are real or just a ploy.

Have I become too jaded, or is that just my gut talking? Sometimes it's hard to tell.

I look down at my yellow legal pad to see where I want to go next, and she lets out a fresh sob. "Dr. Baylor used those," she explains.

Give me strength.

"I feel like you don't believe me," she says.

"About what?"

"What I've been telling you. That I could never have killed him. I love him. Loved him." More sobs.

"Do you think he loved you, too?"

"He must have. It's the only explanation." She dabbed at her eyes. If she pulled herself together, she could be a looker, though I've never liked women taller than me.

"The only explanation for what?"

Weeping conveniently overtakes her again. I try mightily to resist an eye roll.

It's not that I'm hard-hearted. When I meet with grieving widows, or parents who've lost their kids, or, you know, people with legitimate reasons to break down, I feel for them. But in my humble opinion, Lucinda needed to shut off the waterworks.

Greer already told me Lucy's story from dim sum, though I haven't yet let on about that. I'm not planning to. I want to see if Lucinda is going to come clean.

Lucy. That's what Greer called her, same as Flora. Was the nickname a sign they are all buddies, or coconspirators, or something else?

Greer confirmed that Flora was a woman scorned (no, excuse me, that Flora "claimed" to be a woman scorned). The fact that Greer didn't want to believe that the good doc had been sleeping with Flora suggested that she herself was doing the deed, though, of course, Greer denied it vigorously.

And what about sweet little Lucy? What is she going to admit or deny?

I've got to handle her with kid gloves, that's for sure. She's fragile. Both Flora and Greer agreed about that, and they agreed about virtually nothing else.

"What I don't understand," I say gently, "is why you were at the dim sum brunch. Those other women, they hated him."

"I probably shouldn't have gone," she finally says, after an extended nose blow. "I didn't believe what they were saying. Those stories . . . that wasn't the Michael I knew. He wouldn't take advantage of anyone. Whatever they gave, they gave willingly. Like I did. You might have regrets, but you can't take anything back."

"Do you have regrets?" Now we're talking.

She breaks down into tears all over again.

"Tell me the truth," I say. "It'll be better for you that way, I promise."

She looks into my eyes. "I am telling the truth. I always tell the truth. That'll be on my tombstone someday. It'll be my downfall."

"But you didn't answer the question. Do you have regrets?"

"Not when it comes to Michael. I'm at peace with everything I did."

"Did you kill him?" My voice is gentle, the way I picture Dr. Baylor spoke to her.

Another nose blow, which has the convenient effect of allowing her to avoid eye contact. "No," she says, "I could never. I love him."

BEFORE

CHAPTER 25

FLORA

I wished Kate were flying out of the Oakland airport, instead of San Francisco, and that it wasn't a Sunday, so I had a good excuse for making her call an Uber. But no such luck: it was a forty-minute ride, and inside my Lexus, the tension was palpable.

I forced myself to speak. "I know it's been a strange visit," I said, "but I hope you can tell my parents they have nothing to worry about."

"You mean lie to them?"

"They have nothing to worry about."

"I saw what I saw."

I kept my eyes on the road and my jaw tight. "And what was that?"

"I saw you subservient to a man. Playing his game. Dancing to his tune."

"You saw wrong."

But how convincing could I sound when the only reason I was talking to her at all was because of Michael? I couldn't blow up our friendship, our sisterhood, since I needed to maintain my influence over her to protect him and his profession. Kate loved me, I did believe that, but if I told her how I really felt—that I couldn't trust her anymore, that our relationship wasn't what I thought all these years—I would lose all control. Then I'd lose Michael. Lose Michael, and I had nothing. Ergo, just get through this car ride, then send her on her way. End well.

Maybe that was what Kate meant when she said I was subservient to him. I'd never loved anyone like this before, and it was a type of bondage.

But that wasn't all she meant. The other night, I came back from Michael's and shook her awake. She sat up on my couch, bleary-eyed, sans makeup, defenseless. I flashed on the many sleepovers we'd had growing up, all the history we'd shared, the ways I'd always looked after her and she, in turn, had looked up to me, and I felt a searing pain in my abdomen, as if I'd been impaled.

"How could you?" I said. "How could you tell him the truth?"

"I had to," was her reply.

"But your allegiance is to me, not to him."

"That's exactly it. I am loyal to you. I'm trying to help you get away from someone who's only out for himself. You had every right to confide in me, I'm your family, but he doesn't care about that."

"I gave him my word, and I broke it."

"He should never have asked for your word."

This wasn't supposed to be a referendum on my relationship with Michael; it was supposed to be about her actions. But somehow, I hadn't been able to keep that thread going. "I could have told him no."

"No, you couldn't."

No, I couldn't have. Not without potentially losing him.

But regardless of what she thought of him or of me, Kate had no business razing my relationship to the ground. Or trying to. She hadn't succeeded. Or she had, I didn't know. It depended on the hour. Michael had become so volatile and moody, maybe he needed to see a therapist himself.

For the past two days, it had been "don't come around," "don't call me, I'll call you," "forget where I live," "okay, maybe I do need to see you," "I'll come to your house," only of course that wouldn't work, since Kate was still there. Now that she was leaving and he could have me anytime he wanted, he might very well have changed his mind again. My remorse was fraying at the edges, yet my love was holding firm. I just needed to ride this out. Sometimes love was bondage. But it was still love.

"Just because he's a therapist doesn't make this healthy," Kate said to me now.

What did she know, anyway? She'd never had a healthy relationship in her life! I wasn't even sure if ours qualified anymore, after what she had done.

But I promised Michael I'd do anything, so I told her that I appreciated her concern and that I'd think about what she'd said. I had to make nice, for him, but I was burning inside. I kept my eyes on the road.

"All the time you were struggling," I couldn't resist saying, "I never judged you."

"You mean my addiction? That's a disease. You being with Michael—that's a choice."

I bit my tongue. Who was Kate, with her past, to go deciding what was a disease and what was a choice, who should stay together and who shouldn't?

She could claim to be looking after my mental health, but she was the one who'd sent me into this state. I was just lucky that he hadn't dumped me altogether after the betrayal. Now I had to live with that sword hanging over my head. I needed to be seductive, and I couldn't make any trouble; I couldn't state any of my own needs or desires, because I just had to stay in his good graces. We'd been so close to being a normal couple, to going public, and then Kate had to open her mouth. She'd put me back in a subservient position.

I wanted to ask again, *How could you?* but there was no point. She could because she'd felt empowered and entitled. After spending a total of six hours in Michael's presence, she thought she knew him better than I did. She was an arrogant little kid who never grew up. Don't they say that people who abuse drugs are stunted at the age they first started? Kate was still eleven years old.

"I appreciate your concern," I said again, tersely.

"But you're staying with him."

"Yes."

She nodded, looking out the window. "I was right to try to get him to end things, because you never could."

I needed to get her out of my car. The exit for the airport was coming up in less than three miles. The speedometer hit ninety-five miles per hour.

"You're not even sorry?" I couldn't help it; I had to give her the chance. Give our relationship a chance.

"I'm sorry that I hurt you, but I feel like it would be hypocritical to apologize when I'd do it again in a heartbeat. It was like—what do they call those?—an intervention. My version of getting everyone together in the living room to tell you that if you don't stop using, you could die."

Everyone was just her, the ultimate arbiter. "Stop," I told her. "Just stop."

"Stop what?"

"Stop acting like you're better than me."

"Because we both know you're the one who's superior, right?"

It was the fight we'd never had, but maybe it was inevitable.

"I know I'm not better than you," I said. But I was lying, and she knew it.

We were silent for the rest of the ride. Once I pulled up in front of Delta, I considered remaining in the car, but we were family. I wanted to end on a good note. Or if that wasn't possible, at least get out of the minor key.

I popped the trunk and lifted her suitcase out, setting it on the curb. Without looking her in the eye, I pulled her to me in an embrace. I closed my eyes and pretended things were as they always had been, and when I said, "I love you," I meant it.

After what she'd done and what she'd just said, it was more than an olive branch, it was the whole tree, but she stepped away and rolled her bag behind her into the terminal without a backward glance.

What more could she have expected? "Thank you for nearly ruining my relationship"? I didn't understand this girl I'd known my whole life. And I was terrified because Michael was right; she had the goods: the text messages, a few selfies of him sleeping beside me that he didn't know I took. She could turn on Michael, and on me, anytime she wanted.

As I got back in the driver's seat, my phone was pinging. It was Kate. I looked back at the terminal and saw that she was standing to the right of the glass doors, her eyes on me, her expression opaque. I glanced down at the text.

He's done this before.

CHAPTER 26

GREER

It was my weekly meeting with Chenille, and some unusually nervous energy was radiating from her. *Please don't quit on me.* That, I could not handle. I'd offer her a promotion, a 20 percent raise—no, make it 30 percent. I just couldn't do it on my own, not now.

"What's going on?" I asked her.

"To tell you the truth, lately, you've seemed preoccupied. I've tried not to mention it. I've just been doing some double-checking—"

"You check up on me?"

"I've been finding errors," she said softly. "I correct them."

My cheeks grew hot. "What sort of errors?"

"Sometimes it's accounting. Sometimes it's in personnel. Occasionally, a name is misspelled. Balls get dropped. They're not major, but I worry they could be one day." Chenille's eyes were on the desk between us. "I didn't want to have to say this—I know you'll refocus soon—but I got a call from Jon Morrow. He's thinking of moving his business to another firm."

I stared at her. "He told you that, not me?"

She must pick up on something in my tone, an accusation I hadn't known was there, because she turned cool. "I'm entirely appropriate with every client, as you know."

"Of course I know that. I trust you implicitly."

"Even the ones who aren't appropriate with me, and you know who I'm talking about." Now the slight accusation was coming from her, as in, I hadn't protected her adequately. I left her to fend for herself. We all had to. Did she really think I was immune just because I was the boss around here? Sure, CEOs were still resigning over sexual harassment claims, but far more kept their jobs than got ousted. Most of our clients were in Silicon Valley, in Brotopia, and it took a very long time to change a culture. If I confronted every high-ranking executive whose eyes or hands strayed, who made overtures or subtly demeaning comments, then my dance card would be half-empty. I kept mine full. I had to be crafty in my rejections and clever in how I policed my personal space. Chenille needed to learn those skills, pronto.

"I do know who you mean," I said, "and I run interference as much as I can."

"That's not really what I wanted to talk about. I understand our client base." Good girl. "The issue is, I'm fielding more calls from unhappy execs who are on the verge of weighing their options."

"It's not just Jon Morrow?"

Her eyes on mine were moist. I hadn't realized how much stress my "preoccupation," as she put it, had been causing her. "No, it's not just Jon."

"I'm sorry. I hope you know how much I value you and that I would absolutely hate to lose you. Can I ask you candidly, am I in danger of losing you?"

"It's been hard."

"I'll do better. I can promise you that. Also, we need to reevaluate your compensation, and any adjustments will be retroactive. I've made your job harder, and your salary should reflect that." She didn't appear fully reassured, so I added quickly, "Not that it's going to stay this hard. Like you said, I'll be refocusing."

Finally, I was rewarded with a tentative smile.

I could understand her reticence. She wasn't sure what was wrong with me, so she couldn't lay odds on when or how I'd be able to turn it around. Seeing as I'd never been one to share my personal trials before, I certainly couldn't start now, when they were as embarrassingly banal as wanting to be a mommy without the benefit of Chenille's young, fresh, gorgeous eggs. And I didn't have a man, not like Chenille with the small tasteful desktop photo of her and that Adonis who would soon propose. He should hurry up. Maybe a diamond on her finger would help ward off the Jon Morrows of the world. Probably not, though. They hadn't gotten to where they were without rising to a challenge.

I got more specifics about which clients needed tending and the types of mistakes Chenille had been catching, and I issued a final apology. It was the last one she'd need, because I intended to pull myself together. Then Chenille saw herself out, and I walked over to the wall of windows overlooking the financial district of San Francisco. I'd earned this view. I'd done nothing else with my life to get it.

If I couldn't manage the thoughts of a baby and my workload with any degree of competence, I didn't see how I'd be able to balance an actual baby and my career.

The problem was, I didn't care like I once had. I hadn't picked up any new clients over the past month because I couldn't muster any true zeal. My pitches were rote, and their targets must have felt that. My follow-ups were half-hearted. Now my existing clients were feeling it, too, and while some might be relishing the chance to turn to Chenille, others were thinking of defecting altogether. I had the list of those who'd voiced their concerns to Chenille, but the reality was, I was going to need to do damage control with everyone. And I dreaded it. Not just because of the occasional hand on my thigh but because I'd have to playact what used to be authentic. Channel the old me, with conviction. Could I do it, or was I going to lose more clients in trying? Would I be exposing myself?

I had no choice but to try. My business depended on it, and Chenille was counting on me. All my employees were.

Ever since I'd developed baby brain, I'd been uninspired. I'd lost all sense of purpose and meaning. I no longer got why me and not the other guy. I placed expensive talent in top jobs, which was hardly a service to humanity. I kept demanding people happy, for a little while, until they got restless, and then they came back to me for another search. Their inability to find true contentment, to feel any one place was enough to contain their gifts, was my bread and butter. I used to thrive on that. But it was different now. It felt as empty as my womb.

I'd gone from being a pragmatist—which I came by honestly, straight from my parents—to an existentialist. Dr. Michael would have a lot to say about that. He harped on the parent connection like it was the root of everything, and sometimes, I thought he was right.

My work alone wasn't enough anymore; a child would be too much. What was I supposed to do?

Then there was that dream I'd had last night. I was going off to work with this heavy 1950s briefcase, the kind Dagwood would carry in those old *Blondie* comic strips, and I was in a pinstripe suit. Michael was seeing me off, holding our baby's little hand, making it wave, and he was wearing an apron. He was laughing, and I was laughing, and the baby was adorable and perplexed, and the thing was, in the dream, I was absurdly happy. Delighted. When was the last time I'd felt delight? Had I ever?

It probably didn't mean anything that it was Michael. He was the only man I had any sort of significant relationship with these days, so of course he'd feature prominently.

No, it didn't mean anything at all.

CHAPTER 27

LUCINDA

"A leave of absence," I said. "To take care of him."

It was hard to even form complete sentences; the pain was still so acute. I hadn't thought it would be after how I'd pulled away from my mother all those years ago. Just so I could have him. And now she must have been doing the same thing with me, so she could have him just a little longer. We had come full circle.

The strange thing was, I couldn't even remember what I'd seen in him or fathom what she continued to see in him. That wasn't only because he'd been so whittled down the last time I was in his presence. It's that he was just a guy, and she was my mother, and I was her daughter. I didn't understand how it could have meant so little to either of us, to me then or her now.

"You feel like she chose him," Dr. Baylor said.

"She did choose him. She still hasn't called me back. And I keep thinking"—lump in my throat—"about what that says about me."

I was the vixen who tempted her husband away from her. Well, tried to. I failed. She was the one who'd be beside him in the end. The one he loved. And who loved me? No one.

"Don't torment yourself," Dr. Baylor said. "That's what she wants."

"Or she just wants to nurse her husband in peace."

"If that's all she wanted, she could text you to say so. She's punishing you."

"Maybe I deserve to be punished."

He leaned forward in that way he did when he really wanted me to take in something important. "Last week, you overheard something you shouldn't have. Something that a nearly deranged woman wanted you to hear so she could humiliate me." Weird. He was talking about his girlfriend in the waiting room. "She was trying to trap me, and it almost worked. Then I realized: She wants me to feel responsible for her emotions. But we're all responsible for our own. See, even I'm susceptible to that kind of manipulation.

"Think about it. Your mother going MIA—that's manipulation. That's cruelty. But she wants you to feel you brought it on yourself, that you're responsible for her pain. You're not."

There was something off about the parallel he was drawing between us, but I liked it. Overhearing him last week had somehow shifted our dynamic. It was like I'd graduated from the kids' table to the adults'.

When I said again, "Maybe I deserve it," I didn't know if I meant it or I just wanted to be told that it wasn't true, to hear again that Dr. Baylor and I were the same. We were being manipulated, and we could withstand together.

"Whatever age you are, you're still her child," he said. "That's not how a parent behaves."

"Are you a parent?"

He paused a long moment, debating, and then nodded.

"How old?"

"Story for another time." Did I imagine his sadness? "This is your story. And I think it's time for you to start telling it."

I felt a splash of fear. "To who?"

"On the page. You're a writer. Write."

"I'm not a writer. I'm an editor. Not even. A proofreader. I punctuate for a living."

"This isn't about how you make money. You have the heart of an artist. The lived experience of an artist. You don't need to portray exactly what happened. Just sit down and write your way through this and out of it. Write into the light."

From anyone else, it might have sounded cheesy. I'd definitely heard him more eloquent before. But he was so impassioned that it had made him less articulate, less controlled, and that scooped me up. He was passionate about me and what I could do. What I could become.

"I haven't tried to write in a long time," I said. "I'm a little scared to try."

"What are you afraid of?"

"What I'll say. When I'm here with you, I know who I am." When I was being coached, it was all so clear. "But when I'm alone, it's different. You talked about the light, but some of the corners of my mind are so dark."

"Write through that and bring it in for the next session."

"You want to read it?"

"I'd be honored."

That brought up another fear entirely. "What if you don't think I'm talented?"

"I think you're brilliant. I think you're a bright shining star. Write until you know that. Write your way there."

"This is the last thing I thought we'd talk about today. I thought we'd be talking about my mother."

"We've talked about her enough. She's holding you back. Your past is holding you back. Write like an exorcism."

"Do I have to write as myself?"

"Of course not. Be anyone you want. Any character you can think up, that's who you're meant to be."

No one had ever talked to me like this. No one had ever seemed so sure of my talent. My mother never even asked to see anything I was working on. Adam never did, either. In my writing workshops, no professor had anointed me.

But then, Dr. Baylor hadn't seen a word from me, unless you counted my initial intake form. His certainty could be misplaced. The thought of disappointing him . . .

"Do I have to bring it in right away?" I asked. "Can I sit with it awhile?"

"This is your process. You do whatever you want, whatever feels right. I trust you. Follow your muse. It knows where to go."

CHAPTER 28

FLORA

"It's official," Nat said. "No more Tinder."

"Hear, hear!" Jeanie raised her glass. "To being off the market!"

We all clinked. I was happy for Nat, yet I couldn't help but envy how simple it had been. A few dates, mutual enjoyment, and voilà, she had a boyfriend. It wasn't love, though. It might not ever be.

Not that I was rooting against her. Nat was my friend, and she'd never even been married. Things should go smoothly for her, finally. I wanted them to. I just wished I were on the conveyor belt to (re)marriage myself, but if I couldn't even get Michael to be seen in public with me, that was looking like a long shot. And it had been a very bumpy ride this past week, to say the least.

"Tell us more about him," Jeanie said.

His name was Devlin, he worked in finance, he was short but handsome, ready and eager to commit. He wanted three kids, just like Nat did. With the right woman, he'd get started right away.

"He sounds amazing," I said. I downed the rest of my champagne.

"You're next, you know," Jeanie tells me.

Without even thinking, I said, "I'm in love."

Jeanie's mouth was open. Her expression wasn't merely shocked but hurt. She couldn't believe I hadn't told her sooner, that she was finding out for the first time at cocktail hour with Nat.

Speaking of Nat, it was like she and I had been playing poker, and I'd just raised her all in. "Since when?" she asked.

"It happened quickly." I gave Jeanie a conciliatory glance. "A few dates, and we're practically living together." It felt good to say it, though. It was a prophecy and a prayer. Soon it would come true.

Jeanie rearranged her expression. She liked to be happy for people, and right then, between Nat and me, her cup was overflowing. "Where'd you meet him?" she asked.

"We ran into each other at Market Hall while we were buying coffee. Our eyes locked, and it was just one of those things. You know when you know."

"Infatuation," Nat said, a touch dourly. "So what's his name?"

I had this trick I'd mastered a long time ago: I could drink in a way that sent the liquid down the wrong pipe. After a long coughing jag, no one ever remembered the question that came before.

I was not going to say Michael's name. I wouldn't make that same mistake twice, not after Kate.

I never responded to her text about how Michael's done this before. I refused to take the bait. If Kate had information she wanted to share, then she could just come out and say it. But I was almost positive that she was just casting more aspersions on Michael. Her hatred of him bordered on the irrational.

Michael told me that he'd never been involved with a client before, and he'd never lied to me. But Kate used to lie plenty, to me and everyone else. It was what addicts did.

When I was done sputtering and choking, after I'd drained the glass of water that Jeanie procured, Nat said, "So tell us about him."

I'd been thinking during my fit about how to play this. No name, no mention of what he did for a living. No identifying details, like how he told me about his clients. I'd stress the way I felt about him and how he felt about me. "I've never been so attracted to anyone," I said honestly. "He feels the same. It caught us both by surprise."

"You've seemed so jaded. I was starting to wonder if it would even be possible for you." Jeanie smiled. "I'm glad I was wrong."

"Well, who wouldn't have sounded a little jaded with that succession of losers?" I smiled back. "But now I have a good man, and I couldn't be happier."

Nat nodded slowly, taking it in. "Then I'm happy for you."

I couldn't entirely blame her for the tepid response. I had stolen her thunder a bit. She'd found a boyfriend; I'd found love.

I was recalling, with a visceral tingle through my body, the early days when Michael and I had been so certain of our feelings, a surety that was only strengthened by the obstacles standing between us. We'd stayed up all night because we couldn't get enough of each other. Not just sex (though that was spectacular)—no, it was the confessions. I told him all my hurts and all my fears, how it felt when Young no longer wanted me sexually and the way that reactivated all the insecurities I'd felt growing up. Michael took it all in, and he transformed it. He made my pain beautiful. He thought my pain made me beautiful. It made me lovable. I felt completely held by him, in every way. And being secret meant we were separate from the world. It was heady and intoxicating. We weren't like other couples; we had our own cocoon.

We could go back there. Stay up all night talking and making love. Build a cocoon again, even stronger this time.

When Nat asked, "Who wants another drink?" I begged off. I said I was tired, when really, I was anything but. I was still tingling with the recollection of where Michael and I had started. We were meant for each other. We'd known we were worth the risk, that we would navigate every obstacle to be together. And we had. It was our time.

It was after eleven when I arrived at his house, and it took him a while to answer the door. That was my first clue that this might have been a mistake. Another mistake.

His hair was adorably askew; his expression was thunderous. He stared at me, saying nothing, and I felt my liquid courage evaporate.

"Hi." I smiled, a little nervously. At least I knew I looked good.

Didn't I? He was still silent, glowering. He'd never liked being woken up, but this was something more.

Had Kate reached out to him? I'd confided a lot in her over the past two years, things I said or texted in moments of frustration that I hadn't really meant, things I would never want getting back to him.

But she wouldn't do that.

I had to hope she wouldn't.

"I missed you tonight," I said. I was trying to look and sound seductive, but I felt so damned afraid. "I was out with my friends, but all I wanted was to be with you. In your bed, in your arms." If I could just get my feet to move over the threshold, if I could touch him, everything could change back. We'd be transformed into who we once were.

But for how long? He'd been running so hot and cold. In my presence, he remembered; I left, and he forgot. I didn't know what to do to make a more lasting imprint.

"You can't come inside," he said. His lips pressed together tightly to let me know that his proclamation was final.

"I'm sorry. I should have called first."

"My phone was off."

"I thought you'd like the surprise."

He didn't soften. What I needed was for him to harden. *Just let me come inside. Let yourself come, Michael. Come home.*

"I'll call an Uber." I made a move to go inside. He stood firm.

"No. And don't wait in front of my house, either; I have neighbors."

"They don't know that I used to be your client, Michael. This is crazy. Where am I supposed to go? It's midnight."

"There's a well-lit Safeway three blocks away and besides, you should have thought of that."

So scolding, so devoid of empathy. He was a therapist, for fuck's sake. He'd been my therapist.

"Do you have a woman inside?" I asked.

His eyes widened. "Are you serious? You're the one who lied to me. You told Kate about us months ago."

"Do you have a woman inside?" I repeated.

"Of course not." He opened the door wide. "You want to search my house? Go ahead, do it."

It was a dare. Search his house, and it could be the last straw. I shook my head.

This was all my fault. I never should have betrayed him by talking to Kate. If I'd just followed our agreement, if I hadn't invited her to town, if I could have kept my mouth shut and been patient, I could have had everything I'd ever wanted. We'd been so close.

The door was shutting, and I was hoofing it down the street. Safeway was, indeed, well lit, and I was exposed. A crying, humiliated wreck, makeup running in rivers. I'd ruined things for good this time.

CHAPTER 29

GREER

Dr. Michael looked exhausted and out of sorts. Residually surly, maybe, like he'd been stewing over what someone else had done to him, and while he wasn't exactly taking it out on me, he couldn't contain the leftover emotion.

I dealt with wealthy and powerful men all the time. They were often a ball of thinly disguised aggression, so I was largely unfazed by Dr. Michael's bearing. If anything, I was intrigued. He was a real person with real feelings. Real anger. Honestly, it was manlier than I'd considered him before. Nearly sexy.

But then, apparently, I also found him sexy as a manny in an apron.

It wasn't like I'd been nursing that image, but as I sat across from him, I could feel that something had shifted. I didn't know if he could tell. I hoped not. I didn't even understand the nature of the shift. I wasn't understanding much these days. That made me feel out of control and, worst of all, out of character. Was I having a growth spurt at almost forty? Or could it be that my whole life, I'd never truly known myself? I wondered if what Dr. Michael seemed to think could be true: that all this time, I'd just been living out my parents' script, that their boundless ambitions became mine, and maybe, just maybe, the desire to have a baby was the first true motivation I'd ever had.

If I became someone completely different, I might not like her. I'd always had good self-esteem. In college, all those girls with their cutting and their eating disorders mystified me. I would never deny myself food or slash my skin. It was mine.

Now, though, I wasn't sure who was in my skin. Dr. Michael treated it as an evolution, but he was clearly biased.

There were two conversations going on: the surface one about my parents, and then the undercurrent of his anger as it interacted with my—what, desire? I was very aware that I was across from a man and not merely a shrink. I could smell him for the first time. Had he always worn cologne that was like leather and tobacco, or had he recently taken up smoking?

Normally, I hated cigarettes. The old me had, anyway.

I was sitting differently, showing my legs to their best advantage. I was distracted, and so was he. But I didn't think my legs were doing it to him. He was reacting to someone who wasn't in the room, while I was reacting to him. It felt unfair somehow. Unequal.

"I need to apologize," he said. "I'm not at my best today."

"I'm not, either."

"But you don't have to be."

"Because I pay you."

"Because this isn't your job. If part of you is elsewhere, then I bring you back. If part of me is elsewhere . . ." He looked down at his hands. "It's my responsibility to give you my all."

"You're only human." I smiled. "So where've you been?"

"I've wasted enough of your time without answering that question."

"With someone else? A woman, perhaps? Or a man?"

He sighed. "I'm not going to charge you for this session, okay?"

"I'll pay. Then you're free to answer."

"I'm not free. That's the problem." His eyes were still cast downward. "I have to make a tough decision."

"You're debating whether to break up with someone, is that it?" I was rather enjoying this game of Twenty Questions. For once, he was in the hot seat.

I wanted his answer to be yes. I wanted him to say he was about to be free.

I didn't know why I cared. He was my therapist. He wasn't even someone I'd normally date.

"Something like that," he said.

"Could I ask you something else?"

"Seeing as this session has gone off the rails, sure, you can ask. I'll see if it's something I can answer."

"Do you have children?"

He looked right at me. "What would it mean to you if I did? Or if I didn't?"

"It wouldn't change anything."

"Then why should I answer?"

"Then why shouldn't you answer?"

He dipped his head a little, touché-style. "No, I don't have children."

"Have you ever wanted any?"

"I've said enough for one day."

"Given the issues that brought me in here, it would be good for me to know why you never had children. Maybe there are variables I've never considered."

"I guess I should say, I've never raised children. I was a sperm donor a long time ago."

I stared at him in surprise. "And you never said anything, even though you knew I was reading through the profiles?"

"I'm not sure why my being a sperm donor would have any relevance."

Maybe it didn't, but still. He'd been holding out on me. "Why did you do it?"

"I was in college. I needed some pocket money, and I knew other guys who were doing it. It was pseudo-altruistic. Perhaps a touch egomaniacal. I liked the idea that women out there would choose me to father their children, no strings attached."

"You think most sperm donors are egomaniacal?"

"Not necessarily. I can only speak for myself."

There was something arrogant about his very profession, about the presumption that he had the power to help people. But then, I was sure he'd helped many. I just wasn't sure I'd be one of them. "Are you egomaniacal now?"

"A lot can happen in twenty years, Greer."

"Life's cut you down to size, is that what you're saying?"

"I've got a much clearer sense of what I can offer and what I can't."

It seemed Dr. Michael liked his boundaries as much as I did. Well, as much as I used to. The new me obviously felt differently. "Is that why you're a therapist? It's safer than having real relationships?"

"We're having a real relationship." He met my eyes. "Aren't we?"

I stared back. Yes, we were.

CHAPTER 30

LUCINDA

Cassie couldn't stop watching the door. Behind it was her mom and Kevin. Maybe they were talking. Maybe they were having sex. Maybe they were trying not to talk, keeping all their secrets from each other. Maybe Kevin wanted to tell her mom. Maybe someday he would. And maybe that wouldn't be so bad.

Except it was illegal. It shouldn't be, because love was love. That's what Cassie thought, anyway. Kevin said they had to wait. Wait for what? For her to be eighteen? Or twenty-one? Or for her mom to fall out of love with Kevin? No, that would never happen. They'd have to wait for her mom to, like, die.

With how much Mom loved Kevin, it would hurt less that way. But Mom wasn't very old, only fifty, and she was in good health. And she was sitting on that inheritance from her dad, who died before Cassie was born.

Cassie knew this: the waiting was killing her.

In college, I'd never tried my hand at a novel. It was always short stories about people who were entirely different from me. An oil rigger, a Sudanese refugee, a female firefighter—the list went on. Writing was a chance to inhabit someone else's body, to see through their eyes. The most painful critique was when another student said, "Your characters all wind up sounding the same. They all have the same voice." I could never manage to leave myself behind. Wherever I went, whatever I wrote, there I was.

With Dr. Baylor's encouragement, I'd started writing my first novel. It was semiautobiographical, about a teen girl who became involved with her stepfather, but it was going to have a very different ending. It was way more cathartic than I expected and definitely better than what I proofread at work. Who knew, it might even be good.

I'd never try to publish it where I worked (you don't shit where you eat). But maybe it could make its way out into the world, where it could help other abuse survivors.

Because that's what I was. A survivor of abuse. I was stronger than I'd ever been, with Dr. Baylor at my side. He believed I was capable of much more than rearranging commas on other people's manuscripts, that I could use what I'd been through and turn it into art, and I was beginning to believe that, too.

I'd been indulging in a few fantasies about Dr. Baylor. Michael. I hadn't had the guts to ask if he and his girlfriend had officially broken up, but even if they hadn't, it was obviously a matter of time. He was so ambivalent about her. But with me, he was nothing but supportive. Admiring, even. And since he clearly didn't shy away from women with mental health issues, I couldn't help thinking that maybe someday . . .

I pictured the two of us sitting in front of a roaring fire, him reading my latest pages, sipping brandy or cognac or something classy, and then—well, you know. It was funny how PG I could be, how it would basically fade out at the moment when Michael leaned toward me. Strange that someone with a past like mine could be such a prude.

Or it might be that I couldn't really imagine what it would look like, or feel like, to have a man like that interested in a girl like me.

A woman, I had to remind myself. I was a woman. A smart, talented, beautiful woman. He'd told me that before. More than once. Did he really say that to all his clients? Did he work with them all for free?

Of course not. I was special.

I just needed to stand up straight and tall and see myself as he saw me.

I stepped away from my computer and walked over to the full-length mirror. "This is the woman who Michael loves," I said over and over, until I actually sort of believed it.

CHAPTER 31

FLORA

I was in front of Michael's building in a metered space, wearing a scarf over my head and sunglasses, though it was seven p.m. at night. It was the third night of my stakeout. Three nights since he'd last returned one of my calls or texts.

Could it really have just been because I'd showed up unannounced, or was it something else? Someone else?

I didn't want him to see me, not like this. If he walked out of the building, I'd have to duck and hope he didn't recognize my car, not that there was anything unusual about a dark-gray Lexus in this neighborhood. While I had been waiting in front of the Safeway the other night, I had a revelation. Maybe Michael's behavior toward me wasn't about my supposed mistakes at all; it was about my being replaced. If Kate was telling the truth and he'd done it before, he could do it again.

There were several other therapists in the building, so I couldn't be sure that the women coming in and out were Michael's, but I had a feeling about his Wednesday lineup: the blonde giraffe and the chic woman in clothes that managed to be loose and perfectly tailored at once. They were very different types but both attractive. The blonde didn't know it, while the brunette certainly did because she worked at it. Perfect nearly nude makeup, not a hair out of place. I liked my clothes tight and my eyelashes fake, but I bet that the brunette spent as much time as I did to achieve the opposite effect.

Neither was my type, yet somehow, I felt in my gut that if it were going to be anyone, it would be one of them. I hadn't had an instinct this strong since I knew about Michael himself.

It had been during a session. Under Dr. Baylor's tutelage, Young was starting to recognize that my demands for sex were requests for intimacy. Dr. Baylor called them "bids;" he said we were all making bids for closeness all the time. When we say, "So I had a rough day," and our partner says, "Hmm, what?" and doesn't even stop what he's doing, it's a bid denied, and we're less likely to bid again. "It's kind of like being in an auction where no one acknowledges that your paddle is raised," Dr. Baylor said, and Young nodded intently. He was really listening. As much as he'd resisted the counseling process, he really seemed to respect Dr. Baylor.

By my estimation, Dr. Baylor was only ten years older than Young, but he just seemed so much more mature. As I watched my husband get schooled in the intimacy arts, I started to imagine what it would be like with the teacher instead of the student.

We were twelve sessions in, so that meant I'd known Dr. Baylor for about three months, and he'd been doing a good job. As in, Young was making more bids and responding to mine with greater enthusiasm. There was more conversation, cuddling, and closeness; numbers were up in all the major C categories. Only I wasn't happy. I'd initiated this whole thing, and now I was mildly annoyed and bored. But I couldn't admit that. I was just going through the motions.

Did Dr. Baylor see that? If he did, he didn't let on. He kept working on Young diligently, surgically. Young became more vulnerable, opening up about his childhood wounds. He wanted to be with me, fully; he was just now figuring out how to merge love and sex.

Dr. Baylor had gotten me more love; now it was time for him to get me more sex. The only problem was, I didn't want it anymore. I didn't want Young.

I was sitting there in session twelve when that came into stark focus for me. I'd wanted Young when he didn't seem interested. Dr. Baylor was about to make Young available, and I felt this rush of fear. Young wasn't the only one who had trouble merging love and sex. In my case, I wanted sex more when I felt less loved.

I was waiting for Dr. Baylor to call me out on this, but instead, he was working with Young about how he could approach me sexually. "Be more animal," Dr. Baylor was saying, and then he gave me the quickest sideways glance, and I swear, my panties got wet. It was a gusher like I'd never felt in my life.

It wasn't just that I didn't want my husband; I wanted Dr. Baylor—Michael—badly. He was the real man, and oh, the things he would be able to do to me . . .

It was like he was talking right to me, through Young. All his helpful advice was letting me know exactly what I'd be in for if I could trade up, if I could go from the pupil to the master. He was ostensibly trying to save my marriage, but instead, he was showing my husband up.

I listened, and it was hotter than any porn. I was relieved that Young just kept watching Michael closely, like he was taking mental notes. He didn't notice my red face and my shallow respiration. But Michael must have. As he continued to speak, it was like he was masturbating me with his voice. I almost came right there, and I had to talk myself down, like that old joke where guys try to think of baseball or something equally unsexy. I thought about credit card bills until I could pass for normal.

But from then on, I was under Michael's spell, and even though he'd barely glanced at me, he must have known it. He suggested that we each have an individual session: as in, first me, and then the next week, Young.

I was going to be alone with Michael.

And Young—poor clueless Young. He agreed. He had so much faith and trust in Dr. Baylor.

I wished I could feel that way about Michael now, but I didn't even know if we were still together, if I could hold on to the expectation of monogamy. I was entitled to the expectation that he wasn't fucking any of his clients. That was the code of his profession, one that he broke with me only because some feelings couldn't be denied as much as you might wish they could. And even we hadn't been together until after therapy had concluded.

But Kate said there were others, and as I looked his Wednesday ladies up and down, I could easily believe her.

Michael said he never had "true romantic feelings" for any client other than me. I hadn't pressed him at the time, because back then, he'd gone on and on about how unique, special, beloved, and erotic I was. But it was a hell of a cagey statement, now that I was looking back from a much less secure perch.

That was, what, a year ago? He might not even have known the giraffe and the chanteuse back then. Their relationships could have been growing right under my nose for months now, shielded by confidentiality. Plausible deniability was more like it. He was always only too happy to respond, "You know I can't tell you that," and that was when we were on good footing, nothing like now. I couldn't ask anything these days.

That's why I was here, watching and waiting.

Waiting for what? For him to make out with one of them in the street? He was far too discreet for that. I knew that better than anyone.

All I knew was that if I wanted answers, I had to find them myself. And if I wanted Michael—which I did, and had, desperately, ever since session twelve—then I had to fight for him.

CHAPTER 32

GREER

Donor Profile #3731

Interview Notes

Donor 3731 describes himself as "the class clown all grown up." He's quick to joke and quick to laugh. He has many friends, both male and female, though he identifies as gay in his sexual preferences.

He is tall and attractive, with blond hair and green eyes. Someday he'd like to be in a committed relationship and have children of his own via a surrogate.

Family is important to him, he says, even more so because his parents disowned him due to his homosexuality . . .

Q & A

Describe your personality.

Lighthearted. Loyal. Imaginative.

What are your interests and goals?

I read a lot and write screenplays in my spare time. I've been a hacky sack aficionado from way back. I play Frisbee golf every week. My goal is to

make enough money to live comfortably and be generous with my friends.
Toward that end, I work in finance where I uphold a strict code of ethics
and the golden rule: I treat my clients as I'd want to be treated.

Donor 3731 sounded pretty fantastic. I liked that he was gay, so there
were no circumstances under which we would have been in a romantic
relationship. In other words, this was the only way I could have had his
baby. It couldn't have been more natural if I'd tried.

But he was twenty-four years old. Who would he be in another
twenty? Would he turn out as he imagined, as he hoped, or was he an
egomaniac whose subconscious wanted to propagate his gene pool and
prove his worthiness after the most stinging rejection anyone could
receive from his own parents? I couldn't know.

But with Michael, I knew. I had experienced for myself that he
was highly intelligent, attractive, successful, motivated to help people,
able to admit his own imperfections, and that he and I had chemistry.

There, I admitted it. I read the donor profiles and I had no idea
whether I'd mix well with this person at all, and yet, with the way evolution and evolutionary biology operated, I had to believe chemistry
was part of what made a great baby. We were designed to be attracted
to people with whom we'd spawn well. The species depended on it.
Pheromones existed for a reason.

In business, I didn't like to take unnecessary risks, but if I'd sat
around waiting for complete information at every decision point, the
competition would pass me by. There were always variables that couldn't
be controlled and data that couldn't be possessed. In this case, the smart
decision would be to go with what I knew for sure: how Michael turned
out, and our chemistry.

Had I lost my mind? Because asking my therapist for his sperm was
starting to seem like my safest bet.

It was unorthodox, of course. Perhaps even impossible, because he might dismiss it out of hand. I had no idea how I'd even broach the topic. The best course of action might be if I just treated it like business: "I know what I want, now how do we make this happen?"

We'd need to stop working together, of course. But it would be easier to find a new therapist than to find the perfect sperm donor. And if I were pregnant, I might not need therapy anymore. Decision made, problem solved, leap taken.

Perfect was probably an overstatement. Even *ideal* was too much. *The best I can do* sounded negative, but it was accurate. I was under a strict biological deadline.

I did need to ask him some more questions. His health history and genetics, for example. More about his childhood, maybe? I smirked at the thought. But there had to be other things I needed to know. It couldn't be this simple.

It wasn't simple at all. I had decided: a) that the new me needed to have a baby, damn the torpedoes, and that b) I should try to have the baby of my therapist. This was insane. I couldn't really be contemplating this.

Except I most definitely was.

CHAPTER 33

LUCINDA

My phone was ringing, and it returned me to my body and to my desk where I should have been proofreading someone else's crappy novel, but I just wanted to write my own. Not a crappy novel—a good one. I was increasingly sure that I could.

Lately, I'd been catching fire, and all I wanted was to write and to see Dr. Baylor. I was growing more confident about the prose, and I'd even thought of bringing some pages to our next session, letting him see what I could do. I'd make him proud.

Or he might have to psychoanalyze them. After all, that was his job. I wasn't ready for that. I wanted them to be art, like he said.

Oh shit. The call was from Adam.

I'd almost forgotten I left him a voice mail weeks ago. Honestly, I'd almost forgotten how worried I was about my mother. I'd decided to go with Dr. Baylor's take, which was that my mother was an adult who was responsible for her own feelings and behavior, and that she was an adult who was being unfairly punitive with her own child. Besides, I had my writing, and she wasn't going to steal that from me. It felt good to be a creative being, uninhibited, especially after so many years of being racked with guilt and shame.

But I saw Adam's name, and I was sucked back down, down, down in an instant.

"Hello," I said.

"You sound out of breath," he said. "That's my department."

He was wheezing, though it wasn't lung cancer. I never thought before of dying in that way: as the loss of breath. That it was just running away from him, running out.

Adam didn't deserve air.

"Hold on," I told him. I stepped outside. It was just about noon, which meant that there was the most pedestrian traffic the street would see all day. I watched people heading into the vegan diner, wishing I could join them. Wishing I could be doing anything other than talking to my dying stepfather and ex-lover.

Bile rushed up into my mouth. No vegan food today.

"I called you when I was trying to find my mother," I said. Trying. Past tense. I didn't want to hear about how she was nursing him back to health, and I wasn't about to ask how he was. I didn't care. There would be no pleasantries or small talk. He could drop dead tomorrow for all I cared. He had decided to take my relationship with my mother into the grave with him, and he had no right to do that.

Dr. Baylor would probably want me to express my anger to the source of it, but that had never been my style, and I wasn't going to change now. It wasn't because I had compassion for Adam; it was because I didn't see the point. Dr. Baylor always seemed so sure that anger needed to be vented, that it would set me free, but for once, I thought he was wrong. I had my writing for that. I had him.

"Yeah," he said, "no one's heard from her." Each word was a belabored exhalation. I'd like this conversation over as quickly as possible, but I wasn't likely to get my wish.

"Because she's spending all her time and energy on you."

"I haven't heard from her." I . . . haven't . . . heard . . . from . . . her. This was excruciating.

Wait, if she wasn't with Adam, then where was she? I thought of how to ask the question so that the response would require as few words as possible. "Did she leave you?"

"Kicked . . . me . . . out."

It was good to hear that. But it unleashed a whole different set of worries. Blythe said she'd taken a leave of absence from her job and that she hadn't been in contact with anyone. It wasn't just me. Even Adam said he hadn't heard from her.

"Where are you?" I didn't know why I asked; it wasn't like I cared.

"In hospice."

It was real. He was going to die. I closed my eyes and leaned against the building, blotting out all the lunch crowd, blotting out the sun as best I could. "What's that like?" I whispered.

"It's okay here. No treatments, just morphine. Going gentle into that good night."

It took a long time for him to finish, and in the spaces between words, tears slipped down my face, one after the other. I knew he didn't deserve them, but it didn't matter.

I wasn't crying only for him but for my missing mother. She was gone because of what I did. Because I didn't just fuck her husband; I tried to steal him, and I failed.

Did she know everything? Even half would justify her silence.

Dr. Baylor disagreed, and it had been in my interest to believe him. To say that she had been the adult and I had been the child and therefore, it was unacceptable for her to behave so childishly now, to freeze me out. But I was an adult, too. She got to decide who she wanted in her life, same as I did. She didn't want Adam anymore, and she didn't want me.

"I'm sorry," he said.

I'd ask for what, but it would take too long for him to answer.

"I'm at peace. I want you to be, too."

Then why did you tell my mother?

As if he had any right to find peace first. A minute ago, I was crying. Now I wanted him dead. I wanted to do it myself.

I hung up and got in my car. I started driving, and there it was, a space right in front of Dr. Baylor's building. Like this was just where I was meant to be. And his office door was open for once, and he stood up like he'd been expecting me and said, "Come in, I had a cancellation."

I couldn't explain how it happened, who moved toward whom, but I was in his arms. I'd been so upset and furious and confused, and now I was just confused. But happy, too.

"I wish I could stop this," I could have sworn he murmured into my hair.

"I don't."

PRESENT DAY

CHAPTER 34

DETECTIVE GREGORY PLATH

Flora said it was just girl talk; Lucinda said it was all about Michael. That they'd been trading stories. "Why?" I asked her.

"To confirm we were special," she answered, and I could have almost believed her. Except that I don't believe any of them.

Which leaves me where, exactly?

I've still got three suspects.

Obviously, Flora was lying. Greer was, too, making it sound like she was just an observer at the restaurant that day, like she had nothing to contribute because the good doctor hadn't been inappropriate with her in any way.

It could have been someone else, though. The Oakland PD doesn't have the manpower to follow up on every current and former client from Dr. Baylor's file drawers, and I still don't have access to the records themselves. What I can tell is that he had startlingly few male clients. When I asked his colleagues about this, they didn't seem to find it strange; they said way more women than men seek therapy, and besides,

"He was good with women." This was said with a straight face. The follow-up comment? "Whatever you're good at in the therapy business, you get more of it. When it rains, it pours. You get a reputation. Other therapists refer to you; satisfied clients send their dissatisfied friends."

A social media search of the names also revealed a disproportionate number of unmarried women, and a fair number were good-looking. It seemed like Dr. Baylor may have had a type. Or maybe it was pure coincidence. The Bay Area had a whole lot of attractive females, and sometimes they ran in packs. Tell a friend, that's how it works, right?

But why did this guy have so few actual friends? He had colleagues and a good reputation, but who did he meet at the bar for a couple of beers? And he appeared to have no hobbies, no life at all, really, outside of his work.

These three women remain the front-runners. I can tell there's more to Greer's story, but she's going to make me get a lawyer or a warrant to find it out, even though she says what she wants more than anything is to find the killer. More than anything, she wants to find out who offed her therapist?

Lucinda's a disaster; Flora's a manipulator; Greer's a liar.

But so far, I haven't been able to pin anything on them. They've got no alibis, but there's no evidence to tie them to the crime. Lucinda says she's in love with him (present tense) and sure, the flip side of that is hate, but I can't prove she flipped. Greer says it was just therapy, and good therapy at that, and I can't crack her. Flora saw him for couples therapy a while back, but she still wants to have girl talk with his current clients? She says that if I find that odd, it's my problem, and she's right. It is my problem.

So which one killed the good doctor? Could they be in it together?

It's clear that at least two of them—Flora and Greer—hate each other. But they might have hated Michael more. Lucinda's a wild card. Hatred—and murder—make strange bedfellows.

BEFORE

CHAPTER 35

FLORA

I know you're angry, but ignoring me is not okay.

If you want to end things for good, at least say it to my face.

But why would you want to end things? I love you and you love me.

I ended my marriage for you.

You got me to end my marriage for you.

You seduced me right there in front of my husband.

Go ahead, tell me you didn't.

You wanted me, and you made me want you. Now you're treating me like old garbage.

I'm not your garbage.

I don't deserve this shit.

Yes, I told Kate about us. I shouldn't have lied to you about that. But I've never lied about anything else. Can you say the same?

You have to find a way to forgive me.

Please, forgive me, and I'll forgive you. I'll forgive how cruel you've been recently. Because I can see past it. I can see the real you.

Can't you see me?

Won't you see me?

No, he wouldn't, and I was coming unglued. I needed him, and yet to him, I was extraneous. Replicable, was that it? One of those Wednesday women had replaced me. He could be with her right now or thinking about how to be with her.

Neither of the women was wearing a wedding ring or engagement ring, so it would probably be even easier for him than the last time around with me. Week after week, it was just the two of them in his office, growing closer.

I was striding around my apartment, wearing a groove into the living room rug, and all I could see was Michael and those women. Maybe this time, he'd raise the level of difficulty. He'd go for a Wednesday ménage à trois.

I'd have given him that. I still would, if he'd let me.

Fuck, where had my self-respect gone? I'd never been this way before with anyone. You'd think my life depended on Michael.

Forgive me, I texted again. Forgive me. Forgive me. Forgive me . . .

Over and over I typed it, and the repetition became oddly comforting, like when I was a kid and I got in trouble and I had to write the same phrase a hundred times. I will not chew gum in class. I will not talk to my friends. I will pay attention.

I'll do anything. I'll do anything. I'll do anything. I'll do anything . . .

I'd do anything, yes, but still, he gave me nothing. Not a single word. Not a character. Not an emoji. Hadn't he ever made a mistake before? Was he so incapable of compassion, of mercy?

That asshole.

I can talk, too, if I need to.

As in, you leave me, and you expose yourself to a world of hurt, professionally and personally.

Kate wasn't the only one who knew his secret. She wasn't the only one who could bring him down, if it came to that. Not that I wanted it to come to that. All I wanted was him. But I was willing to play hardball because he'd given me no choice. Because he was giving me nothing.

I thought it would feel worse to be reduced to that kind of a threat. Instead, it was a little bit satisfying. It didn't level the playing field exactly, but the grade of slope had shifted.

If you'd asked me a few weeks ago whether I would ever be threatening Michael, I would have thought you were crazy. But then, I never would have thought he would just ignore me. If he wanted to break up, that was one thing. This was another. He was refusing to even acknowledge me. That, I couldn't have. I would say anything, do anything, to remind him that I existed.

I remembered being a little girl. An ugly little girl with a big nose, straggly hair, and bowlegs. You know the old story: picked last in gym class, no one to sit with at lunch. I was invited to the birthday parties only when the whole class was, and my parents would make me go because they said that then I could make friends, which never happened. I wasn't even teased; I was invisible. I didn't rate mockery and disdain. I wasn't worthy of any recognition at all.

Then my breasts came early, and I figured out how to be sexy, if not actually pretty. I taught myself to be gregarious and sporadically outrageous so that people would want me at their parties. I worked hard not to be overlooked. Kate claims she doesn't even remember my awkward phase, that she only remembers me as having tons of friends and guys who wanted to date me. I appreciated her selective amnesia. If only I possessed it.

All those insecurities from elementary school were still alive inside me. Mostly, I kept them at bay, tucked behind glass, but it could shatter. Like when Young stopped desiring me. And now, with Michael.

Do I sense a pattern? I could just imagine Michael—when he's Dr. Michael—querying.

But I was hardly alone. There was nothing more terrifying than the withdrawal of someone you love, when their worshipful gaze turns elsewhere. Sure, I had my work, and when I visited the different male doctors with my pharmaceutical samples and literature, I knew plenty of them would be happy to have a go at me. That was part of what made me successful in sales. I was a good flirt because I liked the attention, instead of merely enduring it like some women do. When men flirted or made a pass, I didn't cry sexual harassment. I earned the self-esteem and the commission.

But no matter how many other men eyeballed me, I needed that gaze of Michael's. Was that because I imagined Michael was more discerning, more refined, a connoisseur of the human condition and psyche, that his lens penetrated beneath my skin, to my very core?

Maybe. It was also because I loved him, passionately, devotedly, irreparably, devastatingly.

I was all texted out. There was nothing else I could say to lure him back. No, there had to be something else to say or do. I just needed to think.

Not tonight, though. Tonight, I was spent. I fell to the couch and sobbed, and then my door was flung open. I looked up with eyes nearly swollen shut, fighting to blink. No, it wasn't a mirage.

His shirt was half-untucked, and his hair was wild. He looked, in a word, frenzied. He was on top of me and neither of us spoke. We made love for an eternity, like we were both afraid to stop. Because then we'd have to talk. We'd have to see where we stood—after my betrayal, and the pain of his silence, and the impact of my threat. Far better to keep lying down, to arch my back and cry, "Oh God," until my voice was hoarse. Eerily, though, he remained silent.

He never came. He just continued, and then, without warning, he stopped. He pulled away and put his head in his hands. "I don't know what I'm doing anymore," he said, more to himself than to me.

"You love me," I told him. "That's why we can't stay away from each other."

"I need to get out of here. I just need to clear my head." He stood up and started putting on his clothes.

"Let me come with you."

"No."

"You love me, though, right?" I hated that I had to ask.

I hated even more that he didn't answer. Not right away. Finally, unhappily, he nodded.

I had no choice but to let him go. He was like that bird you have to set free, and if he comes back, he's yours, and if he doesn't . . .

Maybe he never had been. He came here to hold out false hope, to keep me on a string. All that sex could have been a stalling tactic, a response to my earlier threat. He had to stop me from reporting him. He had to give me just enough.

It could be that he wasn't worried about losing me at all; he was worried only about losing his true love, his work. His other clients. His other women.

Maybe they weren't his mistresses; I was.

CHAPTER 36

GREER

Dr. Michael and I started seeing each other twice a week because my eggs weren't getting any younger. And after three weeks and six sessions, I was convinced that motherhood was for me. I wasn't even scared of it anymore; I was euphoric. Someone would put their tiny hand in mine and look up at me and say, "Mommy, is it going to be okay?" and I'd have the honor of saying, "Yes, it will; Mommy's right here." The dependency wasn't the price I'd have to pay to be loved; it was love itself.

Motherhood was my calling. It was strange that it had taken so many years for the phone to ring, but my focus had been on professional success because it was the only thing my parents really cared about. But I wasn't them, and the recognition freed me. Michael's instinct had been right; we needed to go there—back into my childhood—to get me to where I needed to be.

Yes, it shouldn't have taken me until nearly forty years old to have such an obvious epiphany, but better late than never. Because there was still time. All I needed was the guy.

Three weeks and six sessions, and I was sure that I had him. I just had to get him.

I'd come to like so much about Dr. Michael: his caring nature, his compassion, his intelligence, his erudition (he had way more books than I did), his wit, his smell, his looks, his mannerisms. Today was the day. I was going to propose.

I couldn't concentrate on anything he was asking me. I was too busy looking for an opening, that perfect moment to ask about his sperm, though I knew logically that there was no such moment. Sperm donation was an acceptable topic in therapy only when the desired donor was someone other than the therapist himself.

"What's up, Greer?" he finally said.

"I've been telling you what's up."

"I don't think you have. You're holding back. Is it me?"

I stared at him. How could he know?

No, he didn't know. He meant professionally; he meant was there more that he could be doing as the man whose job was to abet my mental health. It was a reasonable question, given that he'd had to woo me back into therapy not long ago. In two months, I'd gone from running away from him to wanting to have his child.

All the evidence suggested I had lost my marbles. Yet I felt so sane. I was going to be a mother, whatever it took, and hopefully, Michael would sign on. If not, it would be Donor #3731 for the win.

I opened my mouth. Then I closed it.

"How can I make you more comfortable?" he said.

Was that a come-on?

"I meant, how can I make it feel safer for you to say what it is you need to say?"

"I don't think there's anything you can do. I just need to bite the bullet and tell you. Or rather, ask you."

He waited, his hands clasped.

I pushed my hair back from my face, composing myself. It was strange to be so nervous around him, when his job—as he'd just reminded me—was to decrease my nerves.

No, that wasn't how he did his job. He pressed me all the time into uncomfortable positions (psychologically speaking). But usually, it felt more like sparring. Maybe a little like flirtation, like we were one of those classic sitcom couples who start out hating each other and then they're ultimately unable to resist the pull. They're arguing, and one says, "Are you as turned on as I am right now?" and the other says, "More!" Then they're consummating wildly.

I'd gone nuts. Truly.

But it wasn't simple baby fever anymore. Sometimes I still couldn't believe the extent of my current attraction to him. He wasn't the kind of man I ever saw myself with, after all. He was successful for a therapist, but I had a lot more money, not even counting my inheritance. He was an alpha, though. His dominance was subtle. It snuck up on you, sinewy, like a snake.

"What's your question?" he said.

"You know I've been looking for a sperm donor. When you told me that you'd been one in the past, a light bulb went on for me. I think you could be the one."

"Your question is about my sperm?" He was speaking slowly, but he didn't look nearly as surprised as I would have expected. Perhaps I wasn't the first client who'd wanted to reproduce with him.

Not *with* him. It wasn't like he'd be raising the baby with me. "You've done it before. Why not do it again?"

"That was many years ago, and I didn't know the recipient. She certainly wasn't my client."

"I'd stop being your client."

"I think that's a bad idea."

"It'd be easier to find a new therapist than the right sperm donor."

To my surprise, he moved over to the couch and sat opposite me, as if he were trying on this change in roles, what it would be like for us to just be a man and a woman rather than therapist and client. "What does it say about you that you'd decide your therapist is the right sperm donor?"

Was that a yes or a no? An insult or a compliment?

"You might think I don't know you," I said, "but I do."

"I never said you don't know me. Our relationship is very real. It's not one-sided." As in, he had feelings for me, too?

I didn't even know what my exact feelings for him were. But I had to be a mother, and I preferred his sperm to make it happen. Beyond that . . . "In my gut, I know that you and I would make a good baby."

"And have you decided that you'd be a good mother?"

He didn't mean it to be scathing, but it stung. "I'm a hard worker. Whatever I do, I'll do my best."

"You'd run yourself ragged; I'll give you that. But what about the toll it would take on you and on the child? Parenthood isn't just about working hard."

"What is it about, then?" I said, stony. He wasn't answering me about the sperm; instead, he was telling me I shouldn't be a mother at all.

"Are you angry with me?"

"Such a therapist, answering a question with a question."

"So you are angry. Can you tell me why?"

"Because you're questioning my fitness as a mother."

"No. I'm questioning the difference between theory and practice, what it would feel like for you to actually practice motherhood, day after day."

"Do you think I'm incapable of love?"

"Of course not. What makes you ask that?"

I flushed. This was a mortifying conversation. "If you want to say no, say no."

He didn't, though. He was quiet for a full minute.

"So you might say yes?"

Finally, he nodded. "I'm open to considering it. That's if we can do some more work around your decision-making process. If I can be assured that motherhood is really what's best for you and, by extension, best for the baby."

Our baby. This could happen. "You want me to stay in therapy with you and we figure it out together?"

"Let me think on it more, okay? I wasn't exactly prepared for this." He smiled, and I smiled back. Mortifying to exhilarating in 120 seconds.

"And if I decide that it's best—if we decide that's the next step— then I'll be finished with therapy?"

"You'd have met your treatment goal."

"I guess I would have."

His smile was oddly tinged with sadness. He glanced at the clock. "I'll see you next week, then?"

"I guess you will." I didn't know what my smile was tinged with.

As I was leaving the building, I once again managed to stumble. But unlike last time, it was because I was so busy grinning. I stopped and adjusted the strap on the back of my heel, and when I looked up, I saw a woman sitting in her car who appeared to have her attention trained on me. It was hard to be certain, since she was wearing sunglasses. At dusk. And some sort of head scarf, but not like a hijab. No, this was more like a disguise.

I scanned my surroundings. There was no one else she could be looking at. A chill went through me. But I told myself that I didn't know her, and there was no reason for me to be of interest to any strange women.

Then she lifted the sunglasses so that I could make no mistake: She was staring at me. Glaring at me, and she wanted me to feel it.

She was a handsome woman, with olive skin and a slightly bulbous nose. She dropped the sunglasses back down, started her car, and roared out of the parking space without checking for traffic. A horn blared after a narrow miss, but she just took off, as if her mission was complete.

Was I part of her mission? It made no sense. And yet . . .

She was watching me, I was sure of it.

CHAPTER 37

LUCINDA

Dr. Baylor looked up from the pages he was holding. "I knew it," he said.

"Knew what?" I asked, though I was already smiling.

"Knew you were gifted. This story needs to be told."

"Do you think it could go somewhere someday?"

"You mean, could you publish it?" I nodded. "I'm no literary critic, but it seems like it to me. You'd just need to think through all the ramifications."

"Are you talking about my mother?"

"And about you. People will assume this is autobiographical. Are you ready to have your past made public?"

That was all I'd been thinking about—that and Dr. Baylor's arms around me. "I'm an abuse survivor. Yes, I could be ashamed that my abuser was my mother's husband and that I wasn't loyal to her, but . . ."

"But what?" He leaned in. I had him on the edge of his seat. There was something different in how we were interacting. There was a crackle to it. Was he also remembering what it had felt like to hold me?

I couldn't afford to remember it just then. I had something important to tell my therapist. "As I'm writing, some things are coming back to me. Some things about my mother and the years when she was on drugs."

"You've always said you can't recall much about your early childhood. Is the writing jogging your memory?"

"Yes." Another deep breath. "It's nothing concrete. I mean, they're just images, almost like dreaming. I'm seeing the house and men coming through it. Men coming toward me. Then it's black."

"How old do you think you are?"

"Not very. She got clean by the time I was in kindergarten. Then she was the world's best mother. But before that, it was a really different story."

"One you're finally ready to tell." His expression turned admiring. "You are just so strong, Lucy. You amaze me."

With the way he was looking at me, I actually felt it. I mean, I felt sort of amazing. "It's because of you."

"No."

"Yes." Something came over me, and I approached him, kneeling, my chin tipped upward to meet his eyes. I wouldn't be the first to look away. I couldn't. I was too strong for that. I wanted this. I wanted him. "Michael."

He didn't move a muscle. Was there fear in his eyes? "This can't happen."

"I'm not a little girl."

"I'm your therapist. I know it might not feel like it, but that's a position of power. Being with you the way I think you're suggesting is an abuse of that power."

I shook my head, which was still upturned, coy. I hadn't inhabited this role in so long.

Adam. This was how I used to play it with Adam. Me below and him above. *You know so much about the world, and I know nothing. Oh, you big man, I'm just a little girl.*

I got up and walked around the office, trying to shake it off. I'd been the victim. Because I couldn't have been otherwise. I *was* just a little girl. A teenager is a child. My body had been developed, but my brain hadn't. Now it was. Adam had made me a victim; I'd made myself a survivor. Wanting Michael was not the same as wanting Adam. Not at all.

"What's going on?" He was talking in his Dr. Baylor voice, authoritative and soothing at once.

"It's hard to breathe," I said, "but I can't stop moving."

"Is it the recovered memories? About your mother and that man's house?"

"No." I started to wring my hands, which had gone numb. "I don't know."

"I'm going to ask you to do something." Now his voice was slow and deliberate, almost hypnotic, but I was still pacing. I wanted to run, only I wanted to stay close to him. He was the only thing that could save me. Yet he'd rejected me, hadn't he? He'd told me it couldn't happen.

He hadn't said he didn't want it to happen. He said it couldn't. But he was wrong. We were two mature adults, and we could decide to take our relationship in a different direction. We could make the rules together. I wasn't a child.

"Sit down, please," he said, and I found a way to do it, perching on the couch, though my legs stayed in motion, bobbing up and down.

"I can't stop them," I said. "Can you help me?" I meant, would he come and touch me? If he held me again, like last time . . .

"I want you to try to press your feet against the floor as hard as you can. Then just feel them there, flat."

"I can't. They're still going."

"Just try." He was so gentle. So perfect.

I wanted to please him, so I did it. I tried. I pressed down from my heels to my toes, and he was still talking, telling me to feel only my feet, that all my energy and my awareness should go to my feet, and I was listening to him, like I was in a trance. When I opened my eyes, my legs had stilled. I felt something akin to calm.

"You did it!" I told him.

"I'm thinking maybe we're moving too fast, kind of like your feet were. Your body is trying to tell us important information. Between twice-a-week sessions and the writing, it's too much."

"No, it's not!"

"You were decompensating right in front of me. Now, some of that's to be expected when we're doing trauma work, but it can be a sign we need to slow down."

He'd just talked me down off the ledge, and now he was trying to put me right back up there. "What are you saying, exactly?"

"We could go back to once a week and pull back on the intensity—"

I couldn't wait seven whole days to see him. "If this is about the money, I can start paying. I'll pay for both sessions."

"It's not about money."

"Is it about earlier, when I went and sat by you? That made you uncomfortable and now you want to get some distance?"

"No, it's about what's best for you. I don't want to foster an unhealthy dependency, and I'm afraid that's what's happening. I need to get some more consultation on this."

I stared at him. "Consultation? As in, you've been talking about me to other people?"

"To one other person. Her name is Dr. Devers. She's a highly skilled trauma therapist. It's for your protection, a safeguard for the treatment process."

I didn't understand how talking to another woman about me constituted protection. What about confidentiality?

"It's in the Consent to Treatment you signed when we first started. It says that sometimes, I might need to seek consultation from colleagues. Make sure I'm providing responsible treatment. I never use your name."

"And what does she say about me, this colleague of yours?" Had he told her about the other day and how he wrapped his body around mine in a decidedly unprofessional manner?

"I'm sorry if you feel I've betrayed you. In a sense, this isn't about you; it's about me. It's making sure I'm aware of all my blind spots, so I can give you what you need."

"What do you think I need?"

"You need people in your life other than me. You're a beautiful young woman. You should have friends. You should have dates."

"You think I'm beautiful?"

He'd said it before, but this time, he reddened. He'd said it couldn't happen, but maybe he wished it could.

"Are you still involved with that woman, the one you were arguing with?"

"Let's stay focused on you and what you need."

"Was that woman Dr. Devers?"

"No, that was personal. Whatever you overheard, it has nothing to do with our work here." But the high color in his cheeks belied him.

What did he think I'd overheard? And how could I use it to get what I wanted? No, what I needed.

CHAPTER 38

FLORA

"So how are things with you and Michael?" Kate's tone was unusually delicate. She was trying to avoid the trip wire. But she'd already set it off, and I was dealing with the fallout every day with Michael. Kate and I could step around the debris and act like it wasn't there, but all the pretending made me sad. And tired. I was just so tired these days.

I wouldn't say that, of course. Kate would blame Michael, because I was normally a very energetic person, and she'd think he'd sapped me. She would be right. She just couldn't know it, since I intended to get Michael back.

It was late, and I'd called her while I was walking home from the BART station, thinking it would be good to have some company on the darkened streets. For an expensive neighborhood, there were very few streetlights. I wasn't used to my high heels making this particular thudding sound; I wasn't used to feeling so heavy.

Not that I'd put on weight. It was the opposite. As I'd gotten dressed this morning, I noticed my hipbones were sharp and jutting, and my thigh gap was actually too pronounced, which I wouldn't have thought possible. I switched from pants to a dress. My face stayed drawn and gaunt despite a forty-minute makeup application. The situation with Michael was eating away at me.

Since our sex-a-thon the other night, his texts had been perfunctory. He initiated no exchanges; it was all me. I'd text, "I love you," and two, maybe three hours later, he texted it back. But there was no feeling in it. No extra words, no emojis, no inflection—the minimum to keep me from blowing up his life.

"Michael and I are great," I told Kate.

This block felt interminable. Normally, I loved it. It was one of my favorites, with leafy trees and beautiful brown-shingled Craftsman and Victorian houses. But every step drained me further.

"Are you sure?" Kate said. "You sound—"

"It's been a long day at work, that's all."

"You're not yourself. Is that because things are so great with Michael or because they're so bad?"

"I am myself. I'm perfectly and completely myself."

"See, the way you said that—you never would have said that before."

I didn't need an argument right then. Tears of frustration filled my eyes. I missed Kate and the friendship—the love—we used to have. She was right about that, too: this wasn't me, and it wasn't us. I'd prefer to never talk to her than to engage in this exercise in falseness, but if I pulled away, if I stopped returning calls or if I said outright that our relationship was over, then Kate would lose all incentive to keep Michael's secret. She could think that she was protecting future clients from Michael. Kate could get sanctimonious like that. If she ruined him, he would blame me. I was, after all, the one who'd set it all in motion by breaking my promise and confiding in her.

I needed to suffer through these talks, which only reinforced my sense of loss. She wasn't just my cousin; she'd been my best friend.

But she'd done me dirty. She had no business trying to break up my relationship regardless of the reason. Her conscious mind might have thought it was because she was looking after me, but her subconscious was another matter. Michael had told me all about what a person's subconscious could be capable of. Deep down, Kate was just jealous. She didn't even know whether she wanted men or women; she'd spent so much time being with whoever would have her just for drugs, and since she'd stopped using, she had been alone. Really, I was her lifeline. Or I had been.

I still could be. We were family; we could weather this. All we needed was to stop talking about Michael. How hard could that be?

I was about to tell her that the best thing for our relationship was to make Michael off-limits when I was shoved from behind. I went down hard onto the pavement, and the phone went flying. I heard Kate saying, "Flora? Flora, you there? What's happening?"

I tried to get up on my skinned knees, to look behind me and see who had done this, but then I was kicked, hard. "Stay down," a male voice growled. I pressed my face to the pavement. If I listened to him, maybe I'd get out of this alive.

He'd gone inside my purse, and the contents were raining down beside me. He didn't take my wallet, just cleaned out the cash. My ID was mocking me, with its smiling picture. Was that the last thing I'd ever see?

Then he grabbed my phone off the pavement and took off running. I should have gotten up and started running myself, so I could get back to my apartment as fast as I could. Get inside where it was safe. I'd dodged a bullet, really. I could have been raped; I could have been beaten; I could have been killed.

I sat up, scanning my body, gingerly touching my bloody knees and the bruise on my back from his kick. I was shaken, but I was okay.

He'd taken my phone, taken Kate with him. I could still hear her panicked voice, a concern that couldn't be faked.

He had my phone, with all the evidence of my secret life with Michael. He had my phone, so I couldn't even call the police. Not that I could give a description. I'd only seen him from behind as he'd fled the scene, a faceless man in a navy-blue hoodie and jeans. Yep, the overtaxed Oakland police would get right on this.

Michael. That's who I needed to call. Sure, things had been strained between us, but when he heard about this, he'd sound like Kate had. His love for me would assert itself as he assimilated the fact that he'd never lost me for good. You don't know what you've got until it's gone, right?

It gave me an idea.

"Are you okay?" It was a woman's voice. I'd been so lost in my thoughts that I hadn't even heard her approach. She crouched beside me. "Can you stand up?"

I tried, only to crumple back down on colt legs.

"Did you trip, or did someone do this to you?"

So she hadn't seen the mugging. How long had I been here, unable to muster the energy to walk home? I'd been enervated lately, but this was on another level. Was it possible I'd been hurt worse than I thought, that I'd hit my head and been unconscious?

"Someone did this," I said. I felt around my scalp and my face. There were no painful or tender spots. Maybe I'd just been lost in thoughts. In plans.

The woman introduced herself as Kate. It was like a message from the fucking universe, but what was the universe saying?

"I got mugged," I said.

"Oh no!" She was about my age, a little bit overweight, a little bit frumpy, dishwater blonde hair, a kind face. "Have you called the police yet?"

"He took my phone."

"Use mine." She thrust it toward me.

"I didn't see his face. The police won't do anything."

"Maybe not. But shouldn't we call them anyway?"

We. Now I was a we with this do-gooder I'd just met. I was able to get to my feet, with her assistance. I winced at the pain in my knee, which was pretty torn up. Damned vanity. I should have worn pants.

"Could you call my fiancé?" I said. "His name's Michael."

"Do you want to just borrow my phone for a minute?"

"I don't want to have to say the words again, to tell him what happened. Could you just tell him for me, and where I am so he can pick me up?"

Sad that it had come to this, that Michael was more likely to answer an unknown number than mine, more likely to come get me if the request came from a stranger. At the moment, given the state of trust in our relationship, he'd be more likely to believe her. And he wouldn't want to look like a cad in front of this other Kate.

But he would feel differently once he saw me. I'd make sure of that.

"Don't tell him your name," I said. I didn't want him to think it was *that* Kate. "Just say you were passing by."

"What's your name?"

"Flora." I gave her a weak smile. "Nice to meet you."

She was hesitating. Something about this didn't smell right, but she was not the most assertive, this other Kate. She'd rather carry out my request than confront me about its peculiarity.

"Five one zero . . ." I started to reel off the number, and she dutifully punched it in.

"Hello?" Michael answered, sounding a bit leery. But my read on him was right. He did take calls from strange numbers. Was it because he gave certain clients his personal cell?

No. Just because Kate had said it didn't make it true. She had ulterior motives, whether she knew it or not. All she'd kept telling me when I pushed her was that she was trying to help me. But there had to be more to it.

"I'm here with Flora," the other Kate said. "I was walking, and I found her on the pavement. She was just mugged."

"Is she okay?" I thought I could make out urgency in his tone. He cared, or at least, he cared how he looked to this stranger.

"I'm not sure. It was hard for her to get up, and he stole her phone. Could you pick her up?"

One potato, two potato, three potato, four . . . I didn't look at Kate, I was so embarrassed. I'd hate to know what mental calculations he was doing during that time when he should have answered with an instantaneous yes. Finally, he relented. "Where is she?"

Once Kate had hung up, she offered to wait with me. I said no, she'd been too kind already. She insisted, and I insisted no, I'd be fine, and after a couple more rounds like that, I wanted to punch Kate instead of myself. But I prevailed, and she looked relieved. I'd been behaving oddly and so had Michael. I reassured her she'd been an exemplary citizen and that Michael lived very close by, which was true. Then she was on her way, quickly, without a backward glance, which confirmed that what she'd wanted most was to be rid of me while still feeling like a good person. She could join the club.

Once the street was deserted, I had to admit, I was a little spooked. I was surrounded by multimillion-dollar houses, but I'd just been attacked in front of one of them. It was like nowhere was safe.

I was also a little spooked by my decision. What if I misjudged and gave myself a concussion or internal bleeding? I was lucky to be alive. I didn't want to screw that up.

Then there was the fact that my bystander's name was Kate, like the universe was telling me to cease and desist.

Well, I'd always had a rebellious streak, and besides, the universe had also presented me with this golden opportunity to get back into Michael's good graces. If I had to get mugged, I wanted to profit. Make lemonade out of lemons.

There was no time to waste. Michael was already on his way. I hoped.

I surveyed the street. I kind of wished someone was coming so that I could abort the mission, but nope, it was just me, alone, under cover of darkness. You'd think the residents could afford—or would insist—on streetlights, but no, they had other priorities. Really, the moment couldn't have been more perfect.

I sprawled out the way I had just minutes ago, my head to the pavement. Then I smacked my forehead. Holy shit, you really could see stars. And I managed to scrape it, too, so that when I touched my welting head with my fingertips, they came away with a smear of blood. As long as I hadn't accidentally concussed myself, it couldn't have gone better. I stayed there a long minute, waiting for the pain and the disorientation to subside until it was a lucid ache.

I looked around again furtively. Then I sat down on the sidewalk with my feet in the street, and . . . wham. I coldcocked myself right in the jaw. No stars this time, but it smarted, and it was surely going to bruise.

Michael, where are you? He was only a five-minute drive away, seven minutes tops. He should have thrown on some clothes and raced out. You didn't dillydally when the woman you loved had just survived a brutal attack. But then, the other Kate hadn't made it sound very brutal. She just talked about my cell phone. He was going to be surprised when he saw the condition of my face. That would work in my favor.

It occurred to me that I should gather up the contents of my purse and see exactly what was missing. Fortunately, he'd only been interested in the cash and the phone. All my credit cards were intact. My compact mirror had a jagged crack down the middle, and I was shocked to see my face in it. It was unreal, like stage makeup, like I was playing a battered woman. Except for the scraping on my forehead, it was rapidly purpling bruises. I would heal, with no scars. But man, I looked rough.

What would people say at work tomorrow? Maybe I'd call out. I could just stay in Michael's bed all day.

That was, if he ever showed up.

Without a phone, I had no idea how to pass the time, and I had no idea how much time had passed. I couldn't call and demand to know what was keeping him, and he couldn't call me to say he'd decided not to come. I was trapped here, on a street that was demonstrably unsafe, with a bashed-in face and sore knees.

This might not have been my finest hour.

What would Kate—my Kate, or the woman who used to be my Kate—have said if she could have seen me? It would have confirmed that I was not myself. Because this had better not be myself.

I needed to call her and tell her I was okay. I could do it from Michael's phone, if he ever arrived. I'd tell her that I got mugged and Michael was my knight in shining armor. See? Our relationship was going great.

Where the fuck was he?

I might need a plan B. If he didn't show up soon, I'd knock on a door and ask to call a cab. No one would turn me away, looking like this. Of course, they might ask a bunch of pesky questions or be like the other Kate and try to make me call the police.

Calling the police was plan C. Think how bad Michael would feel if he had to pick me up at the police station after I'd been paging through books of mug shots. Was that how it was done? I didn't know; I'd never been the victim of a violent crime before.

No, I couldn't go to the police. The mugger had shoved me, but he wasn't trying to injure me. He just wanted my stuff. If I went in looking like this, it could be a lot worse for him, if they found him. Not that they'd find him, with my generic description.

The strangest thing was that I felt compassion for the guy. I felt a certain kinship. I really and truly understood desperation, and his was probably a lot more legitimate than mine. It was hard to earn enough money to exist in the Bay Area. For all I knew, he had kids. Hungry mouths to feed. He'd tried to do it the right way, the honest way, and life just got away from him. Suddenly, he was doing things he never could have imagined. Like snatching purses. Like smashing his head into a pavement and throwing a left hook into his own jaw. You know, normal acts of desperation.

It had gone way too far. My face was throbbing, and I had my feet in a gutter. Yet all I wanted was to see Michael's frightened face and have him grab me and tell me that he hadn't realized how much he loved me until right that second.

I saw a car moving slowly, and yes, yes, it was him. I stood up and waved with way too much exuberance for a woman who'd been recently assaulted, but I couldn't help myself. I was bowled over. He came for me. He. Came. For. Me.

He stopped the car, and the hazards went on. He got out and regarded me. Then it was like I'd imagined: him pulling me to him ferociously, and then lifting his trembling fingers to my jacked-up face, and he didn't need to say he loved me, it was just so incredibly, wonderfully obvious. I didn't ask what took him so damned long because it didn't matter; he was here now and beside himself. Over me.

"Flora," he said, "I had to come." He sounded so tormented, like he wished he'd been able to resist, like he wanted to quit me but couldn't. I kept pulling him back.

"I need you," I said. It was true. I buried my head in his neck, and then let out an involuntary "ouch." I had to be more careful with my face. I'd almost forgotten it in the joy of seeing Michael and being held by him. I'd forgotten the pain. "I need you," I repeated, in case he'd forgotten.

"I'll take care of you."

"And then?" I kept my head down. I couldn't bear to look and hear the answer.

"And then," he whispered, "I don't know. I've been so angry, Flora. No one in my entire life has ever made me so angry."

"You make me angrier than anyone ever has, too. It's because of how much we love each other."

"It's not healthy, Flora. We're not healthy anymore. I'm not sure we ever were. It's just that we didn't have to face it because we were always in the dark. And since you've wanted us to go public, it's like . . ." He trailed off. "For so long, I was sure you were the one."

"I still am."

"I thought I wanted a force of nature."

I risked picking my head up and grabbing his face. "You do." I kissed him, throbbing face and all, and he couldn't help it, he kissed me back. But the urgency petered out, and when he pulled his head back, his eyes were full of sadness.

He wished he could let me go, but I wasn't about to let him off the hook that easily. He'd made promises for two years, and he was going to deliver.

CHAPTER 39

GREER

"It's been a long time," I told the matching gray marble headstones. The day was overcast and cool, and I hugged myself for warmth. I was in a pair of stylishly voluminous pants, and the wind cut right through them. I hadn't known how to dress for the occasion.

It wasn't either of my parents' birthdays or the anniversary of their deaths, which was when I usually visited. Today, I was there for more selfish reasons. I wanted to be heard.

"I don't know if there's an afterlife," I said. "If there is, I hope you're doing well."

This had been foolish. If there was an afterlife, they could hear my thoughts already. I could have had this "conversation" with them from the comfort of my condo.

Dr. Michael hadn't suggested this, and I hadn't decided whether to tell him in session later. I didn't believe that therapy necessitated full disclosure. He could have access to some of my most private thoughts but not every last one of them.

I must have wanted to at least give myself the option to discuss it, since I chose to come to the cemetery on Wednesday afternoon, a workday (and my therapy day), instead of the weekend. Maybe—and I hated even admitting this—I thought Michael would be a little proud of me. He liked to spend a lot of time talking about my parents, and now here I was, going right to the source.

"I don't know where to start," I said. It wasn't like my parents and I had had a long history of deep sharing. We had tended to exchange information and sometimes opinions, but generally on impersonal subjects. "I mean, if you're somewhere watching over me, you already know I'm not married. I'm not even dating. I've never been engaged. And I've never been maternal. But now I want a baby, very badly. Since realizing that, everything's upside down.

"I don't work the same. I don't sleep the same. I don't care about what I used to, and I care about things—and people—I never thought I would. I'm drawn to strange men. Well, one man. He's my therapist. I actually have a therapist."

My parents and I had never talked about therapy in relation to me or to them, but I knew they thought it was pure quackery. A scam perpetrated on the weak and vulnerable. As they saw it, people just had to find something they were passionate about and work hard at it. According to my parents, that was the answer.

All their opinions had been in stereo. I'd never heard them disagree.

It was only now that I saw how odd that was. That maybe they were the strange ones. That their form of happy marriage was outside the norm. That maybe it hadn't even been happy, that they'd just found someone whose compulsion matched their own, who validated their choice to pursue success above all else, to love the accumulation of accolades and money far more than either of them had loved me. That was what therapy had done to me and for me: it had forced me to realize—no, to admit what I'd always known somewhere inside: my parents had never really loved me.

I watched some leaves skitter down from nearby trees and dance in the wind along the neighboring gravesites. It was almost pretty, in a haunting sort of way. More haunting because no one else was in sight. Just my parents and me, hanging out. For the last time.

"My therapist might become my sperm donor." It was the first time I'd said it out loud since asking him. It was powerful, this saying things out loud. "That's because I'm almost forty, and I've never been in love. And my whole life, I've told myself that's because it wasn't important, because I wasn't one of those people who needed it. But it's not that I didn't need it, it's that you didn't teach me how to do it. Why is that? And why do I have so much trouble remembering anything specific about who you were as people? You're just this assortment of platitudes about hard work and uncharitable judgments about people who didn't do enough. I was so afraid to fall into that second category that it per- verted my whole life."

Tears were dripping down my face. I looked around, but the cem- etery was still. If anyone saw me from a distance, they'd think I was crying for what I'd lost when really, it was the opposite. I was crying because my own parents represented no loss at all.

They hadn't abused me or even neglected me. Sure, they worked a lot, but they made sure I was taken care of, and when they were home, they paid me some degree of attention. They checked my homework. They let me participate in their conversations. It's not like I was told to go to my room or that children were supposed to be seen and not heard. I was allowed to be part of their world.

They just weren't part of mine.

"Did you know anything about me?" I waited, like they might come back with something, like it might be carried on the wind.

I'd begun to wonder who I might have been had I been raised by other people, people like, say, Dr. Michael—someone who cared how I felt and what I really thought. I might have become more imagina- tive or expressive. I might have been a different kind of worker and a different kind of lover. I might have been a mother by now, with a doting husband.

It was cheap to blame them for all my shortcomings, I knew that. But I still felt, just a little, like spitting on their graves.

How had I missed this for so many years? I had terrible parents, and now I was contemplating being one myself. But I was so limited. I could picture myself with a baby, because babies were so immediate, so raw in their needs, and the responses were so clear, so primal. Feed them, change their diapers, love them. But that was where the images ended. I couldn't really see myself with a child at four or eight or thirteen. And even older, an adult who could come back and say, "Why didn't you do a better job at loving me and turning me into someone who could love others? Why didn't you and my father show me what it looked like?"

I had the strangest sensation. I wanted Dr. Michael beside me. He understood what I didn't; he could fill in the gaps. Be what I couldn't. Yin to my yang.

"I don't miss you," I said, "but I wish you were here. I wish I could ask you some questions. Like, why did you have me?"

The wind had no answer.

Hours later, I was telling Dr. Michael everything, except the part about wanting him there beside me. Wanting him, maybe for more than a sperm donor. Because the sperm donor part was outrageous enough. If I let on that I had these other thoughts and feelings, he'd think he was dealing with someone too unstable to have a child, certainly too unstable to have his child.

Besides, this wasn't about him. I was talking about my parents.

I held it together pretty well as I told him the cemetery story, until I got to that final question I'd asked them, and then the pain of it struck me. I should have known why they had me. I should have known that they loved me.

"You deserved so much more," Dr. Michael told me.

That's when I lost it, crying with an abandon that was, well, child-ish. Dr. Michael moved to the couch next to me, and I wished he'd come closer, but he stayed on his side, placing the box of tissues between us. My sobs started to die down. I took a tissue and blew my nose nois-ily. It was a good way to avoid looking at him. I imagined his eyes were all lit up because he had finally done it. This was where he'd wanted me all along, and now he had me. Checkmate.

"Thank you," he said softly.

I still couldn't look at him.

"Thank you for trusting me. I feel really close to you."

I almost smiled. It wasn't checkmate; the match wasn't over. We were still playing the game where I convinced him that I was the right mother for his child. Another mother of his child. There were probably others from twenty years ago. How had those kids turned out?

Not as well as ours would.

CHAPTER 40

LUCINDA

Since Dr. Baylor—Michael—held me in his office, things had moved so quickly that I almost couldn't believe it was real, that I'd made it happen. Was it really just two weeks ago that I'd shown up there, and he'd seemed so somber when he said we needed to talk, and I thought, *Oh no, this is it, no more pro bono, no more anything, I'm too fucked up to be his client even, let alone what I want to be to him,* and instead . . . ?

Instead, we'd talked about the new rules. Vegas rules. What happened in session stayed in session, where he was still Dr. Baylor and he behaved entirely professionally. His domain was my psyche only. We were back to one session a week again, so I wouldn't become "overwhelmed." Then, late at night, we could have this other relationship, which was also therapeutic but carnal. "Have you ever heard of sex surrogates?" he asked. I said I hadn't. He explained that they helped people take charge of their sexuality as a way to heal emotionally.

On Wednesdays, therapy proceeded as usual. It was almost like he was two different people: responsible therapist by day (well, early evening) and lover at night. He changed the lighting, added scented candles, and voilà. I wouldn't have thought a few sensory cues could do that much heavy lifting, and yet, oddly, they did. He flipped a switch, lit a candle, and transformed from Dr. Baylor into Michael, though even as my lover, he was still concerned with my therapeutic goals. He wanted me to own my power in all arenas, including sexual, so I could realize how wonderful I was.

He didn't just tell me, though; he showed me. To a casual observer, it would seem illicit, but it was actually beautiful. I was learning that sex wasn't about one person being in charge. Love was sharing power and control, passing it back and forth.

Not that we used the word *love*. We didn't talk about anything other than what we were doing and feeling in that moment: what we wanted, what we were willing to give. We didn't need to label it or promise a future. Whether that was because it was so obvious to him that we'd have one or because it was obvious we wouldn't, I didn't actually know. For the moment, I didn't need to know, and that in itself was revelatory. I was simply experiencing, and enjoying, and growing. Each time, I grew. I became more myself.

I'd only been with Adam before, and this was so different. But then, Adam and I had barely consummated. Almost every night for the past ten days, Michael and I had been consummating, and consecrating, everywhere in his office.

Sometimes it was tender, sometimes wild, but it was always, always amazing. Otherworldly. I hadn't known what I was missing, which made sense. Since Adam, I'd steered clear of all entanglements.

I was entangled now, all right.

Rules defined the boundaries, and Michael was a big believer in boundaries. I got what he meant, since Adam had violated mine, even though I hadn't recognized it at the time.

Yet somehow, when Michael and I were together, I felt unbound. Really, I'd never been so free. Michael wanted me to express myself, which was another way it deviated from my time with Adam. Back then, I'd been so pliable, so eager to please, and sure, I wanted to please Michael, but he told me that his enjoyment was derived from mine. "Say what you want and do what you want," he told me. "I'll follow your lead. You're in control."

I'd never felt in control with Adam. He kept me off-kilter. I could see that now, the ways he'd dominated me through his age and experience. It wasn't in a sadomasochistic way—at least, not overtly. But he'd kept me waiting and wanting and uncertain. It wasn't like the second my mother left, he would be in my room. No, I had to lay in my bed, agonizing, and sometimes, he wouldn't come at all. When he did, I was so grateful. He snapped his fingers, and I jumped. I gave that guy blow jobs until my mouth went numb. A hundred of them, maybe. He went down on me four times, and three of them, he stopped before I came. He was always pretending he heard my mother's car in the drive. Seriously, Adam? When his cock was in my mouth, I never heard phantom tires. I committed.

Michael had gone down on me twice already, and we'd barely begun. But oh, what a finish. And his office was conveniently soundproofed. I never imagined I could feel so unselfconscious. So myself.

Really, it was an extension of treatment. Treatment with benefits.

PRESENT DAY

CHAPTER 41
DETECTIVE GREGORY PLATH

"I didn't expect to see you back here," I tell her. "Not without another invitation."

"I felt like it was my duty," Flora says, almost primly. She is definitely a piece of work. "Like I owe it to Michael to help you catch his killer."

"And you didn't owe it to him that first time we talked?" I can't help it; I give her a smirk. She might think it's flirting, since that's how she's wired. Maybe it is flirting. Her tits are half hanging out; it's an involuntary response.

"I was trying to protect the other women. I didn't think that any of us would have harmed Michael; we were just blowing off steam—"

"I thought you were having some girl talk."

"Girls talk about boys. We talk about men, especially when we've been sharing the same one."

I sit back in my chair and give her an appraising look that's got nothing to do with her tits. "Go on."

"Have you gotten the records yet? If you have, then you'll know everything I'm about to tell you is true."

"Sadly, no. The judge decided to uphold therapist-client privilege beyond the grave. That's part of why I appreciate you coming here today to fill in some holes."

She might be relieved; I can't quite tell. She's not unhappy about my answer; I know that much. "Well," she says, "it's a good thing I'm here, then."

"I want to believe you, but I've got a boss. He'll want corroboration."

"Get Lucinda's records."

Oh, so she's here to talk about Lucinda and not Greer. I had the impression that Flora liked Lucinda and hated Greer. Was it possible that's just what she'd wanted me to think? Or that she had a change of heart for some reason?

"I was thinking about your records," I say. "Then I can prove you're the reliable witness I know you are. You ready to turn those over?"

"I don't want to contradict the court."

I almost laugh. "The judge denied the subpoena, but you're in charge of your own records. You can hand them out on College Avenue if you want."

"Let me think about it." Okay, she's thought. I can see the answer is no. "Lucinda had a really messed-up childhood, and Michael took advantage of it. Did she tell you they were lovers?"

"No, she must have forgotten that part."

"I'll tell you everything I know."

What she's about to say might very well be true, but she's not here because she suddenly caught a conscience. Something's spooked her. She must think I'm onto her, though actually, I'd started to put my money on Greer. Now, though, I'm thinking Flora. Though I might be open to persuasion.

"Start talking," I say.

BEFORE

CHAPTER 42

FLORA

I listened at the door as Michael was in the shower. I wished I could hear him singing. Sometimes he did, and then I knew he was happy to have me here, in his bed. But maybe he wasn't singing this morning out of respect for me and what I'd been through in last night's attack.

It hadn't occurred to me when I bashed myself in the face that I was putting myself in the same category as his clients, but it was rather brilliant. Now I needed him just like they did. I was vulnerable, just as they were. Whatever they were offering him, I could, too. I was finally able to compete. I would win.

I smiled to myself as I rolled over. At some point, I'd get him to upgrade these sheets. The thread count was way too low, practically burlap. Or I'd just move in here and bring my own sheets. They'd become ours. Everything would.

Last night, after he picked me up and brought me back here—brought me home—he was so solicitous. He set me up in bed with a tray and some food and an ice pack. He nursed me with great tenderness, never even making a move toward sex. Before we fell asleep, I pulled him toward me so that he could cradle me from behind. "Are you sure it's okay?" he asked. "Nothing hurts?"

"No," I said. For the first time in weeks, nothing hurt.

I didn't like how I'd gotten here, the manipulation of it. But once we were back on track, everything would be aboveboard. No more lies. I'd tell people about him only with his full consent. If we needed to stay secret longer, that was a small price to pay for knowing that eventually, we'd be free and open and legitimate. Michael thought we'd become unhealthy, but we could get healthy again, together.

Love is patient. Love is kind.

Last night, Michael demonstrated that. It reminded me of our first individual therapy session.

I'm not a natural type in general, but for that meeting, I was truly over the top. I bought a new outfit. I left work early so I could take an extended bubble bath, layering fragrances from body lotion to oil to perfume, but only a little of each so that the effect was subtle and wafting yet unmistakable. My makeup was nearly an hour of artistry. I blew my hair straight and then worked just a hint of a wave back into it. Good thing Young was working late, so that I could undo it all before he'd get home that night. If he'd seen me, the jig would have been up.

Did I feel guilty about my feelings for Michael, for the ways I was contemplating betraying Young? Of course I did. But not just then. I was too wound up.

I was nearly panting with anticipation as I sat in the waiting room. Why so many *Psychology Today* issues? I'd never remembered to ask why he didn't have a subscription to anything else. Or why so many of the issues were about sociopaths, narcissists, and those who love them.

His door opened, and he and the previous client were laughing as they said goodbye. It was clear they liked each other a lot, which made sense. Who wouldn't like Michael? The woman was pretty, I couldn't help noticing, in a simplified way, in her athleisure with no makeup.

I felt a second's despair, like maybe that was what he was into and I'd gone in the wrong direction. I'd misread him during the sessions with Young. He wasn't attracted to me at all. He thought I tried too hard, which was practically the biggest insult there was. And in my case, it was true. I had tried way too hard.

She's his client, I reminded myself, *not his girlfriend.*

Oh, right. He could have a girlfriend. Somehow that hadn't occurred to me before. He wore no ring, and my Google-stalking hadn't suggested a wife, but it was possible he was with someone. It was possible his interest in me was purely professional.

"Flora!" He gave me a warm smile. I was pretty sure he was happy to see me, but then, he'd been jovial with Athleisure, too. "Come on in."

"Hi." My smile was wan. I followed him inside and arranged myself on the couch. My skirt was short. Too obvious? Should I have worn some yoga pants?

"How do you feel about being here?" he asked. He'd resettled in his chair and looked entirely in his element.

My stomach plummeted. If he were into me, he wouldn't look quite so comfortable. He was wearing a rumpled plaid shirt and some corduroys, for fuck's sake. He hadn't tried at all. He might not even have remembered it was our first day alone until he got to work and looked at his schedule.

Somehow, in my mind, it had been so different. He'd been in a state of expectation all week, like I had.

"I feel fine." Now my smile was tight.

"You seem a little nervous. I get it. You're used to having Young here with you, and the risk is distributed."

"Risk?"

"Figure of speech. What I mean is, you're not in the hot seat the whole time." The way he looked at me when he said "hot seat" . . . was I imagining that? "This is tough stuff we're talking about. Sex and intimacy. It goes to the core of who we are as people."

"I hadn't thought of it like that." I looked up at him admiringly from under my false eyelashes.

"In my experience, a staggering number of people don't think of it at all. We're either doing it or we're not doing it."

I held his gaze. Were we—he and I—going to do it? I couldn't be imagining the current flowing between us.

"And you and Young, you're not doing it, even though we're seemingly making progress in therapy. So that's why I thought it would be a good time to meet with you each individually. Explore the impasse."

"Yes," I said, "let's explore that."

He laughed. "You're a funny one, Flora."

"I am. But how do you mean it?"

"There's just something about you that makes me smile. I suppress it during the sessions. It wouldn't be appropriate then. But later, I'll remember things you said."

I felt myself beginning to glow, like I'd been on a dimmer that had just been turned up. "I remember things you said, too."

"I talk a lot to Young. I thought he was the one who needed the help most, to be honest. I needed to get him reinvested in your marriage. What I didn't realize then was that your investment was only surface deep."

That was the thing with Michael—he was always right. I just hadn't formulated it so concisely for myself until that second. "What do we do?"

"Either we raise your level of commitment to match Young's or . . ." He let his voice trail off suggestively. He wasn't going to say it, but we both knew what was happening. We both knew where I had to end up. "You deserve the best, Flora. Maybe that's Young and maybe it's not. But that's what we'll explore." Our eyes met. "No rush."

It wasn't just one individual session but multiple (a foreshadowing of what delights were to come). He was ultimately coaching me in how to leave my husband for him, without either of us ever acknowledging what was going on in that room between us. We didn't speak of what would follow after I ended things with Young, but we both knew that we'd come together. That there was no resisting for either of us. But it wasn't overnight, that was for sure.

Love is patient. Love is kind.

Michael was back, a towel around his waist. He started to get dressed nearly silently, creeping around the room.

"Good morning," I said, and he visibly startled, his belt halfway through the loops.

"Good morning. I wanted you to sleep in."

"It wasn't in the cards. I was having nightmares." Untrue but effective: he came and sat on the edge of the bed, instantly tuned in to me. I was going to need to play the victim for a little while longer, because I had been. The mugging was real. But since it had brought us back together, it didn't feel like a trauma; it felt like a blessing.

"I was surprised that you seemed so peaceful. I'd expected you to thrash around."

I fingered his belt loops. "It must have been your presence."

"I could go with you to the police station this morning if you want. Do you remember his face?"

"No. I didn't see it."

"He punched you in the jaw. That means he was in front of you."

I had hoped he wouldn't reenact it in his mind. "I must have been looking at his fist, then. It was all so fast."

"So he was walking toward you and punched you, and then shoved you the other way? I'm trying to picture exactly how it happened."

Why? Was that some weird sexual fantasy he'd never told me? "I don't want to talk about it."

"I'm sorry. It's too fresh. But fresh is better for going to the police."

"Would you push one of your clients like this?"

"You're not a client."

I wasn't sure if that meant I was more precious or less. "I need your support, Michael. I've been through a trauma."

"I know. I'm trying to support you. I want to keep you safe. He's still out there." He was quiet for a second. His hair glinted dark and wet. I wanted to grab him and fuck him senseless, but that wouldn't fit the profile. I was a victim. "What if this wasn't random?"

"Muggings happen all the time near the Rockridge BART station. I shouldn't have been walking there at night."

"But if it wasn't random, he can get to you somewhere else. I mean, this attack was pretty vicious. Normally, they just shove you from behind and grab your things. And didn't he only take your phone and some cash?"

"I think that's all he took." Now I was getting frightened. It hadn't even occurred to me that the attack wasn't random. I mean, who would target me? I didn't have enemies.

Kate?

No, that was insane. Kate had been on the phone with me; I could hear her reaction.

Michael, trying to get rid of a problem. Trying to be done with me once and for all.

No, that's totally nuts. Besides, if he had somehow orchestrated the mugging, why would he suggest that it wasn't random?

Besides, all the guy did was shove me from behind. The vicious part was all me.

Why had Michael said that, though, about shoving from behind and grabbing? It was so specific and so accurate. Not the version I'd choked out last night through tears. The version that I was fast realizing didn't fit the forensic evidence.

I definitely couldn't go to the police.

"Give me time," I said. "You always say that when you work with trauma survivors, you need to go at their pace."

"You're right, I do say that."

"I just need to go to the office and forget about this." I hadn't been planning to do that; I'd wanted to loll in Michael's bed, preferably with him, but now it seemed like it'd be prudent to get away. Then he couldn't badger me about the police. "Maybe you could drive me and pick me up? I'm still a little shaky."

"I have clients later."

Right. It was Wednesday. "Maybe you could cancel. We could go out to dinner tonight."

He looked down at the bed, like he didn't know how to break it to me.

"We could have dinner here," I amended. "I just really don't want to be alone."

"I'll be home by eight thirty. You can come by then."

"After you see all your clients?" I tried not to sound too spiteful on the word *clients*.

"What would you suggest?" There was an edge to his voice.

"I already suggested. That you cancel."

"I'm responsible for them."

He was responsible for me, too, wasn't he? We were responsible for the people we loved. Unless my worst suspicions were true, and it really was better to be a client than a girlfriend. Not that I was necessarily his girlfriend. Not that they were necessarily just clients.

Time to go for broke.

"I'm afraid to drive myself," I said. "Afraid I might have flashbacks or something and then, I don't know, maybe I'd careen off the road or something. You've told me weird stories about what can happen with trauma. And I'm afraid to be alone."

"Do something with Jeanie, and then take an Uber at eight thirty."

He had all the answers. Finally, I nodded. It was the most I was going to get out of him, and it was certainly progress from how it had been between us lately.

His eyebrows knitted together with concern. That was more like it. Then he said, "Whoever stole your phone has access to all our texts, right?"

Kate wouldn't have been stunned by his self-absorption, but I was, momentarily. "You know your real name isn't in my phone. No one would figure out who you are." I decided against adding, *And no one would care.*

I also didn't add that I'd downloaded all the photos I'd taken of him from my phone to my computer. I'd wanted to make sure I'd never lose any of our precious memories. But maybe it was also insurance. Against what? I'd never fully articulated that to myself.

I didn't go to work. I preferred not to answer any questions, and I was on a reconnaissance mission. On the surface, Michael and I were back on track, and I hoped fervently it was true, but things had turned on a dime before. He'd turned. Now I had to stay vigilant. Trust but verify.

I couldn't help thinking that with my head scarf and sunglasses and bruises, I officially looked like a battered wife. I reminded myself that Michael would never abuse me. Not physically, anyway, and it wasn't like he took pleasure in causing me emotional pain. I was the one who'd betrayed him. It wasn't on purpose; I didn't see it that way at the time, but that was the net result.

He never should have known. For that, I blamed Kate. Maybe that's why I waited so long to text her and tell her I was all right, it was just a mugging, nothing to worry about. I did it at almost five p.m. (eight in Miami) as I was sitting in my usual parking space, the one I circled an hour to get, directly in front of Michael's office building. I pretended the delay was because I hadn't gotten a new phone until then, when my first stop that morning had been the Apple store.

There she was, approaching the office. The blonde giraffe. My jaw tightened as I noticed that she had a spring in her step.

I reminded myself that it was before her session. She hadn't even seen Michael yet, so most likely, it had nothing to do with him. She'd won the lottery, or gotten a promotion at work, or her boyfriend proposed. It was a new pair of shoes. It could be anything.

But I didn't like how she was moving. She was way too confident.

And she was the one going to him while I was the one on the outside, looking in, hoping to avoid detection. Just hoping I wouldn't be seen.

CHAPTER 43

GREER

Chenille looked worried, and I could hardly blame her. While I'd been much more diligent of late, not wanting any mistakes of mine to lead to further discomfort for her, my heart simply wasn't in it. She must have sensed that. It seemed that my clients had, which was another reason for my decision. Better to step aside than to destroy everything I had built. Then I'd be able to come back to it later, fresher, with greater purpose, with a child to support.

"I've been thinking," I said, "that I could use some time away."

She blinked her beautiful brown eyes at me, clearly taken aback.

"You're meant for this industry. You have all the diplomacy and all the passion." I'd never had passion, only drive. I'd just wanted to make my mommy and daddy proud, as it turned out, only neither of them had lived long enough to see it. Oh, sure, they saw that I was moving up in my previous corporation, and I'd asked them for their advice if I were to start my own firm down the line, but they never saw me have my own independent success. If they had, if they were still around to disappoint, I might never have had the courage to do this. I might still have been trying to earn their love and attention at almost forty years old. In a way, I was lucky they were gone. It had opened up the possibility of true love, finally.

"I do feel passionately about the work," Chenille said. "I learned from you."

"You learned to do the work from me. But the passion—that's something else. Don't sell yourself short. Women do that far too often."

"That's why they need us to get in there and play hardball with their contracts. They need you."

She was afraid. She suspected what was coming and didn't think she could do it on her own. "Don't sell yourself short," I repeated firmly. "I plan to spend the next month or so grooming you to take over."

"During your sabbatical?"

"That's a good word for it."

"How long will it be?"

"I don't know yet."

"Are you going somewhere?"

"I don't know that, either." Travel seemed like a no-brainer, but honestly, I'd never felt the need. I'd been all over the world for conferences, but the hotels were largely the same, and I never ventured far afield. I hadn't really learned much about local culture in Brussels, Tokyo, Helsinki, or Hong Kong. That was what I should do. Maybe I could move and start over, far from where my parents had lived and where they'd died. I could be reborn. Then I'd have my baby.

But did I want to be that far away from my baby's father?

That was if Michael decided to honor my request. The fertility center had done all the basic tests and assessed that I was within normal limits for a woman my age. I'd been hoping to hear I had the ovaries and eggs of a twenty-five-year-old. He warned me that miscarriage rates were higher for "geriatric pregnancies" (yikes!) but that most likely, I would be able to conceive. In my mind, it was all systems go.

I could sell my condo and buy a house outside the city. Sausalito or Marin, someplace beautiful and bucolic, by the ocean or amid the trees. Someplace child-friendly, without so many hills and so much traffic. I could afford most anything I desired, and I didn't need to work. I made a healthy income, I invested and I saved, but moreover, my parents had left me tens of millions, also well invested, and given how much I had, my current lifestyle was practically frugal. My condo had cost only a million but was worth triple by now. I could go wherever I wanted.

It was a frightening prospect, thinking for two. And while no one had ever had a more first-world problem than this, it remained a problem.

If I stepped away and Chenille performed as well as I envisioned, it would be hard to come back. My name would be on the masthead, but she'd have the real power. She'd have the relationships: with staff, with clients. There might be no real place for me. I'd never been a figure-head, someone to sit back and let others do the work while I reaped the rewards. I'd been a hustler, like my parents taught me. In their world-view, you could never have too much ambition or too much money; there would never be too much success.

But as Michael had excavated, what I wanted was love. I'd subli-mated that desire for as long as I could, channeled it, and eventually stopped trying to attain the unattainable from my emotionally unavail-able parents. Stopped trying to attain it from anyone. Intimacy, who needed intimacy? Not me, that's what I told myself. In the end, though, our deepest desires always won out.

"Once you left, would I be able to reach you, or would I be on my own?" Chenille asked.

"I'd like you to do your own problem-solving, but I'm not falling off the face of the earth."

"Are you sure I'm ready for this? I've been your assistant. I'm not even a recruiter."

"So you won't have a lot of clients we'd have to place with other recruiters."

She was still hesitating. "How do you think the rest of the staff would feel? One minute, I'm beneath them, and the next, I'm doing your job."

"You've never been beneath anyone. If that's how they feel, then fuck 'em."

She smiled, just for a second. "Maybe I should become a recruiter first. That's the trajectory I was expecting. Honestly, it's what I thought this meeting might be about, you offering me a promotion. A chance."

"Well, you nailed it. That's exactly what I'm doing."

"I'd be jumping about eight rungs on the ladder."

"You're that good. You've proven it of late, when you handled all the situations I put you in with my mistakes."

I could see she was struggling with whether to say something.

"Out with it. If this is going to work, I need to be able to trust that you'll tell me the truth, even if it's bad news."

"Some of the staff think you're gay. They might wonder if you and I are involved."

"Who's spreading those rumors?"

"I can't tell you that. Not if I'm going to be managing these people."

No one had ever seen me on a date or heard me talking about one, but that was because I observed appropriate boundaries. And at times, I could take on a certain male energy in my professional dealings. But gay?

Not that there was anything wrong with it, to quote *Seinfeld*. I just didn't like the speculation, even if it was only natural that in the absence of information about their boss, they'd come up with their own theories. I'd kept them from knowing me, though as it was turning out, I hadn't really known myself.

If I came back, I might be a different manager than I'd ever been. But hearing this made it easier to go.

"I can handle it," Chenille said, sitting up a little straighter. "I can do this."

"We haven't even discussed compensation yet."

She smiled. "I'm going to be a tough negotiator. I learned from the best."

CHAPTER 44

LUCINDA

Cassie was five, and she spent a lot of time in the closet. That's because she didn't like the looks of the men or their smells. She didn't like how they'd lay on her pink princess bed, whether she was in it or not. She didn't like that Mommy went in her own bedroom and didn't answer when Cassie knocked on the door. She didn't like being left to take care of herself, while the men prowled the house like jungle animals. She didn't like the feeling that something was always about to happen, and she didn't know what that thing was, but it would be bad.

She kept all her toys in the closet just so they would be there when she needed them. She'd do Legos in the dark, by braille, because she couldn't turn on any lights. And she couldn't make any noise, because then they'd know—that one man would know—that she was there, and then the bad thing could start happening, and maybe it would never stop.

"An older man taking advantage of a young girl," Dr. Baylor said. "Seems like a theme."

"That's as far as the memory goes," I said. "Just the anticipation of something bad, and of course, as an adult, I know what that something bad would be. But when I'm writing—when I'm in Cassie's five-year-old head—I don't know."

"So you don't know if something bad ever happens to 'Cassie.'" He didn't use air quotes, but he might as well have. Other than the third person and the name change, my semiautobiographical novel was really a memoir. When I tried to write as myself, I faltered. It was instant and immutable writer's block. When I was Cassie, it flowed.

"I'm afraid of what happens to her," I said.

Dr. Baylor nodded slowly. It was so hard to believe that this was the same man I regularly saw naked. In a way, he wasn't. That man was Michael. Dr. Baylor was still my therapist, and I could focus more in session now that I didn't have that distracting crush on him, now that I'd separated the two out. I wouldn't have thought myself capable of that type of compartmentalization, but it worked. I no longer wanted Dr. Baylor; I just wanted Michael, and other than Wednesday evenings, I had him.

Sometimes we did the mornings, if I couldn't wait until nightfall. We'd had a few assignations at lunchtime. I'd text him, and if he was available, we'd meet at the office. He never texted me. He said it was important that I called the shots completely. This was about my needs, not his. We were there to fulfill my fantasies, not his.

"Go on," he said.

"My mother got clean when I was six," I said. "If anything happened, it couldn't have been going on for very long. A year, at most."

"The length of time doesn't determine the extent of the trauma. It's about the imprint."

"The imprint?"

"You know how after ducklings hatch, if the mother isn't there, the ducklings will follow whoever they see first? It could be another animal entirely. They could follow around a human, if that's who's within eyesight. It's because that's what imprints on their mind. With trauma, there are imprints."

"Are you saying that my being with Adam was about some nameless man making an imprint on me?" I nearly shuddered. It was just so gross. But then, I had been his trained puppy, hadn't I?

"I don't know that yet. We're still at the beginning of this thing. You're just now recovering memories that you'd suppressed because they were too dangerous. You weren't strong enough. Or rather, you didn't think you were strong enough."

Now that was an idea I liked. "Do you think I've always been strong enough?"

"Yes. You're coming into the recognition of your full power."

I smiled to myself, thinking of my extracurricular "sessions" with Michael. I sure felt powerful then.

But I hadn't written since that closet chapter. It was only two days ago. Still, before that, I'd had so much momentum, so much fire. I was worried that it was gone for good, that I'd retreat back into my proofreading and my powerlessness. Michael, Dr. Baylor, and my writing were what buoyed me.

Or maybe it was my own strength that had been there all along.

"How do I get myself to write again?" I asked.

We talked about coping skills and self-talk, all the tools I could use to get myself back in front of my laptop, to stare down the bogeyman of my past and remember that it was, in fact, the past, that the days of my being helpless were long gone. I came into the session a little bit hunched, making myself small, but I left walking tall again. I smiled at the thought of coming back later.

Out on the street, in the line of metered spaces, there was a woman in a sedan who I'd never seen before, but I could swear she was staring right at me. It was pretty creepy, because she was in some sort of headdress and sunglasses, like a disguise, which paradoxically made her way more conspicuous. I noticed a large bruise on the lower part of her face, like a purple jellyfish spreading its tentacles, and I was sorry for finding her creepy. Really, she was more sad. She might have been hiding out from whoever did that to her.

Maybe it was because of the talk with Dr. Baylor about the abuse, and the empathy I was rediscovering for myself as a former victim, twinned with the newfound assurance from my lovemaking with Michael. But suddenly, I really wanted this woman, whoever she was, to know she was stronger than whoever had done this to her. She deserved better.

I approached her car and knocked on the passenger side window. She looked skittish, like she might just bolt. Her hand reached for the gearshift. "No, please," I said loudly. "Wait. I need to talk to you."

She hesitated and then rolled down the window, but she stayed in profile, like she didn't want to be seen. She must have been ashamed. I related.

"It's not your fault," I said.

She was still facing forward. "What isn't?" Her voice vibrated with nerves.

"Whatever he did to you. To your face."

"I don't know what you're talking about. I need to leave now. Could you step back from my car?"

I didn't move. "I know what it's like. Lots of women do." No one had ever hit me, but there were other ways to be demeaned and made to feel like nothing. "Is there anything I can do to help?"

"Just step away from my car, okay? That's all the help I need."

I did as she'd asked, and she peeled out. She was lucky not to hit or get hit by another car. I watched her go. There was a woman who didn't yet recognize her full power. Dr. Baylor could have done wonders for her.

CHAPTER 45

FLORA

I needed to stop this. The stakeouts, the getaways. One of these times, I was going to rear-end somebody or worse. But for now, I had to get out of there.

The blonde giraffe actually pitied me. I saw it in her face. And speaking of her face—up close, it was beautiful, like some sort of Scandinavian goddess. Those cornflower-blue eyes and that perfect pale skin without any makeup whatsoever. She was the anti-me. And I couldn't get over how she'd walked right up to my Lexus. So bold, like she'd become a different creature entirely. A gazelle, maybe.

Michael had to be fucking her. That was how a well-fucked woman walked. I used to walk like that. How did I look now?

Like an object of pity.

I told myself it was just the bruise. Also, I was dressed to obscure. If she could have seen me properly done up, it would have been a totally different exchange. I would have intimidated the hell out of her. But what had just passed between us was a *Freaky Friday* moment, a role reversal. I was mousy and meek, and she was so full of herself that she could just stride right up and ask if *she* could help *me*.

She said that she knew what it was like. That meant she was one of Michael's trauma victims. Effortlessly beautiful and newly confident—I couldn't compete with that. I wondered what precisely she was being treated for. How she was being treated—that might have been the better question.

But Michael wouldn't be fucking her while she was still his patient. He'd have to stop the therapy and then wait two years, or pretend to wait two years. That was, unless his MO had changed.

I drove to his house, pulling into the space right in front. It wasn't quite eight yet, and he'd said eight thirty. I'd just get the spare key from under the flowerpot in his backyard and make myself at home.

Only it wasn't there.

He used to like it when he came inside and found me in my negligee, tidying up or putting takeout in pretty bowls. Back then, he liked being surprised.

No, he liked me as his geisha. Now that I was trying to be more, he was locking me out, literally.

What was he hiding?

I lifted every one of the flowerpots. Nothing. Then I looked under the hedges and under rocks. I was on my hands and knees feeling alongside the hot tub, like one of the contestants on *Survivor* searching for a Hidden Immunity Idol. An unsuccessful contestant, who was about to get voted out at the next Tribal Council.

I walked to the front of the house and, on a whim, lifted the mat. *Oh, Michael. I never knew you were so unimaginative.*

I was about to put it into the door lock when I noticed a sticker in the corner of the window, facing outward: Weymouth Security. As in, the house was guarded. Booby-trapped.

The sticker was new; I was sure of that. Property and personal crime had been on the uptick in Rockridge—case in point, last night—but it was hard to imagine that Michael just happened to take security precautions around the same time we broke up. Sort of broke up. He'd been too ambivalent to make it official.

Was Michael scared of me? Did he think I was some kind of psycho?

I had bashed my face in for him last night. Maybe I was some kind of psycho.

Consider the evidence: I'd been digging up the backyard to find my sorta-boyfriend's spare key. I was basically about to break and enter. I'd been stalking him outside his office.

Ohhhhhhh . . .

He'd seen me sitting in my car. I'd been assuming that if he knew, he would have confronted me, but if he really thought I was crazy, he wouldn't.

But he'd been so tender toward me last night and this morning. He wanted to go to the police station with me. He wanted to keep me safe (and he'd wanted to make sure the texts and pictures we'd exchanged over the past two years were safe, too).

There'd been no sex, though. I thought it was because he was being my caregiver. It could be that he'd just lost interest. He'd replaced me with the blonde giraffe.

To win him back, I had to stop the crazy. Or at the very least, I needed to hide it better. For example, what would a sane person do after she couldn't find the spare key to her boyfriend's house?

She'd text him to say that she was going to sit on the front steps and wait.

That wouldn't work for us. He didn't want to advertise our love. It might take a while for us to declare ourselves a couple with the way things were going. But we'd get there.

We'd made progress last night, and I couldn't afford any backsliding. *Think, Flora. Think. What would a sane person do?*

I did have something of an out. I'd undergone a trauma last night. Not wanting to be alone was a perfectly reasonable response. He'd said that he was going to support me through this, so there was that.

I could sit in my car in front of his house until he got home from work.

No, too much like a stakeout.

I could circle for the next half hour.

No. Too close to psycho.

I could go to the Safeway with its well-lit parking lot and kill some time picking up wine, cheese, and olives. Then all I needed to do was act totally normal when I saw him, but in a recently traumatized sort of way. Demure. Like I was scared but doing my best to overcome. That's what bravery was: being afraid and doing it anyway.

And I was afraid. I was afraid of the Wednesday lineup and what kind of hold they might have had on Michael. The blonde giraffe with her trauma that was probably way bigger than a mugging. She'd probably overcome more and been braver, and he was her cheerleader now. I was afraid that I'd driven him into someone else's arms by first betraying him with Kate, and then doing the kinds of things that could mistakenly be interpreted as psycho. I shouldn't have stormed into his office that time, or texted him so much, or made that threat. I shouldn't have been surveilling his clients.

No wonder he'd said we were unhealthy. He thought I was unhealthy. I had to prove otherwise.

I'd just apologize for all of it. A blanket apology, rather than itemizing, in case he didn't know about my stakeouts. I'd tell him that the mugging had set me straight, that it had put everything into perspective. I was so sorry, my behavior had been out of control, but this could be our fresh start . . .

Yes, that's what I'd do.

I didn't love it, but it was my best play.

CHAPTER 46

GREER

"I'm moving forward with my sabbatical," I said.

"Your sabbatical?" Dr. Michael tilted his head quizzically.

"That's what Chenille called it. I like that term, though I'm keeping it open-ended. I'm not necessarily returning in a few months like a professor would."

"You talked to Chenille about it?" He looked concerned, like he'd thought it was going to remain hypothetical for a while longer.

"You know I've been mulling it over for a while." A week, actually. That wasn't my usual timetable, but then, I was changing. Growing. Evolving. The woman I had been before wasn't fit to be a mother. My own parents hadn't been fit.

"Therapy is an ideal place to explore decisions before they're made."

Sometimes he could be so pedantic. It was a mildly annoying quirk of his. But then, that was what let me know this was a real relationship, as he'd said before. It was no fairy tale. He wasn't my fantasy. But he was a good man, an interesting man, and the best I could do on the short notice that my ovaries were giving me.

"I've made a whole lot of decisions in my life before I met you, and I'm going to make a whole lot after," I said.

"You seem a little prickly. What's that about?"

I was prickly because of the tenterhooks. I was waiting for him to tell me his answer, but all through our last session and all through this one, he hadn't even brought it up. "Have you thought more about what we talked about? The donation?" It was about the most delicate way I could put it, and still, I felt heat rising to my cheeks.

He shifted in his chair. Not a good sign. "Honestly, I thought that since you hadn't mentioned it in the last session, you'd realized . . ." He looked away. "My answer has to be no."

"Because of some handbook? Some ivory tower ethics committee?"

He sat bolt upright. "What about the ethics committee?"

"Whoa. Down, boy."

"I take my profession—and its ethics—very seriously."

"I never said you didn't."

"You implied that I shouldn't."

"What I'm saying is, you didn't say no when we first talked about it, and now you are. I deserve to know why."

"Once you breach certain boundaries, you can't go back."

"I don't want to go back. I want to go forward. How about if this is our last session?"

He didn't speak for a long minute. It was hard to wait, but I did it. I liked that this wasn't a simple answer. Did he have feelings for me? It should have occurred to me sooner, but I'd been too focused on all the new and strange feelings I was having.

"You need a therapist," he said finally.

"But it doesn't have to be you."

"Maybe it should be. We can work through this transference you're having."

"Come again?"

Now the heat was in his face. He was feeling something, that was clear. "Transference. You're relating to me like a past figure in your life. You're projecting thoughts, feelings, and hopes onto me. That's why sometimes you get mad at me. It's why you're thinking that I could be the potential father of your child when you know so little about me."

I shook my head. "No. I get mad at you because sometimes you're really infuriating."

He almost smiled. "I could say the same about you."

Our eyes met, and it was still there. That warmth. The tingle. The chemistry. "This is my last session with you. I've decided. The only question is, will you let me get to know you more so we can see if whatever this is translates to the real world?"

"Are you asking me on a date?"

"I want to vet you as the potential father of my child. Does that scream 'date' to you?"

"You just decided you want to be a mother. You just allowed yourself to see that your own parents were largely incapable of love. You need time to process and to grieve—"

"Pregnancy is forty weeks. And it's not like I'll conceive instantly. There's time. I'm going to work hard to emotionally prepare myself for all the changes. That's what the sabbatical is about. That's what seeing you outside of this room is about."

He creaked backward in his chair. "I can't date a former client for two years. If I do, I can lose my license."

"I told you, it's not dating. Does your handbook outlaw sperm donation to a former client?"

"It can't cover all contingencies. There has to be room for sound clinical judgment."

"I'll protect your identity and your livelihood. I have an excellent attorney on retainer who'll draw up paperwork to indemnify you. It'll ensure that I'm not able to sue you or file any complaints against you.

Not that I would ever try to do those things, but I'd want you to feel comfortable."

He stared up at the ceiling as if something were written there. A way out of this, maybe. Or a way in. I had the feeling that Dr. Michael had chosen this line of work because he liked complications. He liked challenges. He liked to be tied up so he could Houdini his arms free.

"Professional guidelines exist for a reason," he said. "They exist because the people who come to see me, who place their trust in me, are vulnerable. I need to be careful not to abuse the power they've given me."

"Look at me. Do I look vulnerable to you?"

"It's not about how you look. You're in crisis."

"In transition. And trust me, any power I give you, I can take back. I just did. I make my own decisions like a big girl. I've been doing it my entire life." I stood up. "This was my last session." I stepped toward the door. "I've made my choice. Now you need to make yours."

CHAPTER 47

LUCINDA

The room was dark, lit only by pillar candles. Sandalwood, by the smell of them. The sound machines were on full blast: two of them inside the office, one in the waiting room, and another in the hall. All precautions were being taken so that no one could hear me. I'd discovered that I could get loud.

We were on the couch, and my legs were in the air, with Michael's mouth in between them. He lifted his head. "Talk to me."

I moaned.

"Tell me what you want."

"I want you to keep going." I was naked and glistening with sweat. I thought, just for a second, about the other women who sat on that couch. Did other women lie on it, too?

No, I was the only one. I had to be.

"I want to hear your voice," he said. "Tell me 'there.' Or 'no, not there. Over here.' Pull my hair. Show me. Faster. Slower."

"Or just right."

He smiled, resting his head against my thigh. "Yeah, sometimes it's just right."

"Will you let me return the favor tonight?" I said.

"No," he said. "Not tonight." Another grin. "I've got a headache."

It wasn't that I liked giving blow jobs or anything, but I couldn't tell Michael what I really wanted: for things to stop seeming so one-sided. For this to become mutual, something we could continue outside the office. But Michael said this was my time, not his. What about our time?

"Get back to work, then," I said.

He did, and so did I. I gave directions, through my hand in his hair. A caress, a yank, a push against the back of his head. Deeper, I needed it deeper. Then I was screaming.

He laughed as he came up for air. "Shh," he said. "I've got neighbors."

It was past midnight. Even the cleaning people had gone home. But I didn't bother telling him that; I was finished.

I rolled over sideways as I waited to get my breath back. He was spooning me, but it wasn't a large couch, so I had to squeeze in tight against the pillows. Hard to believe this was the same couch where I'd be sitting on Wednesday night, talking about Cassie and her mother. About Adam and me.

"Are you ever disgusted by me?" I asked quietly. I could get the words out only because I didn't have to look at his face; I stared, up close, at the tufted buttons of the pillow.

"Never. What made you say that?"

"Sometimes when I think back to what I've done, I disgust myself."

"After all our sessions, you still feel that way?"

I rolled back toward him. "Don't take it personally, okay? You're a great therapist. It's just me."

"'It's not you, it's me'?" He was trying to smile, but I could tell he was a little hurt.

"I don't think it so often anymore. Mostly, I feel good about myself. Like with all the writing you encouraged me to do. Haven't you seen the change in me lately? Don't you feel it?"

It was strange to see that I could bring out his insecurity. He'd told me that I was starting to own my power, and he was right, I was. I had some of what I craved: mutuality. I didn't only depend on him to feel better; he also depended on me.

He smiled and kissed me. We didn't normally kiss much, and he'd never initiated it before. He must have been feeling truly close to me. Or he was grateful for the ego stroke I'd just given him. They could be one and the same.

"I love you," I said. I didn't mean to; it just slipped out.

He brushed my hair back from my face, his gaze steady. He couldn't say he loved me, too, but he must.

Then again, if he could make me come five times a night, why couldn't he say what he really felt?

"Are you still with her?" I asked. "That woman I heard you arguing with in the waiting room?" I should have asked sooner (I'd wondered, of course), but I'd been too afraid. I thought that mentioning his real life would give him pause, that he'd reconsider our unorthodox treatment. Or had he done this "treatment" with other women, too? It would devastate me to think so.

But if that other woman was the impediment to his telling me how he really felt, then I needed to know that.

"That's over," he told me.

Then am I the only one? I was dying to know, but I wasn't strong enough to handle the answer, not yet.

PRESENT DAY

CHAPTER 48

DETECTIVE GREGORY PLATH

"You're saying that Flora's cooperating?" Greer asks.

"Yes."

"Don't you mean deflecting?"

She probably was, but so was Greer. So was Lucinda. It would be refreshing to sit in a room with a woman who was being straight with me. In a very strange way, it made me miss my ex-wife. She's a good woman. I screwed that up, because back then, I was screwed up myself. That divorce was all on me.

But I need to pay attention to the woman in front of me.

"The subpoenas have been quashed," I say. "The judge decided to uphold patients' rights." That fucker. He doesn't care about justice; he cares about letting me know he's the one with the power and the long memory. "That means I'm stuck getting all my information from you. You and others. I need to ask you, have you told me everything you know about Flora?"

"I'm pretty sure she stalked him."

"You forgot to mention that last time?"

"I wasn't sure if that was her I saw outside his building one time. There was this woman wearing a scarf on her head, like a disguise, and she was staring right at me. She had daggers in her eyes. It took me a while to piece it together and realize that the first time she approached me and introduced herself, it wasn't the first time I'd seen her. She'd been stalking him for a while."

"Or she was stalking you."

Greer stares at me, and her whole cool-as-a-cucumber routine falls away. She looks genuinely scared. "What I know is, Flora has a lot of fury."

"I don't think she's the only one."

"You think I do?"

"Still waters run deep."

"What did Flora tell you about me?" Greer asks, trying to put that fear back under wraps. "Because she doesn't know anything. I didn't tell her anything, because I didn't trust her."

"But what did Michael Baylor tell her?"

Her mouth falls open, like it never occurred to her that the doctor could have betrayed her. He was fucking two other women, one current patient and one former, and it never occurred to her?

"I thought you were smarter than that, Greer," I say.

She stands up. "If you want to question me again, it'll be with an attorney present."

"If that's how you want to play this, that's fine by me."

I'm pretty sure I've got my murderer. But I can't charge her based on intuition. I don't have records, and I don't have physical evidence. Speaking of the latter, my gut tells me that Greer is the only one of these three who could cover up a crime so completely. Lucinda's an obvious mess, but Flora's a mess, too, just better disguised. They would have left hair fibers and fingerprints all over that body. They're shedding little bits of themselves all the time; they can't be contained. But Greer—she's hiding something, for sure. Whatever the motivation, it's got to be big. He crossed her.

I need those records. I can feel that they'll show a woman who's lost control before. They'll show me who she really is.

And I know where that file is. I know anything in it is inadmissible, and I can never tell anyone if I take a peek, but it could point me in the right direction of something I can use. Even if she doesn't crack, I can take her down. We're talking about justice here.

BEFORE

CHAPTER 49

FLORA

I was learning how long it took for a bruise to fade. I didn't want to burn through all my PTO waiting, so I was back at work, having also learned the inadequacy of makeup. As I was out on calls in various doctors' offices, I found that the men—particularly the self-involved doctors who ought to know better—immediately accepted my explanation that I took a tumble down my stairs. I embellished it with a dingbat smile: "Klutzy me!" I stuck out my chest. Worked every time.

But once I was back in the office, Jeanie wasn't buying it. She pulled me aside, into a conference room. "You can't fool me," she said. "I know the signs. And you know I know all the signs."

Somehow, though, I'd forgotten. I'd forgotten about the man she was with before she found her sweet, kind, milquetoast husband. I'd forgotten about the man who almost killed her. I hadn't known her then, but we used to be close enough that she told me anyway.

"You're projecting," I said. Projecting. A Michael word. It meant that people see in others what they are themselves, or what they hope to be, or what they hope to avoid. Jeanie was seeing the life she never wanted to return to. She was trying to save me.

She shook her head. "I'm seeing what you can't. I should have left him a whole lot sooner than I did, but I was telling myself all kinds of bullshit. That I shouldn't have made him mad. That it was somehow my fault. If I just did everything better, if I could only be what he needed, then he'd stop."

"I'm sorry that happened to you, but that doesn't mean—"

"You didn't fall down any stairs."

Her eyes were penetrating, but I couldn't squirm. It would make me look like a liar. "Yes, I did."

"Who is he, really? This guy you're involved with."

"I told you and Nat all about him."

"No, you didn't. He sprouted up out of nowhere, after months of shitty Tinder dates, and I'm starting to think you were hiding him for a while. That you were just feeding us those stories to buy you some time." Shit, she was smart. I always knew that, but I didn't know she could be this challenging, that she could pin me to the wall like a bug. "And you weren't returning my texts very much, and that's not how it is with just any new man. That's how it is with an abuser. He isolates you. You're prey, and he's circling you and closing in."

I laughed, with effort. "You're way off, Jeanie."

"So tell me about him."

"What do you want to know?"

"His name, for starters."

"I'm sure I told you this. His name is Michael." I figured I'd minimize my outright lies. Michael was a very common name.

"What's his last name?"

"Why the inquisition?"

"Why can't you just answer the question?"

258

I decided to try a different tack. "I don't have anything to hide and neither does Michael. But you're right, I didn't fall down the stairs. I just didn't want everyone to know that I was mugged."

"You didn't want me to know? After everything I've told you over the years?" There it was again, the hurt. I hated doing that to her. She was a loyal friend; I just couldn't afford that right now.

"I knew you'd ask if I went to the police."

"You didn't?"

"No, I didn't. I didn't see his face. He pushed me down from behind and stole my cell phone and my cash. It was awful, and I didn't want to relive it for nothing, because that kind of stuff happens in Oakland all the time. Without a description, what would be the point of talking to the police?"

She stepped closer. "Come on, Flora," she said softly. "You don't need to protect him. What you need is to go to the police. Domestic violence is a crime. He assaulted you."

"Someone assaulted me, but I don't know who it was."

"I'm not going to judge you. I've done this dance myself. I walked into walls. I fell down stairs. I slammed my hand in a door. I was 'klutzy,' too."

"That was your dance. It's not mine."

She ignored me, caught up in a terrible reverie. "It starts with little things. He needs to know where you are all the time. He's jealous and possessive. He doesn't want you out of his sight; he needs to be in touch all the time." Boy, was she barking up the wrong tree. "At first, it seems flattering. You've never been with anyone so attentive. But he'll get more and more controlling, and he'll explode into anger, and he'll do—well, you already know what he'll do. He's doing it so early, too. Usually they wait longer before they pound your face." I tried to say something, but she wouldn't stop talking. It's like she couldn't. "I've told you all about how I covered up the bruises and I lied for him. I lied to myself. I was in deep, but you don't have to get there. Get out now."

"I don't want out."

She gripped my arm. "Tell me the truth, and I'll help you."

"I'm telling the truth! I was mugged. I can prove it." I wriggled out of her grasp and held up my phone. "See? It's new. A mugger stole the last one."

She hesitated. "I want to believe you."

"I know you're looking out for me. And seeing my face obviously triggered you." Triggered. Another term I'd learned from Michael. "Maybe there are things from your past that you still need to process."

"You're telling me that I need therapy?"

"You're seeing things that aren't there. I was mugged. My boyfriend doesn't abuse me; he cherishes me."

I was remembering last night—how he'd accepted my apology and the lovemaking that followed. It must have helped me to sound convincing because Jeanie looked troubled, like she was starting to question herself and not me. She was wondering if she was still so damaged that she was seeing things that weren't there.

"You amaze me," I said. "You come out of this horrible relationship and go on to find a wonderful husband and create a family. You're an inspiration. I want what you have, and I might have found it. Michael has been taking such great care of me since the mugging."

And before that? Fortunately, she didn't ask.

I hugged her. Then I wouldn't have to look into her eyes. "I'm good. I'm in love."

She wasn't going to let me off quite that easily. She retracted her head and searched my wrecked face. "For some men," she said, "this is love."

CHAPTER 50

GREER

"I'm so sorry," the harried-looking mom told me.

"It's fine," I said, smiling down at the ginger-haired little girl who'd wiped her grimy hands on my jeans and who was looking up at me with great curiosity. She sensed that I was an interloper, that none of the children running around the goat pen at the children's zoo belonged to me.

But they could, that was the thing. They easily could.

Maybe not easily, given my age. But plenty of the mothers looked older than I did, and there was no shortage of options with my bank account.

"It's completely okay," I told the little girl's mother. "She's adorable. I know how it is." Or I would.

She smiled at me gratefully. Then she addressed the child. "Let's go, Livvie. We've got horses to brush."

"Bye!" I waved at Livvie in an exaggerated way, and she gave me a delighted grin back. How old was she? Two? Three? I had no facility at guessing the ages of children. I'd never paid attention before.

But I could learn. I was a hard worker, and I'd become a full-time student. After all, I was already down to half days and titrating fast as Chenille had taken to her new role with alacrity. Power suited her. Power suits did, too. It was looking like I might never go back.

I would never have guessed that I could feel this way, that I could abdicate control happily. Yet here I was, in the middle of the afternoon at the children's zoo, and I felt if not at home, then the possibility of home. There were moms who were messy and moms who were put together and those in between. I didn't know what my mom wardrobe would be like, but the shopping could be fun.

I was observing the world of motherhood like an anthropologist in a foreign culture. In a way, it was. Typically, I went to the types of restaurants and bars for working lunches and dinners and drinks where no one would bring a child; I shopped at the same types of boutiques. I didn't go to Golden Gate Park on weekends or to summer festivals. Unintentionally, I'd ordered my life in such a way that I ran into kids as little as one could. Now I was tracking families like they were Bengal tigers, fascinating and rare.

What I was finding was that for as many moments of irritation, frustration, and horror I witnessed, there tended to be a corresponding number that elicited contentment and joy. I watched parents help their little ones feed a goat, and sure, there was corralling (of the children, not the goat), but it was accompanied by such unfettered delight (again, the child's, not the goat's). If you could slow down, if you had nowhere else to be, if you could stop the world and just be there to bask in it—what could be better or more precious?

There was no reason I couldn't be a stay-at-home mother. Devote myself entirely to the development of a human being. I could be the absolute opposite of my own parents, an idea that was enormously appealing.

It wouldn't be forever, of course. Soon enough, the little bugger would be headed off to preschool and then kindergarten. But for a while at least, I could be all about my child. That little boy or girl would know how valuable they were to me, that they were everything, and everyone wants to move through the world with that type of assurance. When they have it, they can do anything, be anything. They don't have to be a success, even. They don't have to pursue it with all they have, to the exclusion of relationships, to the denial of self. They don't need a lifetime of hollow victories.

I could do that for someone. Be that. What a staggering idea.

But first, I needed to hear from Dr. Michael. I couldn't call him first. I'd look desperate. After an exit like mine, you couldn't slink back. You had to wait until you were pursued. He'd come crawling. He had to. I couldn't have been so wrong in my read of him. I read men all the time for a living. Or I did.

He must have been thinking about me. He was just having to wrestle with his professional ethics, his conscience, whatever. He'd call.

If he didn't do it soon, though, I'd have to figure out how to prod him a little. How to push the thought of me to the front of his brain.

I'd been doing a little cyberstalking, trying to get some clues as to the best way to approach without approaching. I couldn't just send him a friend request—again, too desperate. But could I show up in his social media feeds by some other, subtler means? Perhaps a targeted ad that he wouldn't know was targeted, one for my company, with a great press shot of me.

The problem was, I hadn't been able to find him on any social media, not under the name Michael Baylor. It's possible he was protecting his privacy by using a pseudonym to avoid situations just like the one I was mulling. As a therapist, he probably wanted to remain a blank slate for his clients so they could do all their transferring. Wasn't that what he called it? Transference, that was it. He said that was why I wanted him to impregnate me, because I was confusing him with someone else. Like with my father.

Bullshit. That wasn't at all what this was about.

I didn't have to date him. I didn't need to hear a bunch of his high school anecdotes or get the rundown on all his ex-girlfriends. I'd felt him in the room with me. I knew him.

I could tell he had a good heart and he wanted to help people, but he was no altruist. No goody-goody. He had a more dangerous side that he had to rein in, and that was part of what attracted me. He'd get close to the third rail and pull back.

He was going to call. He wouldn't be able to resist.

The fact was, the kind of therapist who was always by the book wouldn't have lasted more than a session with me. And he definitely wouldn't be the man I wanted to father my child.

The problem with donor profiles was that the people (women?) who wrote them sanded off all the men's rough edges. They'd been neutered. No hint of danger there. It'd be like mating with Big Bird. It might sound crazy, but even though we were just talking about sperm, I wanted to feel like the donor was sexy.

Dr. Michael was, for some complicated reason, sexy.

Though I didn't intend to sleep with him. I planned to get his donation, go to the clinic, and have the professionals handle the rest. That was the safest route, for many reasons.

Dr. Michael was the one. Now I just had to become the one myself. I had to be mother material, and fast.

Call, Michael. You know you want to.

Before I had to do something truly desperate.

CHAPTER 51

LUCINDA

There were houses, other people's houses. Men's houses, mostly. Cassie was told to wait somewhere—it could be any room; it didn't seem to matter to her mother. Mommy had other things on her mind. Mommy wanted the men to put the needle in her arm, though there was no thread attached to it, and then she'd get that look on her face, like she was floating, and afterward she'd sleep. Sometimes the men only waited until the floating, and sometimes they waited for the sleeping. But that didn't matter, either. Cassie knew Mommy wasn't going to help her, even if she screamed.

She never screamed, though, because she knew these were not good men. Why didn't her mommy know that? How could Cassie tell her? Cassie was only five. She didn't have the words, even if she hadn't been so scared. She was a late talker, and she didn't have all the words the other kids her age had.

The closet could save her at home, but she was too afraid to go opening doors in the men's filthy apartments and houses. She thought that if they caught her, they might do something awful. More awful than what they already sometimes did. But they didn't always do it, and that's why she needed to just stay as small and quiet as she could. She hoped they wouldn't notice her. Just don't move, *she'd tell herself.* Just stay still and maybe . . .

But maybe not. One of the worst parts was that she never knew. She might be left alone, or she might have their dirty fingers or their dirty mouths on her body, or they might want her fingers or her mouth on theirs. Sometimes they tried to bribe her with candy; sometimes they didn't bother, they just grabbed her. She was only five. It was a small mouth, and one time she threw up, and the man threw her. She smashed into the wall and she cried, but silently. Her mommy didn't wake up, not for a long time.

So at home, the closet saved her from the bad thing, but the bad thing got her anyway, in the end.

Poor little Cassie. Poor little me.

"That's it," Dr. Baylor said. "Let yourself go there."

"I don't want to."

"The sadness is better than the shame. The sadness is deserved. The anger, too. You can get mad at her."

"I don't want to do that, either." Every day, a small part of me was waiting to hear from her. All this time, and I still didn't know what to say. I wanted to start from now, as if none of it had ever happened. As if she hadn't failed to protect me when I was little, and as if I hadn't failed to protect her years later, when I should have gone to her and told her that Adam was . . . that he was . . .

Dr. Baylor scooted his chair forward. "Pretend I'm her. You're not five years old anymore. Find your words."

"There's nothing to say. It was a long time ago, and she tried to make it up to me. She was a good mother."

"I took you to those places because I needed my fix. Because for a while, I loved drugs more than anything else, including you."

Tears ran down my face. "Please stop."

"I was a terrible mother for years, Lucy. No wonder you were so furious with me. No wonder you wanted to get back at me by seducing my husband."

Even though he hadn't made his voice higher, it was like I could see her there, talking to me. I could see myself through her eyes.

"I wasn't furious," I said. "At least, not that I knew."

"And I wasn't a terrible mother. At least, not that I knew."

"You weren't terrible! Don't say that."

"I was, until I wasn't. Then I tried too hard, but maybe it was too late. The damage was done."

I stared at him—at her. "You mean I'd already turned bad?"

"I mean the damage to our relationship had been done. And yes, you were harmed, but you've gone on to become such a beautiful person. A talented, beautiful, loving woman."

"I'm not. I'm a mess." The snot was flowing down to my mouth; I could taste the salt. Where was his trusty tissue box when I needed it?

"No, that's an old story. Look at yourself now."

"I can't."

"You have to. See what you've become, and then you can forgive us both. You can forgive me for how I neglected you and exposed you to abuse, and you can forgive yourself for what Adam did to you."

"For how I seduced him. You said it yourself. I did it to get back at you."

"But he was the adult, and you were the child. I get that now. And I forgive you."

I let out a sob. "No, you can't. I don't deserve it."

"Of course you do. But can you forgive me?"

"There's nothing to forgive. You got clean, and you were a loving, attentive mother. You went back to school, and you helped other people. I was so proud of you. You're a good person, and I'm not."

"That's an old story, Lucy."

I put my head in my hands, weeping. "It's the only story I know."

I felt Dr. Baylor's weight on the couch beside me, his voice close to my ear. "It's time to tell a new story."

I'd always felt so much guilt—how could I have done this to the mother who'd been at every school assembly and baked so many cookies and loved me, oh, how she'd loved me?—but Dr. Baylor had his hand on my shoulder, and he was telling me that my anger was righteous; it had been directed at the mother who came before. "Even though you didn't remember," he said, "you knew. You were a small child, left to fend for yourself, and you were victimized. Consciously, you were only allowed to feel love for your mother, but subconsciously, you were full of rage. That was how you protected yourself. You thought you loved Adam, but that wasn't love. You're just coming into your ability to love."

I lifted my face. "Here, with you. I'm learning to love, here, on this couch, with you." I meant on non-Wednesdays.

"Our work is for you to be able to separate love from hate. To be able to love in a pure and healthy way. To take care of someone and be taken care of."

"Right," I said. "With you."

"I'm just the vehicle. You need to find your love outside this room." Was that a promise? That someday he and I would emerge into real life?

I hoped so. I'd make it so.

I started to smile, just a little. Dr. Baylor left the couch and returned to his chair. "Thank you," he said.

"For what?"

"For letting me be a part of your recovery. For letting me bear witness."

"You do a lot more than that."

"It's all you, Lucy."

When I stepped out onto the street, it was like I was levitating. But then I saw that woman again, the one with the bruises, now considerably faded or possibly concealed, inside her parked car. No sunglasses today. Last time, I hadn't been sure if she was really looking at me. But this time, it was undeniable. In her eyes was pure hatred.

I stopped, staring back. She dropped her gaze first, and then I got it. I knew who she was.

Dr. Baylor had said that assertiveness is a little bit of anger crossed with self-esteem. It's knowing that no one has the right to mistreat you. Not ever again.

I strode up to her car. I felt this tingling all through my limbs, and it was probably adrenaline, though it felt like the origin story in a superhero movie, the moment when someone got bitten by a radioactive spider or drank an isotope. When that person was infused by a force greater than themselves.

She was doing that same thing as last time: staring straight ahead, her windows rolled up. I knocked on the passenger side. I could see her jaw working, just a little. She was nervous again. She was also ignoring me.

I walked around to the driver's side. "I know who you are," I said loudly. "I heard you and Michael that day in the waiting room." Then, still at top volume but tinged with empathy, I added, "I know it's hard, losing a man like him, but this isn't good for you."

Her jaw twitched, but she wouldn't give me the satisfaction of looking at me. She was trying to maintain her pride. I could understand that. But stalking her ex wasn't going to help, and from her reaction, I could tell I was right. She was there about Michael.

"Does he know you're out here?" I said.

She started up the engine and yelled, "Get away from my car!" And I listened, because I had the distinct feeling that if I didn't, she might just run me over.

It was only after she'd left, tires squealing just like last time, and I was alone on the pavement, that I wondered: Last time, she'd had a bruise on her face. Had Michael put it there?

And was she really his ex?

CHAPTER 52

FLORA

It hadn't been my fevered, jealous mind. It was true.

The giraffe had called him "Michael," and she knew about me. That must mean he told her. And he must have also told her he was done with me. Otherwise, why would she have talked about losing a man like Michael?

Her voice was kind, but she was threatening me. She was going to tell him that I was out there. I'd still been nursing the hope that he didn't know. The apology the other night had gone so well, and so had the lovemaking.

No, it hadn't been lovemaking. Not if he could turn around and tell the giraffe that he'd broken up with me.

My hands were shaking on the wheel as I drove. I knew I shouldn't have done it again; I shouldn't have gone back to watch the Wednesday lineup. But my intuition had guided me there. I'd known that however things appeared on the surface, the center could not hold. Our relationship was fragile. We were inside a snow globe, and it could be dropped, and shattered, at any time. Was it in the blonde giraffe's hand right now?

He was lying to her, though. We weren't over. I was the one in his bed, not her. He was ministering to me, helping me recover from the mugging.

But she was the one on his couch, and maybe that was the better spot.

I'd already apologized in a general way; I could get more specific. I could tell him that I'd gotten insecure and decided to check up on him. I could say, truthfully, that I hadn't even known what I was looking for. It wasn't like I thought he wouldn't be there, that he was pretending to be at work. He was dedicated.

Too dedicated.

He was cheating on me with his client, and I was the one panicked about how I'd explain myself. He should explain himself. I was the one with the evidence. I could go to his licensure board anytime and blow the whistle. I had the selfies I'd taken in bed with him while he was sleeping, date-stamped. Almost like I knew it would come to this someday.

No, I'd just wanted to be able to see him throughout the day. To stoke my memory. To remember every second with him. To feel loved. To know it had been real.

My cell rang. I went ahead and pulled over, since I was shaking too much to drive safely. The highway overpass was on my left; beautiful houses were on my right. I didn't know how they could stand the noise. But then, I did know that over time, the intolerable became bearable. It could seem almost normal.

Young was the one calling, and curiosity compelled my hand. "Hello?" I said.

"Hi, Flora. It's Young. How are you?"

271

"Fine."

I didn't sound at all fine, but he wasn't going to step in that. "Good! Me too! I mean, I'm fine, too. A little better than that, actually."

"Glad to hear it," I said flatly.

"There's something I wanted to tell you myself. I know it's been a long time since we were together, and you might not care about this at all; you probably don't"—he wasn't normally a babbler—"but I wanted you to hear it from me and not the grapevine. Not that I'm sure if we have a grapevine between us—"

"What is it?"

"I'm engaged. We're getting married in a few months."

"Short engagement."

"You always were astute." He sounded admiring. The prick. "She's pregnant."

"On purpose?"

"We were planning to start a family someday, and God decided to bless us early."

I felt like pounding my steering wheel. How did he get there first, the prick?

I'd met Michael so long ago, as early as I could meet him, really, and here was Young, happy and starting a family. And worried about how I'd take it. After everything, he was the one worried about me.

He wasn't really a prick.

He went to couples therapy. He tried to save our marriage. He listened to everything our therapist told him, to the letter, and it all just made me think of him as weak and unattractive. He was sharing his feelings, being sensitive to mine, initiating sex in romantic and thoughtful ways, being an attentive husband and lover.

But it just drove me away. Like our therapist knew it would. Because our therapist had my number. He knew that what would get me was the push-pull: the "you're my everything" paired with "no one can know about us." The mixed messages. The drama. That was what had kept me in my marriage for all those years, that Young was . . . not indifferent but a little bit inaccessible. The same thing that had kept me in heat for two years, like our therapist knew it would.

He'd been playing me this whole time, hadn't he?

Not Young, of course. He was too simple for that. Michael.

But why? Could it be because he really did love me? He was desperate to keep me. He knew that everything was psychology, including (especially) love.

I remembered when I told Young that our marriage was over. I'd been so concerned about his feelings, not wanting to hurt him after he'd done everything in his power to make us work. He was blameless. But I didn't feel like I was to blame, either. Meeting Michael was fate; it was bigger than all of us. There was nothing I could do but submit.

Not that I told Young that. I just said that in my individual sessions, I'd been learning how screwed up I was, and that I'd realized I needed to be alone. "You're a wonderful man," I said, "and I appreciate all you've done, but I need a divorce."

In short order, he agreed that I was too fucked up to be married. Not in those words, but I got the gist.

In the weeks that followed, as arrangements were made, I could see relief peeking around the edges of everything Young said and did. Everything had been working out better than I could have hoped: Young would be okay, and I'd get Michael. Ha.

I'd been so careful with Young's feelings, so kind, like how Young was being with me now. He was returning the favor.

He wasn't a prick. He might have been the one that got away.

"I'm happy for you," I told him, and I tried to sound sincere, I really did.

"Are you okay?" he asked. "You seem like you're . . ."

Like I was crying. Somehow, I hadn't even noticed the tears starting. I hadn't known that the life I'd given up could still hurt me.

But what had I given it up for?

"I'm sorry," Young said. "I never meant to hurt you. I should have had more guts."

"What do you mean?"

"You must have realized it by now. You were always way smarter than me."

"Realized what?" My voice was loud and squawking.

"That I was doing what I always did, taking the easy way out. Coming at you with all the cheesy romance and the heavy talks, knowing it would just make you cringe. I got you to end things because it was easier than taking responsibility for what I really wanted."

Just when I thought I couldn't feel any more rejected.

"And I'm sorry for that."

He was a prick. Apologizing after all this time in a backhanded, I-never-wanted-you-anyway-that's-why-I-couldn't-get-hard-and-now-I'm-going-to-be-a-father-and-you're-all-alone-forever way?

"Fuck you," I said, hanging up and hurling the phone across the car.

CHAPTER 53

GREER

Technically, San Francisco was my turf, but Michael had picked such an unusual meeting spot that it was practically neutral: a Russian sweet shop in the Richmond neighborhood, where it was foggy all year round. We sat at one of the three iron tables. The proprietress had droopy skin and potato-sack clothes, and she gave us a wide berth. She may have been used to people choosing her establishment to discuss their unmentionables.

"How did you even find this place?" I asked him as I removed a candy from a bright-blue wrapper emblazoned with a dancing bear and popped it in my mouth.

Michael had eschewed all the sugar and was having a coffee, black. He looked different outside the office. More tired, maybe. Older, absolutely. He couldn't control the lighting in here, and it had never occurred to me before how forgiving his office was in that respect, softened light like Vaseline on a camera lens.

But his eyes were bluer than I'd realized, and I liked that his hair was tousled. His fisherman knit sweater made me want to curl up next to him and buffer myself against the miasmic weather outside.

Only this was business. I was here to broker a deal.

He ignored my question and asked one of his own: "So how are you, Greer?"

He didn't normally use my name. It was sexy, coming from him. We hadn't seen each other in more than two weeks. It felt long. "The sabbatical's going great. I've been visiting new parts of the city. The other day, I went to the children's zoo. And now, this place."

"The children's zoo, really?" He couldn't help it. He was insatiably curious. It was one of the qualities I wanted in my child.

"I'm like Jane Goodall with her chimps, only with motherhood. It's going to suit me."

"You're absolutely sure that this is what you want?" He took a sip of his coffee. I noticed that his hands were trembling the slightest bit as he replaced the cup.

"Yes. I don't care if I ever return to my company. Motherhood will be my life's work."

He nodded slowly. I assumed that he'd want to "unpack this" or maybe "explore it further." But he just drank his coffee.

"I didn't think that was an option before," I said, "with the way I was raised."

I was baiting him. He'd have to probe now that I'd opened the parent door. I didn't know why I even wanted him to do that, except that there might have been some things I'd inadequately considered. I told him I didn't need a therapist, but I wouldn't have minded thinking this through a little more with someone I trusted.

"I'm glad you're doing well," was all he said, and I had no right to feel disappointed. I'd flounced out of his office, effectively ending that relationship, on the gamble that I wanted his sperm more than his help.

"I'm glad you called. Does that mean what I think it does?"

Another slow nod. He was going to do it, but he was none too pleased. Or he was just in a lousy mood; what did I know? I couldn't let that deter me. I was going to get what I wanted.

"You're going to do it?" I said.

He paused. "I want you to have what you want."

It sounded practiced. There was no true feeling behind it. "It's not what you want, though."

"If it's not me, it'll just be someone else, and I don't want that."

Was he telling me he had feelings for me, that he couldn't imagine me pregnant with another man's baby, even if that man was basically anonymous?

"I'm healthy," he said, "and I'm from a strong gene pool. No cancer, no heart disease, no diabetes. Everyone dies peacefully in their sleep in their eighties and nineties. My grandmother lived to a hundred and four."

"You're saying you're better than anyone else I can find."

He met my eyes finally. "You and I have a lot in common. I'm not cut out to be partnered, either, or a full-time father. But to have some sort of relationship with a child, however unconventional—the more I think about it, the more appealing it is."

"You want to be involved?" I hadn't dared hope for this. The idea of not being entirely on my own, and of having a male influence, and of having Michael still in my life in some capacity . . . Let's just say, it wasn't unpleasant.

"I don't want custody. I don't want to step on your toes. You'd be the mother, and you'd make all the decisions. But yes, I'd like to have some involvement."

"I'm open to that."

Then he said something else unexpected: "So that's one of my terms, and the other is a fair compensation."

I was momentarily speechless. I'd come to make a deal, and I had all my arguments lined up. But I'd thought it would be pass/fail, a yes or a no. I didn't think what it would be worth to me or if the fact that he could be so mercenary should be a rule-out.

Then I smiled. He was a therapist and a businessman. I always knew he was too smart to be a complete altruist. In other words, he had the left and the right brain. Rule him out? This was a bonus.

"What's your number?" I said.

He smiled back. It was like we were flirting, except we both also knew it was serious business. Which could be flirting. A negotiation was a dance.

For me, this interaction wasn't about the money; I had more of it than I could spend. It was about the dance. How we moved together. The chemistry.

"What's it worth to you, Greer?" he said.

My name again. Did he know how that affected me, hearing it from his lips?

"Our baby. What's she worth?"

"You think it'll be a girl?"

"Apparently I do."

Our smiles broadened, as joyously as if she were already here.

This was crazy, wasn't it? We were talking about money and babies in practically the same breath. But the fact that we could do that so easily, that neither of us was spooked, that, if anything, we were turned on . . . we were great dance partners.

A partner. I could have a partner on this life-changing adventure. Not in a traditional sense, but that was okay by me. Better than okay. As he said, neither of us was cut out for conventional.

"What do you need?" I asked him. "Give me your number."

His smile wobbled, just a little. He wouldn't be asking if he didn't need to, and he had hoped he could flirt and shimmy and keep me from seeing.

"If we're going to do this, we have to be honest," I said.

"A hundred thousand," he said.

I could have played hardball. I could have made him work for it, but this was my future baby daddy. I wanted to start off on the right foot. "Deal."

CHAPTER 54

LUCINDA

Ten minutes till five, and I was behind on my proofreading. I'd have to work at home tonight to get it done by the deadline, but I was confident I'd be able to. I was confident about everything these days.

"Lucinda."

I startled. Christine's voice was deep and raspy, startling under the best of circumstances. I swiveled in my chair to face her, forcing a smile. "Hi."

"Come in my office." She didn't bother with the smile. As usual. I followed her, not unduly alarmed. "Shut the door."

I took the seat across from her. The office was a mess. As usual. I didn't know how she could work that way. No, I did know. She was a lousy editor. She insisted she couldn't read anything on the computer, it all had to be printed out, so she was surrounded by towering piles. She must have thought it made her look literary rather than disorganized.

She pushed her glasses up, turning them into a headband for her artificially black curly hair. She squinted at me. Normally, I'd hate the scrutiny, but with the way I'd been feeling lately, I stared back. Bring it on.

"It's come to my attention," she said, "that you've been doing your own writing during company time."

I didn't think she could see past the end of her nose, or past these piles. I had no prepared answer.

"That's time theft. You could be fired for much less."

Should I deny it? Apologize and throw myself on her mercy? I didn't want this job, but I didn't want to start looking for another one, not when I was halfway through my book, when it and Dr. Baylor/Michael were all that mattered.

"But you're very lucky."

"Why's that?" I finally managed, since she was obviously waiting for me to draw my good fortune out of her. She was enjoying this, having me on the hook, in the same way she'd always enjoyed rejecting my suggestions. Now that was an abuse of power.

"Because I'm going to allow you to complete the book—not on company time, of course—and submit it on an exclusive basis. As in, I have the right of first refusal. There are obviously significant structural problems, and sometimes it's a bit overwrought. Melodramatic, even. But it has potential, I'll give you that."

She read my book, without permission. She read my life.

She must have been able to see the pure hatred in my eyes, because she shut the fuck up for once. It was her turn to be startled.

"You had no right," I said.

"It was on your work computer." She said each word slowly to emphasize my stupidity.

"But you knew it wasn't a work product. You knew it was mine."

"I have every right to know what my employee is doing on my time."

"Once you realized it was my private property, you should have stopped reading."

Her eyes widened. "Are you actually questioning *my* ethics? You've been caught red-handed! I could fire you right now!"

I dropped my eyes. I needed to look ashamed, and I had plenty of practice at that. "I'm sorry," I nearly whimpered. Be subservient. Beg for mercy. It was what she wanted. Well, that and to have the first crack at my book. But I knew she'd give me some shit offer. Those were the only offers she was authorized to make. This wasn't a major publishing house, and if I sold it to her, I'd get basically no publicity or marketing support. It'd be like flushing all my hard work down the drain.

And Christine would be my editor. I couldn't even . . .

But I needed to keep the job. I'd just say what she needed to hear and work the rest out later. I could tell her I got writer's block and wasn't able to finish. Meanwhile, I'd be shopping for a literary agent, and then my agent would shop for a publisher, and once I had a deal in my hand, I'd throw it in Christine's nasty blackmailing face.

Because that was what this was, essentially. She was saying that she wasn't going to fire me, and in exchange, I'd let her have my firstborn. That's if she wanted it.

Of course she'd want it. It was a hundred times better than anything she was currently publishing, and even she must have been able to see that. Not that she'd admit it. Oh no. There was no use paying me a real compliment when she could insult and extort me all at once.

"Why do you hate me?" I asked her. I made my tone pitiable, piti-ful, even, but it was a genuine question.

"Hate you?" She couldn't have been faking shock like that. "I barely think of you!"

It was about the most rotten thing anyone could say, and it was obviously true. She hadn't had time to calculate a dagger. "But you like my book."

"I'm willing to *consider* your book. That's if you stop writing during the workday, and that includes lunch."

"I can't write on my lunch break?"

She shook her head. "You have to earn my trust back, Lucinda. Don't you see that this is a huge violation?"

Like she knew anything about violation. But I kept my eyes averted. Shame, think shame. Portray shame. "I do," I said, sotto voce. "I'm really sorry, Christine."

"That's not really good enough." She sighed. "But that's all for now."

I was being upbraided and dismissed. And I had to take it. For now. I stood up. "Thanks for giving me another chance. You won't regret it."

"I hope not." Then her face changed, practically liquefying with sympathy. "You're Cassie, right?"

I hadn't thought she could say anything worse in this conversation, but there it was. "No. She's a character. It's a novel."

She didn't believe me. "Well, then," she said, "good work. She's very realistic."

I thought she'd said it was melodramatic.

"Thank you," I said again, and as I started to leave, my limbs threatened to buckle. I couldn't tell if I was more scared or angry or humiliated. It could have been an amalgam of all three.

It was hard to drive home, but the alternative was staying in the lioness's den, and that wasn't going to happen. Before I left, I emailed my latest draft to myself, and then I deleted it from the computer. But I was sure it was stored somewhere else, that IT could recover it, or that Christine had taken the liberty of saving a copy. I didn't think she'd post it anywhere or share it with my colleagues, but I couldn't know for sure.

She'd used the word *violation*, like she had any fucking idea.

I'd been writing my life, and now it was in the possession of my narcissistic boss. She must have printed it out, and it was sitting there in one of her paper stacks. It was in her brain. She knew it was me, and I couldn't do anything about that, short of giving her a lobotomy, and with the way I felt right then, it seemed like a very real and tempting option.

How proud Dr. Baylor would have been. I was so in touch with my anger.

I pulled up in front of my house, and I blinked. Was that a mirage?

No, it was my mother, on the front steps. She stood up and waved. She looked so gray in her hair and in her pallor. So old. But it was my mommy.

I ran to her, and she held me as I cried. "I'm so sorry," she said over and over. She thought she'd done this to me. But I knew I'd done it to myself.

Finally, I was cried out. We sat down on the steps. "I'd invite you in," I said, "but I have roommates."

"We could go out to eat."

"I don't think I can eat."

"I made you a pie. Apple rhubarb." She patted the paper bag I hadn't noticed.

She'd disappeared for months, refused to answer any of my calls or texts, and she'd brought me pie, like that was supposed to make it all okay?

But it was my favorite, and I really could have used pie right then.

Like she could hear my thoughts, she pulled it from the bag, removed the cellophane from the top, and handed it to me, along with a fork. I devoured it, which was both a stalling tactic and a comfort. She was a great baker. It was something she'd taken up after her recovery, and during my elementary school years, the house had smelled heavenly.

"I wanted to reach out to you sooner," she said, "but I didn't know what to say. I was having so many feelings; I didn't know how to sort them. Feelings about you, and about Adam, and about me and my role in all of it. I was having to rewrite my whole life, if that makes sense."

I certainly understood about rewriting, and about too many feelings to sort. But I just kept eating and let her keep talking.

"Not for the first time. The truth is, before Adam got sick, before he made his big confession, we were already in trouble. Things had been deteriorating for a while." So that was why the house looked like that. "I'd found out that there were a few other women, and he swore it was nobody serious, so I was trying to forgive him. When he started losing weight, I thought it was guilt eating away at him. Once he got the diagnosis, it sounds so stupid, now that I know what he did to me all those years ago, but I panicked at the thought of losing him. It reactivated all my love for him. He seemed like he was giving up, refusing the chemo, and I was trying so hard to keep him alive. And then he told me the first time he cheated on me had been with you."

I put my fork down. I was bloated and sick.

"I went back over everything, dredging up all my old memories. I should have seen what was happening back then, but to tell you the truth, I had no idea. Zero. As in, not one suspicion. Not even when you started to pull away from me. I just thought it was teenage hormones. I thought it was developmental. You know, like teenagers aren't supposed to be as close to their mothers as you and I were."

She was right; we had been. Until Adam, we used to talk for hours, and cuddle, and laugh. We were the envy of every other mother/daughter pair we knew.

"My friends with older children said that's just how it was, that I needed to let go and let God, like they say in the meetings, and you'd find your way back to me. But the distance remained, long after you grew up, and I still didn't get it. I just thought you stopped liking me or something. I didn't know, and what I realize now is that I never asked. I was too afraid to hear the answer."

"Because on some level, you did know." If not about Adam, then about what one of her dealers had done to me all those years ago.

"No. I didn't. That's what I mean about going back over my story, over all the stories. I'm looking for moments when I overruled my own

285

intuition, but they're not there. I wish they were, believe me. But I was just oblivious, and that's the worst part. Denial would be preferable to this kind of blind ignorance. To being so disconnected from you that I had no idea you were being abused by someone I'd brought into your life."

Tears pricked my eyes. "Adam wasn't the first," I said.

"What?"

"When you were still using. When I was five or even younger. I'm in therapy, and I've uncovered all these old memories. I used to hide in my closet when we were home. But there was this one man, and you'd take me to his house with you, and there was nowhere to hide."

She closed her eyes. "Oh God," she moaned. Then she was the one shaking and crying. I should have reached out to hold her like she held me, only I couldn't do it. I hated that some part of me wanted her to hurt, but I couldn't deny that it was there.

CHAPTER 55

FLORA

"You want to know how I'm doing? You really want to know?" Kate demanded.

"Yes, of course I do. That's why I'm asking." It really was. This was my first night in my own bed since the mugging. I had curled up and called Kate, hoping that we could push past the bullshit chasm and just be friends—be family—again. "I don't want to fight with you. I love you."

She snorted. "Yeah, you've been acting like it."

"Things have been tense since you came out here, that's true. You hate my boyfriend."

"It's bigger than that. I think he's a monster."

"A monster? Seriously, Kate?" I kicked off my covers. I was overheating.

"Two women have filed complaints against him with his licensure board. Both were withdrawn. Has he told you that?"

No, he hadn't. But of course he would have been embarrassed, and his accusers must have been lying. Otherwise, why would they have withdrawn their complaints? They were probably in love with him, like the blonde giraffe. Women were territorial. It was a dangerous business, being a desirable man treating needy women. Disturbed women, like the giraffe. The way she charged at me—it was like she really was an animal sprung from the zoo. So much aggression. I wanted to warn Michael, but how could I? I shouldn't have been there.

I'd been rethinking that confrontation with the giraffe. She said she'd overheard me in the waiting room, so it must have been the day I stormed in. Based on her eavesdropping, she could easily have assumed I was Michael's girlfriend, and given the vitriol, she further assumed that Michael and I had broken up. He hadn't told her anything.

In other words, nothing had changed. Michael had accepted my blanket apology, and now we were getting back on track.

Since the mugging, every time I was with Michael I'd been emphasizing my victimhood, acting like I couldn't handle normal life quite yet, in the hopes that he'd relish being my protector, that he wouldn't kick me out or confront me. So far, so good.

But it was hard to be in my own apartment, even for one night. I could understand why Michael wanted a little time to himself, with how solicitous he'd been. It must have been exhausting. I told him that we could just hang out, in different rooms, even. He didn't need to take care of me every minute; he could have some space. But he said he wanted to drink beer in his underwear and watch porn. He was probably kidding.

It was perfectly normal for him to want to be alone, and I had no real problem with beer or porn. But not knowing what he really was thinking or what he felt, not being able to read his face—it scared me.

"Yes, he told me what happened with those women," I lied to Kate. "Or rather, what didn't happen, which is why they withdrew their complaints."

"And you believe him?"

"Yes, Kate!" I nearly yelled, exasperated. "I believe him! I love him."

"Love is a terrible reason for believing him." Then she turned accusing. "But I thought we were going to talk about me."

"I'd rather talk about you! I'm sick of talking about Michael. You hate him, fine. You think he's a monster, which is ridiculous, but okay, I have to accept it. And you have to accept that he's not going anywhere."

"You only want to talk about me to avoid talking about him?"

I walked around the room, trying to discharge the energy coursing through me. "No, that's not it. I want to know how you are because I care."

Another snort. "Yeah, you care so much. That's why you took a full twenty-four hours to call and tell me that you were okay after the mugging."

"I'd just been attacked. I was trying to figure out whether to go to the police or not. You weren't the first thing on my mind, okay?"

"Did Michael tell you not to call me?"

"No." By a tacit understanding, neither of us mentioned Kate anymore.

"Did he tell you not to report it to the police?"

"No. He wanted me to. But I couldn't describe my attacker, so why bother? Why put myself through that?"

"Do you know what you put me through? I couldn't reach you. I was debating whether to call your parents and see if they'd heard from you, but I didn't want to freak them out. I was awake all night." She sounded like she was on the verge of tears, and I was chastened.

"I'm sorry. You're right, I should have called sooner."

"I've given this a lot of thought, and all I can tell you is, it's him or me. I can't be in your life and watch him destroy you."

I spun on my heel. "If you really think he's such a monster, you're going to leave me to him? Whatever happened to loyalty?"

"You won't let me help you, and I can't stand it. It's getting so that I . . ."

"You what?"

"It's not just him. I'm starting to hate you, too," she said, just above a whisper.

"You can't mean that."

"I've looked up to you my whole life, and I can't stand how you are now. You're weak and pathetic. You lie to me. You lie for him. You're choosing him over me—"

"You're out of your mind, do you know that?"

"You've got that backward." She was speaking in a way that was clipped and deliberate, very un-Kate. "You're going to find that out someday, and I'm not going to be around to see it."

CHAPTER 56

GREER

It shouldn't have felt like a date, but it did. Maybe that said something about how little dating I'd done over the past few years, or ever.

We'd hit the pavement after a multi-hour consultation with my attorney, working out the myriad protections for both Michael and me, given the peculiarity of our situation. We were heady and exhilarated. We were in this together, and we were starving.

Two hours later, at an old-school Italian joint in North Beach, we were stuffed full of pasta and cannoli and three cocktails apiece. "Once you're knocked up," Michael said, "there won't be any more evenings like this, not for a long while."

"Are you trying to scare me off, Baylor?" He laughed. "I can afford all the babysitting I want. I might get an au pair, brush up on my high school French."

"Is that the language you want the little one to pick up? Not sure it's got the most practical applications."

I polished off my martini. "I'm not sure you get to have an opinion on matters of the little one. Isn't that what we were just discussing with my attorney?"

"We haven't signed anything yet."

It was a high-voltage version of the sparring we used to do in session. Funny to think where we could take it if we wanted.

Did I want? Not tonight, good as I imagined it would feel. I didn't like dating, but I did like sex, with an actual human, and I hadn't had it in well over a year. Tonight, though, was too soon. Too fraught. As Michael pointed out, we hadn't signed anything yet.

"I'm not going in for all that your-life-is-over talk," I said. "Honestly, I feel like my life is just beginning."

He held up his cocktail as if in contemplation, ruby liquid glinting. I couldn't even remember what he'd ordered. "Don't be one of those women who lives through her kids, though, okay? I can't stop you; you're going to have all the control, but promise me."

"Was that the kind of mother you had?"

"Hey, I told you I'd give you my medical history. I didn't say I'd let you psychoanalyze."

"Oh, so you can do it, but I can't?"

"You paid me for it."

"Now I'm paying you for something else."

He leaned forward, his eyes intent on mine. "And what's that?"

"My future. I deserve to know."

"Know what?"

"Who and what shaped you."

"Isn't it enough that you've seen the shape I'm in?"

He could act cute—he *was* cute—but he wasn't going to skate out of my grasp that easily. He needed that $100,000, and he was going to earn it.

"Okay," he said finally, "what do you want to know?"

I stroked an imaginary beard and made my voice deeper. "Tell me about your mother."

He told me that she'd been the opposite of mine—utterly suffocating. Her happiness entirely depended on him. He was terrified to disappoint her. He had to move across the country to escape the weight of her expectations, and even now, her neediness could feel overwhelming, but still, he tried. You would have thought that with a mom like that, he would have retreated into a selfish profession, but instead, he tried to help even more people.

The waiter dropped off the check, and Michael grabbed for it. I appreciated the gesture, though it was a little silly given the apparent disparity in our finances. Not that I'd asked him for a bank statement, or that I would, but if all was well and solvent, I liked to think he would have donated gratis.

I didn't want to insult his manhood by insisting on paying. I thanked him and suggested we go to a bar up the street. "I'm buying," I said, "and I won't take no for an answer."

"Somehow, I knew that about you," he said, and we both laughed.

We stayed at the bar until closing. I found out more about his childhood and about how he sowed his oats into adulthood. He confessed that he'd been with a lot of women. "But when I'm committed, I'm committed. If anything, I try too hard to make it work. I hang around too long. I'm the one who's saying, 'Don't go, let's give it one more chance.' I don't want to give up if there's even a single ember burning."

"So you're needy and pathetic, basically."

He laughed, but I realized it was nervous. "Have I scared you off?"

I shook my head. I'd already sensed he was complicated, and I didn't want to create a simple human being.

No, there was nothing simple about any of this, and that suited me fine.

CHAPTER 57

LUCINDA

Michael's (ex?)-girlfriend wasn't in her car when I arrived, and I knew that because ever since my boss hacked my computer and my mother showed up on my doorstep, I'd been twitchy, perpetually looking over my shoulder, stomach pretzeled. I couldn't write anymore. I could barely think, except that I was thinking all the time at a terrifying velocity. I was panicked, wondering who knew my past, my secrets, who could see my shame, which was back, full-force, like riding a bike.

My mother took full responsibility, said everything had been her fault, she'd been derelict of duty, but somehow, that had made me feel the opposite, like I was entirely to blame. Now I was all pure, roaring feelings, every one of them bad. It was like I was back in those men's houses—there was no place to hide.

I didn't even know who I was upset with anymore, if there was anything or anyone I wasn't upset with, and of course that included me. For the first time, it also included Dr. Baylor/Michael.

He wanted to be Dr. Baylor tonight, but I needed him to be Michael.

"I see that it's hard for you to sit still," he said, looking down at my gyrating legs. "Has something happened?"

"Too much," I said.

"Let's start with some deep breathing. Just breathe with me." He inhaled, watching to see if I'd follow suit.

"That's not what I need." I approached him. "What I need is for you to fuck me senseless."

He got this shocked look, as if we'd never done it before. "What you're asking is—"

"I'm not asking. I'm telling you." I grabbed his hand and put it on my breast. He pulled away immediately. "Isn't this what you wanted? For me to assert myself? To find my power? Well, I'm doing that. I need you to fuck me now."

"Sit down, Lucy," he said. His face and voice were stern. He was letting me know he was in charge. And what pissed me off was that I could feel it working. I never had a father around, but I was still somehow programmed to listen to male authority.

I flopped down on the couch, my legs spread wide in defiance. "Fuck you, Michael." Now I sounded like his petulant child.

"I'm worried about you. You're decompensating."

"What does that even mean? Don't talk to me like that." Like a shrink, when I needed a lover. Our arrangement was bullshit, and I could see that now. Bifurcating our treatment, trying to keep things separate—that wasn't how people worked. I needed him now, and he didn't even care.

"It means you're unraveling. Things are moving too far and too fast. It's possible I'm out of my depth."

"What are you saying?" My legs had gone still. Too still. Like they were paralyzed or belonged to someone else.

"We may have taken things as far as we can, in terms of our work together. I know a very good trauma specialist—"

"That's one of your specialties, isn't it?"

"A very good female trauma specialist." He didn't particularly emphasize the word *female*, but it ricocheted through me like a bullet. "Dr. Devers, remember? I told you that sometimes I consult about you."

"You can't just throw me away."

"It's not like that. This is about what's best for you." He ran his hand through his hair, visibly distressed. About losing me? About screwing me up? About screwing me?

"You're what's best for me."

"It wouldn't have to happen immediately. We could take some time with the transition. You and I have a few more sessions, and then a joint session with Dr. Devers. A medication evaluation with a psychiatrist would be recommended."

I glared at him. "Recommended by whom? I'm an editor. I don't like the passive voice. Be active. Say what you mean. You think I need to be drugged?"

"It would just be an evaluation. You'd gather information and then make a decision about whether medication is right for you."

"You sound like an ad. 'Talk to your physician and see if Happy Pills are right for you!'" I made my voice high and mocking.

"There are no happy pills, Lucy." As if to underscore that, he sounded truly sorrowful. Because he was going to miss me? Because he regretted what we'd been doing? Because he thought I was beyond repair, a car in flames, and he was just trying to get away, un-singed?

"Why do you think I need drugs?"

"You've been having mood swings lately. You've been so up and so down. Problems with stability and impulse control."

"My mother showed up! My boss read my book! Who wouldn't have problems with stability and impulse control?"

"I didn't know about any of that. You didn't tell me."

Unbelievable. He wanted to off-load me, and he was going to make me sound as bad as he could to make it happen.

All these sessions where he'd tried to empower me, and now my therapist was trying to convince me I was crazy.

". . . I care for you so much, Lucy, and I just want you to find relief, to find some peace—"

I couldn't listen anymore. Pure, roaring feelings, all of them bad. He was supposed to help me, but he just wanted to get away.

I stumbled out onto the street, and there she was in the car. Michael's ex, or maybe she was his current. She was his future, and I was just a joke.

Then I couldn't see her anymore because tears blinded me, and all the confidence I had, all my supposed power, was long gone.

PRESENT DAY

CHAPTER 58

DETECTIVE GREGORY PLATH

"Am I officially a suspect now?" Lucinda asks. Her legs are like twin tuning forks.

"You're a person of interest," I say.

"But I'm of greater interest than I used to be, it feels like. Should I have a lawyer here with me?"

These women and their lawyers. I feel a little bad for Lucinda. In a way, she's here because she's easier to bully than Greer, not because I think she's guiltier. Though I do think she might be guilty. I haven't ruled her out, not after what Flora told me.

"You can always have a lawyer," I tell her.

"But are you going to provide one for me?"

I smile. "Me, personally? You mean, am I going to spring for your representation? I can't really afford it on my salary."

Her legs are moving even faster now. "I mean the state or the city. Whoever it is who protects my rights."

"You're talking about a court-appointed attorney? A public defender?"

"Yes, a public defender."

"You have to meet certain criteria to be assigned a public defender, and it won't be until you're charged. If you think you need an attorney here during questioning because you've got something to hide, then it'll be on your dime."

"It's not that I have something to hide. It's that things are being misconstrued. Honestly, it feels like someone wants you to misconstrue them. Misdirection, is that the word?"

"You think one of your friends is making you look guilty on purpose?" Maybe both your "friends." I think both Greer and Flora are afraid to gun for each other, and they're both trying to make Lucinda the patsy. Or maybe Lucinda really is the killer.

"Couldn't you see through her? You're a smart guy." Suddenly, she's smiling at me. A Flora kind of smile. Seductive.

Where the fuck did that come from? She's a pretty girl, but it's more unsettling than it is sexy. "You seem different," I say. "Seems like you're done crying over this guy."

"Sometimes when I'm threatened, I get really calm. I'm good in a crisis."

"And I'm a threat? This is a crisis?"

"Wouldn't you think it was a threat and a crisis if someone was trying to pin a murder on you?"

"That's not what's happening here. I'm just trying to get some answers."

Her eyes burn into mine. "Yes, I was home alone, but I never would have done this to Michael. I don't hurt anyone except myself."

BEFORE

CHAPTER 59

FLORA

It hadn't been fifty minutes. The blonde giraffe should still have been in session, but there she was on the street, weeping, an absolute mess.

Good. Served her right.

But there was no time to gloat, because Michael had appeared. He looked frantic, about to give chase, though she'd gone only ten feet. She must have wanted him to come after her. That was the reason for her little performance. She had his number; she was speaking his language. She knew that he needed pursuit, and that was why she was going to win, and I was going to lose. He had me, but he didn't have her.

As if to prove it, he didn't see me; he only had eyes for her, but still, I sank down in my seat, my heart pounding.

I shouldn't have come here, obviously. But I couldn't stop myself. It was an addiction. I wanted a hit of the truth, and I just kept feeling like it was going to come out here, on this street.

I snuck a glance. Michael had gripped her by the arms, and he must have been telling her not to go, not to leave like this. Please.

That's what I imagined the closed captioning would read. From his body language, he was pleading with her.

He hadn't been pleading with me to stay lately. It was pretty much the opposite.

That was what I'd been doing wrong. His weakness was women who spurned him, like his mother had. In second grade, he'd come home to discover she was gone for good. In a way, he'd never really stopped searching for her. He was always looking for intense connections to women that were impossible to sustain. He made them impossible, throwing up roadblocks, and then he tried to get away. He told me about all the women and their grasping fingers and how he'd had to learn to be direct and somehow, I'd never thought that eventually that would be us. It would be me.

Michael had initially seen me as desirable and untouchable, incapable of metabolizing my husband's love. He'd pegged me as the perfect woman for him: the one who wasn't built for the long haul. We were probably supposed to burn out before the two years had been up. Great passion, insurmountable obstacles, that was what Michael was into.

What if Young and I had gone to see a different therapist, one who'd been trying to bring us together instead of tearing us apart? Ever since that talk with Young, my mind had been returning to those old sessions. Michael had pitted us against each other. Young had been trying to turn me off so that I'd end things, because Michael had tapped into Young's pathology. And Michael had also tapped into mine, which was why I'd resisted what I had thought were Young's sincere attempts to be close to me.

But Michael had a subconscious, too, and maybe it had been orchestrating the sessions. Maybe he'd wanted me so much that he couldn't help himself.

That had to be it. Because the alternative made him a monster.

CHAPTER 60

GREER

As I was lying in my paper gown on the exam room table, I could hear my parents' voices in my head, overlapping in their usual duet: "This isn't how things are done." "Listen to your mother." "Listen to your father." "You don't just rush in. Due diligence takes months if not years. You don't take unnecessary risks."

Well, this was a necessary risk, as I was on borrowed time. I had to go with my gut and put a baby in my uterus as quickly as possible. I didn't control when I ovulated, and why wait another month when I knew Michael was the one? We had the same deficits—I couldn't be a wife or have an equal partner in parenting beside me, I wanted the control too much, and he couldn't be a husband and a full father—so we were two wrongs that made a right. We were perfect for each other.

The sperm analysis showed that his was of high quality, and it had already been washed and processed by the fertility clinic. All dolled up for its big day. Now I was just waiting for the doctor to show up and perform the insertion. Michael and me and the doctor made three.

I'd been assured that intrauterine insemination (IUI) was likely the fastest route to where I wanted to go. There were no guarantees, either of pregnancy or of my being able to carry the baby to term, as I'd been reminded on countless forms. But I was hopeful. I had unlimited sperm (per my contract with Michael) and unlimited funds and unlimited determination. I wouldn't stop until my child was in my arms.

The thought made me smile. That was the endgame, and every day, I was surer of it. Surer of myself. I wasn't one of those women who was born to be a mother, but neither was my mom. No wonder it took me extra long to reach this point. Really, it was the same way with Michael. No one in his house made parenthood look appealing, either.

I kept thinking back to the other night in North Beach. I'd been a bit worried about how our chemistry would be affected by the change in venue, but it was still there. If anything, it had gotten stronger because now I knew so much about him: his past and what he wanted for his future.

I had to admit, I was excited to see where it would lead. I even had a dream the other night about his being in the delivery room when our baby was born, and I woke up as happy as I had after the manny dream. We still had so much to learn about each other. There was so much potential. It was an unconventional love story, of course, but those were the most interesting.

Not that it had to become love. That was the beauty of our arrangement. It didn't have to be anything other than a means to an end, but it could wind up surprising us. We'd left open the possibility.

There was a knock on the door, and Dr. Salton bounded in. He was young and handsome, the junior member of the practice. Since I had no known issues, no long history of disappointments, I didn't need the senior. "Good to see you again!" he said. "How are you feeling?"

"Excited."

"No nerves?"

"No. I've had plenty of Pap smears in my life. Use a small speculum, and we should be fine."

He laughed. "I like a woman who knows what she wants." From him, it was boyish rather than gross. He had me slide down the table (just a little farther, just a little farther, that's it) and I placed my feet in the stirrups. Then came the narration: first the speculum, might be a bit cold (it was), and afterward, "the sperm sample is being prepared for insertion." I stared up at the ceiling, wondering where Michael was as he was impregnating me. "Now you'll feel the catheter being inserted. There might be a little cramping," and just as he said it, I winced. It could have been the power of suggestion or the syringe pumping sperm into my cervix, but before I could determine, he told me it was over. He'd placed a sponge that I'd remove in a few hours. "It'll keep the sperm where we want it," he explained, removing his latex gloves and tossing them in the garbage.

"That's it?" I said. I'd expected something more momentous somehow. It didn't seem like new life—mine, a baby's—should start with disposable gloves.

"If you've got fifteen or twenty minutes to keep laying down, it could boost your chances."

I laughed. "Yes, I think I can find the time." I settled myself back against the exam table.

"Any questions for me?"

"No, I've read through all the paperwork. Now I just need my body to do its part. Could you hand me my cell?" It was stacked on top of my folded clothes on a chair.

"Sure thing." He handed it to me. "Enjoy your day."

After he'd left, I called Michael. One ring and into his voice mail. Had he sent me straight there? I shouldn't have felt hurt. This was a business arrangement, after all.

With potential.

"Hi, Michael," I said. "Well, it's done. I've taken the first step, the first insemination. Hopefully, it's the last." I could practically feel the cells proliferating. Or maybe that was just another cramp. I wished I could talk to him live, because my excitement was yielding to anxiety. But he wasn't my therapist anymore; it wasn't his job to talk me through this. Oddly, his job (the one I was paying a hundred grand for) might already be done.

I was hit with a wave of sadness. Someone should have been there with me, holding my hand. Someone should love me and the zygote inside me.

"If you feel like talking, give me a call. I'll keep you posted." My voice echoed in the room that suddenly felt so empty.

I didn't even know where the possible father of my baby was, who he was with. I didn't even know if he was in a relationship with another woman. He hadn't volunteered that he was, but he hadn't reassured me that he wasn't. I'd felt it would be inappropriate to ask.

I felt myself laughing, even as the tears rolled down my face. Like I knew anything about appropriate anymore.

What I knew was that I really, really wanted him to call me, but there was nothing in our contract that said he had to.

CHAPTER 61

LUCINDA

Love you! Hope you're having a good day!

For weeks and weeks, my mother had refused to text me back. Now I couldn't go more than a few hours without a text from her. She wanted me to absolve her, but I was in no position to absolve anyone.

I turned my phone off and got back to my work. In the office, I'd been trying to act normal, whatever that was. I'd planned to lie to Christine about writer's block, only it had manifested. It was a self-fulfilling prophecy, or perhaps a punishment. Without my novel, I was just a proofreader again.

I couldn't afford to do a shoddy job or miss any deadlines, because Christine was watching me. About once an hour, she circumnavigated the cubicle area before returning to her office. She wanted me to feel her eyes on me. Then when she stopped by my desk, she made it clear that she expected a continuous IV drip of gratitude for not having fired me, saying things like, "Another manager might not have been so forgiving."

The groveling stretched out before me, a road to nowhere. But I couldn't lose my job, since I didn't have the wherewithal to find a new one in my current condition. My destabilization. Mood swings and impulse control issues, wasn't that what Dr. Baylor had said?

Maybe I did need a psychiatrist and some medication. But what I didn't need was a new therapist. The thought of starting all over was heinous. The thought of losing Dr. Baylor/Michael was worse.

Outside his office building, under the watchful gaze of his (ex?) girlfriend, he'd wooed me back. "I was wrong," he said. "I make mistakes, too. Could you please forgive me?" He was so sincere, and I melted. He still wanted me.

Only I didn't feel as secure as I once had. The fact that he could even talk about foisting me onto someone else was telling, regardless of how fervidly and convincingly he'd walked it back. He'd been ready to let me go. I couldn't forget that.

I was hemorrhaging. Having sex with Michael last night temporarily stanched the bleeding. It was angry, and I'd pummeled him with my fists. He seemed to like it or, at least, feel he deserved it. The sex acted as a tourniquet, but the wound was still there. I felt it with each breath.

I was grateful for the proofreading—the commas, the semicolons, the minutiae, the complete insignificance of the manuscript. I couldn't be a part of anything that mattered right then. But when I wasn't working, my thoughts jumbled together, a discordant cacophony. I couldn't quiet them; I could only try to drown them out. I wasn't sleeping. I kept the TV on all night, Netflix marathons that were touted as 95 percent matches for me. Dysfunctional family dramas, one after the other. People breaking apart and coming back together. I lacked the volition to tell Netflix that was no match at all.

CHAPTER 62

FLORA

"Where've you been?" I snapped as I turned on the lamp beside me.

Michael blinked like he'd never seen his own living room before.

"You moved your key, but I found it under the mat. And you don't actually have an alarm system." It had occurred to me that after he ignored all my texts about Kate, he'd have to respond to Weymouth Security when told that he had an intruder. But they'd never shown up and neither had he. I'd been camped out in the living room in the dark for three hours, working myself up into a froth.

It wasn't all his fault, what happened to Kate. I let him come between us. I defended him until the end. Until what might be her end.

"Why didn't you answer my texts?" I said. Just ten days since the mugging, since we'd gotten close again, and now . . .

He closed the door behind him and sat down heavily on the couch opposite me. He looked terrible. Worse than exhausted, he was like a scooped-out melon. But this wasn't the time for my compassion. It was his moment of reckoning. He needed to face what he'd done.

"I'm sorry," he said. "I know you said it was an emergency about Kate, but I just didn't have it in me to—"

"My cousin, my best friend, is in a coma!"

"I didn't know that. You didn't say what the emergency was."

"She relapsed. I deserted her, and she overdosed, and she's in a coma. She might not wake up. She's probably a fucking vegetable, and her parents will have to pull the plug, and you didn't have it in you?" I thought I might honest to God smack him, at a minimum. I was up on my haunches, about to pounce, and he'd just collapsed into the sofa cushions, which infuriated me more.

"I'm sorry."

"That's all you've got?"

"What do you want me to say?" He sounded truly defeated.

"You're a therapist; this is a crisis! Say something that will help me!"

He shook his head. "I'm all talked out, Flora."

I leaped up and moved in front of him, shouting into his face. "She told me you were a monster! I said no way, you're a good man, you're my man, but you know what? She's right!"

But even as I said it, as I yelled it, I wanted him to prove her—to prove me—wrong. He stared down at the floor, and that made me even madder.

"She told me the truth about you. She told me you'd done this before. Two different women lodged complaints against you. This is a pattern for you, huh? It's just how you roll, taking advantage of women."

That got him. He was on his feet, screaming, "I tried to help you! I try to help everyone!"

"You helped yourself to me and to those other women! You took advantage of us!"

He sat back down, shaking his head, fighting to contain himself. I towered over him, feeling like some ridiculous impotent giant, but to sit, to follow suit, somehow felt like a concession. Now he was talking low, practically a mumble, more to himself than to me. "These fucking women. She breaks into my house to tell me that it's my fault her cousin overdosed." Then he looked right at me. "News flash. People are responsible for their own actions. If she felt like using, she should have called her sponsor. She should have done anything—except use. Did you ever think maybe she wanted to die? She had practically nothing in her life besides you. Would you want to live if you were her?"

His blow landed. When Kate said that I barely asked about her, that wasn't a recent development. Kate went to work and back home after. She had a few Twelve Step friends. Ask her what's new, and she'd say, "Nothing. What's new with you?" It was almost no life, and instead of my encouraging her to get one, I capitalized on it. She was just this waiting receptacle, someone I could always lean on, always so eager to listen to me, to laugh and to cry with me, until she got strong opinions about Michael, and then I turned against her.

No, it couldn't be. She hadn't tried to kill herself because of me.

"You see it now, don't you?" he said. "She was your therapist, and you took everything out of her. It does that, being there for people. She had nothing left in the tank. That's how I feel."

My head was spinning. Somehow, he'd gotten the upper hand, when I thought I finally had. I'd finally seen through the haze of my love for him, and I was going to confront him. Bring him low. Get him to admit to everything. Then I could forgive him. Maybe.

"This is crazy," I said.

"Yep. It's crazy that you're lying in wait for me so you can make me the bad guy and feel better about your cousin. I'm not the bad guy, but you're not, either. She's her own bad guy. She did this. She chose this."

"She didn't choose a coma."

"She risked a coma. Maybe it was because she wanted to die, or maybe it was because she wanted a few hours of oblivion and instead she got eternity. We can't know." For a second, I felt just a little comforted. He could be right, and we were all responsible for our own actions, and I could let go of the intolerable guilt I'd felt since I got my parents' call earlier tonight. "But you know what's also crazy? That you came here to play the victim."

"No, that's not me."

"Yes, apparently it is. Ever since the mugging. I know trauma, and you, Flora, were not traumatized. You saw an opportunity to get back into my bed, and you took it, and I was too weak to fight. I was too tired." He gave me a penetrating stare. "You're the one who's been taking advantage of me all this time. You seduced me in the sessions. You used all the compassion I had for you about your inability to love a man who was learning to treat you well. I'm a sucker for damaged women, and you must have figured that out. You all do."

All. As in, there had been others. Kate had been telling the truth.

Michael's the one with all the reasons to lie. How many reasons? How many women? At least two, based on those complaints that were filed and withdrawn.

He must have manipulated them into withdrawing the complaints, the same as he was manipulating me.

Because he was a monster, just like Kate said. I chose a monster over her, and now . . .

I stormed out of the house. There was no way I was going to let that monster see me cry ever again.

CHAPTER 63

GREER

"This is the first time it's even seemed possible that someone is growing inside me," I said. "I've always been so careful to avoid it." I was curled up on my sofa in front of a roaring fire (it's electric, but top-of-the-line and entirely convincing). I was drinking hot cocoa. Nesting, is that what they called this feeling, this pursuit of coziness, this need for home?

"You've never had a pregnancy scare?" he asked. I wished he were there in the room instead of on the phone, but tempting as it was, I wasn't going to be issuing an invitation. Therapists were big on boundaries, and I had always been, too. Maybe that was part of why I'd never had a pregnancy scare. I'd put up so many barriers in my life. But I was ready to let some of them drop.

Tonight was too soon, though. Michael and I could afford to wait for the right moment. Forty weeks of pregnancy, and afterward, we'd be bonded for life by having created a life and then by nurturing one.

"I've always been extremely careful." Also, I hadn't had that much sex in my life, by the standards of what would be termed my advanced maternal age. Only twelve partners, which meant that if Michael and I decided to give it a whirl, he'd be lucky thirteen. If the IUI had worked, then he already was lucky thirteen. Could we have gotten that lucky? My gut said yes, but it had no experience in these matters.

"I can't believe I might be a father soon!" He laughed, as if dazed.

"Haven't you done this before?"

"Honestly, no one chose my sperm the last time around. I guess I don't look that good on paper."

Huh. I'd come away from our conversation that day thinking he'd already made someone a mother. I must have misunderstood. "Were you bummed? Or were you relieved? You got to take the money and run."

"It wasn't much money. But yes, I was both bummed and relieved. Remember, I was young. I didn't know what I wanted."

"Do you know now?"

Another semidazed laugh.

"Well, I know what I want," I said. "And she—or he—might be inside me." Now I was the one laughing, with pure anticipatory joy. The joy of soon being joyous. "Do you think she's listening right now?"

"Your gut still says girl?"

"It's hoping for a girl."

"How come?"

I contemplated the crackling of my pseudo-fire. "I don't know. Girls seem easier to understand."

"Because you are one?"

"Can't you tell?"

"Just to play devil's advocate, boys are less complicated. They're more primal, less evolved, and they're more likely to worship you."

"Stereotype much?"

He chuckled. "You've found me out. Therapists can be judgmental, too."

"Were you judging me all those sessions, and you're good at concealing it?"

"I'm a human being. Judgments come with the territory. But when I'm in that chair, in that office, I'm a better version of myself. I can stay open-minded and suspend disbelief, and I'm seeing the best in other people. And I'm always getting surprised."

"So it's not an act; you just change once you walk out of the office?" That wasn't exactly welcome information. My initial affinity had been toward Dr. Michael. But no need to panic. I reminded myself that since Michael and I had been—what to call it? Courting?—I was still drawn to him.

"You make it sound like Superman and the phone booth," he joked.

"Don't flatter yourself."

"I like you, Greer. I like that you're just the same inside that room as you are out. You're a challenge. You challenge me."

There was nothing to worry about. Michael and I had been feeling each other since the day we met. It could be that I was finally part of some great romance that started with a very unusual meet-cute and ended with a family. I noticed that I'd been unconsciously running my hand over my flat belly.

"Hello?" he asked. "Have I made you uncomfortable?"

Quite the opposite. "I'm just reflecting."

"On?"

"How we started."

He let out a little sigh. "Part of me wishes we could freeze this moment and just live here in the fantasy, where anything's possible. Reality kills everything."

"What do you mean?"

"Nothing. Don't mind me. It's been a long day."

It was the first time in the conversation we were on different pages emotionally. His melancholy was bleeding through the phone line. "Has something happened?"

"I just had a breakup, that's all."

It wasn't a betrayal. It wasn't. I'd never asked, just assumed. Just hoped. "Did you break up with her, or did she finally manage to shake you off her pant leg?" I was trying to sound light, but the answer made a big difference.

"I broke up with her. The last embers were extinguished last night."

"Is it because of our arrangement?"

"No, it had been coming for a while. She didn't know anything about this or about you."

That was a sign of how wrong they'd been for each other, that he couldn't even tell her about something this life changing. Unless it was a sign that he didn't intend to have it change his life at all.

That was his prerogative. We'd signed all the papers, and he was free to do whatever he wanted. There was no obligation for him to be involved; I'd made sure he had no parental rights. The paperwork was written up much like that between an adoptive parent and a birth mother: If he wanted visitation, he could see the child up to twice a month, but he could never sue for custody. He was guaranteed limited access; I had control. He wasn't forced to have a relationship with his child or with me, but I'd been hoping that he'd want them. That he'd want us, me and the baby likely growing inside me.

"I'd want her to have your eyes," he said. "You have beautiful eyes." It was a non sequitur but a damn good one.

"I'd want her to have your emotional intelligence."

"Your grit."

I laughed. "I didn't know anyone said 'grit' anymore. Do you want her to have my gumption, too?"

"Yes, absolutely. But let's not stop there."

I settled back into the couch and let him sweet-talk me, my hands roaming over my abdomen lightly, like a prayer.

CHAPTER 64

LUCINDA

Dear Lucy,

They tell me it's just a matter of days now, and I don't have much energy left. I'll keep this short and sweet.

I don't know where I go after this. I don't know what punishment is coming to me. But in a weird way, I'm glad it's so close. I don't have to wait and wonder anymore or deal with my conscience. It's almost here.

But I hope it's not too hot. I always hated the heat.

Before I go, I want to say how sorry I am. At the time, I made so many excuses. You were so persistent, Lucy, and even though I said no a hundred times, even though I dreaded the sound of the front door closing behind your mom, even though I felt like maybe what you needed was a doctor, none of that matters. Because in the end, I did what I did. You were beautiful and you were telling me you loved me and I just broke. And there's no excuse for that, because you were supposed to be my daughter, and I was supposed to protect you, even from yourself.

I just hope you can have a real relationship with a man someday. Someone normal. Something normal. But the best kind of normal, you know? I hope you find true love and happiness.

From beyond,
Adam

The letter arrived the same day I got the message that he was dead. Divine intervention or just a fluke of the hospice mail? I didn't know.

What I knew was that Adam had no reason to lie. Which meant that what I'd told Dr. Baylor—what I'd been telling myself—was the lie.

I'd thought Adam and I were both eagerly anticipating the slam of the front door, that we couldn't wait to be together. I recalled it as so much love, and so much passion, that neither of us could resist. Instead, I'd just worn him down with my youthful vigor and my determination. Eventually, he'd given in, and I'd said to myself, "See? I knew it! He loved me all this time!"

Since reading the letter, I'd been drinking all night. That made it hard to think too clearly about what was real and what wasn't. My whole life, I'd avoided alcohol and drugs because of my mom. I'd feared my genes. But I read that letter and I headed to the store, straight for the booze aisle. Apparently, vodka and cranberry juice was my drink of choice.

I was flooded with things that (I thought) Dr. Baylor had said, across our sessions:

It's not uncommon for clients to develop feelings for their therapist. It's called transference. We can work through this. It can be grist for the mill.

It can't happen, Lucy.

No, Lucy.

You need to hear me, Lucy. No, it can't happen.

You're a beautiful, wonderful person, and I'm your therapist. Whatever feelings surface can't be acted on.

You might think it'll help you, but it'll only hurt you worse.

Trauma repetition is when you keep trying to replicate the past. You keep hoping for a different ending.

I'd pursued him relentlessly, just like I had with Adam. Then when Michael gave in, I tried to believe it was love. But maybe he'd always been Dr. Baylor; it had always been about his trying to fix me.

Case in point: He was avoiding me now. I texted him about meeting at his office, but he told me he couldn't. We'd see each other in session.

Just before I fell asleep, I finally returned my mother's myriad text messages: **Adam's dead.**

A smiley face came back.

CHAPTER 65

FLORA

"Maureen Hillard?" I said.

The woman looked up at me with a "do I know you?" expression. She'd just left her house and was about to get into her car, an Audi that looked to be new—purchased in the last year, which was when she'd withdrawn her complaint against Michael. She had lodged the complaint six months before that, though the alleged incidents occurred five years ago. Repeated sex in his office. He'd smartened up by the time he got to me.

I hadn't been able to find out the other woman's name, but I'd gotten lucky with Maureen. Some asshole was running a misogynistic website where he posted complaints that were later proven false or the accuser reneged; his point was that women weren't victims; they were liars. I have no idea how he got the paperwork or why it hadn't been taken down. Maybe it was because you had to be a real keyword jujitsu master like me to find it. But find it I had, and from there, it hadn't been hard to find Maureen Hillard.

She was pretty, if somewhat harried, and in her midthirties. Her hair was dyed dark red and parted in the center. Her roots needed to be retouched. Her eyes were bright blue and already suspicious.

"I wanted to ask you about Michael Baylor."

She yanked open the door. "I don't have anything to say about him."

"Did he really do what you alleged in your complaint? And if he did, why did you let him get away with it?"

She shot me a glare. "You don't know anything about me."

"But I know a lot about Michael. He doesn't use Tinder to meet women; he uses his office."

"Are you saying that you . . . ?"

I nodded. "Yes. I'm in the club. Are you a member?"

"I can't answer that."

"Because then he'd stop paying you?"

It was just a guess, but from her obvious surprise, I'd say it had been an accurate one. Then the glare was back. "Don't ever come near me again." She got in her car and drove off. I saw her looking at me in the rearview mirror. I could hardly blame her. I'd totally botched that.

But I could get better.

Michael had given her money. Now whether she blackmailed him or he just offered so that she'd make her complaint go away, I had no idea. But he'd been sleeping with her, I was sure of that. Nasty underground websites aside, women didn't lie about sexual abuse. They could, however, be persuaded to go silent about it—with money, or because of the humiliation of the investigation, or both.

Wednesday night. The slot before the blonde giraffe seemed to be available. The self-assured brunette in the flowing clothes hadn't been coming. I had a little time to grab a falafel and strategize.

I positioned myself inside the building (the code hadn't changed, fortunately). Right near the door, beside the stairs, in a small vestibule. We'd have to talk close, which worked for me. Michael's sound machines would be going full blast upstairs. He'd never hear us, unless the giraffe screamed.

Since my fight with Michael last night, I'd been piecing things together, realizing how calculating he'd been, how far back it went. I recalled the time during Kate's visit when I stormed into his office, and he headed me off in the waiting room with all those words of love, so many promises. But then by the time I saw him later that night, he had already confronted Kate, which allowed him to renege on everything he'd said. I couldn't push for us to go public anymore because now I was groveling.

His sweet talk had been the most efficient way to get me out of his office. I didn't know who'd been behind his door, and he didn't want me to. That's who he was protecting. Her, and his relationship with her. And his reputation. Everyone had to think he was the greatest therapist around.

He'd said what he needed to say, and then later, he got to tell me what he really thought, directly. He could vent his anger and take back control. But it was all a game to him. He must have already suspected that I'd told Kate long ago; he just kept that in his back pocket until it was time to deploy it for his own ends. He shouldn't have been a therapist; he should have been a general. He was Machiavellian. And he was going to pay for what he'd done to me, and to Kate, and to whomever else. I just needed ammunition.

The door opened. Nope, not her. I turned away, no need for anyone to recognize my face, and the man clomped upstairs to his own therapist.

Then it was her. "I'm Flora," I said gently. "I should have introduced myself sooner. I think we have a few things to talk about."

Her eyes widened. She'd already looked distraught, and now she added a top note of fright. When I last saw her up close, I had been struck by how pretty she was. Now I was struck by how fragile. Her formerly perfect skin had one perfectly round pink pimple, and there were bluish circles under her eyes. Her hair was always a little flyaway, but today it was running amok. Not only had it not seen a comb, I didn't think it had seen shampoo. Conditioner was a distant memory.

He'd done this to her, I knew it.

"I have an appointment," she nearly whispered. None of her bravado from our previous interactions was in evidence.

I wasn't the most empathetic person, but this little giraffe could break your heart. "I'm sorry to bother you. I know that I wasn't the nicest when we spoke before. I'm here to warn you, but I feel like you already know everything I'm about to say."

"I don't want to be late."

She was loyal to him. She still thought he was helping her. "I'll pay for your session. Just let me talk to you, please. Now, or we can meet somewhere later."

"You don't need to pay for the session."

"Where should we meet?"

She looked down at the floor. A strand of hair worked its way into her mouth, and she didn't even reach up to remove it. She was just wrecked. And so young. How could Michael have done this to her? He was probably done with picking strong women like me.

"Just tell me now," she said.

"I was Michael's client a little more than two years ago. I went to see him with my husband. The whole time he was supposedly 'helping' us, he was systematically exposing my husband's weaknesses and getting me to focus on his—Michael's—strengths. Getting me to want him." I squirmed a little. "I let him in, and he used me. He told me he loved me, but now I know it was all a game to him, and he plays it with a lot of his clients. There are at least two others that I know of. They filed complaints against him." I tried to catch her eyes, but it was impossible; they were still on the floor. The hair was still in her mouth. "Are there at least three?"

She didn't answer, but she heard me. Her discomfort had ratcheted up.

"Has he been sleeping with you or grooming you to sleep with him in the future? Like, in two years?"

Her blue eyes suddenly met mine. "Why two years?"

"In the ethics of his profession, he can get romantically involved with a former client after two years. He's kept me hidden for all that time. But we've been together I don't even know how many times. Just no one is supposed to know about it. I was his dirty secret."

Something in that last phrase resonated with her. The eyes dropped again. "He's not grooming me," she said.

"You're already sleeping together." She didn't answer, which meant yes. "He's abusing you. He's abusing his power over you."

"No." It rang out in the vestibule. "I've been finding my power."

I let it hang there a long minute so she could feel the disconnect between her words and how she appeared tonight. She had been fiery that day by my car, but she was shrinking. Whatever power he was supposedly granting her with his magic cock was an illusion.

"I hope that's true," I said. "But whatever he gives, he takes away in the end. I used to feel that way, too." I stepped toward her, and she looked like she wanted to curl inside herself. "This is my card. Call me anytime."

She took it, but she wouldn't look at it or at me.

I stepped back. "I'm Flora," I repeated, in case she'd missed it the first time. "Could you tell me your name?"

"Lucy." It was a true whisper.

"It's good to meet you, Lucy. Call me if you want to talk or to meet up somewhere. We could help each other."

"What? Like a support group?"

The sardonic nature of her comment surprised me. But I liked it. She still had a little fire in her; it hadn't been totally extinguished.

"Maybe. Or like a revenge group. He could use a taste of his own medicine."

She was about to say something, and then thought better of it. "I'm late."

"Just think about what I said. And if you can, keep it between us, okay? That gives us the upper hand."

"I don't even know you."

"You don't know him, either. Trust me."

CHAPTER 66

GREER

I woke up that morning, and I knew. It was like I could feel the migration of the cells, arranging themselves into a double helix.

I ran to the drugstore in my pajamas with no bra and a coat over the top. Vanity was a thing of the past. The baby I was so sure was inside me had already vanquished it, and good riddance. I was going to change, all for the better, starting now. I got the twofer pregnancy tests, and back inside my condo, I took them both simultaneously. It was confirmed, in tandem.

But I didn't want to leave even 0.01 percent to chance, so I did a test at the doctor's office. Then I was out on the street, grinning madly. I was 100 percent, absolutely, certainly pregnant.

From the back seat of a cab, I dialed Michael. Whenever it wasn't too inconvenient, I took cabs instead of Uber or Lyft. I liked the plastic divider. It wasn't genuine privacy protection, but it was a boundary of sorts.

"Take Gough," I told the driver. "The lights are timed."

"Hello?" Michael said.

"Hi," I said. "You'll never guess why I'm calling."

"You missed me already?"

"Guess again."

A long pause. "Are you . . . I mean, did it really happen that fast?"

I didn't love that response. "Sorry, my ovaries aren't on your timetable."

"No, no. It's incredible. Congratulations. I just thought it would take longer, that's all."

"Because of my advanced maternal age?"

I noticed the driver glancing at me in his rearview mirror. When he saw I'd caught him, he immediately shifted his eyes back to the road.

"You're beautiful for any age, Greer," Michael said. "I can't wait to see you."

"You don't need to flatter me. I'm already having your baby." He went quiet for just a beat too long. "What's up?"

"I'm just floored." He sounded tremulous. Moved. Excited. He really wanted this.

My eyes filled with tears. "We shouldn't get our hopes up too much. Miscarriage rates are high in the first trimester, and it's even higher when you're pushing forty." I looked toward the driver, daring him to take his eyes off the road. He didn't.

"I know," he said. "But we're allowed to feel some joy, right?"

"Yes." I smiled. "That's allowed."

I wasn't going to tell anyone until three months, no need to tempt fate, but in my heart, I felt like this was it. We'd done it, a hole in one. For the next ten weeks, it would be our beautiful secret.

"Could we celebrate?" he asked.

"With sparkling cider."

"As long as we can toast, I'm happy."

We agreed that I'd meet him at his office and go from there. I thought maybe that meant that the toasting would happen in his office, since that was where we'd met. Or we could walk up the street to one of the restaurants. Or he might invite me back to his house; I knew it was nearby. At that thought, I felt a stirring that was in my loins, not my womb.

It seemed fitting, finding out on a Wednesday. Our lucky day.

Hours later, I was still riding high, full of anticipation about the night to come. I was almost to the door of Michael's building when I heard staccato steps behind me. Then there was an urgent voice in my ear: "I need to talk to you."

I looked over at a woman in tight jeans and a tight sweater, designer and expensive, sexy but in the most effortful way. Her hair was lustrous and black, probably flat-ironed and then each wave was twirled back into it. Her nose was prominent, though it didn't detract from her attractiveness; it made her more imposing, handsome rather than merely sexy. She didn't appear threatening, but even so, my hand reflexively went to my abdomen.

I stopped walking, because I didn't want her following me inside. "Do I know you?"

"No. But I know Michael Baylor very well. And you haven't been part of the Wednesday lineup in a little while, which means this might be a social call, and that means you're likely in need of a warning."

I hesitated, trying to fit the pieces together. "So your relationship to Michael is . . . ?"

"I'm his ex. His ex-girlfriend and his ex-client. We met when I was his client. It was couples therapy. He stole me out from under my husband fifty minutes at a time."

"You're making him sound diabolical."

"He is."

No, if anyone was off, it was her. "How do you know that I haven't been coming to see him for a while?"

She obviously didn't like the turn this conversation was taking. I was supposed to just accept everything she said at face value. Was that how she was used to operating in her life? Spoiled brat. I could believe she'd been a client, but the rest must have been her fantasy. The man I knew wouldn't be romantically involved with someone like her.

Wait, he'd said he just had a breakup. Could it be . . . ?

No. Absolutely not.

"Excuse me," I said, and went to walk around her.

She planted herself directly in my path. "No one wants to believe it about him. He's that good."

"Excuse me." It was angrier this time. This was the father of my baby she was talking about. She had no right to interfere in my happiness.

"There are other women who've lodged complaints against him, and then withdrew them after he paid them off."

I didn't want to, but I found myself thinking of the $100,000 deal. Michael was a successful therapist; why did he need that money?

I'd told myself it was the high cost of living in the Bay Area. Everyone needed more money.

She could see that she'd struck a chord, and she moved a little closer. In for the kill. "He's sleeping with another of his clients right now. Her name's Lucy. She's the tall blonde woman, his six o'clock. You've probably run into her before."

I knew just who she was talking about, but it was too fantastical. That woman was obviously coming apart at the seams. Michael would never.

And this woman in front of me . . . She'd been seeing him for couples therapy, she said, but she could still have been deranged. If she hadn't been then, she was now.

"We can't let him get away with it anymore," she said. "We need to band together."

I laughed at her. "Mete out some vigilante justice? Is that what you're talking about?"

"I'm talking about stopping him. Exposing him. He's abusing women."

"He hasn't abused me."

"If you're sleeping with him, then he's abusing you."

"Well, good thing I'm not."

Her face turned sympathetic. She thought I was lying, covering for him. "I was in love with him, too. I wanted to spend the rest of my life with him."

"I'm sorry that he didn't feel the same."

"He doesn't feel that way about you, either. He's incapable of true love. He's a monster, and I refused to believe it."

Just like I was refusing. I couldn't stand to hear it, not now. What I wanted was to go off and have my sparkling-cider toast with the father of my child.

Could I really be carrying the baby of a monster?

No, it couldn't be. She had to be out of her mind.

I needed her to be out of her mind.

"Don't feel bad," she said. "He's good at what he does—at seeming to be what you want most. Or he's just good at picking women who see what they want in him. Projection, or transference, or whatever."

"I forgot something in my car," I said, as if it was any of her business. I started to walk away, and she chased me again, this time pressing her card into my hand, and I took it, because this woman, this Flora, needed to be investigated.

I went around the corner, out of her line of sight, and leaned against a building, trying to catch my breath.

The night was ruined. There were too many questions, too much to think about. I couldn't go forward with our celebration, not like this. I had to delay it until I could look him right in the eyes and raise a glass to all that was ahead of us.

I texted Michael. Have to cancel, sorry. Who knew you could have morning sickness in the evening? Talk soon!

I was putting Flora's card inside my purse and saw there was writing on the back. *Call me. I have the proof.*

CHAPTER 67

LUCINDA

During the session, I couldn't stop looking at Dr. Baylor/Michael. I mean, normally I looked at him, but this was different. I was wondering what he was capable of, whereas typically, I was thinking about what I was capable of, for better and for worse.

It was impossible, what Flora had said, and yet, she'd been so convincing. On the back of her card, like a little teaser, it said that she could show me the proof.

I almost asked him about her, but I knew he'd have some explanation, some story, and he'd be convincing, too. I needed to see her proof first. I didn't want to believe it, but I'd been duped before by a man I loved.

Still, hours later, I was sitting in my room, struggling not to call him. Sex was where I could lose myself, and I really needed that. It was itchy inside my skin, where I couldn't scratch. I needed Michael.

And I needed Dr. Baylor, too. There was so much I didn't understand about my own life, my past, who I used to be, who I was right then. He'd been my conduit for more than a year; he connected me to myself. Without him, what did I have? Without him to narrate my story, who was I?

I'd been there in his office, dying to tell him about Adam's letter so we could make sense of it together, but I couldn't. Not after what I just heard from Flora. The office had been my safe space, and now it wasn't.

He could see something was going on as I babbled in obfuscation. When he probed, I was bobbing and weaving like a boxer, and finally, at the end of the session, he said, "I expected this, that I'd have to regain your trust." I gaped at him. He knew what Flora had told me? Then I realized: he was talking about when he'd threatened to refer me out to another therapist, when he'd nearly abandoned me.

Even if Flora was telling the truth about their relationship, it didn't make him a monster. It could be the opposite, that he was only human. He couldn't control who he loved or who he stopped loving. I'd replaced Flora in his heart, and he couldn't help that. Now she just had to accept that.

I recalled how angry Flora was when I'd approached her car, and how she'd sounded in the waiting room. No wonder Michael had broken up with her, and now she had an ax to grind. She might have changed her approach with me so she could seem nice, but I had no reason to trust her. Dr. Baylor—Michael—he'd given me lots of reasons.

Plus, I knew from the Adam letter that I did seduce men. I pushed until they relented. I outlasted them. That meant I was at least partially responsible for how this had played out. I'd wanted Michael to put aside his professional and personal ethics; I wanted him to love me. Maybe you couldn't entirely fault me for what happened with Adam because of my age, but I was an adult now. I'd made choices, too. Flora might want to put it all on Michael, but she was obviously pretty persistent herself. And good-looking. I could see that woman wearing a man down.

I was so alone. I couldn't stand to be this alone, so I had to call.

"Mommy?" I whimpered.

"Oh, sweetheart." My mother's voice commingled abundant love and relief. "I'm so glad you called."

"I didn't know who else to talk to. Things are just so fucked up."

"I know. Adam's death is bringing up a lot of feelings for me, too."

"It's not about Adam."

"What is it, then?"

I'd called her because I was that desperate, that low on options. Because I needed to get these things out of my head, and I hadn't been able to write in weeks.

But could I really go through with this and just blurt it out? Michael and I were in this together, and if I told anyone else—

He didn't have to know. He might not even deserve to know.

I trusted my mother. Since she'd been clean, she'd always been good to me, if you didn't count when she went MIA after learning about my affair with Adam, and she'd apologized for that a hundred times already. If there was anyone on this planet who wanted only the best for me, who was singularly invested in my happiness, it was Mom.

I jumped off the high dive, and I told her everything: about Adam, and my therapy, and the unorthodox treatment sessions late at night.

She asked the occasional question just to clarify, but mostly, she was listening. When I'd finished, she said, "Your therapist knew all about Adam and had sex with you anyway. He wanted you to think that you could exorcise the demons of one old pervert through another."

I wanted to protest, but she was right. Dr. Baylor had told me about trauma repetition, and that you couldn't resolve what happened before by doing it over and over. Then he'd fucked me.

Over and over.

PRESENT DAY

CHAPTER 68

DETECTIVE GREGORY PLATH

Another call from the victim's mother. She's been crawling up my ass since I got assigned this case, and she's been no help at all. It's like she didn't know her own son. She doesn't have one scrap of useful information to contribute to the investigation. She just goes on and on about how he wouldn't hurt anyone, it must be a random act of violence, he had no enemies, he was the best human being, did I know how much he'd done for her, how he paid all her bills and listened to her, he'd been the only one who listened to her and now she's all alone . . .

What's that pop psychology term that's all the rage? A narcissist, that's what she is. I feel for the doc, having to put up with that. No wonder he didn't tell her anything; it's not like she would have heard him anyway.

But I might have a break in the case. I resisted the temptation to go through his records because I don't know this guy; I'm not going to risk my career just because one of his women gets under my skin, because she looks down on me like she's daring me to officially call her a suspect and bring her in with her $1,000-an-hour lawyer, because (I wouldn't admit this to anyone) she reminds me of my own mother who I had to stop talking to twenty years ago for my sanity.

Instead, I go through the doc's house, inch by inch, and I can't believe what I find, that the jackpot is hidden under his couch cushion. A key under the mat and a file folder under the couch cushion. People, what are you going to do with them?

Inside this folder is a contract between him and Greer. It says he's going to father her child, and not only that but he's going to have some rights to see the kid as s/he grows up. And then I remember this funny thing I noticed the last time I saw her: the way she draped her arm over her stomach and it tightened at one point, almost protectively. I'd thought I was giving her a stomachache, but no. All those loose clothes and that arm—she's pregnant.

Picture it: You're newly pregnant, you've got all these hormones coursing through you, you're at dim sum (where both Lucinda and Flora happened to mention Greer didn't eat a thing and ducked out early, probably sick from the smells, not to mention the conversation), and besides, you've heard enough. The guy's—what's the other pop psychology term?—a sociopath who's been fucking two other women, and you've got a baby on the way and you've guaranteed that sociopath access because he snowed you, too.

I've got her. I've got motive.

BEFORE

CHAPTER 69

FLORA

I was tempted to make him stand outside my apartment so he'd see what it felt like. He could position himself beneath the window and call up to me, like I was Juliet on her balcony. But my neighbors didn't really need to be privy to my destroying the good doctor.

I stepped aside without a word and let him cross the threshold, shutting the door behind him. I crossed my arms over my chest to emphasize how closed I was to him.

"I've been thinking about you," he said. "How's Kate?"

"Like you care." The truth was, she was no better. It was likely that she'd never be any better. My aunt and uncle weren't yet "making any decisions," and I wasn't planning to fly out to Miami until they had. As in, I'd fly out to say goodbye—not that Kate would be able to hear me, or, even if her ears worked, her brain wouldn't register what had been said. Still, I needed to see her one last time.

But Michael didn't care about any of that. He didn't care about her or about me. He never had.

"Could we sit down?" he asked. "It feels strange to talk in the entryway."

I walked to my couch and took a seat—on my hands, for self-restraint.

He sank down on the other side, his eyes on his feet. "I need to apologize." His body language was clearly intended to convey how hard this was for him, that he couldn't even look me straight in the face because he was so very ashamed, so entirely chastened by the recent events.

I didn't buy it for a second. He wasn't here to repent; he wanted something. I could guess what it was, but I was going to make him say it.

I wouldn't even ask the obvious question: "Apologize for what?" Nope. I was going to let him hang there in the silence, stewing in it. He'd done that to me enough times. *How do you like your own medicine, Michael? Pretty rancid, eh?*

"I've treated you really poorly, and I have no good excuse. I think I just got scared." Oh, please. "You're a formidable woman, Flora. At times, it was overwhelming."

Huh. Interesting. So that was how he was going to play this. No declarations of love; he was going for fear.

What was most interesting was that I could be this detached from someone I'd thought I loved so deeply. It was almost like he was a lab rat I was studying. Yep, he was a rat all right. I didn't even remotely want to fuck him. I couldn't believe I ever did.

When I was done with someone, I was done completely. It had always been that way. Like the boyfriends before Young, who I never loved, and even with Young, who I did. I suspected that even if Michael hadn't been waiting in the wings, I wouldn't have spent much time pining. It was like there was a valve inside me that shut off at will. Not my will, or I would have turned it long ago with Michael. But once it was off, watch out.

Watch out, Michael. You're not dealing with the same woman who slept in your bed like a mewling kitten after the mugging, who was trying so hard to elicit your sympathy and your love.

It made me cringe to even think of all my machinations. I'd debased myself for this guy here, this mealymouthed loser?

Now he was going on about how much he loved me and what a beautiful relationship we'd had, but it had grown so toxic and he should have been more direct with me, he should have ended things sooner once and for all, and he hoped there could be forgiveness. Closure.

Seriously? Closure? That was the best he could do?

I still hadn't spoken, and he'd kept his eyes on his feet. But he must have sensed that his little speech wasn't going over so well, since he'd always been able to read a room, because he lifted his head and turned to me. "I'll always have love for you, Flora."

I could have clawed his eyes out. "Cut to the chase. What do you want?"

"I told you. I want forgiveness, and healing, for both of us. We've both behaved badly."

"I behaved badly in reaction to what you did. You drove me to it."

He visibly chafed at that, and I enjoyed the sight. He was battling himself, deciding whether he could contradict me or if he had to continue this little routine of contrition. His pride was vying with his pragmatism. "I'm sorry," he said. Apparently, pragmatism had won out.

"You're sorry for your pattern of seducing your clients? For making me feel special when I'm just one of a long list? For convincing me that I'd be better off with you than with a husband who was actually trying to make me happy?" The news of Young's engagement still burned. Sometimes I had the crazy thought that if we'd just picked a different therapist, we might have had a different outcome. That I could be pregnant right now with my husband's child. Another therapist would have used our individual sessions to teach me to love what I have. What

I had. Who I had. The bird in the hand. Now my bush was empty, and it was all Michael's fault.

"I see that you've worked yourself up, that you've started to believe this narrative—"

"It's not a narrative. It's the truth. I'm alone because of you."

"We're both alone because we weren't good for each other. It wasn't healthy, for either of us."

I gave a nasty laugh. "Oh really? You're alone? You're not with Lucy or with that other woman, the one who used to see you on Wednesdays?"

He paled. So it was true.

Kate had told me, and I hadn't wanted to listen. Now he was walking around, and she was in a hospital bed, the living dead.

When he spoke, he was trying to control his voice, just like he'd tried to control me for so long. But he couldn't anymore, and that was fast dawning on him. "I don't sleep with my clients. You need to stop this obsession. It's no good for you."

"You don't give a shit what's good for me! You don't want me talking to your clients because it's bad for you."

He shook his head, as if I'd gone truly crazy but he was willing to bear with me. For my own good, surely, so I could stop this obsession. How arrogant and infuriating. "You're hurting my ability to treat my clients. Now we have to spend valuable time in the sessions with me clearing my name."

"You mean covering your ass. Lying to them. I'm sure you tell them I'm some stalker nutjob."

"Aren't you?" He must have seen how dangerous that remark was because he backtracked. "I know you're not. I've made mistakes, but I'm hoping you can separate those mistakes from my work. My clients shouldn't have to pay for them."

"When I told you I'd made mistakes, you weren't willing to forgive me. You tortured me."

"That's one of my mistakes. I am truly sorry." He was able to look it, but that didn't mean shit. He was a monster who could behave like a human, and he could behave well. I'd been fooled, and how many other women had, too? He was dangerous, and he had no conscience. If I didn't stop him, I didn't know who would. Like he said himself, I was formidable, so the job fell to me.

"You want me to stop talking to your clients. What about the licensure board?"

"Are you saying you've filed a complaint?"

"I haven't decided what I'm going to do with you yet. Because if I try to punish you that way, I get punished, too. Scrutinized. Humiliated. Is that part of why you were able to pay off those two women to withdraw their complaints?"

"I didn't pay anyone off." But he was clearly rattled. "They realized what they were doing was wrong."

"Oh, what *they* were doing was wrong." The chutzpah of this guy.

"It's hard for you to believe that, since I violated the ethics of my profession to be with you. But you know that our relationship was entirely consensual. It had been building for months during the therapy, and yes, I should have resisted. But you were irresistible."

Had he always been this lame, this transparent, and I'd been blinded by what I thought was love? Kate told me to choose, and I chose Michael. That meant I was as much to blame for her destruction as he was, but he had so many more crimes under his belt and the potential to keep on committing them. I couldn't go back and change what I'd done to Kate, but if I stopped him, I could start to rebalance the ledger, in some cosmic sense.

"Save it, Michael. You're just going to have to wait and see what my next move will be. You'll live knowing I'm out here, and I understand exactly who and what you are, and I'm not going to let you get away with it." I stood up, walked back to my front door, and opened it. It was his turn to get kicked out onto the street. His turn to feel powerless.

349

CHAPTER 70

GREER

Maybe I shouldn't have left my company in Chenille's capable hands quite so soon, because now, I had way too much time on my hands, time to contemplate what a colossal mistake I may have made. I finally decided to trust my instincts, and now, what if I might have chosen a monster for the father of my child? That was the word Flora used.

Might. That was the operative word as far as I was concerned. I didn't have any proof yet. But if this was a *Rosemary's Baby* situation, what could I do? She was in there. Or he was. Someone was growing inside my uterus, and I couldn't just boot him or her out.

My run-in with that Flora woman had been two nights ago, and after I texted Michael to cancel at the last minute, he went on a texting spree. It was like he was looking for reassurance, like he knew there was more than what I was telling. I kept responding minimally, hoping to allay his suspicions, because what if he was a monster? I didn't want to get on the wrong side of that. It wasn't just about me anymore; I had to look after my baby, too.

I was able to verify that there had been two women who filed and then withdrew complaints. But that was all I really knew.

I'd been falling in love with him. I had to admit that now. Flora seemed awful, but that didn't mean she was lying. It was possible that what she said was true: that he was very good at what he did, at being what women wanted him to be.

Why hadn't I done a background check, like my parents would have insisted?

Because I'd been mounting a rebellion against them, though they were too dead to know it. I'd been defiantly going with my gut, and now . . .

I couldn't stop thinking about—and rereading—the papers Michael and I had signed. I had a good lawyer, which meant that the contract did just as I'd asked: it reduced Michael's risk, ensuring he couldn't be held liable in any way, and that while Michael had no parental rights and could never sue for custody, the visitation was fairly liberal. He was guaranteed at least once a month, with more at my discretion. He was entitled to pictures and updates at predetermined intervals. It was modeled on the contract between a birth parent and an adoptive parent in an open adoption.

Open. As in, my baby would be exposed to her (or his) father. I'd given Michael access to my child, and I didn't have to be present if he didn't want me there.

I'd been so stupid. So crazy. Baby crazy. Baby blind. I'd wanted to be pregnant, and Michael was the only man immediately available. I'd convinced myself that everything I'd seen and heard from him rendered him legitimate and trustworthy. And I told myself that was my gut speaking up, and I needed to listen, for once. It felt like a triumph. Paying a man a hundred K for sperm, and I'd been proud of the deal I'd brokered.

If I'd done even a fraction of my due diligence, I would have known about those two complaints. Of course, if I'd asked him about them,

I would have been desperate to believe any explanation he gave. I still was, which was why I hadn't yet asked him about Flora.

It hadn't felt desperate, though. I'd felt excited. I'd felt like I was on the verge of the best choice of my life, practically the only choice of any consequence that I'd made without the influence of my parents, an influence that had extended beyond the grave. Michael had, in remarkably few sessions, managed to deprogram me. But then whose influence was I under?

No, it wasn't possible. He couldn't have conned me into this, into becoming the father of my baby, so he could get a hundred K. For one thing, it wasn't even that much money in the Bay Area. He lived in Rockridge. I'd looked up his house on Zillow and it was worth $1.5 million.

Then there was Flora. That was a conniving woman if ever I'd seen one. Women didn't often make false accusations, but it happened. There was a reason people were innocent until proven guilty.

I needed to see the proof. She'd written on the back of her business card that she had it, and she told me the blonde woman on Wednesday was another victim. I'd have to meet up with them and see what was really true. Most likely, it was a bunch of garbage from a few disturbed women. I'd tell Michael afterward what they were saying and that he needed to watch his back.

Thanks to Amazon Prime, I already had the beginnings of a library for my little one. I'd been reading aloud, hand on stomach, doing different voices for all the characters in *The Giving Tree*; *Oh, The Places You'll Go!*; and *Guess How Much I Love You*.

Just my baby and me. I'd hoped for more, but if not, this was enough.

The pages blurred before me. I kept on going.

CHAPTER 71

LUCINDA

I'd been reading the same sentence for the past ten minutes. It was a horrible sentence, for sure, from a book about making cocktails that taste craft on a beer budget, but normally, I could have rewritten it in seconds.

"Problems?" Christine asked, just over my shoulder. I jumped. I didn't know how long she'd been there, watching.

"No problems," I said. It came out curt when I meant it perky, like I was a good little employee who danced to my boss's tune instead of a woman in the grip of a slowly simmering rage.

"I thought maybe you were working on your own book again."

"No, I haven't done that since our conversation."

"Or should I say, our book?" Her smile was small and mean. She was reminding me that I owed her, and that, in effect, she owned me.

No one owned me.

That book was my life. It belonged to me alone. I had suffered for every page, and there was still so much left to write. The story of a therapist who told me that my stepfather was in a position of power and that made me a victim, and then that therapist did the very same thing, which made him even worse than my stepfather. I stayed up all last night writing, stoking the flames of my anger, and now I could feel them burning bright.

"That's my book," I said. "I'm not writing it at work, and I'll decide what I do with it."

"Someone's feisty today." Christine's lip curled in displeasure. "Have you forgotten what was said in the conversation where I spared your job?"

"I'm trying to forget."

"Why's that?"

Everyone has his or her boiling point, and I was fast approaching mine. "Because I'm not going to be blackmailed. I don't need any job that badly."

Her mouth actually fell open. She was speechless. I refused to drop my gaze in submission. It was another of those moments, the ones Dr. Baylor encouraged, when I acutely felt my power. Like when I'd confronted Flora that time. But this one had nothing to do with him.

Or did it? The fury he engendered was coursing through my veins. It was like a second heartbeat.

"You're fired," she finally said.

I stood up so we were nose to nose. Something skittered across her face. She was afraid of me.

I grabbed my bag off the floor, put it over my shoulder, and pushed past her. Better to say nothing. Not because I'd regret it but because anything I came up with wouldn't be nearly as strong as the power of my silence. She wasn't going to get any more apologies out of me, or a goodbye, and whatever came next for me wouldn't require her recommendation.

I was sure everyone was staring from their desks, but I was looking ahead, at the straight shot to the door. The fresh air was a chilled and welcome blast. It smelled like brunch. It also smelled like freedom.

Was this the first time I'd literally had nothing left to lose?

I was almost smiling. Then I walked up the street to the vegan breakfast joint and chowed down on faux eggs and what their menu termed fakon (fake bacon), and it might have been the best meat I'd ever eaten. I felt inside my bag, to the very bottom, where my fingers closed around a business card. I placed it on the table beside my plate.

Somebody needed to pay. Not Christine—she'd be paid back just by having to exist inside her own body. Being her was its own punishment. But Michael had his alter ego, Dr. Baylor. He got to walk around pretending that he was helping people. He got to feel good about himself. He'd painted Adam as a villain, and then he took advantage of me himself, calling it an alternative treatment. He literally got off on my pain. Adam never did that.

I looked down at Flora's card. A fellow victim. A fellow vigilante. There was strength in numbers. It would be harder to ignore multiple women coming forward.

But not impossible. He was the one who'd written about all my sessions. Who knew how his records made me sound? I didn't know what was wrong with Flora, what her diagnosis was. I wasn't even sure what mine was, but I was pretty sure it wouldn't play well in front of a board or a tribunal or whatever. Even with Flora beside me, I'd still have to testify. I'd probably have to talk about Adam and relive everything in front of an audience that may be more sympathetic to their colleague than they would be to me. Poor Dr. Baylor, with his stable of the unstable. They might think that we'd formed a mob and turned on him, when all he'd wanted was to help us.

He could make me look crazy. It wouldn't be that hard to do.

And after all that, what would be the worst that would happen to him? He'd lose his license. Or more likely, he wouldn't. It would all have been for nothing.

I'd need something more fail-safe. Since I didn't have a job anymore, I could devote all my time and energy to figuring out just what that should be.

I polished off my almond milk *horchata* (also delicious). Was this place really that on point, or was it just me? I never knew that having nothing to lose could feel so exquisite.

CHAPTER 72

FLORA

"I just wish you'd been here, *zvezda moya*." Mama's voice was a sigh. I'd never heard her sound so small before. And she hadn't called me by that Russian diminutive in years. *My star,* she was saying. When had I stopped being her star? Was it gradual or all at once? But I knew that her saying it then had particular meaning. She was lost; she needed a light to guide her. "You and Katya, you always had such a special bond."

Mama thought that I had the power to save Kate; she didn't know that I was the one who'd pushed her over the edge, with a huge assist from Michael.

Kate still hadn't woken up. The doctors held out little hope that she ever would.

She was lying there because of me. Because I believed Michael instead of my own flesh and blood. And now my family was devastated, and my frail mother was having to take care of her broken sister, and why? Because of what I'd done to Kate, all for that monster. Because of that monster.

I hadn't slept or showered in two days; I was still in the same hoodie and yoga pants that were now food encrusted, though I couldn't even remember having eaten. I'd called out of work—wait, *had* I called out of work, or had I just failed to show up? I was ignoring Jeanie's repeated texts saying she was worried about me, including the pointed one about whether I'd had another "accident." She'd put the quotation marks around it, even.

I replayed my confrontation with Michael over and over again, his asking me to leave him and his precious clients alone. Saying that he'd made mistakes. Mistakes! As if I'd cease and desist because of all the clients he was supposedly helping. Helping himself to them was more like it. The good-looking ones, the weak ones, like Lucy. I used to be weak for him, too. Greer said she hadn't slept with him when we spoke on the street, but she called me yesterday and we were going to meet up soon. Then I'd find out what he'd really done and what she was really made of.

But as I listened to my mother sob, I started thinking that slowly circling Michael, amassing evidence, and ultimately destroying his practice wasn't nearly enough. Kate was gone, and he was still here. Was there any justice in the world?

There was only what you made. What you took.

It was Friday night. Michael didn't work on Friday nights. He would be home, since he had no freaking friends. Unless, of course, he was out with his latest woman. Latest client, maybe? I'd spoken to Lucy, who was pretty shaken up, and she was keeping her distance. Greer supposedly wasn't even fucking him. While I thought that was a lie, I couldn't imagine that either of those two women was going to be with him before we all met up for our little powwow. But I wouldn't put anything past him. He could be very persuasive.

I headed for his house, my hands trembling on the wheel with adrenaline. I was driving with purpose, though I had no plan. I'd never felt this before, like I didn't even care what happened to me; it was all about stopping this feeling. Stopping him. He couldn't do this anymore. I wasn't going to let him.

His car was out front. Images were flashing in front of my eyes, bloodred: Kate in her hospital bed, my mother distraught, Michael inside the house that I'd thought would someday be our home together. All the lies and the machinations and the terrible consequences, not just for the two of us but for my whole family. They didn't deserve this. I was a kaleidoscope of rage. I was lit up, psychedelic, drunk with it. Uninhibited. I wanted him looking over his shoulder, feeling hunted. It was the least I could do. It was a start.

Since the mugging, I'd been carrying a small knife on my keychain. It was the one Michael had bought for me. Such sweet irony.

I walked across the street, popping it in and out of its protective case. I felt like I was in a movie about the fifties, where there was about to be a street fight and everyone was readying their switchblades.

He was so cocky, so sure he could control everything and everyone when the time came.

Well, time's up.

I was almost to his car when I heard my name. I spun around, the knife still protruding, and saw Jeanie.

"Oh my God," she whispered. "Put that away, please."

The knife, she meant. I was still holding an unsheathed knife. Seeing the expression on her eminently sane face made me realize just how insane I looked.

I did as she'd instructed. She came up the stairs, putting her arm around my shoulders and ushering me down, like I was a small child. One of her twins, maybe. And inside the circle of her maternal energy, I let myself be led. I leaned into her, feeling the emotional exhaustion of the past weeks.

Her Mercedes was parked behind my car. She helped me into the leather passenger seat and then took the driver's seat. "Should we get you to a hospital, do you think?" Her tone was halting. This was clearly new territory for her. It was Michael's territory, committing people to psych hospitals, but I didn't think we'd be consulting with him tonight.

"No, I'm fine," I said in a small voice.

"You were holding a knife."

"I was just going to slash his tires."

"Just?"

I tried to smile. "Carrie Underwood did it, right?"

"No, she sang about it."

"Shocker. I'm not Carrie Underwood." I wanted to seem breezy, like the version of myself she used to know. But I wasn't her. I was unhinged, and I wasn't fooling anyone.

"Oh, Flora," she said sadly. "What's he done to you?"

"I'm fine," I repeated. Or I would be, as soon as he'd paid for what he'd done to Kate, and to me, and to who knew how many others.

Really, slashed tires were too good for him.

I could see that Jeanie wanted to believe me, like always—that I was fine or would soon be. But how could that happen when Michael was walking around free and easy?

"How did you get here?" I asked. "Where did you come from?"

"You didn't answer any of my texts, so I drove to your apartment. I rang your bell a few times, and you didn't answer, but your car was there. So I waited, and then you came out and you looked—you know, like you look." Disheveled. Bedraggled. Unkempt. Utterly unlike myself. That was what Kate hated most about Michael: how he'd transformed me, entirely for the worse. "I called your name, but it was like you didn't hear me."

"No, I didn't." I'd been possessed.

"You got in your car, and I didn't think you should be driving, so I ran back and got in mine and followed you here, and I called your name again."

Now that made me smile for real. I hoped his neighbors had heard (though I hoped no one else had seen the knife).

"Sorry I put you through all this," I said.

"It was just so familiar. Even tonight, the way you looked. Like you'd gone into some kind of fugue state. When I was being abused, there were times where I'd basically sleepwalk while awake and I'd come to somewhere—one time it was a Laundromat—and I couldn't remember how I'd gotten there. I was literally out of my mind."

"All I could think about was putting him on notice," I whispered. "Making him stop."

"Making him stop what? What, exactly, has been going on?"

I'd been denying it for so long. Kate had been the only one who knew, and not because I'd told her. She just knew, and now . . .

"I would never judge you. I was nearly killed, and the guy was sent to prison before I broke free. I had this sixth sense, and that's why I came out tonight. I was meant to find you so that you couldn't pretend anymore. So you'd finally let me help you."

It was all hitting me at once: that Michael had abused and manipulated me from the first; that he'd driven me to this point; that I'd been pretending to be traumatized by the mugger, but I'd been genuinely traumatized by Michael. Trauma distorted and contorted, until you didn't even recognize yourself.

"His name's Michael Baylor," I said. "He was my old couples therapist, and we've been involved since Young and I split up."

She did a double take. "You've been with him for, like, two years?"

"He didn't want me to tell anyone."

"Of course. That's what they do. They isolate you, and they break you down mentally. And if he used to be your therapist, he must have had all kinds of tricks up his sleeve. He must have been using all your secrets against you, everything he learned from when you and Young were seeing him."

"It wasn't his style to use things against me like a threat. It was more, he knew where my wounds were, and he healed them. Or he seemed to, until he got tired of me or until I asked for too much; I don't know." I couldn't be sure what exactly had happened in his mind, but I knew that it hadn't been love.

"He must have known from your therapy that you wouldn't report him. You're a very private person. Secretive, almost. It takes a long time to really know you."

Was that true? I'd never seen myself that way. I'd thought the Tinder tales were only for Michael's benefit, but maybe a part of me did like to keep people far away. Jeanie and I had bonded when she cried over her failed IVF treatments; I'd never cried to her. As Michael discovered, I love you best when I can't really reach you.

"Well," she said, "domestic violence is a crime. If you're willing to testify, we can try to get him that way."

"We can't. It really was a mugging."

She shook her head in frustration. "You have to stop protecting him."

"Oh, I've stopped." I gestured across the street.

"If I hadn't been here . . ." She shuddered. She didn't believe I had my eye on only his tires. "I don't even want to think about it. But I do get it. I had those thoughts myself when I was going through the worst of it. I fantasized."

Nothing wrong with fantasies. But I couldn't go around losing control. I wanted to destroy Michael; I didn't want to go down with him. I needed to be strategic.

And I needed to get my life back, with people who actually cared about me. Jeanie had been right about the isolation. If I hadn't pulled away from Kate, she might be okay right now.

He'd never laid a hand on me, but he'd been every bit as destructive, and he was going to pay.

CHAPTER 73

GREER

Let me go on record as saying I didn't like these women at all. It could have been my hormones, or that if Michael had actually done something to them it had distended their personalities, or I might have simply resented being shoehorned into keeping this new company.

I'd had quick run-ins with Lucinda before, ships passing in the night, and I'd always had the impression she was sweet but scattered, unaware of just how beautiful she really was. But from the moment I sat down across from her at the dim sum restaurant, I had an entirely different sense. There was something almost cannily unhinged about her. Somewhere along the line, she'd learned that the world likes a tall drink of water who averts her eyes and bumps into walls, so my initial perception had been a reaction to a performance, an act that was wearing thin. This was the real Lucinda, the one with a furious radiance in her blue eyes, who was eager to tell her tale and exact her pound of flesh from Michael, and she wanted my help to do it.

Mine and Flora's, that was. Flora was another real winner. Just like last time, she was done up to the nines, with so much makeup she might not even have had flesh under there. I could tell that she was used to being the bawdy sexpot, the one who went out with her friends to bars with twenty-dollar cocktails and said outrageous things to all the men who came up to hit on them. It strained credulity, frankly, to think that the same man would be interested in the three of us.

The first ten minutes were taken with figuring out which items we should mark with a pencil on the dim sum menu. Flora wanted us all to split so she'd get to try everything, but this plan soon fell apart. Lucinda was a vegetarian (of course). She was already thin as a bean sprout, might as well eat them, too, and I had to decline anything with fish. Even if it was cooked, I didn't know if I could trust Oakland to get it fresh enough for the precious cargo I was carrying. But I had to hand it to Flora: this restaurant was an inspired choice. Everyone in there except the three of us was Asian, both the customers and staff. They were all speaking Cantonese. Silver carts were pushed along the thickly carpeted floor, and the tables were covered in white linen. It looked like a banquet hall, and it absorbed sound just as readily, which was perfect, since the one thing we could surely agree on was that we'd prefer not to be heard.

Finally, we placed our order: dumplings and buns for me, since I'd been craving starch; some exotics like edible fungus and chicken feet for Flora so she could prove how badass she was; and an assortment of vegetables for Lucinda.

"So," Flora said, "where do we start?" She tossed her dark hair back, but it immediately returned to the same spot, as if magnetized.

"Let's compile the data," I said. "What do you know about Michael?"

"He grew up in Oakland," Lucinda answered.

"On the East Coast," Flora countered, "like me."

"The Midwest," I said quietly. My stomach lurched, and it wasn't from what looked like pig intestines being doled out from a silver cart onto a plate at the next table. "He said he was raised by a mother who was intensely needy and smothering. He needed to get away."

Flora gave me a look like I must be some kind of fool. Of course she thought the version he told her was the truth. "His mother left when he was a little kid."

I turned to Lucinda, like she might be able to settle this. "What did he tell you?"

"He didn't talk about his childhood." I picked up an air of defensiveness from her. Or maybe it was defeat. She didn't like that he had revealed himself more to Flora and me than he had to her, even though what he'd disclosed to at least one of us was bullshit.

I wanted to think that he'd been telling me the truth. The other two could either be misremembering (in the case of Lucinda) or lying (Flora). Flora seemed absurdly competitive, wanting to prove she knew Michael better than I did. If she thought he was the Antichrist, why did she even care?

I was making mental notes for when I talked to him later. Both of them lacked credibility, as far as I was concerned. There could be a simple explanation for the childhood inconsistencies. Flora seemed like a terrible listener, and Lucinda was so scattered.

All I knew was, I wanted to get the hell out of here ASAP.

"Let's come at this another way." I pushed my hair back, and, unlike Flora's, mine receded. "What happened between you and Michael?"

"Who are you talking to?" Flora asked, a bit sharply.

"Both of you. Whoever wants to talk first."

"Maybe you should go first." So Flora didn't like me, either. Somehow, I'd survive.

We were in a staring contest when the first of my dumplings and Lucinda's vinegary cucumbers were heaped on our table. We waited until the cart had moved on, and then I returned to looking at Flora expectantly. The smell of the BBQ pork filling was making my mouth water, but I could hold out. Lucinda, however, began to eat her cucumbers, one after the other, almost compulsively. Maybe she had some kind of eating disorder.

I put my hand to my stomach, picturing the growing baby inside, no bigger than a legume.

Abruptly, Flora started talking. She gave so many details about her couples sessions and her individual sessions that it seemed like at least some of it must have been accurate. But how stupid could her ex-husband have been for Michael to get away with all that under his nose? It was tragic that her cousin was in a coma, but that didn't make sense, either. What person has a relapse and nearly dies because her cousin won't break up with her boyfriend? There had to be more to the story. Flora must have been more culpable than she was letting on. But she wanted it to be all Michael's fault.

And what was the big deal, really? So he hadn't waited the requisite two years after therapy. She hadn't, either. Still, I hated thinking of them together, and it was hard not to, since she pulled out her phone and showed us her proof. It was the pictures she'd taken of him asleep beside her. The father of my baby had been with that woman.

And then I started picturing the cousin in the hospital bed, never being able to walk or talk or think again . . .

I'd never even pulled the dumplings toward me, but I pushed the plate away anyway.

Next up was Lucinda. As she spoke, she stared down at the tabletop. Her fingers were kneading the white linen that rested on her thigh. It created a creepy juxtaposition, how she appeared to have regressed twenty years, even as she was detailing illicit sex acts.

It was harder to dismiss what Michael had done to Lucinda. She did not appear to be a woman of sound mind, and even if she was giving consent, Michael should never, ever have touched her. But then, she'd been victimized before. That could have caused her to misinterpret . . . No, if he was really fucking her in his office, that was pretty depraved.

If he was fucking her. It wasn't like she had any proof. Flora had the photos (as if she'd always been preparing for this moment, which was, in itself, rather suspect). But I didn't have any way to verify Lucinda's story. I just had to trust her, and, who knew, maybe with Flora there to egg her on, Lucy was exaggerating. She might have wanted to be in Flora's club. She seemed very suggestible.

Only I glanced at Flora and saw how genuinely sympathetic she seemed. She believed Lucinda.

But I couldn't. I was the only one here who couldn't simply walk away from Michael forever. He had no claim over either of them, but he did have some rights over my child.

As Lucinda reached the conclusion, her voice was suffused with anger. "He told me that I need to own my power," she said, "but he didn't think I could ever use it against him."

"That's going to be his downfall," Flora said. "He underestimated all of us."

I almost contradicted her; he had never underestimated me, but then, he was getting $100,000 out of me. Lucinda had been seeing him pro bono. Was that part of how he justified what was happening between them?

What she *said* happened between them. It was her word against his, and I would let him have his day in court. I'd hear him out.

Flora was on a diatribe about how Michael should pay, that he was the devil incarnate. Then Lucinda joined in, and there it was again, that glow from earlier. She was incandescent with righteous anger. In a sick way, they were both enjoying this.

Well, no one had taken advantage of me. I'd propositioned him. I had always owned my own power, and I had nothing in common with these women.

They were both watching me. It was supposed to be my turn. "I'm so sorry for what you've both been through," I said, "but it doesn't really have anything to do with me."

"Then why are you here?" Flora said, her eyes blazing, and Lucinda was looking at me with venom, too. Maybe they'd simultaneously had the thought that I could be a spy for Michael. I was the traitor in their midst.

"Did he try to have sex with you?" Lucinda said it accusingly. Really, she was accusing me of not having had sex with him.

"I told Flora when she first accosted me that Michael and I never had sex."

They could never know that I'd had his sperm. With the way they felt about Michael, who knew what they might do with that information? They could decide to harm my baby with the justification that the world would be better off without Michael's spawn.

They didn't know who they were dealing with, what I'd sacrifice, how far I'd go in the name of protection. I was already a mother.

Flora and Lucinda hadn't moved a muscle, yet it seemed like they'd drawn together, closed ranks against me. They thought I just came here for the gossip. Let them think that. They couldn't know that I had a vested interest.

"I'm sorry," I said again. "I wish I could help you."

They wore identical frowns and glares. I hadn't meant it as patronizing as it came out. There was no graceful exit. I stood, dropping money on the table, more than enough to pay for all of us.

"Is this just a game to you?" Lucy asked.

"No," I said, "it's most certainly not a game."

It was my baby's lineage we were talking about, my baby's life, because genes were destiny, weren't they?

No, they couldn't be. Because if that were true, I'd have as little to give my child as my parents had given me, and there was no way. I couldn't let that be true. Couldn't let a few uncorroborated accusations rob me of my happiness, of the first time my heart and my gut had been in utter alignment. What had Michael said? That that was the definition of progress? And these two women were the definition of unreliable sources.

Still, I was glad I'd already dropped the money so they couldn't see my hands trembling. I didn't want them to know they'd gotten to me, not even a little. They could have their cabal, but it would be without me.

CHAPTER 74

LUCINDA

And then there were two.

In the wake of Greer's departure, amid a flurry of silver cart activity, the table filled with food, a third of it hers, underscoring our abandonment. I shouldn't have thought of it that way. I didn't know her. I didn't know Flora, either, despite the intimacy of what she'd just shared. Her cousin. Wow. I had no idea how she was holding herself together. Maybe she needed her fury at Michael or she'd fall apart completely; she'd get lost in her guilt. Because underneath all her ranting about Michael, the subtext was that if she'd never let Michael into her life, her cousin would be truly (and not just technically) alive.

"She's hiding something," Flora said, chewing ferociously on one of Greer's dumplings. "More must have happened, or she wouldn't have shown up here."

"Or she just had nothing better to do."

"No. She reached out to me. I gave her my card, same as I gave it to you. She and Michael have to be involved somehow. Maybe she's his girlfriend, and he sent her."

I didn't think so. Greer didn't seem like the kind of woman who got sent anywhere. She was way too smart and confident to fall for Michael's tricks, not like Flora and me (not that I was about to say that to Flora). "Maybe she came here to rub her superiority in our faces. Like, ha, I got away scot-free and you two are permanently scarred."

"We're not. Don't say that."

It sure felt like it. How was I ever going to recover? I'd never gotten over what happened when I was five years old or with Adam. I thought I did, but that was just the euphoria of new love. I'd fallen for Michael, and it made me believe I could do anything. I even thought I was a good writer, with something important to say. He'd gone on and on about my talent, but he'd been playing me the whole time.

We ate our way through everything. I didn't know about Flora, but I couldn't even taste. I was uncomfortably full, and still, I couldn't stop until it was all gone. I wasn't a true vegetarian, I just lean that way, so I was eating chicken feet and BBQ pork and who knew what all else. Flora's ordering had been bananas.

She was eating manically, too, as if her chewing was keeping time with her racing thoughts. She kept talking about how we could get back at him, but it was all just wishful thinking, not planning. Even Flora must have known that he still had the upper hand; she just wasn't the type to admit it.

I wondered if the conversation would have been different had Greer stayed. That woman could get shit done.

Also, two felt like so much fewer than three when it came to proving Michael's wrongdoing. Greer seemed like the sanest of us. Maybe that was why she was the one to quit therapy. To quit Michael.

My stomach was ballooning outward, and the waistband of my jeans was probably leaving indentations. I felt worse and worse about myself with each bite, and still, I didn't stop. It was punishment. I'd been so stupid. I was a little girl and Greer was a woman and Flora was—well, Flora. She'd always land on her feet like a cat. She was a survivor, and I was a jobless disaster.

Finally, the table was cleared, and we paid the check with Greer's cash (it was way too much, and Flora divvied up the overflow and gave me half). If I'd told her I was unemployed, I probably could have gotten it all. But I didn't like how any of this felt, the weight of the dirty money in my palm.

"Well," I said, "it was nice to have met you."

Flora laughed, and it was a natural, sweet sound. "You too. We're in this together now." She pulled me into a hug, and my body was rigid in her arms. There was so little touch in my life, now that Michael's . . .

He didn't know it was over. I was thinking that I just wouldn't show up for my next session. I couldn't have stood up to his questioning about why I was ending things. I'd get sucked back into his web because I had so little else.

But not nothing. Which was why I hit the pavement and texted my mother.

There were at least two others.

She texted back immediately, offering to come see me, to stay the night, to mother me. But even though I'd been the one to reach out, the thought of her being there brought up too much turmoil, too many memories. I turned off the phone, took some Benadryl, and fell asleep until morning.

That was when I saw Mom's latest text: Have you heard? That pig is dead.

PRESENT DAY

CHAPTER 75

DETECTIVE GREGORY PLATH

"Boy, am I glad to see you." I smile at Dr. Devers. Her name's Marilyn, though she didn't tell me to call her that. She's a little haughty, but still, I am glad to see her. I'm desperate for a new lead.

I've hit a wall. The boss didn't think that the contract between Michael Baylor and Greer was enough to officially declare Greer a suspect. He said he'd gotten a complaint from her already about my "strong-arm tactics" and a veiled threat that she'd be filing a lawsuit if I continued to "harass" her. He'd said that I couldn't bring her back in until I had something ironclad, but how was I supposed to get something ironclad unless I brought her back in and made her crack?

That's why I need Dr. Devers.

"I'm happy to cooperate," she says. She's an ash blonde in her early sixties in an expensive pantsuit. She looks a lot like Hillary Clinton. "I always go traveling for the month of August and I unplug completely, so I hadn't heard about Michael."

"I appreciate you coming in now." I've checked her out, from her reputation to her alibi. She's solid. She's got nothing to gain by lying. And she shouldn't be bound by patient-client privilege, since they weren't her patients. "Could you tell me about your relationship to Dr. Baylor?"

"We consulted about cases. It was an informal arrangement. We generally met about once every month or two, more frequently if needed."

"Who tended to need it?"

She stiffens, though I wasn't meaning to offend. I thought since she was a fellow professional, I could leave off the kid gloves. But detectives and therapists aren't really the same kind of professionals. "It's a difficult line of work, Detective. Colleagues help you maintain perspective, keep you focused on the best interests of your clients."

"Did you feel that Dr. Baylor acted in the best interests of his clients?"

"Yes. He genuinely cared about them. If anything, he cared too much."

I'll circle back to that, for sure. But kid gloves. "How long had you known him?"

"About fifteen years. We moved in the same professional circles. He was very highly regarded, as I'm sure you've uncovered in your investigation."

I'm not touching that one. "Has he brought any unusual cases to your attention over the past year?"

"Several."

"Could you say more?"

"Not about their identities."

So much for cooperation. But I've got to keep the frustration out of my tone. "Is privilege in effect? They weren't your clients."

"That's not it. I didn't know their identities. Michael was very respectful of confidentiality, so much so that he always made up names for them."

"If I ran a few names by you, could you tell me if any of them sound like the pseudonyms he was using?"

She pulls out a notebook she can consult. "I'm game."

"Lucinda or Lucy?" Headshake. "Flora?" Headshake. "Greer?" Headshake. "None of those is familiar to you?"

"Not the names. The stories might be."

"Did he tell you he was sleeping with any of his patients?"

She looks shocked. "Absolutely not."

"Then you probably don't know these stories."

"Have you checked out these stories? That really doesn't sound like Michael."

"I've got some reliable sources." *Reliable* might be a stretch, but still.

She seems to be carefully considering her words. "Truthfully, over the past six months, Michael hasn't been himself. He was clearly under enormous strain, and he was experiencing a lot of conflicting emotions."

"What kind of conflicting emotions?"

"Sometimes when I saw him, he was euphoric. Sometimes he was despondent. Sometimes he even seemed frightened. He could move between those emotions in a single conversation. I'd advised him to seek personal therapy."

"Isn't that why he was seeing you?"

"No. Consultation is definitely not the same. For one thing, it's not even confidential, which is why I can talk to you. For another, our focus was the clients, not his mental health."

"But you were concerned about his mental health, which is why you advised him to get his own therapist?"

She hesitates, then looks down at her hands, her eyes moistening. "I have a lot of guilt about what happened to Michael. I should have done more, but I didn't want to get more involved. I didn't want to ask more questions because I was uncomfortable with what he told me."

"Which was?"

"He told me he was falling in love with one client, and that another seemed to be in love with him, and a former client was stalking him. But he told me explicitly that he wasn't sleeping with the woman for whom he had feelings, and that she'd ended treatment with him." She grabs for a tissue. "I should have asked more questions. If I had, maybe . . ."

But I'd stopped listening.

It's like that game Fuck, Marry, Kill. He was fucking Lucinda, he wanted to marry Greer, and he wanted to kill Flora. Only one of them got to him first, the one with the motive—no, the biological imperative. Women are wired to save their kids, no matter what.

I know which one got to him, only I can't get to her.

I was warned by my sergeant to stop leaving her voice mails. That's what she was calling harassment, but everything I said in my messages was true. That I understood it, I really did. She'd gotten tricked into that contract, and after all she'd learned, she couldn't have him out in the world. He could get to her kid. She'd guaranteed him a certain amount of visitation and even if she managed to block him, the kid would get older and go looking. An absent father can make as much of an impression as a present one. And if Michael wanted to get to that kid, he'd find a way. He could inflict some serious damage; he was adept at psychological warfare. She's practically a mother; she had to do what she had to do. No one would fault her.

Unless Dr. Devers can give me something specific enough to take to the sergeant, I might have to bend a few rules. Those records are so close, and they must hold some clues. Sometimes you have to go gray to do the right thing.

BEFORE

CHAPTER 76

FLORA

If anything was going to happen to Michael, I needed to make it happen. Lucinda was lovely and delicate and useless, and Greer was just a liar. She had no sense of sisterhood whatsoever. She cared only about herself, and her story that she was the one that got away.

Like I was buying that.

I fingered her money in my pocket as I walked back to my car. It niggled at me, why she'd called me and shown up here today, and why she was at his office the other day—on a Wednesday—after the evidence suggested that she was no longer in therapy with him.

She had to be sleeping with him, and that was a crime. He was supposed to wait two years before being with a former client, and he waited, what, a month or two, at most?

I could really use Greer's testimony. She'd be able to convince a jury, whereas I shuddered to think what would happen to Lucinda if you put her on the stand. She'd splinter into a million pieces. But she was obviously telling the truth; she'd been ruined by it.

Somehow, Michael had brainwashed Greer. Just because she looked together and competent didn't mean that he couldn't work his magic on her. He was a master at that, at finding the chinks in someone's armor. Now I needed to find that same chink, and what he had on her, psychologically speaking.

Let the cyberstalking begin! Back home in my apartment, I had at her. I already knew that Michael was a nonpresence online. I used to think it was because of his profession, but now I understood the real reason he needed to protect his privacy.

Greer had a large footprint when it came to her work. The company she built looked impressive. But weirdly, she was on sabbatical, and as I continued to search, it looked like she had started it right around the time she ended therapy.

Coincidence? I thought not.

I'd say that she and Michael had some sort of love shack, but I'd stalked him enough during that time to know that his routines had stayed largely the same.

Greer's personal life was a blackout, internet-wise. I needed to come at this another way.

I knew a couple of Michael's passwords, managing to lurk nearby while he was logging in, but he'd long since changed them. Still, I tried them on his email accounts, because you never know.

No luck. But then I had an inspiration: His bank accounts. He might be foolish enough to use one of the passwords he'd discarded from his email for his bank accounts. Might think I'd never look there.

Bank of America. I can have a photographic memory when I need it, and I'd seen him toss mail on his counter with their red-and-blue logo on it.

I went to the website and tried to log in. The first password failed. But with the second, I got a message on the screen saying that my computer hadn't been recognized and I'd need to answer a few verification questions. There I got lucky. He'd told me some things that were true, like the name of his first pet, a golden retriever named Biffy. I was in.

And shocked. Because I found that Greer had transferred two payments of $50,000 each, weeks apart.

One hundred thousand dollars! That was not payment for therapy services rendered.

I also found that he'd made payments to a Cyrus Hillard. As in, a relative of Maureen Hillard, one of the women who'd withdrawn her complaint?

I hadn't even bothered to check for a husband; I'd just assumed there wasn't one. But if Maureen had been married and had an affair with her therapist, she might have withdrawn the complaint on her own, for her own reasons, not due to pressure from Michael.

A quick search revealed that yes, Cyrus was Maureen's husband. And he looked like kind of a scary, beefy dude. I wouldn't want to be the one sleeping with his wife.

The payment had been made just a few days after the first money transfer from Greer. Michael put up the alarm system sticker just about then, too. So maybe that hadn't been for me at all but for Cyrus. Just because Michael had paid Cyrus didn't mean he'd feel safe. There was no honor among blackmailers. Maybe the money hadn't been enough to make up for the assaultive visions of Michael with Maureen. Michael had been acting strange and jumpy for the past few months. He might have feared for his life.

When he'd sobbed in my arms that night and I thought it was about his terror at losing me and what we had, it probably hadn't been about me then, either. I said I was so sorry, I'd do anything, and he'd responded, "No one does anything." He was probably talking about the police or just expressing his general helplessness. It had nothing to do with loving me. I was a footnote.

The upside was that I might not have to do much at all: Michael was already getting what was coming to him.

No, I wanted him to know it was me.

Now there was a paper trail. Proof of his misdeeds. I'd caught him red-handed, or as close as I could come to it. This, plus my testimony and Lucinda's testimony—we had him. We were going to take this fucker down.

I couldn't believe it. That he could be that full of himself, or that dumb, as to transfer money directly from his account to Cyrus's. He wasn't even worried about a trail, though I'd warned him. I told him I was coming for him, and here I was.

But what about Greer? What could he possibly have on her? If Cyrus and Maureen were blackmailing Michael, with Greer it seemed to be the other way around. Maybe she'd told him something in therapy and he was using it against her . . . ?

Or more likely, Greer was so lovesick she'd lost all common sense. He could have told her some cockamamy story about his needy mother and she bought it. But did she know she was subsidizing his payments to a former accuser's husband? She might be interested in that information. It could be enough to get her on my side.

All night, I was strategizing, and then in the morning, I did one last online trawl and nearly fainted.

Michael was dead.

I never thought . . .

When Lucinda and I had been talking, I was just spitballing. Fantasizing, like Jeanie said. I told Lucinda we were in it together.

I hadn't meant . . .

I never thought she'd have the guts. But then, Michael always told me that people were surprising.

I'd caused Kate to be in a coma, and now I might have set things in motion for Michael's death.

Sure, I'd snapped the other night, and sure, I'd wanted to make him pay, and sure, I'd wanted him to know that I was the one behind it. But I'd been thinking the cost would be his reputation, not his life.

I staggered to the floor. He was dead.

Was it Lucy? Or could it have been Greer? Was this all my fault?

PRESENT DAY

CHAPTER 77

GREER

It was my usual routine upon waking: check my phone for messages and my computer for news.

Today, it was the most awful stereo. In a truly surreal experience, I heard Michael's voice as I was reading, *PSYCHOTHERAPIST FOUND DEAD IN HIS OFFICE*.

"You've been avoiding me, and I think I know why," he was saying. "I have a feeling someone's gotten to you . . ."

The body of Michael Baylor, a licensed clinical psychotherapist practicing in the affluent Rockridge section of Oakland, has been discovered.

". . . and you're either hearing or are about to hear a lot of—well, not misinformation, exactly, but very skewed information. I want to tell you my side.

"I know I've done some bad things; I've hurt people. I can't blame them for wanting to hurt me back, but please, just let me explain myself. I need you to know the whole truth because I think I could love you."

The police are not yet releasing any firm details but at this time, the death is being investigated as suspicious.

"I know I could love our baby, and for the first time in my life, I want to make a real go of it. As in, I want to do the right thing by you and by our child. I want to be a family. We can take things slow, really get it right. There's a rule about not sleeping together for two years after terminating therapy, and I've pretended to follow it before, but I haven't. With you, I want it all aboveboard. We can take our time, just let our relationship grow organically, along with your belly." He laughed self-consciously. "That came out wrong. Please, could we just talk?"

The phone clattered to the floor. I was crying and crawling under the bed to get the phone so that I could listen to the message one more time. A thousand more times. It was all I had left of him.

I was moaning and cradling the belly that was too small for anyone to suspect, but it was substantial. I could already feel the weight of my baby in my arms. Michael's baby.

Oh my God. It had to be a mistake. He couldn't be dead, not when I was still listening to his voice. As long as I kept listening, he was still alive.

I let it play again, and my tears dried. He was with me. He was right with me, me and this baby. Our baby. He was right with me, the man I love. It couldn't be too late to tell him. No, he must have known, must have felt it. I was with him in the end. My love was.

Did he die fast or slow? Quick or agonizing? Had there been time to remember me, to let the life we were about to have flash before his eyes and bring him peace?

Noooooooo. He wasn't dead. It couldn't be over. We'd barely begun. That's what he was telling me in his message. We were going to do this, for real. We were going to be a family.

It had to be a mistake. He couldn't really be gone.

I played the message again, holding the phone tight against my belly so my baby could hear it, too. Our child could come to recognize his (her?) father's voice. I just needed to keep listening, that was all.

We were going to be a family.

CHAPTER 78

LUCINDA

I didn't know what time it was, just that the sky had darkened. I'd had nothing to eat or drink. My tear ducts could no longer produce moisture. It was like I'd been wrung out to dry.

Michael Baylor was no more. The me who had existed in the room with Michael Baylor—his client, his lover—was no more. Most of me was bereft and terrified, but some small piece of me thought it had been poetic justice.

Other than my mother, the only one who'd reached out to me was Christine, and her call had nothing to do with Michael. I mean, why would it have? She didn't know about my therapist's untimely death. She left a voice mail saying that I'd been fired for failing to meet deadlines and for my poor attendance. "When you didn't show up today, that was the last straw," she said.

So like Christine, to try to take away my victory, to pretend that our scene had never happened, to act like I'd never declared my independence from her. How like an editor to rewrite history and tell me, "You can't quit because you're fired."

But it wasn't like it mattered now. This was life and death, Michael's and mine. Because Michael was most likely in hell, burning right alongside Adam, but someday, I might be there, too. I didn't know how Michael had been killed; I just knew I'd participated in that conversation yesterday where we kicked around various scenarios, and now he was dead. I was an accessory.

When someone began knocking persistently on my front door, refusing to be ignored, my first thought was that it was the police, and if I didn't answer, they might just break it down. I had no idea if they had that authority, but we were talking about murder.

I smelled terrible, and I looked worse, in a pair of threadbare flannel pajamas, my hair half-fled from the confines of its bun. If the police didn't think I was guilty before, my appearance would certainly suggest guilt or some other pronounced disturbance.

But it wasn't the Oakland PD. It was my mother.

She embraced me, and I sobbed in her arms. Could I ever see her again without weeping? She must be mortified that she'd raised such a disaster. I was mortified to be me.

"Is anyone else home?" she asked.

"No." Otherwise, they would have answered the door ten minutes ago.

"Let's go inside. We need to talk."

She thought I'd done it. What was I going to tell her?

We sat on the living room couch, an aged navy-blue chaise longue that had probably been here through the last five successive cycles of roommates. I licked my parched lips, and then bit at the flaking skin.

"How are you?" she said. I noticed that her lips were just as dry, that other than the fact that she was dressed in clothes rather than pajamas, she looked as bad as I did.

"It's been a very strange day," I finally managed.

"For me, too." Her eyes darted around nervously, and I had this feeling, like I wasn't the only one worried about a knock from the police. Could it be . . . ?

No. My mother was no killer.

"I've done a terrible thing," she said.

Oh my God.

She started to cry. "When you told me you weren't the only one, it made me think of what happened to you when you were little, and then with Adam, and I just went into this spiral. It was like your therapist had become every man who'd ever hurt you, and he was out there doing this to other women, damaging them or preying on the damage from when they were little girls, and I can't even tell you what happened to me. It was like something took over my body. I just started driving."

She squeezed her eyes shut as she continued. "The outer door to his office building was propped open, and I went upstairs to his office. He was alone. I told him who I was, and he turned away from me and went to the window, almost like he didn't want to look at me, like he was ashamed, and I saw that heavy statue; it was the perfect weight, and it was like, this might not even make sense, but it was like he was giving me the opportunity. Like he wanted me to do it, you know? Like he wanted it to be over. Like he couldn't stop himself any other way and I needed to do it for him."

She was shaking, and I couldn't speak. There was no way Michael wanted to die. She was rationalizing.

But maybe it didn't matter what he'd wanted. Maybe he'd deserved to die. She was right; he was destroying people, and she'd stopped him. For me. "Mommy," I whimpered.

We were in each other's arms, sobbing. "I'm so sorry," she said. "I meant to be a good mother, and I wasn't. And now I'm . . . Now I've . . ."

"You protected me," I said. "Because the truth is, I would have gone back to him. I would have kept going back because he had this hold over me."

"You were addicted to him, and I could feel that. I get that. One of the scariest things was how I felt when I went to his office. I had all this fury and adrenaline and excitement. I was high, like I hadn't been in years. And I'd missed it, Lucy. Later, I was so horrified by myself. I still am."

"No one would blame you if they knew what he'd done."

She pulled away. "Do you think I should turn myself in? I will, if that's what you think I should do."

"Do you think anyone saw you?"

"No, I don't think so. It's not like he and I were yelling, and when I did it, it was quieter than I would have thought." She swallowed and stared down at her hands. "I can still feel the weight of that statue. I can see what he looked like lying there on the floor."

At the image, I should have felt horror. I should have felt something. I'd loved him, or thought I had. But knowing that my mother had risked her future, and her freedom, to stop Michael—that put everything else to shame.

I laced my fingers through hers. "We'll get through this together. Should I be your alibi?"

"No. That's too risky. This is what I had to do for you. And if I go down for it, I can be okay with that."

For the first time in my entire life, I felt truly and completely loved. All those pies and showing up for dance recitals and being everyone's favorite cool mom hadn't done it, because deep down, I'd known that she had failed at her primary job: to keep me safe. But she'd changed the narrative.

My book just got a whole new ending.

THREE MONTHS
LATER

CHAPTER 79

DETECTIVE GREGORY PLATH

The Michael Baylor case is still open, but the active investigation is done. The killer's still out there, and in a way, that eats at me, and I still have my suspicions, but I just couldn't reach any conclusions and I certainly couldn't make any arrests, not without going into those records. I'm pretty sure it wasn't Flora, which makes it a toss-up between Lucinda and Greer, and I have to content myself with maybe never knowing.

I suck at not knowing. You would have thought I'd improve over the years, but I don't get a ton of practice. The majority of cases are easy: you find the most obvious suspect and they wind up confessing. Sometimes you have to dig deeper, and then you solve it, and you get to pat yourself on the back. And then there are cases like this one.

Dr. Devers and I went through her consultation book case by case, and you know, Dr. Baylor really did seem like a hell of a therapist. None of the initials she was using corresponded with the list I had of his current and former patients, and for a while, I was a dog with a bone. I started working my way through all of them, attractive or not, just to see if I could get at what made this guy tick. To see if he'd been inappropriate in other ways or maybe he'd slipped and told one patient about another, like maybe he'd somehow mentioned my three suspects.

Sure, there were some who'd ended treatment early or who thought Dr. Baylor was just okay, but no one said anything too bad. They all thought he'd tried hard to change their lives. And for most, he had. Changed their lives. They raved about him. They had stories of how he'd gone above and beyond for them. A bunch had abusive ex-husbands and boyfriends and fathers, and he'd helped them see that men could be good and kind, that they could want nothing but the best for you. "He saw me for free," one woman told me, "for years. I got away from my ex, and I got back on my feet, and I learned to love myself and to be someone my kids could look up to." Her eyes were full of tears. "How could anyone do this to Dr. Baylor? He was like an angel on Earth."

This was one of the women who had no social media, so I hadn't known until I saw her how attractive she was, which was plenty. Any man sitting in a room with her an hour a week would have some impure thoughts. Dr. Baylor must have had some untoward impulses that he resisted.

So why those three? What about Flora, Greer, and Lucinda was so irresistible to the guy?

That I'll never know.

But I know I did the right thing, not going into those records. Not doing something unethical for the greater good. Who am I to determine the greater good? Rules exist for a reason. You start deciding which ones you want to follow and which ones you don't, and it's a slippery slope. You slide down, you can become Michael Baylor.

That's what I've come to think about him, after everything I've been able to learn and all I have to guess: He bent rules and he justified. He took one step, and then another, and he was in deep. He lost his moral compass, he lost his way, and maybe part of his rationalization was all the other times that he'd done the right thing by other people, by other women, even other good-looking ones. Almost every other time, he'd resisted. Why not just this once? Hadn't he earned it with all his other good deeds?

I don't know if that's how he thought. I don't conveniently have some journal of his, and he didn't have good friends who could tell me. Flora, Greer, and Lucinda might have been the closest people to him, and unfortunately, anything they tell me is colored by self-preservation. Even if they think it's true, it might not be. It's not just the guilty who are scared, it's the ones who might look guilty. And all three of them look guilty as hell.

I can get all tormented about my failure to solve the case, or I can be glad that I didn't do anything unethical, that I don't have to cover my tracks and look over my shoulder. I can learn from Dr. Baylor's mistakes.

From my limited vantage point, he was no monster. He was a man who lost control of his emotions in a profession where he was helping people gain control of theirs, and what's that corny saying? He paid the ultimate price. Corny but true.

Part of why I hate not finding his killer is because of my ego; I hate to lose. The other part is that I came to feel a strange responsibility to him, a sort of kinship. Not that I've ever crossed the line with any women professionally; I've never slept with a suspect or anything like that. But in my personal life, I've cheated and I've lied. I've paid the price—not the ultimate, but a high one. I still miss my wife. Every day, if I'm not careful.

And I get what it is to be a man in over his head with various women, trying to be what they want him to be. I think of all that stuff in his Consent to Treatment about how he'll be whatever you need, all he asks is that you give him a chance. That's a man spilling his guts on the page. That's a man who's painfully trying to overcome his lack of self and his inadequacies after having spent his life tending to his narcissistic mother.

Yeah, I can do armchair psychology. And don't tell anyone, but sometimes I think that shit's true.

CHAPTER 80

FLORA

Old habits die hard. Once a stalker, always a stalker.

No, this was purely an accident. Or fate, maybe. I've got only a week left in the Bay Area, and I'm in the Westfield, kissing this particular retail promenade goodbye, when I see her from behind. That blowout with just a hint of wave worked back into it, the diaphanous clothes, and she does live in the city. Even from a floor above, given the rotunda architecture, I know that it's got to be her. We must have found ourselves under the same shopping dome for a reason.

I've put aside so much of my anger, nearly all of it, over the past few months. Greer is my test.

I curve my way down to her, dodging the other shoppers. She stops to look in a store window where baby clothes are on display. As she rubs her belly in that subconscious and unmistakable way, I think how long Michael's been gone, and the time line fits.

Other things fit, too. Like how standoffish she was at dim sum. Now it makes sense. She didn't want to believe anything we were saying; she was already in deeper than I'd ever been.

Better her than me.

But even as I think that, what I feel is hurt. Even from beyond the grave, he can stick the knife in. Because while I hate him, I can't help loving him, too, and it comes back up on me sometimes as if it's all present tense and I might see him around a corner and I don't know if I want to kiss him or slap him and I think that when he said he would always have love for me, it was the truth. Or maybe I just don't want to believe that it was all lies, that I got taken on a two-year ride. I can't know anything for sure, because I can never ask him another question, and if I had been able to ask him more questions, would I ever have believed another word out of his mouth?

She's walking inside the upscale kids' boutique. I watch her lift onesies with this sweet—dare I say maternal?—smile on her face, and I just can't hate her, not that I ever did. Really, I hated him. And loved him. And still do.

It's been rough, and I imagine Greer would know what I'm talking about.

She looks up and sees me. I don't want to admit it, but pregnancy suits her. In addition to the smile, she's got that fucking glow, and she can use the weight.

Her expression becomes uncertain, probably mirroring my own, and it's that kinship that pulls me inside. Also, I don't want her to see me running away.

There are a few people lined up in front of the register, which is where the salespeople are, too, which means that no one can overhear us. "Hi," she says. "It's been a while. How are you?"

"I thought about walking on by, pretending I hadn't seen you, but—"

"There's no point in that. We know each other, right?"

As in, we know things no one else does. We've loved the same man. Maybe it's because of the pregnancy, but Greer seems unguarded and sad, where a minute ago, she was stroking baby clothes.

"I shouldn't miss him, but I do," I blurt.

She's surprised to hear it, like I'm surprised to have said it. She nods slowly. "I know," she says, and I can tell, she does.

"I thought you'd done it." I'm not going to spell out what I thought she did; this is still a public place. "But now . . ." I gesture to her belly.

"I thought you'd done it." She doesn't add the "but now."

"That's Michael's baby, right?"

She hesitates, and then finally nods.

"So you were sleeping with him." I can't help it; I want to needle her a little, pin her down on her lie. She'd been so holier-than-thou, but Michael finds a way. Found a way.

"No. It was an insemination, actually."

The money transferred into his account. She paid him for his sperm. "It was a business deal, then? You paid him to father your child and that's all?" I don't know why, but I sound hopeful.

"No," she says softly, "it wasn't only a business deal. But we never even kissed."

Michael wants what he can't have. Wanted. We all do. "Was he really going to wait the two years to be with you?"

"We were going to try."

I don't know why she's being so honest with me. It could be that she's trying to hurt me, and it's working.

I'd thought it was a compliment that he couldn't wait, that he had to have me right away, but now it just seems like a lack of respect. True love is patient. True love is kind.

Greer is looking at me with compassion, which is more humiliating. "So what brings you to the city?" she says, almost brightly. That subject change might, strangely, be the most awkward part of the world's strangest, most awkward conversation.

"I work in the city," I say, and then I correct myself. "I used to work in the city. I recently"—I debate on the wording—"gave up my job. I'm moving back to Miami."

It's been much easier to pack up my life in California than I would have thought. It could have been because, like Jeanie said, it takes a long time to know me, or because Michael had intentionally isolated me, also like Jeanie said. But really, she's the only person I'm going to miss. She says she'll bring the twins down for a beach vacation, the kind where you can go in the water without freezing your ass off. Florida's got it all over California in that regard.

"My parents are pretty old," I say, "and I should spend more time with them and help them when they need it." Since I don't have Kate to do that anymore. "It'll be good to have a change of scenery. Too many memories here." She bobs her head with feeling, and I wonder if she's thought of taking off herself. "And my cousin Kate, the one I told you about at dim sum? She woke up. She needs to learn how to do everything all over again, how to walk and talk and feed herself, and I'm going to be there every step of the way. I'm going to take good care of her."

I don't know why I'm telling Greer all this. Maybe it's because I want her to think I'm a good person, because she basically told me she thought I was the killer, and she hasn't yet walked it back. Or maybe it's because I want to convince myself that it's all going to turn out all right. That I am, in fact, a good person. Sometimes I have my doubts. Michael wasn't in our relationship alone. And the way I threw shade at both Greer and Lucy when I talked to that detective, trying to get him to focus on them—I don't feel good about that. Well, before today, I'd felt fine about Greer, but I always felt a little guilty about Lucy.

She never got arrested, though. No one has.

"It sounds like a really good plan," Greer says when I've stopped babbling. "I wish you and your family the best."

She sounds sincere. I think.

I indicate her pregnant form. "I wish you and your family the best, too, Greer."

And that's it. We're parting ways. I've gone from floored to hurt to proud of myself for my maturity in, like, five minutes. But that kind of roller coaster of emotions has gotten to be routine over the past months. Hell, if I'm honest, it's been a lot longer than that. My time with Michael was no picnic.

But things are going to be different now. It's funny that circling back to the beginning, to my roots, can be a fresh start. I think it will be, though. I'm not even bitter about getting fired. It's been a blessing in disguise, and the timing was incredible. Within a week, Kate woke up. That gives me a chance to be the friend, and the family, I should have been. The human being I should have been.

Kate's going to need a ton of rehab, and I'll be right there with her. Like Michael said, I'm formidable; I'm a force of nature, and I'm going to send all that Kate's way. Every bit of my energy is going to her. I'm swearing off men for a long, long time.

I text Lucy.

Hi, stranger! Hope you're doing well. I'm moving back to Miami and I'd love to see you before I go.

And I've got the scoop on Greer and Michael. You're not going to believe this.

CHAPTER 81

GREER

These days, I spend almost all my time nesting. I sit in the rocking chair in the nursery, singing to my unborn child. He's healthy and beautiful. The ultrasound has been blown up and framed and, in profile, he looks like his daddy.

Yes, it's a boy. That particular instinct had been wrong.

My instinct about Michael was right, though. He made mistakes, and he was flawed, but he did a lot of good in the world, too, and he was ready to change, and he loved me. I still listen to his voice mail at least once a day, and I can hear it in his voice. I can hear the man he was becoming and the life we would have had together. It breaks my heart and restores it at once, which is very complicated, much like Michael was. Much like I am.

I still miss him and the vision of what we could have had, but this way, I'll have full control. I'll get to tell my little boy any story I want. Like I can say that his father was a hero. He helped people. Disturbed people. And one of them killed him.

I visit the police regularly to remind them that Michael's case is important and he still needs justice. The detective hates me because I went over his head after all his harassment, but he has to do his damn job. The last time I saw him, he stared pointedly at my belly, and I stared right back. I've got nothing to hide but no reason to share unnecessarily, either.

It was crazy, running into Flora yesterday. I've been so sure she was the one, and now . . . I don't know. The fact that she's still so obviously grieving for him doesn't rule her out, but there was just something about her.

So that leaves . . .

It's ironic that my attempt to exact vengeance backfired. Flora seemed so much more peaceful and so much more likable than she had at dim sum. Getting fired suits her. Since I wasn't about to get my hands truly dirty, not with my baby to consider, I'd thought that the least I could do for Michael was use my contacts over at Flora's company to get her ousted for unethical conduct. So what if I had to invent the actual charges; I'd believed the underlying accusation. That Flora's a loathsome human being. A murderer.

I'd thought she was getting off too easy, that it wasn't an eye for an eye, it was an eye for a pinkie toe. But maybe I was wrong.

It could all be for the best, though. She'll go take care of her cousin, and I'll never have to run into her again. San Francisco will be all mine.

But does this mean that Lucy . . . ?

Now that I think about it, I really had tunnel vision about Flora. She'd just been so flamboyant in her rage. But it's too obvious. Lucy's the much more obvious candidate.

I'll have to hire someone to follow her, see what he can find out. I can't be going on stakeouts like Flora did, not in my condition.

I need to keep my focus where it belongs, on my baby. He's all I have left of Michael, and I'll cherish them both. But that doesn't mean I'll give up on justice.

CHAPTER 82

LUCINDA

I should have turned off my phone; I'm in a business meeting here. But I'm still not used to that whole idea.

And I definitely shouldn't have glanced at the texts because now I'm thinking about Michael, which I try to do as little as possible. I've become quite good at it. He didn't teach me compartmentalization (he might even think that was avoidance or denial or some unhealthy defense mechanism), but he doesn't get to weigh in on my life anymore.

I sneak another look at the text. Nothing in there says that there's been a development in the investigation. That's what I think about most. I want to make sure my mother doesn't get punished for what she did. She's a hero, in my book.

As far as I know, the investigation stalled out. Detective Plath brought me in a couple more times. I think he expected me to break. But I'm stronger than I gave myself credit for, and really, that's what my memoir is about.

I changed my book from fiction to nonfiction at the advice of my literary agent. My incredibly high-powered literary agent, that is. It's turned out it's much more marketable as a memoir than a novel, especially given the weird true-crime angle about the therapist who abused his power and then wound up dead.

I didn't break through all of that, though I have to admit, some moments over the past three months have been touch and go. Fortunately, I had my mother there for it. I moved back into the river house with her, after a whole lot of cleanup. Not just the dust and garbage but all reminders of Adam got purged. She cooks and bakes for me and just generally looks after me, and I do the same for her, minus the cooking and baking. It's felt good, like we get a do-over.

The detective never even asked me about Mom. And she must have done an amazing job on the crime scene, so there's no physical evidence she was ever there. I'm pretty sure we're in the clear.

The fact is, I'm in the clear because I didn't do anything wrong, except pick the wrong man. I did it twice, and they're both dead. I'm the survivor.

I need to pay attention. My editor is telling me what I need to revise. She thinks I really need to focus on the ending, on the uplift. She tells me, "You're going to be an inspiration to so many young women."

I'm writing a dedication in my mind:

To Michael, for showing me the path, and to my mother, for clearing the debris.

Or something like that.

CHAPTER 83

Client: Lucinda
Date: January 14
First session with new client. She appeared disheveled and disorganized. Indications of trauma, in that she vacillated between being extremely open and extremely guarded. She states that her presenting problem is difficulty forming relationships, a dead-end job, a lack of assertiveness, and self-hatred . . .

Client: Lucinda
Date: March 29
Client seemed alternately tearful and seductive, and the shifts did not match the stated problem (feeling unappreciated by her boss). The sudden and uncontrollable mood changes may indicate the initial diagnosis of major depressive disorder is incorrect or insufficient. Rule-outs include bipolar disorder and schizoaffective disorder. This would then necessitate a modification of the treatment plan, though client may not have the insight or stability to contribute meaningfully to such a plan.

Client: Lucinda

Date: May 10

Client spoke about a need for a "different type of treatment." Upon probing, it was clear that she was talking about a sexual relationship and proposing that it happen at another day and time from the usual sessions. For example, she stated that it could occur spontaneously late at night, that she would make herself available to this therapist whenever it was convenient for him. She said that she felt that being sexually in control, even dominant, over this therapist could be curative for her.

Explored her countertransference as normal, while reiterating the boundaries of a responsible therapy relationship . . .

Client: Lucinda

Date: June 20

Client disclosed today that her stepfather had sexually abused her, though she did not speak of it as abuse; she spoke of it as a love affair that she had initiated and perpetuated.

This history makes sense in the context of client's inappropriately seductive behavior toward this therapist . . .

Client: Lucinda

Date: August 3

Client's diagnosis has been updated to erotomanic delusional disorder, in light of her continued insistence that she and this therapist have been having assignations in this office after hours. Given the liability issues and clinical considerations, this therapist has sought outside consultation (documented separately; client is referred to as J.R. to protect her identity and maintain confidentiality). The pertinent question is whether it would be better for the client to be treated by a therapist who is not the object of her affection/delusions or whether that would be more dangerous, as it risks her feeling abandoned. While she hasn't disclosed any previous history of self-harm or suicidal ideation, that doesn't mean it hasn't occurred. As noted in other progress notes, there are holes in client's short- and long-term memory, as well as evidence of denial and her choice not to share details that she feels may cast her in a negative light.

Through consultation, this therapist has decided to continue to treat client, while documenting exhaustively what is said in session and the clinical decisions being made by this therapist . . .

Client: Lucinda
Date: September 22
Client continues to believe that she is having a sexual relationship with this therapist, imagining that there are two sessions a week: one that's "normal" therapy and another that's supposedly designed to facilitate her sexual liberation, to help her find her voice, and thereby allow her to heal from her past sexual abuse. She reports these not as fantasies but as encounters that have already occurred (i.e. they are psychotic symptoms of her disorder, though this therapist cannot challenge them without posing psychological risk to client).

It appears increasingly untenable for this therapist to continue treating her. But because of the traumatic origins of the delusional disorder, that it's rooted in sexual abuse and how she seems to see this therapist as a father figure who she then turns into a sexual figure, it could be profoundly destabilizing to her to terminate the therapeutic relationship.

Client: Lucinda
Date: October 19
Client continues to decompensate. The combination of her stepfather's impending death and her mother's disappearance, along with the weight of her own delusional fantasies related to this therapist, seem to be too much for her.

In today's session, this therapist broached the subject of switching to a female trauma therapist (with whom this therapist has been regularly consulting about client, using the moniker J.R.) and getting a medication evaluation from a psychiatrist for client's mood symptoms. Client is not sufficiently stable to handle knowing her true diagnosis. This therapist hopes that he can convince client to sign releases of information and then brief the new therapist and the psychiatrist about the erotomania and related psychosis.

As of this writing, client remains extremely resistant to both recommendations. She appears to feel wounded and rejected. Trust may have been damaged, and given her fragile state and her lack of a support system, this therapist has no choice but to continue treating her while attempting to repair the damage. This therapist will also continue to document the process in great detail through these progress notes, while seeking further consultation for client's own protection, as well as his.

ACKNOWLEDGMENTS

I'm so grateful to my first Lake Union editor, Danielle Marshall, for seeing the potential in *Neighborly* and for handing me off to the incomparable Alicia Clancy for *Confidential*. What editor is so excited to get your new draft that she reads it that day? Alicia, that's who! And rounding out the editorial team is Sarah Murphy, who is so full of enthusiasm, insight, and acumen. Thank you both. Here's to many more!

The bounty continues, as I couldn't be happier with my agent, Elisabeth Weed. I thank my lucky stars for this partnership.

And speaking of partnerships . . . big thanks and love to my husband, always and always.

ABOUT THE AUTHOR

Photo © 2013 Yanina Gotsulsky

Ellie Monago (not her real name) is the author of the bestselling novel *Neighborly*. She is also an acclaimed novelist—under her given name—and a practicing therapist.

As well as being a wife and mother, Ellie is an avid tennis fan, a passionate reader of both fiction and nonfiction—especially memoirs (because nothing's as juicy as the truth)—and a firm believer in the restorative value of a good craft cocktail.